HEAVY METAL SYMPHONY by Alyssa Palombo

First Edition

Published in 2021 by
Kaledena Press, LLC
P.O. Box 602
Fredonia, NY 14063

Please visit our website: kaledenapress.com

Copyright © 2021 Kaledena Press, LLC

Editor: Amanda Vink
Interior Design: Amanda Vink
Cover Design: Jennifer Hark-Hameister
Album Cover Designs: Jennifer Hark-Hameister

The interior of this book was designed using the following fonts:
Charcuterie Ornaments Regular
Garamond
Mason Serif
Origins
Sabon LT Pro
Steelfish

Image Credits:
Cover © Adobe Stock Photo: Cristian (221364740); olgavisavi (140129208)
Album Covers © Adobe Stock Photo: fergregory (367266171); Rudy Matchinga (216526274); Fernando Cortés (59847693); Fotokon (86871840); Obsessively (274422182); ParinPIX (99611462) © Shutterstock Khomenko Maryna (372206572)

This is a work of fiction. Names, characters, places, and incidents either are the product of the author's imagination or are used fictitiously. Any resemblance to actual persons, living or dead, events, or locales is entirely coincidental.

All rights reserved. No part of this book may be reproduced in any form without permission in writing from the publishers, except by a reviewer.

Printed in The United States of America

Paperback ISBN: 978-1-7368603-3-5
Ebook ISBN: 978-1-7368603-4-2

Heavy Metal

Symphony

A Novel

by

Alyssa Palombo

For all the women in heavy metal: musicians, songwriters, road crew, fans, everyone. We rock, and the heavy metal scene is our scene too.

chapter 1

✦

**Album #5
2016**

For the first time, Ava thought maybe she could live without him. She was standing in the doorway of the recording studio, waiting for him to look up and notice that she was leaving, and it occurred to her that yes, maybe, just maybe, her life could go on without him. What kind of life? Now, that was a different matter. Even just imagining it was a sort of cold, bleak hell; more screaming than music, more brutality than beauty, more static than sound. But still, life it would be. It would be something, which was more than she had been able to admit until that moment.

"I'm leaving," she called to him when it was plain that he was too lost in his own head to notice her, even should she stand there all night. He looked up at her then, the candlelight deepening the planes of his face, casting his eyes into shadow. There were lit candles everywhere; on the floor by the grand piano at which he sat, on the piano's lid, on the chair beside him, on the table behind him. He claimed he worked best with darkness and candlelight and "atmosphere". For so long it had been so romantic to her, so mysterious and sexy. Now it just seemed too dramatic. "I'll see you in the morning."

Killian studied her for a moment, and Ava felt her heart catch in her throat. *I take it back,* she said to herself wildly in that one, fragile instant, regretting her traitorous thought of just seconds ago. *I didn't mean it.* Maybe, Ava thought, he was going to ask her to stay or tell her he would come to her apartment later. As he once would have.

But he didn't say either of those things. Instead, he nodded and turned his attention back to the score on the piano in front of him. "All right. See you tomorrow."

She stood there and watched him for just a beat longer, but she needn't have bothered. As far as he was concerned, she was already gone.

Ava was exhausted by the time she got back to her apartment, much more so than the day in the studio had warranted. Creating music was always exhausting in so many ways, but usually it was

CHAPTER 1

an exhilarating kind of exhaustion from accomplishing something momentous. Tonight all she felt was tired.

She tossed her leather jacket and bag on the love seat near the door, not bothering to hang them up—they'd be there when she needed them again in the morning, bright and early. She showered, changed into a pair of soft cotton pajama pants and an old Evanescence t-shirt, and made herself a cup of tea with honey in the small kitchen. She loved her apartment: bigger than the one she'd had when she first joined the band, but in a building just down the street. She didn't want to leave her beloved Elmwood Village, and they were on the road so much that she hadn't felt the need to buy a house yet. Maybe someday.

She sat down in her favorite armchair with her mug and the book she'd been reading, ready to take her mind off of the day. Yet once she was seated she didn't so much as pick up the hardcover novel, instead staring off into space as she sipped her tea.

That day hadn't been the problem, not really. She and Killian had been perfectly cordial, kind even; able to work together without any problems, able to keep it strictly professional in front of the rest of the band members. Yet the rest of the guys knew something was wrong. How could they not? Everyone could feel it, a physical presence in the recording studio, an extra musician who was louder than the rest of them combined.

They couldn't go on like this. Yet the question—the terrifying question, the one that came for her with teeth and claws in the night—was how they would change.

There are so many ways I drown without you, she thought, that one lyric never quite leaving her head.

Her tea gone, she stood up, restless suddenly despite her weariness. She went out into the living room and sat behind the Yamaha baby grand piano, its shiny black varnish reflecting her face, slightly distorted, back at her. The piano had been a gift from Killian, early in their relationship. She had protested, saying that she could buy one for herself if she wanted (though she couldn't have afforded it then; not yet), but he had insisted. She had come home the day it had arrived to find him waiting for her, the piano in place, angled against the corner, with a black vase of dark red roses—her favorite—on the lid. In spite of herself, in spite of feeling afraid that it was too much—both the piano and what had grown between them—she had been thrilled and excited. She had told him that he should be the first one to play it.

She ran her fingers listlessly over the keys. She began by playing a Chopin prelude, then one of Schumann's *Scenes from Childhood*. Then she paused, staring at the gleaming black and white keys for a few moments. When she started to play again, it was something entirely different, something she had never heard before. Something no one had ever heard before.

It had been years since she had begun to play like this, let the notes flow from her unchecked, hearing the mistakes and imperfections and things that needed to be changed and yet not caring, playing on anyway, knowing that she could go back and fix it later. What was important right then was to just let the music come, to let the ocean of heartbreak and desire and fear swell around her, but never to let it drown her.

When it finally stopped, she waited a moment, then went back and started at the beginning. She remembered most of it, the keys her fingers had pressed, where they had lingered and softened and rested and pounded. Certain measures she forgot, and so she filled in something else that may or may not have been just like the original.

Then she played it a third time, knowing that it was now etched into her brain, carved there as surely as the grooves of a vinyl record.

It had been a long time since she had been able to improvise so freely, been able to let a song flow from her fingers rather than laboring over every chord and note. Not since around the time she had first played one of her songs for Killian, she thought.

Those songs were gone, and she knew she'd never get them back.

This one, though. She played through it once more. This one showed every intention of sticking around.

chapter 2

EP,
2007

"Who is that?" Ava asked, stepping hesitantly into her roommate's room. It looked like Denise was studying, but Ava couldn't help but interrupt—she had to know the name of the band Denise was listening to.

Denise swiveled around on her desk chair, the music spilling from the tinny speakers of her laptop. "Handel's Messiah," she said. "My brother's band. He's the keyboard player. They're great, aren't they? Really different. I think so, anyway. But I might be biased."

"Yeah, they are good," Ava said, knowing she should reply—she had started the conversation, after all—but mostly just wanting to hear more of the music, trying to hone in on it beneath their voices. "I've heard of them before, but I've never listened to them."

"Oh, really?" Denise asked. "I thought you were into this kind of stuff. They actually remind me a little of that other band you like—Wavelength, right?"

"Yeah," Ava said. Wavelength was one of her favorites, and the lead singer, Marissa Martin, with her powerful yet beautiful voice, had long been one of her heroes. Yet Handel's Messiah was different, somehow; more metal where Wavelength was hard rock, and with a scope that was more epic and grandiose but still somehow managed to be achingly beautiful at the same time. "I can't believe I haven't heard them before, either."

"I should have know you'd be into them!" Denise said. "I should've played them for you before now."

"Well, I'm glad I finally heard them," Ava said with a smile. "Vivian's coming to meet me for dinner, if you want to join us."

"Oh, I'd love to, but my Bio midterm is tomorrow, so I'd better keep studying," Denise said. "Thanks, though!"

Ava left Denise's room, summoned by Vivian's knocking on the door of the dorm. But all night—even though she'd only heard a portion of one song—she couldn't get that music out of her head.

CHAPTER 2

The next day, in between Music Theory III and Music of the 19th Century, Ava walked to the indie record store a few blocks from campus and found a copy of Handel's Messiah's EP, as she'd hoped she would. She loaded it onto her laptop as soon as she got back to her dorm that night, plugging in her massive, ear-covering headphones, and listened to the entire thing all the way through.

The music was brutal and beautiful, a perfect marriage of strings, choirs (samples only, but still), piano with bass, drums, and distorted guitars.

And that voice. Celeste Perinot, the lead singer, was a classically trained vocalist, and she used the full extent of her abilities on the six songs—even, Ava thought, to the point of over-singing. Yet still. Ava had never heard anything like it before, and as a voice major, it was exactly the music she envisioned herself singing, even if she hadn't known it before hearing this.

And the lyrics. They were dark, theatrical, romantic, and larger than life. It was as though someone had taken all the dramatic thoughts Ava had tried to get down in (often bad) poetry since high school and given them their most beautiful possible incarnation. It was everything she had always felt and wanted to say, but had never been able to find the words herself.

※

Around the time Ava first discovered them, Handel's Messiah got signed by a big metal record label. Ava was a senior in college when they released their first album, *The Art of Escape*. This time, the production was all top shelf: live choir and orchestra, the best quality instruments and recording space. They revamped a couple tracks from the EP, but most of the music was new and even better than the old songs.

Then, of course, came the big world tour and interviews and music videos. The band remained fairly underground, as metal—and particularly their brand of metal—was hardly mainstream, but for those who were into that scene, they became huge. And, of course, they were hometown heroes. Ava saw them live twice, both times at the Town Ballroom; they were one of those rare bands that managed to sound even better live than they did on the record.

Ava not only had a new favorite band, but she had a new dream. The vision she had so long had of herself on opera stages and in recital halls and standing in front of an orchestra slowly began to be eclipsed by a very different picture: her onstage, leading a heavy metal band, pouring passion into her voice and sending it through the microphone and into the ears of a rapturous, headbanging crowd.

It seemed like an impossibly distant dream, the kind that required lightning to strike. And yet Ava dreamed anyway.

But in the meantime, there were classes and lessons to attend, recitals to give, and soon Ava was graduating from college. Then it was time to find a job—which she did, at a call center for a bank that was hardly what she dreamed of, but at least it paid the bills—and try to make her dreams happen on the side, like so many artists. She gave local performances in collaboration with other artists, sang at weddings and funerals, saved her money to be able to rent a space and hire an accompanist for recitals of her own as much as she could. In the face of all of that, in the face of real life, her dreams sometimes faded, but were never forgotten.

chapter 3

Album #5
2016

The next morning, Ava woke up and drove back to the studio. It was in a big old brick building on the West Side that had been remodeled and outfitted with all the best, top-of-the-line equipment. She parked outside in the small lot and allowed herself to soak in the quiet of the early morning. Bright sunshine splashed on one half the street, illuminating a few people dressed in sharp suits on their way to work downtown. Ava could barely hear their movements, their voices, the barrier of the car muffling sound and separating her from them.

Taking one last deep breath, Ava exited and slammed the car door shut behind her. She entered the studio, which was already buzzing with activity.

Rafael was in the booth already, finishing up recording his bass parts, his eyes closed and his long brown hair hanging over his face as he dialed in on the part he was playing. Raf had been the first member of the band Ava had met after Killian, and perhaps for that reason Rafael had always felt like Ava's closest friend among the band members, even if the three of them all felt like her brothers.

Ben, who had finished tracking the drums a couple days ago and was sitting on a couch against the wall, nodded to Ava as she entered and hung up her coat and bag. Ben was a tall Black man with a shaved head and thickly muscled arms, in part from years of playing the drums. Ava returned the nod and took a seat on the couch beside him.

Joel, seated on a stool in the corner and noodling a bit on his guitar, jerked his chin in her direction. "Sup, Ava," he said. Joel was on the shorter side, white, and skinny, with shoulder length blonde hair that he tucked behind his ears.

"Hey, Joel," she said.

Killian was seated at the sound board with Rich, their engineer. He glanced over his shoulder and gave Ava a brief nod, then turned his attention back to Rafael in the booth.

"I should probably be able to recognize the song just by the

CHAPTER 3

bass line," Ava said in a low voice to Ben beside her, "but I can't. Which one is this?"

"'Map of the End of the World'," Ben replied.

"Oh, right. Shit, he's almost through them all now, isn't he?"

"Yup."

Next up recording would be Killian with the keys, and then Joel with guitar; and finally Ava on vocals. Then would come the fine tuning, the tweaking, perhaps re-recording a part here and there. Maybe they'd decide, last minute, to do a new song.

That had happened, not with the last album, but the one before that: *Terra Nova,* Ava's first with the band. They had recorded all the songs they'd planned and rehearsed, and then one night Killian had come to her apartment flushed and excited. He'd kissed her, then run right to the piano and began to play something new. She came to stand beside him, eyes closed as she listened, felt. When he'd stopped playing, she opened her eyes, and he stood up and kissed her again. "I've been writing that all week," he said, "after listening to you record. I wrote it for you. You have to sing it."

He'd given her the sheet music where he'd written out the vocal line and some harmonies and the lyrics. Oh, the lyrics. They'd practiced it together a few times that night, then brought it to the rest of the band the next morning. With everyone on board, they recorded it quickly, and the song made it onto the album. Called "The Lighthouse", it had been the second single off of that album, for which they'd made a gorgeous video, with lots of shots of the band on a rocky coastline in California. The song had quickly become a fan favorite, one they played at almost every show, and a song that—or so Ava liked to think—had truly won Handel's Messiah's fans over to her side.

She knew, though, that there would be no last minute song this time, no loving, beautiful surprise from Killian to her. Unless…

She thought about the song she'd written last night at the piano. Or started to write, anyway. Just the memory of it was enough to make her fingers itch for the keys. She looked toward the grand piano in the studio, the one Killian had been working at when she'd left the night before. She was dying to sit at it during one of their breaks, in between takes, and revisit that song.

But no. She couldn't do that here, not in front of everyone. The song wasn't ready. She wasn't ready.

She could, she thought, play it for Killian, the way she had played him things she'd written in the past. She hadn't done that recently—and for good reason. Still, Ava knew that, even with everything they'd been through, she could ask him to sit down and listen to this song, and he would do it gladly. He would be encouraging, enthusiastic, would say all the right things, and then…that would be it. Nothing more would be said about it after that moment. It would have existed for him only in her one performance of it and never beyond that. Not for him, not for anyone else, and so maybe not for her either. And Ava wondered when she had first realized that there was a difference between the things that Killian said to her and how he really felt.

This song, though. It needed to be heard, even if the hearing would destroy everything. She heard the music again in her mind, and this time lyrics began to form as well. First they came as just a rhythmic whisper, accompanying the music; then louder and louder as they found their melody and began to take center stage.

That night, upon arriving home from the studio, Ava glanced at her phone and saw a text from Vivian.

Vivian: Hey, where you been? Let's get dinner. Text me when you're out of the studio.

Ava hesitated for a moment. It was true, she and Vivian hadn't seen one another in a couple weeks, maybe three. They texted regularly, but that was still a long time for them to go without getting together—when Ava wasn't touring, anyway. But she'd been so consumed with rehearsals and then the start of recording the new album that she had spaced on making plans with her friend.

CHAPTER 3

And she hadn't eaten yet. She started to text Vivian back, tell her to come by the apartment and they'd figure out where they wanted to go, but then she stopped and deleted what she had so far. The song was haunting her, and she knew it was not going to let her leave the apartment that night.

So instead, she sent:

Ava: I'm pretty wiped tonight, babe. Sorry. But soon, I promise!

Vivian replied almost immediately.

Vivian: No worries. But soon, and I'll hold you to it!

She ended with a kissy-face emoji.

Ava felt guilty for a moment as she tossed her phone onto an end table beside the couch. She thought of all the times that Killian had disappeared for days because he was composing, hardly answering her texts, not seeing anyone. She understood—or she'd thought she did—and certainly the end result was worth it, but she always missed him during those times. And now she'd just done the same thing to Vivian.

But Vivian did understand, or she'd always seemed to. She didn't know what she'd done to deserve a friend like that. She just had to hope that Vivian never got sick of her rock star drama.

After scarfing down a sandwich she'd quickly thrown together, Ava went straight to the piano and played her song twice through. Then she got her notebook from her bag, where she had scribbled the beginnings of her lyrics earlier in the day in a quick moment when no one was looking for her, when no one needed her to listen to anything or try out a revised part in one of the songs.

She placed the Moleskine on top of the piano, opened to the page with her scrawled handwriting on it, and started to play the song again. This time she started to sing, letting the melody that the lyrics brought with them unspool in her voice, tentatively at first, then stronger and bolder as it grew more certain of its place in the world. Just as when she had first played the piano part, certain words and notes here and there didn't fit, but she just continued on, knowing she'd go back to fix them later.

When she reached the end, her heart was pounding. She stared down at her hands on the keys for a moment. She hadn't written this song so much as it had written her. It was the most honest she had ever been in her life.

Ava picked up her pen and went back to the lyrics, crossing out a few words and adding new ones, rewriting two lines entirely. She closed her eyes, hearing it once more in her head before beginning to play again. This time, her voice never faltered, and her nerve endings tingled and her stomach fluttered and her skin broke out in goose bumps, and that was when she knew she had something.

Ava played the outro, and then, because she couldn't resist, because she loved the song as much as she was afraid of it, she played it a third time. This time, almost in spite of herself, she found herself mentally swapping out the left hand part for a bass line, the chords for guitar riffs, adding drums to solidly underpin everything as the original piano melody floated over the top. And strings, too, she thought, drifting unobtrusively throughout, and then heightening to an almost unbearable urgency during the bridge.

Once finished, she pulled out her book of staff paper and began transcribing, playing a few chords here and there to be sure, making notes in case it ever came time to fill in the rest of the band's parts. She even clumsily tried her hand at scoring the strings, though she'd never done it before.

She didn't have any concept of how much time had passed when her buzzer rang. She nearly jumped out of her skin at the loud, harsh sound echoing through the apartment. Rising, she walked to the door and pressed the intercom button with a hand that was still shaking slightly. "Who is it?"

CHAPTER 3

"It's Killian. Let me up."

She was nearly as surprised and startled as she had been when she heard the buzzer. She hesitated for a moment—long enough that she knew he felt it—and then buzzed him up.

That was a mistake, she told herself, even as she withdrew her finger from the button and opened the door a crack.

She went and sat back on the piano bench, brushing her fingers silently over the keys, as if to draw strength from them. It didn't work.

A minute later, he stepped inside and shut the door behind him.

Seeing him here was so different than being around him in the studio. There, the professional space kept them safe; the other guys kept them safe; even the music, to a degree, kept them safe. Here there was no such safety, no buffers between them and everything that had gone wrong, was going wrong.

He stood in the doorway for a moment, his black leather coat damp—it must have started to rain outside—as he took her in, sitting there at the piano with her notebook and staff paper scattered around her. He stepped further into the room, and still she didn't get up.

"What do you want, Killian?" she asked, but there was no bite in the words. Even to her own ears, she only sounded tired.

"To see you," he said.

"You saw me earlier today."

"You know that isn't what I mean, Ava."

The sound of her name in his voice, of him rolling it across his tongue, almost undid her. She tried to remember what it felt like, last night, to think that she could live without him, and couldn't quite do it. And yet the fact that she had thought it at all kept her in her seat.

"Really. What are you doing here, Killian?"

"Where else am I supposed to go?" he asked.

"Your house, maybe?"

He shook his head. "That isn't what I mean," he said again.

"For Christ's sake, what *do* you mean, then?" she asked.

Suddenly in a rage, she stood swiftly and stepped toward him. Her palms found his shoulders, and she shoved him. Even though he was a few inches taller than her, he was surprised and stumbled back. "Why can't you ever say what you really mean, Killian? Why is that so hard for you?"

He caught her wrists in his hands. "I do," he said. "I've told you—"

She backed away, weary. "Not in plain words, you don't," she said. "You give me music and poetry and songs and nothing else."

He looked at her as if he didn't know who she was. "That is me saying what I mean," he said. "You know that. I don't have any other way to say it." He paused. "I thought that was what you loved most about me."

Ava turned her back to him. She couldn't answer him, couldn't even look at him, because he was right. Where was a musician more honest than in his—or her—music? "This is real life, Killian," she said. "It isn't a song."

He came up behind her and slid his arms around her waist. "Who says it isn't?" he murmured in her ear.

She pulled away from him. "What the fuck?" she demanded. "You practically ignore me for days, and now you show up here and—"

"I thought that was what you wanted!" he shouted, finally angry now. "I thought you wanted space!"

"It's not!" she cried, and tears stung her eyes. *Damn him,* she thought furiously. *Damn him to hell and back for making me cry and for being here to see it.* "I...I don't *want* it to be like this—"

But she was interrupted when he wrapped his arms around her waist again and kissed her.

She wanted to pull away. She knew she should, but she couldn't. Or didn't really want to. *Damn him,* she thought again, as she felt her arms drape around his neck, as she kissed him back. But the angry voice in her head was fainter now.

He drew back suddenly. "If you want me to go, I'll go."

CHAPTER 3

There are so many ways I drown without you.

She wanted so badly to be able to tell him to get out. Or she thought she did. Ava, who had always been so driven, so clearheaded, who knew herself so well, was suddenly floundering. "You absolute bastard," she said under her breath, and this time she kissed him. She could feel him smiling, and it made her want to slap him even as they stumbled down the hall to her bedroom, shedding clothes and shoes as they went.

It had been so long, and so there were very few preliminaries. Ava practically fell onto the bed, and Killian didn't even bother to unhook her bra. She drew him onto her eagerly, and he thrust into her quickly, almost roughly, and she bit down on his shoulder to muffle her cry, hoping that she hurt him, that she would leave a mark. She came quickly, this time not bothering to be quiet, and he followed soon after, groaning as he buried his face in her hair. He lay atop her for a moment, still inside her, and she kept her legs wrapped tightly around his waist. Part of her wished that they could just stay like this, entwined forever. *Making love has never been one of our problems,* she mused idly as she tried to catch her breath. *It's everything that happens when we're not in bed, lately.*

Eventually he rolled off of her onto his back. He stared up at the ceiling, not touching her, not drawing her against him as he usually did after sex. She remained where she was on her back beside him, not wanting to turn either toward him or away from him. And just like that, the doubt, the fear, the anxiety, the uncertainty that had been wrapping them in its frigid embrace so often of late was back. Ava could trace the path that had brought them here—or she thought she could, if she tried hard enough—and even still she couldn't quite bring herself to believe it. Nor could she, for the life of her, see the way out.

She got up to use the bathroom, which adjoined her bedroom. As she washed her hands, she stared at the outline of her reflection in the dark mirror. *I could be anyone,* she thought, even as her eyes adjusted and some of her features began to emerge: long curly hair, wide eyes, silver hoop through her left nostril. *Maybe someday the dark will swallow me. Or Killian will.*

She went back into the bedroom and saw that he had fallen asleep. She rolled her eyes. So much for the vague idea she'd had of kicking him out.

She got back into bed and dozed off as well. When she woke up again she found that she had moved toward Killian in her sleep and was nestled against his chest. He was trailing one hand over her hip and smiled, ever so slightly, when he saw that she was awake. "Having sweet dreams?"

She chuckled. "Not with you here."

He laughed. "Next time I'll have to make slow, sweet love to you, then."

Next time. She didn't know what those words meant or what she wanted them to mean. Not anymore.

He brushed a curl away from her face. "What were you working on when I came in?"

Her heart started beating out an alarm. *Danger. Danger.* "A song."

"I figured that." He waited until she made the mistake of glancing up to meet his eyes. "Can I hear it?"

She shrugged.

"I want to hear it, Ava. You haven't played anything for me in a long time."

And whose fault is that? She wanted to spit the words in his face. But this was not the time to hash this out, not when they were in bed together for the first time in—weeks? Had it been months? Surely not.

Or maybe it was the perfect time. She couldn't be certain of anything anymore.

"Please, Ava," he said. "I want you to play it for me."

"No, you don't."

She felt his whole body tighten. "What is that supposed to mean?"

She was fully awake now, the blood raging through her veins

CHAPTER 3

again. She wanted him to drop it, to stop insisting. Why couldn't he have insisted before? With the last song she'd played him? Why did he have to pick now, why did he have to pick this song?

She wasn't sure which she wanted more—to play it for him or not to.

She heard, again, the arrangements for the band she had been plotting out before Killian interrupted her and was struck with an almost physical need to hear it aloud for real. But was that more important than whatever was left between them?

"Fine," she said out loud. "Since you insist."

She got out of bed and pulled on her robe—Chinese silk, which Killian had bought for her on their last tour through Asia. *Do I have nothing that doesn't come from him?* Ava wondered irritably.

He pulled on his pants, leaving his shirt draped over his arm. On the way back out to the living room, he picked up his boots from where he'd left them in the hallway and placed them next to the door.

"All right," he said, sprawling on the couch beside the piano. "Let's hear it."

She *hated* that voice—his maestro voice. It reminded her of a horrid choir director she'd had in high school, who was always keen to cut down any who were guilty of even the tiniest mistake. Any doubts she may have had about playing the song because it might hurt him crumbled into ashes. "Okay," she said. "This song is called 'Appassionata'."

So she played, and she sang.

There was one word
At the top of the pages you gave me:
'Appassionata', you bade me,
And I obeyed.
And I sang.

The strings of my passion

HEAVY METAL SYMPHONY

Are held between your fingers,
Be merciful now, puppet master.

Love with passion,
Sing with passion,
Bleed with passion,
Hate with passion.
And someday I'll have the strength
  to bid you a passionate goodbye.

Are the words on my lips
Mine or yours?
"Save me", I begged you,
And you obeyed.

The strings of my passion
Are held between your fingers,
Be merciful now, puppet master.

Love with passion,
Sing with passion,
Bleed with passion,
Hate with passion.
And someday I'll have the strength
  to bid you a passionate goodbye.

The strings have turned to steel,
Cold steel that binds me fast,
I cry into the night
And don't know if you hear;
This passion can kill,
But it won't let us die.

Love with passion,
Sing with passion,

CHAPTER 3

Bleed with passion,
Hate with passion,
Die with passion.
And someday soon I'll have the strength
  to bid you a passionate goodbye.

And in the darkest night
I whisper to myself
That only I can save me.
Only I can hear me.

Her voice was a bit scratchy with the remnants of sleep at first, but as she went on, it smoothed out and soon she was singing at full voice, without hesitation. She wished she could lose herself in the song as she had before and forget that he was there, but she couldn't. He was there, and he was listening, and as uncomfortable as she was, his presence made the circle complete.

Yet even as she wished it could be over, she forced herself not to speed up, to play the song exactly as it was meant to be played. She owed it—the song—that much. As to what she owed Killian, well, she did not stop to consider that.

When she finally reached the end, she didn't look up for a moment. She withdrew her hands from the keys, waiting for him to speak. When he did not, she glanced apprehensively over at him.

He was sitting forward, his elbows resting on his knees, his head down. His long, dark hair was wild, spilling down his bare back and over his shoulders. When he sensed her watching him, he looked up, and she saw that his eyes were rimmed with red.

"It's beautiful," he said, and she could hear that, no matter what it cost him to say so, he meant it. "It really is, Ava. I hope you know that."

She didn't speak.

He stood up and pulled on his shirt, then he grabbed his jacket from the back of the couch, where he'd left it. He walked to the door and pulled his boots on.

Ava rose from the piano bench and started toward him, but when she saw the ravaged look his eyes as he looked up, she stopped short. "Did I break us?" she whispered.

If he heard her, he didn't respond before he left.

chapter 4

The Art of Escape
2009

They had met the way most people met in Buffalo: introduced by a mutual friend. In this case, Killian's sister and Ava's former roommate Denise.

Ava recognized him, waiting patiently at the edge of the crowd of people who had come to congratulate her. She was flushed and smiling, gratefully accepting everyone's kind words. She knew it had been one of her best performances, and that the time she'd spent rehearsing and the money she'd spent preparing and renting the church and paying the accompanist had all been worth it.

When she saw that Killian Sterling had apparently been in the audience, she was doubly glad she'd knocked it out of the park.

They waited until the rest of the audience members had drifted away before approaching: Denise with her brother Killian in tow. Ava found herself wishing Denise might have given her a heads up that she was bringing Killian to the performance.

Maybe it's better that she didn't, Ava thought, her heartbeat tripling as Killian met her eyes. *After all, had I known I would have been nervous, and I don't think I could have sung any better than I just did.*

"Ava, that was amazing!" Denise said as they drew closer. "That was the best I've ever heard you sing! Anyway, I have someone I want you to meet and who wants to meet you." She motioned to Killian. "Ava, my brother, Killian Sterling. Killian, my friend Ava Tomei, my roommate from college."

Killian reached out to shake her hand. "Wonderful to meet you, Ava. You were absolutely phenomenal."

"Wow, thank you so much!" Ava said, trying to keep her tone as professional as possible so she didn't sound like a complete fangirl. "And thank you for coming! Denise probably told you that I'm a huge fan of the band."

"She did mention it, yes," he said. "I'm honored that such a great musician is a fan." He smiled, and Ava felt herself go a bit weak at the knees.

In addition to being—in Ava's opinion—a musical genius,

CHAPTER 4

Killian was also good-looking. Extremely good-looking. He had long, wavy dark hair that he had pulled back and that complimented his pale skin; high, sculpted cheekbones; a neat moustache and goatee; and—Ava's weakness—bright blue eyes.

"I've been wanting to introduce you two for a while, but it never worked out," Denise said. "I figure you'll have a lot to talk about!"

"Yeah, I think maybe we do," Killian said, his eyes still on Ava. "Shall we all go out for a drink?"

"Yeah, that sounds good!" Denise said, looping her arm through Killian's.

"That would be great," Ava managed. She couldn't quite believe that *Killian Sterling* had not only come to her recital, but had asked her out for a drink on top of it.

But then, it wasn't like he was asking her *out* out, right? After all, his sister was with them.

Get it together, Ava told herself sharply. *You just met him. You're going for drinks. You'll likely never see him again after tonight, so none of this matters.*

Ava popped back into the sacristy of the church to collect her coat and purse. When she came back out into the nave, she saw Killian waiting for her, alone. "Denise went to get the car," he explained, "so I offered to wait for you. We can drop you back at your car after, if that's okay?"

"Perfect," she said. "Thanks." She was about to start down the long aisle that led to the main entrance when he gently grabbed her left wrist, studying the tattoo that twined around it. It was a music staff with notes placed along it. He hummed them as he turned her wrist slightly, reading the melody. "Puccini's 'Vissi d'arte'," he said, glancing up at her. "Gorgeous."

She smiled, enjoying the heat of his fingers on her wrist. "Thank you. I just got that less than a year ago."

"Why that piece?" he wanted to know. "It's a great choice; I'm just curious."

She explained as they walked slowly toward the door. "Well,

I've always loved it," she said. "And being a mezzo-soprano, it's not quite right for my voice, but I finally ended up learning it anyway for a recital I gave last year. I got the tattoo after I performed it. And I'm sure you noticed that the notes are just the first phrase: *'Vissi d'arte, vissi d'amore'*. It's my reminder to always live for art and for the people and things I love."

He was smiling when she looked over at him again, but it was a small, quiet smile; an intimate smile, just for her. "That's beautiful," he said. "Really beautiful."

The three of them went to a nearby bar for a drink and spent a pleasant evening talking about music and what acquaintances the three of them had in common. Before the night ended, Killian had asked for Ava's phone number, which she happily gave him. She didn't know if he was interested in her romantically or musically or both, but whatever it was, it was more than just simple politeness, that she could tell. There had seemed to be a connection, both in the church and then again a few times at the bar, when their eyes had locked and held for a few moments before one of them—usually Ava—looked away.

As she drove back to her apartment that night, she tried to tell herself not to get her hopes up, that he probably wouldn't call.

She hoped he would.

chapter 5

Album #5
2016

The next morning, Ava was the last one to arrive at the studio. Killian merely nodded in greeting once again, as though he hadn't shown up at her apartment and seduced her the night before.

The rest of the guys greeted her as cheerfully as ever, yet she couldn't help but feel as though, somehow, they knew all about what had happened last night. There was no way they could; Killian would never have said anything. They were all too aware of the tension—to put it mildly—between her and Killian of late, but how much they knew about its sources Ava could only wonder. What was plain was that things were not as comfortable as usual among the band members, and that, perhaps more than anything else, could not go on. For the first time, Ava thought that maybe she should bow out. She was the newcomer to Handel's Messiah, after all; it was Killian's baby, really. Yet hard on the heels of her visions of noble self-sacrifice came indignant fury. First of all, they were in the middle of recording; second of all, there were things of hers here, in this band, things that she had helped to build. She would be damned if she would walk away from it. Even if they were nothing else to one another again, she and Killian would need to learn to work together professionally.

These thoughts, she found, were akin to carrying hot coals in her pocket: she could not forget about them for very long.

The whole band was in the production room, playing back the last of Rafael's bass parts. When Rafael nailed a particularly challenging riff in the recording, Ben slapped him on the shoulder.

"That sounds killer," Ava said.

Rafael beamed, but, ever the professional, he quickly turned back to work. He asked, "Should we keep going? Killian, are you ready to record today or do you want to come back fresh tomorrow?"

"Maybe we should wait," Killian said. "I may have a new song to learn. We all might, actually."

Ava froze in her seat. She stared determinedly at the floor, picking at the fraying upholstery of her chair. She would not

CHAPTER 5

look at Killian. He did not mean what she thought he meant. He couldn't.

"Another new one, huh?" their sound engineer, Rich, asked, managing to sound both exasperated and excited.

"What new song?" Rafael asked doubtfully. "Killian, we've got more than enough songs. I don't know if we should really take the time out from recording to rehearse it."

Ava saw, out of the corner of her eye, Killian shrug. "It's up to Ava."

"Ava?" Joel asked.

"Yes. It's Ava's song," Killian said.

Ava finally looked up, and she wished she hadn't, wished she had never seen the look on Killian's face just then. He looked, somehow, both furious and devastated at the same time. *Who exactly is he torturing here?* Ava wondered angrily. *Me or himself?*

But the rest of the guys were looking expectantly at her, so she had to say something. She sighed. "It's not a big deal. I just wrote it, and Killian insisted on hearing it." She looked right at him as she said those last words. "I didn't write it thinking it would go on the album or anything."

"Why did you write it, then?" Killian asked.

It took everything she had not to explode at him, right there, in front of everyone. *Not the time, you asshole. Not the place.* "Why does anyone write a song?" She waved a hand dismissively. "Let's just forget about it."

"I don't know," Joel said slowly. "I'd like to hear it."

"Yeah," Rafael added, and Ben nodded in agreement.

Killian's eyes bored into her. "Do you have the score? Your notes?"

"No."

"Why not?"

"Jesus Christ, Killian. I said I didn't write it for it to go on the record. Why would I have brought anything with me?"

The rest of the guys were starting to look uncomfortable

now, and Ava hated it. If there was anything they could break that absolutely should not be broken, it was the band.

"Can you play it for us from memory?" Killian asked. "Then at least everyone can decide if they like it and if we want to record it."

You sadistic, masochistic bastard. "If you *really* want me to," she asked him.

"Yeah!" Rafael said, the most oblivious—as usual—to the mood. "Come on, Ava, let's hear it."

Ava got up and led them—except Rich, who stayed in the control room—like the Pied Piper, back into the recording room with the grand piano. She felt as though she were walking to her own execution. *Apt,* she thought, *because something is going to die here today.*

He did this, she reminded herself. *He did this, and he can never blame me for it.* But she knew Killian well enough by then to know that that wasn't exactly the way his mind worked.

Somehow, playing the song for the whole band was far less excruciating than playing it for just Killian had been. Now it felt more like a performance, instead of something painfully, terrifyingly intimate. She found herself slipping into her performance persona as she played and sang, which was really just a bolder, more confident version of Ava.

When she finished, there was a moment of uncomfortable silence, and she could almost hear the mental reassurances each of the guys was reciting to himself: *Shit, that song is about them, right? It must be, and that's why they were arguing. But...Killian had already heard it, right? If it was about him, he wouldn't have asked to play it for us, right? He must be okay with it. It must be fine.*

"Shit," Rafael said finally. "That's kickass, Ava."

"Yeah," Joel chimed in. "I don't think I've ever heard anything you've written before, but that's awesome."

"Yeah," Ben added. "You started to arrange it for the band? Is that what Killian said?" He glanced at Killian for confirmation.

CHAPTER 5

Killian nodded, keeping his eyes fixed on Ava. "I told you it was beautiful," he said to her.

And I didn't doubt you, Ava longed to say but didn't. *Things can be true without you saying so. You're not the only one who can have pride and confidence in your own talent.* "Thanks, guys," she said aloud. "Seriously, though, I didn't write it thinking it would go on the record. It just sort of…came out, you know? We don't need to spend the time rehearsing, and we already finished recording the drums and bass, so—"

"No," Ben interrupted as they all went back into the control room. "We can do it. If you already started arranging, we can figure the rest out pretty quick."

"Yeah," Rafael said. "I think it should go on the album. I really like it, and I bet it'll really rock once we get all the parts together."

"Definitely," Joel said. "It'll be great live for the tour, too." He glanced over at Rich. "As long as Rich is on board, too, and we have the time."

Rich threw his hands up in the air. "It's your studio, folks," he said. "You're the ones signing my paychecks. I'll record whatever you want me to record."

Ava looked up at Killian again, wanting to make sure that he saw and understood the monster he had unleashed. It was out of either of their hands now, and he had done that.

For once, though, she couldn't read the expression on his face. His eyes were full and dark, almost navy blue, and she, even after years with this man, years of being at his side, of talking to him about everything, of making music with him, of making love to him, could not tell what they were saying to her.

Only later would she realize that it had been sadness.

"Alright," she said then, standing up and heading for the door. "I'll run home and get my notes."

Home alone again that night, after an afternoon of explaining to each of the band members what she had in mind for their parts, of watching them learn what she had written and add to it and improve upon it, she felt like a dam within her had been shattered. She sat at her piano for hours, and by the time she got up, almost shaky from sitting so long, from her single-minded focus, she had written another song, music and lyrics. She had no plans for this one either and vowed that she wouldn't let Killian press her into playing it for him—not that she expected him to ask. No, her one song—a blood-spattered creature of pain and desperation—would be given life, would go out into the world fully realized, and that was more than she had ever thought to ask for. This second song, and any others that came after it—for there were more; she could feel them inside her, writhing like snakes in their gestation—she would write and keep. Maybe someday they would be Handel's Messiah songs, maybe not. Maybe no one besides her would ever hear them. That wasn't the point, not really. The point was creating them; the point was that they existed and were hers. The point was that feeling she got when she sat at the piano and forgot everything else, escaped into another world and brought back with her what she found there. It was a similar creative immersion, almost an ecstasy, as she had when performing, but different. Not better, just different. The world she escaped to when writing was one inside herself, whereas when she stepped onstage, she stepped into a world others had created for her, albeit one she loved to visit.

Killian did not show up that night. She hadn't expected him to.

chapter 6

The Art of Escape
2009

He called. And he kept calling.

The week after they met, Killian took her for drinks again; then he took her for dinner a few nights later on Friday. He also took her to see the Buffalo Philharmonic Orchestra perform Vivaldi's *The Four Seasons,* one of her favorite pieces. She felt a little like Cinderella, with Killian as a heavy metal Prince Charming.

Ava *thought* these were dates, but honestly it was a little difficult to be sure. When he dropped her off after taking her to dinner, he'd gotten out of the car and walked her to the door of her apartment building—certainly a chivalrous gesture in the Elmwood Village where parking was hard to come by—and as they'd said goodnight he had hesitated, leaned in for a moment, and Ava had been sure he was going to kiss her. But he hadn't—had simply held her gaze for a moment, then looked away and taken a step back—and she wasn't sure why.

She was attracted to him in all the ways that it was possible to be attracted to someone: physically, emotionally, mentally. Musically. She was attracted to his talent, that was for sure—it was a major turn on. She thought all of that was clear to him, but maybe not. Maybe she wasn't any good at this. At the ripe old age of twenty-four, she had only had one serious boyfriend, and he had been a fellow music major in college named Dan. They had carried out a slow courtship freshman year that involved using adjacent practice rooms accidentally-on-purpose for a few weeks before he finally invited her for coffee, and things had gone from there. Ava had lost her virginity to him, and they had dated for two years before he dumped her for a girl Ava knew vaguely from seeing her around campus. A pre-med student. Ava had been devastated.

Dan had been a piano major, so it could certainly be said, Ava thought wryly, that she had a type. She didn't know if she was Killian's type or not, but she desperately wanted to be. He was already thirty, six years older than her—could that be his hang up? But, as sexist as it was, what guy had a hang up about *not* wanting to date a younger woman? Ava wasn't quite sure what to make of him.

On perhaps their fourth date—if that's what it was—he took her to Hutch's, where she had never been before but had always wanted to go.

After they'd ordered and the waiter had poured their wine, Killian said, "I've been meaning to ask you, do you have any more performances coming up?"

"Nothing planned, unfortunately," she said. "There's an opera

CHAPTER 6

audition coming up that I'm getting ready for, but as for another recital like the one you saw..." She shrugged. "It's tough. I have to rent the hall or the church and hire the accompanist. It's worth it because I love doing it, but it costs a decent amount of money, and so I have to save up before I can do it again."

Killian was frowning as she finished speaking. "People should be paying to hear *you*, not the other way around," he said.

She laughed, somewhat self-consciously. The more time they had spent together, even in spite of her uncertainty about what their relationship was, the more relaxed she had become around him, for they really did have a lot in common, and he was fun to be with. Yet every so often, she would remember: he was *Killian Sterling*, rock star and one of her favorite musicians. "Yeah, that would be nice," she said, picking up her wine glass and taking a sip.

He spun the stem of his own wine glass between his thumb and forefinger, thinking. Finally he looked back up at her. "What if I helped you?"

For a moment she truly didn't know what he meant. "If you... what? With what?"

"Helped you put a performance together," he clarified. "I could accompany you myself. I know a few people in the music department at Buff State—I'm sure I could get them to let us have Rockwell Hall for a night." He smiled. "And not to sound too high on myself, but I am rather well known around here. If I was playing, I could guarantee you a good-sized audience."

She was speechless. Just the fact that Killian Sterling wanted to spend time with her still occasionally blew her mind; that he wanted to work with her musically was a completely different level of fantasy.

"Oh," she said intelligently, when she finally found her voice. "That's...I mean, that's an incredible offer, but you don't have to...I'm sure you're super busy with the band and all..."

Killian shrugged. "I'm here for another few months," he said. "I'm writing new music for the next album—and seeing you, of course," and here he gave her that smile that made her knees go weak, even when she was sitting down. "We go back out to Los Angeles in early October to record. So say we schedule something for some time in September—would that work for you?"

Her head was spinning. Was this really happening? It was July; this would give them plenty of time to work together, select a program, and rehearse. To spend more time together. "What's the catch?" she asked suspiciously.

"The catch?" He reached across the table and took her hand. "You're a beautiful woman with an incredible voice that I'm pretty sure you can do anything with. The catch, I guess, is that if we're going to work together we should keep it professional."

At this, her heart sank even as the musician in her rejoiced at this chance that she had never dared to dream of. It seemed it was too good to be true that she could date Killian and collaborate with him musically, but one out of two wasn't bad. And having the choice to make, she would choose her music—if only by a slim margin. "Okay. Yes," she said. "I accept your offer."

He smiled at her again and poured some more wine into her glass.

The next morning, Killian texted and asked if she'd like to come to his place on Tuesday with some of her sheet music so they could start putting together a program. He'd just emailed someone he knew at Buff State about picking a date and getting the hall, and he said he was sure it wouldn't be a problem.

Ava had half expected to wake up and find that his offer of the night before had been a dream. But it hadn't been, and so she texted back that she could come over Tuesday after work. Then, starting to get excited since it seemed that this might really and truly happen, she went to look through her scores to see what she'd like to perform.

Killian was renting a house in North Buffalo, off of Hertel Avenue. It was a smaller house on a street full of larger ones, and it was in a quiet neighborhood that felt almost suburban. "It's not much, but it suits me for the time being," he said as he let her in and gave her a quick tour. "I'm not home enough to buy something, and I don't really have the money for that right now anyway. I've been subletting this place for the last couple years while I'm not here, but once we go back out to Los Angeles in a few months the lease will be up and I'm going to let it go. After this next tour, we'll see."

They went back into the living room, where a baby grand piano dominated most of the room. "So what have you brought?" he asked, leaning his forearms on the piano's lid.

She pulled a pile of scores out of the tote bag she always used

CHAPTER 6

for her sheet music: it was printed with a treble clef and the words "Treble Maker". Dorky, but it had been a gift from her parents, and she loved it. "I've got some things here I've performed before that we can definitely include, and then some new things I've been meaning to learn," she said, passing the pile to him. He began to leaf through it. "I'd love your opinion, of course."

He was silent for a moment as he looked through the music. "Alright," he said aloud. "Which pieces are you wanting to have, for sure?"

"I think 'Vissi d'arte',"—here they exchanged a quick smile—"since it's been a while since I've performed that one." She paused and considered. "I think this Vivaldi aria, too—'Tu dormi in tante pene'. You heard me do that one, I know; I really love that one. The Card Aria from Carmen." She hesitated. "Maybe 'Una voce poco fa' again? I don't know, I'm a little sick of that one. Everyone does it."

He laughed. Killian had heard her sing that piece at the recital where they'd met. "No one does it like you, though. But okay, we can keep that one on the back burner. What else?"

"Probably 'Voi che sapete'. A lot of people know that one, so it's usually a crowd-pleaser." She smiled. "I don't always worship at the altar of Mozart, but a lot of his opera music is really fun to sing."

"I agree—I wouldn't know how fun he is to sing, but some of his music has always left me kind of cold." He wrinkled his nose. "And what's with 'Cosi fan tutte'? Is there a more sexist opera?"

Ava was pretty sure she felt herself fall in love with him at that moment. *But we need to be professional,* she reminded herself, except now that seemed like a bigger downside than ever before. "I know, right?" she said in response, and they both smiled at each other.

She could feel herself flushing and quickly looked back down at the music. "These two: 'Forgotten' by Amy Beach and 'Liebst du um Schönheit' by Clara Schumann, since I like to highlight female composers when I can."

"That's great," Killian said, looking at the sheet music. "The Schumann seems vaguely familiar, and I know Beach's name, but not this song. They both seem perfect for your voice, though."

"Yeah, they lay really nice. I've performed them both before." She handed over her last two scores. "Then I have two I definitely want to learn—'Stride la vampa' from *Il trovatore* and the first movement of Vivaldi's *Stabat Mater*." She handed him the score for the latter.

He flipped open the cover and paged through it. "I don't know this one, but it looks beautiful." He hummed softly under his breath for a moment.

"It is. I have a recording of it that I just love. I don't know why I haven't learned it before now. That first movement isn't terribly complicated, vocally."

"No," he agreed, reading through it. "Simple but powerful. For contralto." He closed his eyes for a moment. "Yes, I think this'll be perfect for you. It'll really let you show off your lower range."

She blushed again at his praise.

"Okay, I think that's plenty to work with." He looked up at her. "Where do you want to start?"

She hesitated. "Let's start with the *Stabat Mater*. I'd like to take a stab at it."

He let her use the piano to go through her usual warm ups—she felt extremely self-conscious warming up in front of him, but forced herself to *be professional* and let it go. Then she gave up her seat at the piano so that he could play. He read over the piece once more, than began to play the haunting, melancholy opening of the *Stabat Mater*'s first movement.

A few bars before her entrance, Ava took a few deep breaths as she usually did to prepare—and today, this time, she was in even more need than usual of calming down and gathering her focus.

This was a chance beyond her wildest dreams. She could not blow it.

chapter 7

Album #5
2016

The next day in the studio, Ava arrived to find the guys all just as excited about the new song—*her* song—as they had been the day before. They had hammered out most of the parts the day before, and once they all got there, they decided to rehearse the song before starting their recording for the day.

Ava had yet to copy out the piano part for Killian—it was changing, anyway, with the addition of the rest of the band. "Sorry," she told him as she sat down behind the piano. "I'll transcribe it today."

He nodded, arms crossed over his chest. "Sure. No problem," he said, his voice blank.

"You can listen," Ben said to Killian, positioning himself behind his drum kit, "and let us know how it's sounding."

"Yeah," Rafael agreed. "That'll actually be really helpful."

Killian lowered himself onto a stool along the wall and leaned back against the wood-paneling. "Works for me."

Ava felt nervous as she started playing, the piano beginning the song before being joined by the guitar, bass, and drums. *Will I spend the rest of my career anxious about playing this song?* she wondered, even as she began to sing.

Will I spend the rest of my career hurting the person I'm supposed to love best?

Or will I spend the rest of my career letting him hurt me?

It all fell away, though, as she played and sang, as she listened to the rest of the band's parts out loud, in a space other than her own head. Goosebumps tracked their way up and down her arms, and she wished she could stop and stand apart to hear this thing that she had created in its entirety. She wanted to just be able to listen and sink into it in a way you couldn't while you were performing it, not totally. She wished she could hear it the way Killian was hearing it just then. And she wondered if, at that moment, he wanted to be able to trade places with her.

When they stopped, Killian got to his feet. "It sounds great," he said. To Ava's surprise, he sounded genuinely enthusiastic.

CHAPTER 7

Joel nodded. "It felt great, too. It really meshed together already."

"Yes," Killian said. "I think there are still some things that need to be tweaked before we can think about recording it, but we shouldn't spend any more time on it now." He paused for a moment. "What if we all meet at my house tonight after we leave here? We can really rehearse it and polish it then."

Ava nodded and agreed along with the rest of the guys, even as she felt dread hatching in her stomach. Killian was taking this struggle—and her song—onto his own turf. Could she really play and sing it there, in his space? Or was she reading way too much into this?

Not everything he did was a challenge to her, she reminded herself, even if it sometimes felt that way.

Still, everyone was in agreement, and they got down to work beginning to record Killian's keyboard parts for the other songs. True to her word, Ava found a corner of the studio where she'd be out of the way and began copying out the piano part for "Appassionata" on some sheets of blank staff paper. It would continue to change as they rehearsed it some more, and that was as it should be. No doubt it would change a bit more once Killian got his hands on it, just as Ava would change her vocal lines and Raf his bass lines and Joel his guitar licks. She continued dutifully copying out the music.

She laid low for most of the day as Killian recorded. Hearing his keyboard parts made her fall in love all over again with this album they were recording, made her as excited and passionate about the songs as she had been when she'd first heard them, ready to get out onto the road and play them live for the fans. She tried to remember to hold onto that, even when everything else felt like it was unraveling. Her love of the music, at least, would never change.

Later that night, as planned, they all went to Killian's house. Just last year he had bought a big old house from the turn of the century on Bidwell Parkway, barely a block from Elmwood. It was one of Ava's favorite areas of Buffalo, and the parkway—with lots of green space in between the two roadways where there were often community events and farmer's markets—had some truly gorgeous old houses. Killian's had a grayish brick façade that had always made Ava think of a castle. He had soundproofed and remodeled the basement to make it into a perfect rehearsal space. He had a spare set of drums there, as well as an upright piano and an electric keyboard, and assorted instruments that he dabbled with here and there: violin, viola, harp, flute. Scattered around as well were amps, effects pedals, mics and mic stands, and what had to be miles worth of cord.

Ever since Killian had bought the house, they had tossed around the idea of Ava moving in, but they spent so much time on the road that it had never ended up happening. Ava had always felt that it was probably a good idea for them to each have their own space, since they spent so much time together already, and she liked her apartment. Lately, she was especially glad they'd never taken the step of moving in together.

Ava was—purposefully—the last to arrive, and by the time she made her way down into the basement the guys were almost finished setting up their gear. Killian stood expectantly next to the keyboard.

"Here," she said, handing him the sheet music she'd copied out earlier. "You left the studio before I had a chance to give this to you."

He studied the pages for a moment, then set them on the music stand attached to the top of the keyboard. "I had a thought," he said slowly, and the rest of the band members looked up, giving him their attention. "Since we're a little pressed for time in terms of recording this song, what if I don't play the piano on the album?" He glanced at Ava. "What if you just do it instead?"

CHAPTER 7

The basement went silent at this. *What is he saying?* Ava wondered anxiously. *Surely now the rest of the guys must know something is up with him—when has Killian ever stepped aside musically? Or in anything related to the band?* "No," Ava said, when it seemed as though no one else was going to speak, hating that what should have been a debate amongst the whole band was becoming a conversation—an argument, potentially—between Killian and herself. "You're the pianist, Killian. I'm not trying to take over what you do."

He held up his hands, palms open, in a placating gesture. "I'll learn to play it for the tour, if we decide to put it in the set list."

"And we should, I think," Joel interjected. "It rocks, and it'll rock even more live."

Killian nodded but kept his eyes on Ava. "You would just play it to record it. It'll just make everything easier and faster that way. Besides, I can never know it as well as you do."

Ava held his gaze, searching his eyes for answers that she knew she'd never find. *Do you not want to play it on the record yourself out of the principle of the thing?* she wondered. *Because no matter how much sense your reasons make, everyone in this room knows you can learn to play it in just a couple of hours. What game are you playing? And why do you have to do it with my song?* "Whatever you guys prefer," she said out loud, turning to the rest of the band. "Killian, it's up to you, I guess." She caught his eyes again. "At this point, I just want it to go on the record, however we've got to do it."

I can play the game, too.

⁓⁕⁓

They practiced for a few hours, and despite Killian having apparently decided to cede his position to Ava for this song, he did step in to play certain sections so she could hear it. They played it through without the vocals a few times, allowing Ava to rearrange a few parts and the guys to make suggestions based on the sound and whatever felt best. Ava, like Killian whenever they were rehearsing one of his songs, had a clear idea of how she wanted the song to sound, but as she wasn't a guitarist or drummer or bassist, she generally agreed with whatever Joel, Ben, and Rafael had to say, as they were the experts in their instruments. Then they went through it several times with the vocals. They paused for a break around eight, ordered some subs, ate, and then went right back to work.

It was getting close to midnight when they all agreed the song was as good as it was going to be, and everyone knew their parts well enough to record it. "How do you want to do this, then?" Rafael asked, as everyone was getting ready to leave. "Should we keep going with the keyboards and then guitar and vocals, and then go back and do this whole song from the ground up?"

Killian thought about it for a minute. "Why don't we do this," he said. "I'll finish the keys in the next couple days, and then we'll go back and have Ben do the drums and have you do the bass for the new song. Then Ava can record the piano, and then we can have Joel record all the guitars in one stretch and have Ava do all her vocals at once." He looked around at the rest of them for approval. "This way the song has a few days to kind of sit in our heads, too, since we really wore it out tonight."

There were general nods of assent. "Works for me," Ben said.

Joel punched him and Rafael on the shoulders at the same time. "Just when you jackasses thought your work was done," he joked.

They all laughed, and everyone gathered their things—coats, bags, instruments—and headed upstairs to the front door. "Thanks for coming by, everyone," Killian said, walking them all to the door.

"Yeah, thanks for having us, man," Rafael said. "It was a good idea. We got a lot done."

"See you tomorrow," Joel said.

Ava was behind the three of them as they headed out the door, yet as she went to leave she felt a hand on her arm. "Wait,"

CHAPTER 7

Killian said, his voice low. "Can you stay for a bit?"

Ava bit her lip, hesitating, and did not turn to face him. This was exactly what she had been trying to avoid.

"Please," he said, still lightly holding her upper arm.

She sighed and turned around, shutting the door behind her. "Just for a little while," she stipulated. "I want to get to bed soon. I haven't been sleeping well lately."

She saw as Killian registered her words, could almost see him thinking through the possible implications. She mentally cursed herself for revealing so much. Then, right away, she felt tired, exhausted by the games she herself was playing with both of them. And it occurred to her that that seemed to be the way her relationship with Killian made her feel most often of late: tired.

She followed him back through the living room and into the kitchen. "Do you want some wine?" he asked. "Or a beer?"

She thought about crossing her arms over her chest and just telling him to get to the point, but that seemed too aggressive, unnecessarily so. What if he had no point to make, no master plan in asking her to stay? What if he just wanted to spend time with her again, try to get things back to normal?

"Sure," she said. "Wine sounds good."

He went into the dining room, where his wine rack was, and came back with a bottle of their favorite red. He got two glasses down from a cupboard, and without being asked she uncorked the bottle and poured. They both took a sip at the same time, looking away from each other.

Ava was just about to suggest they go sit in the living room or even at the dining room table—anything rather than just standing awkwardly in the kitchen—when Killian spoke.

"It really is a wonderful song, Ava," he said. "I mean it."

She met his eyes. "I know," she said. "You wouldn't have even told the guys about it if you didn't think so. You would never have suggested it go on the album, no matter how much you're trying to punish the both of us."

He looked taken aback at her words. "Is that what you think I'm doing?" he asked.

"Isn't it?"

"Have you done something you need to be punished for, Ava?" Killian asked.

Ava felt her face go red. "Maybe you think so."

"I don't. I promise you I don't think any such thing. We've disagreed, we've fought, so what? Every couple does. So, no, that is sure as hell not why I want us to do this song. You don't think I'm capable of putting art before my personal feelings? Or yours?"

"No," she said. "I didn't think you were capable of that, honestly."

They were both silent for a moment before he spoke again. "I guess…I guess that's fair," he said. "Is that what you were doing when you wrote that song? Trying to punish me?"

She hated the tone of his voice, the cool, impersonal way in which he asked or said the things that were most fraught between them, as if he didn't care one way or another. He was always like this, whenever they had fought or disagreed about anything. Ava wished he would get mad, shout, yell, slam his hand on the counter. This controlled coldness infuriated her more than his anger ever could. She was afraid of it because she didn't know what to do with it.

She took a deep breath to calm herself and tried to answer as casually as he had asked. "Of course not. The music came first, and then the words just followed. You of all people know how it is. And I can't not write about what I'm feeling."

He studied her for a moment. "You are writing a lot, then? Before this song, I haven't heard anything in…I can't think how long."

"I stopped playing them for you. My songs."

He fell silent again. Then he shook his head. "I don't know what you want me to say, Ava. If you don't know what you want, then you can hardly expect me to give it to you."

These words cut deeper than anything he had said thus far,

CHAPTER 7

than any of the tense silences and brief spats that had happened in the days prior. Because he was right. Ava didn't know what she wanted from him anymore, and she couldn't go on punishing him for that fact. "You're right," she said, setting her still mostly full wine glass down on the counter. "You're absolutely right, Killian." She turned and made for the door. "I'm leaving. Goodnight."

He came up behind her and caught her around the waist. "Ava, don't leave like this."

She pulled away from him and turned to face him again. "I am *not* going to bed with you again."

The finality of her words hung in the air between them, bringing into sharp relief the question that was unspoken but very much present, now: *Not tonight or not ever again?*

Killian sighed. "The other night," he said. "That was—"

"A mistake?" Ava spat, only because she knew she would not be able to bear hearing him say it.

Finally, finally, he began to look angry. "That is not the word I would use. But have it your way."

"I wish I could get away from you, Killian," she said before she could stop herself. "I wish I could go without seeing you for a while, so I can figure this out."

He laughed mirthlessly. "That's the problem, isn't it? We're stuck with each other."

"I guess we are," she said. "Because I am not walking away from this band, Killian. I'm not Celeste."

Killian's face betrayed his hurt for a moment before he composed himself again. That had been a bit of a low blow, and Ava knew it, but she didn't regret saying it. "But I'll tell you this," she went on. "Be that as it may, I don't want you to be 'stuck' with me. I don't want to be with you because I'm your default."

With that, she turned and walked out, and this time he didn't try to stop her.

chapter 8

The Art of Escape
2009

CHAPTER 8

Ava and Killian spent the next few weeks rehearsing for her recital, when both their schedules allowed. She learned the first movement of the *Stabat Mater* quickly, and they both found that the piece fit her voice perfectly and didn't require much rehearsal. Ava was almost disappointed by this, as she absolutely loved singing it. It felt effortless in her voice, like rolling a ball down a hill: she only had to give it a little push to get it started. So, somewhat reluctantly, she set it aside and turned her attention to the more difficult music.

Killian had talked her into including "Una voce poco fa" in the program after all, telling her what a showstopper it was when she sang it. She eventually agreed, and so spent a bit of time polishing and improving her performance of it, wanting to live up to his assessment.

She also took her time with learning "Stride la vampa", which was different from the rest of her repertoire: darker and heavier. Yet she found it suited her voice well, and knew she'd be learning more pieces like it in the future. For now, though, she focused on taking it apart, phrase by phrase, word by word, and note by note, and reconstructing it from the ground up until she knew it backwards and forwards.

She put off Killian for a while when he would ask to rehearse it, wanting to make sure she could do it justice before letting him hear it. When she finally agreed that it was ready for him to hear, she held nothing back and gave perhaps her best rendition of it to date. After her initial nervousness with working in such close proximity to him, she had found herself growing more and more relaxed and less self-conscious about him hearing her mistakes.

In that particular performance, though, there weren't many of those. Once the piece had ended, Killian sat with his hands still on the keys, looking almost baffled. "Jesus," he said. "I was wrong. 'Una voce poco fa' isn't going to be your showstopper. This is." He paused. "Or maybe the Card Aria," he said, referencing the other piece Ava had, in both their opinions, been knocking out of the park. He grinned. "Seems like they're *all* showstoppers."

Ava grinned in return. "I guess all my practice is paying off. I really do feel like I'm sounding better than I ever have before."

He reached out and grabbed her hand, pulling her down onto the piano bench beside him. "You're incredible," he said softly, brushing aside a strand of hair from her face. "And you're becoming more incredible every day."

She felt her face flushing, and she knew he wanted to kiss her. She wanted him to kiss her. And why not? She had just decided to lean in and take the initiative when he drew back and turned his attention to the sheet music again.

"Okay. So, it doesn't seem like that one is going to require quite as much rehearsal as I'd thought it would," he said. "But that's good…because I have a question for you. A favor, of sorts."

"Oh?" she asked, struggling to regain her composure after that strange, aborted moment of intimacy. She already knew she could deny him nothing.

He reached behind the *Il trovatore* sheet music and pulled out more music, a handwritten—albeit neatly—score. "I…well, I guess you could say I've been inspired lately, working with you. So I wrote something for you. If you think you'll have time to learn it, I'd love to include it in the program."

Ava's voice, her most reliable asset, fled her as he handed her the sheet music. She read the title of the song at the top of the page: "Starlight". She looked over the lyrics, the melody, the piano part, and felt her breath catch in her throat and her face flush. It was beautiful; she could tell that just at a glance. And he had written it for her, said it would be a favor if she would learn it for the program. And yet the favor and honor was all hers, to sing this. To be the first one ever to sing it.

"Ava?" he prompted, and she was surprised to hear a note of nervousness in his voice. "What do you think?"

She looked up, resolutely forcing back the tears that had begun to well in her eyes. "I…I can't believe you wrote this for me," she said in a whisper. "It looks…beautiful. I…yes, of course, I'll sing it. I'll just need a little time to learn it, and…"

CHAPTER 8

"Of course," Killian said, and their eyes locked again. Neither of them moved or spoke for a moment, his blue eyes on her green ones. In the end, it was Killian who broke the silence. "So," he said, finally looking away. "Should we do...um...maybe 'Voi che sapete'? We didn't do that one last time, and then maybe after we can go back to 'Stride la vampa'."

"Sure," she said, getting slowly to her feet. She returned to her spot a few paces away, facing him, and after shuffling the music around he began to play the introduction to the Mozart piece.

She began to sing, and as the piece went on her racing mind quieted somewhat, and she focused on the words she was singing, on what they meant in English.

Sento un affetto pien di desir
Ch'ora e diletto, ch'ora e martir.

I have a feeling full of desire
That now is both pleasure and suffering.

She realized she was still holding the pages of his song in her hand.

When Ava got home that evening, she went right to the Yamaha electric keyboard in her apartment and sat down with the pages of Killian's song. She played the flowing, glistening melody for herself a few times, humming along with it, then played her way through the accompaniment—she struggled a bit, as it was a difficult part: complicated chord progressions in the left hand and shimmering passages in the right. She played it twice through, not terribly well, but as she wasn't responsible for learning the accompaniment she didn't trouble herself. She had just wanted to feel his music with her hands, the way he felt it.

Now to feel it with her voice. She had sung his music plenty of times before, of course, all of the Handel's Messiah songs on *The Art of Escape*: while rehearsing, when she would tire of singing the music of dead men and instead put on the album and sing along, whole-heartedly, with her full voice. She would use that time to experiment with her voice, try different things; she would change from the classical style in which Celeste sang, and which came naturally to Ava herself, and try to sing the songs in a belting style, closer to musical theatre or perhaps to more traditional male rock singers. With some of the songs—such as the high, intense, operatic "Gothic Romance"—this wasn't possible; they simply weren't written in a way that made belting them out doable. But others, she found, were, and she loved playing around with the sound of how her voice fitted into the band's music, both in her stricter rehearsal settings and also just singing along in her car—which she'd always found to be very valuable as a singer.

But this was a new song that—or so she presumed—the rest of the world hadn't heard yet, one that he had written expressly for her, and with her voice in mind after hours of rehearsing with her. This would be a very different experience, indeed.

She removed her hands from the keyboard and picked up the pages, allowing herself to fully read through the lyrics for the first time without considering music or melody at all. She wanted, for this moment, to just consider the poetry.

> *Sparkle and shine*
> *Off in the distance;*
> *I get close enough that you can see me*
> *But cannot get closer than that.*
> *Your eyes have more light*
> *Than exists in all the heavens.*
>
> *The light is too bright*
> *Until we are inside it;*
> *We cannot see beyond,*

CHAPTER 8

Only within;
And in the starlight all our dreams and wishes
Will be realized.

Bathe me in your glow,
I would sooner be blinded than look away;
Tell me all the secrets
There are to be found in the starlight;
Your voice for me
Is the music of the heavens.

The light is too bright
Until we are inside it;
We cannot see beyond
Only within each other;
And in the starlight all our dreams and wishes
Will be realized;
And in the starlight, all our dreams and wishes
Will be realized
If only until morning comes.

The lyrics were beautiful, as all his lyrics were; but this, somehow, was different. It was still unmistakably Killian's work, still bore his personal stamp and style; yet the words were simpler, somehow, than his lyrics for Handel's Messiah, and the song itself had the structure and feel of a traditional art song.

She could not resist asking herself the question: had he not only written the song for her to sing, but written the lyrics for her, to her? Was he regretting his insistence that they keep things strictly professional between them, and that was why he had written in the lyrics that he could not get any closer? She read them again, and again, and it seemed that each line certainly fit their relationship and the attraction that clearly existed between them. Was he saying that even if they both wanted to be together, it couldn't last, because their lives were so different?

Or was he not truly speaking to her at all in this song?

She took a deep breath and did her best to put those thoughts aside, trying to shift from being a lovesick girl back to being a professional musician. She had a song to learn, after all—and not only learn but master so that she could perform it in the biggest recital of her career so far.

Still, as she worked and began to take apart the song and to carefully start to sing, she could not shake the feeling of a shiver about to come on at any and every moment.

Ava let a few rehearsals go by before she sang "Starlight" for Killian. He would always ask how she was getting on with the song, if she had any questions, and if he could hear it. She would demur, say that it was going fine but that she needed a bit more time to work on it before she was ready to sing it for him. He never pressed the matter, but Ava could tell that he was anxious to hear her sing it and to hear how she liked it, perhaps, as well.

But she was nervous as well, and she knew she needed to get that under control before she could sing the song for him. Never before had she sung something for its composer, and that was a level of pressure that she needed to adjust to.

A little over two weeks after he had given her the song, though, she knew she could put it off no longer—and in truth she knew the song as well as she was going to, and at that point needed another ear to evaluate her performance. So at the start of the rehearsal, after her warm-ups, he asked what she'd like to begin with and she said, "Let's do 'Starlight' first."

He paused for a moment in his arranging of the scores on his piano, glancing up at her. "Okay. Yeah. Sure. Yeah, I'd love to hear it."

"I hope I do it justice," she murmured, hating the lack of confidence in her own voice but seemingly unable to get rid of it.

CHAPTER 8

It was almost as if she needed a disclaimer, something she could point to afterwards if she did not sing it well or sang it not as he'd imagined, and say "See? I told you it might not be any good." She realized that going on the record as claiming she might fail was probably a habit that needed to be broken.

She took up her usual spot facing the piano, and Killian placed his hands on the keys. She realized that he didn't have the sheet music in front of him; realized that he didn't need it. Nor did she need her copy. "Ready?" he asked.

She smiled. "Ready when you are, Maestro."

His lips curved into a half-smile as he began to play.

She listened to the introduction then, heart pounding faster than was strictly necessary, she began to sing at her entrance. Yet after the first few notes, her confidence in her voice came back to her, and so too had her confidence in the music Killian had written for her.

Her voice slid over the gorgeous melody, luxuriated in the way it fit her voice like a skintight silk dress, allowing her to embrace the bottom half of her range as well as letting it make its way up to a higher note here and there. Most of the melodic line, though, stayed right in the middle, in her sweet spot, as if Killian knew it as well as she did—and perhaps he did, by that time.

When she finished, she knew she had sung it well, though there was certainly room for improvement. And who better to help her improve it than Killian?

He played the outro, and when he was done he remained still for a moment, head bowed, fingers still embracing the final chord. When he finally looked up at her, she was taken aback by his expression: wonder and joy and something a little like pain, too. "Beautiful," he said, his voice slightly raspy. "Ava, that was beautiful. You sang it just how I heard it in my head, just how I imagined you'd sing it."

She felt her face flush and looked down.

When she glanced back up again, he had turned away from her and was searching for her copy of the sheet music from the pile she'd put on the piano when she'd come in. "Just a couple spots I want to take a look at," he said. He retrieved the music and put it on the stand in front of him. "You were a little sharp right here," he said, pointing to a measure.

She stepped closer so that she could see. "Yeah, I know; I knew it as soon as I was on the note," she said. Without thinking about it, she placed a hand on his shoulder so that she could lean in closer. Swiftly, he reached up and grabbed her fingers with his own, squeezing them once. Then he released them and pointed to another measure of the song as though nothing had happened.

chapter 9

Album #5
2016

Killian continued recording the keys, which was always Ava's favorite part of the recording process, save for when she recorded her vocals. The piano was, after all, her other instrument, and while she didn't play quite as well as Killian, she could understand what he was doing in a way that she couldn't always understand what Ben, Rafael, and Joel did, despite noodling around on a guitar herself from time to time. And furthermore, Killian's keyboard parts were always gorgeous and interesting, but sometimes—especially live—they got drowned out a bit by the louder and heavier instruments. When he recorded them, stripped down, Ava got a chance to really appreciate how beautiful and intricate they were.

Despite their fight at his house, things loosened slightly between her and Killian in the days that followed as he recorded, as if having said some things they needed to say had been cathartic for both of them. They were having fun in the studio again, as were the rest of the guys, who seemed to sense the lessening of tension between their keyboardist and lead singer and were almost giddy with relief.

"That was perfect," Rich murmured one day as Killian finished a take of the piano part for "Depths", a heavy, sexy mid-tempo song.

"Yeah, I'll say," Ava said.

He clicked the recording light off, gesturing for Killian to come back into the production room.

"Good?" Killian asked, as he came back through the door.

"Yeah, killer," Rich said. "Want me to play it back so you all can hear?"

"Yeah, for sure," Killian said.

He took a seat at the control board next to Rich, who started the play back. They all listened, and from the couch, Ava grinned, but waited until the track had finished playing before speaking. "I finally figured out what the piano part in the bridge reminds me of," she said.

"What?" Killian asked.

CHAPTER 9

Ava began to sing a few bars of "Come Little Children" from the movie *Hocus Pocus*.

Rafael burst out laughing. "No shit," he said. "It does sound like that."

Ava kept singing, and Joel grabbed a guitar and began accompanying her.

Killian laughed. "I never realized it, but you're right."

"What song is this?" Ben asked.

"From *Hocus Pocus!*" Ava exclaimed. "You've heard this before!"

"Is that that Halloween movie white women all like?" Ben asked.

Ava laughed. "Yes," she said. "It's one of my favorites."

"Figures," Ben said, but with a grin.

"Which explains why it was in my head," Killian said with a groan. "Ava makes me watch it like five times every October."

"It's for your own edification," Ava teased.

"Wait," Joel said. "This would actually sound kickass as a metal song. What if we covered it?"

Ava shrieked. "Oh my God! We have to! How have I never thought of this before?"

"It would be pretty easy, actually," Joel said, fingers flying over his phone as he pulled up a video of the song from YouTube. He turned up the volume and held up his phone so they could all hear it. Setting it on the arm of the couch, he began to play along.

"Yeah," Killian said, nodding along, "and kind of a creepy, tinkly piano part with that, and then Raf—"

"Hold up," Rafael said excitedly. "What if, live, we key change after the bridge of 'Depths' and segue right into this? How sick would that be?"

"Now you're getting crazy," Joel said, nodding approvingly. "I like it."

"Maybe too crazy," Killian said. "I don't know about that, but if we do the cover..." he trailed off and headed back out into the recording both where the piano was set up. "I'm thinking something like this," he called back to the rest of them, then sat at the piano and began to play an eerie melody.

"Fuck yes," Rafael said. "That's *exactly* what it should sound like."

The rest of the band had gotten up to follow Killian into the booth when Rich made a big time out symbol with his hands.

"Folks," he called. "I love the creativity, I do, but we've got an album to finish here. Maybe work out the cover in your rehearsal time for tour?"

Ava and Killian's eyes met, and they both rolled their eyes slightly, giving each other a *Here's Dad keeping us on task* look, and Ava couldn't help but burst out laughing. It had felt like too long since she and Killian had been on the same side, had been able to know what the other was thinking with just a look. In that moment everything—between her and Killian, and in the rapport among all the band members—was at its best, was exactly as it should be.

Thanks, Hocus Pocus, she thought.

"Fine," Killian said, getting up from the piano and coming back into the production room. "I guess Rich has a point. But let's remember this for tour rehearsals, okay?"

"Oh, I am not going to let anyone forget this," Ava said. "And I will be forcing Ben to watch Hocus Pocus this year."

Ben grumbled, albeit good-naturedly.

"Way to ruin our fun, Rich," Rafael complained, and Rich threw an empty Styrofoam coffee cup at him.

Killian finished up the keys within that week, then they moved back to drums and bass again as Ben and Rafael recorded their parts for the new song. Ava's song. It was really happening, Ava realized the day Ben recorded his drum part. They were really recording this song, and soon it would be out there in the world where she could never take it back. And why would she

CHAPTER 9

want to take it back? Finally, a song of hers was being played, recorded, heard. And the damage was already done, had been done that night in her bed when Killian asked her to play the song for him.

Of course, just because they were recording the song didn't mean it would make the album automatically—they'd come into the studio with sixteen to record, knowing they would need to whittle that down to thirteen or fourteen for the album. Ava's song made seventeen. Yet everyone's enthusiasm about it, the way they had all eagerly jumped in to learn it and rehearse it, made Ava certain it would make the final cut. They wouldn't be bothering to record it at this point if everyone didn't think so.

What was happening, then, was what she had always feared would happen, perhaps even her greatest fear: her own creativity, her own ambition, was driving her and Killian apart.

Despite their fight at his house that night, things remained largely unchanged between her and Killian. They spoke and interacted because they had to, because they needed to be professional with one another. It was almost more frustrating than if they outright hated each other, Ava thought at times. *How long,* she wondered, *can we go on talking about the same things, but still not saying anything?*

What she wanted, desperately, was some time away from him to clear her head. But that was not likely to happen, not for at least the next year and perhaps two. Preparations were already underway for a massive world tour to begin around the time the album would be released, and press and promotion for the new album would begin soon after production had wrapped up. Ava would have a couple weeks, at most, to herself before she would need to jump fully into the events of another revolution of the album cycle.

Would a couple weeks be enough time for her to figure out her life, and their romantic future? She certainly didn't think so. Perhaps the better question was whether there was anything else she could do. But carrying on with this stalemate for the next year and a half to two years was equally impossible.

She kept hoping a day would come when the answers would present themselves to her, but it hadn't happened so far.

Or was the problem that she already knew the answer, knew that things between them had run their course, that they wanted different things, and she simply refused to admit it to herself?

If their relationship could be saved, then she wanted to save it. Yet more and more she felt like Killian couldn't—or didn't want to—hear her true voice, hear all the things she really wanted to say.

Ben and Rafael wrapped up their recordings for the new song in a day, and as it wasn't too late they decided to have Ava also do a take or two of the keys for the song, the idea being that if all went well they could start fresh with Joel on guitar the next morning.

Ava waited patiently as Killian and Rich got the grand piano miked for recording again. They had decided that, since her song had piano throughout (rather than synths or organ or other effects that Killian sometimes used), it would be best to record it on the grand, for better quality of sound. Ava couldn't wait. She loved this piano, a gorgeous old Steinway that was kept in near pristine condition. She had learned to play on a Steinway; her first piano teacher had had one in her studio. This one, though, was the nicest piano she had ever played, with a rich, full, vibrant sound that modern pianos—to her ear, anyway—just couldn't match.

Once the piano was set, the guys retreated back into the control room and let her know when to begin. She took a deep, silent breath before beginning, then placed her hands on the keys and began to play.

Her first take was somewhat rocky, as was probably to be expected. She had never recorded piano before, so the thought of playing it perfectly—so different, somehow, from singing perfectly—got into her head a bit. The second time, though, it seemed she had gotten all the jitters and surprises and mistakes

CHAPTER 9

out of her system. This time she managed to go back to when she was playing it in her apartment, just for herself, with no expectations. That time, she thought, she played it not only right, but with just the right amount of passion and longing and pain.

When the red recording light flicked off and she got up from the piano bench, she felt shaky, off-balance, as if she had left some part of herself on the keys, in the recording. Not a part so big that she could not live without it, but big enough that she noticed its loss. It was different from singing, even when she sang something so true and full of emotion, something she felt and connected with. *It's different,* she realized, *when you are using words to say what you need. Does Killian feel like this all the time? How has he been able to do it for so long?*

Even now, even after everything, her default thoughts were still respect for and awe of his talent. She didn't know if that would ever change.

chapter 10

The Art of Escape
2009

CHAPTER 10

"That was great," Killian said enthusiastically, as Ava finished a rendition of the Card Aria from *Carmen*. "Perfect, Ava. You really nail that one, every time."

She smiled widely. His praise never failed to thrill her.

It was three days before the recital, and their last rehearsal. Their schedules weren't conducive to having another one beforehand, and in truth Ava preferred it that way. She never sang the day before a performance anyway, to make sure her voice was rested. Killian had lamented the timing, but she'd talked him around to accepting it was a good thing. "It'll feel more fresh in performance that way," she'd said, and in the end he had agreed. There was nothing that could be done about it, in any case.

So that day, having decided on the performance order the week before so that programs could be printed, they were running through the whole program from start to finish, and then they would be calling it a night. "Starlight", the debut of Killian's new work, was to be last on the program.

He had gotten the printed programs the day before, and he excitedly handed one to her when she came in. "They came out perfect," he'd said, and she'd taken it from him, eagerly scanning the pale blue cardstock and the flowing, cursive type of the header.

A Recital Performance by
Ava Tomei
Mezzo-soprano

Killian Sterling, piano

Vissi d'arte (Tosca)—Giacomo Puccini
Stabat Mater (1st movement)—Antonio Vivaldi
Forgotten—Amy Beach
Voi che sapete (Le Nozze di Figaro)—Wolfgang Amadeus Mozart

HEAVY METAL SYMPHONY

Tu dormi in tante pene (Tito Manlio)—Antonio Vivaldi
Liebst du um Schönheit—Clara Schumann
Stride la vampa (Il Trovatore)—Giuseppe Verdi
Una voce poco fa (The Barber of Seville)—Gioachino Rossini
Card Aria (Carmen)—Georges Bizet
Starlight—Killian Sterling

It give Ava a thrill to see Killian's name beside those of so many great composers, and she wondered if he felt the same way.

They ran through the program, both of them completely in tune with one another, and Ava knew she sounded great. Everything was polished and prepared, but not *too* much so.

"Okay, last one." He placed his hands on the keys again. "'Starlight'."

She nodded. "Let's do it."

He began to play, and she came in at her entrance. Over the past few weeks they had honed their performance of every piece—not just "Starlight"—so that they knew each other's patterns and preferences; Killian knew just where Ava would take a breath, and she knew the places where he would slow the tempo for her or speed it up. Yet it seemed to Ava that with "Starlight" they were the most in sync of all. It was hard to tell where his performance ended and hers began, so much did they feel of a piece. Perhaps it was because Ava had never sung this piece with anyone else, nor had Killian played it for anyone else. She was the only person he had ever heard sing it.

The song had taken a bit of work for her to get just right, for her to render it as he wanted and also in a way that satisfied her own inner critic. Yet the reward for all that work was that now it felt effortless, like a favorite song that she had learned as a child and been singing her whole life. She no longer had to think about it, no longer had to constantly attend to her breathing or the placement of the pitches or how she shaped the vowels. It was all in her muscle memory, and instead of thinking she could just feel.

CHAPTER 10

As they reached the end of the piece, Killian remained where he was, head bowed over the keys. When he looked up, she was startled—were those tears in his eyes? Yet he seemed to blink, and they were gone, so quickly she thought she must have imagined it. "Ava," he said, his voice low. He rose from the piano bench and came towards her, taking both her hands in his. "I've never heard you sing better. And I've never heard someone sing anything I've written better, either."

The admission startled her—what about Celeste, the way she performed the music he wrote for Handel's Messiah? But she had no time to puzzle over that, for suddenly his hands released hers and were sliding around her waist instead, drawing her closer to him. For a moment she was too surprised to react, then once she realized what was happening—that it was really happening—she let herself melt into his arms, closing the rest of the distance between them so that their hips touched, and their lips were just a breath apart.

"Ava," he murmured, and she felt the word more than heard it.

"Yes," she replied in a whisper, and in that one syllable were so many things: a reply and an acknowledgement and an invitation and permission.

She was sure he was going to kiss her, and she couldn't wait for that moment, but also to see where that moment might lead. Yet suddenly he released her and stepped away. "I'm sorry," he said. "We shouldn't. We said we were going to be professional, and I…"

Ava didn't speak; she didn't know what to say. It was obvious she had wanted him to kiss her—thought that it was obvious that she wanted him. Yet once there was space between them again, she remembered all over again—like the cold light of dawn after a dark, sultry night—that he was right.

"I…it's important for you that we keep it professional, I think," he said. "I want to help your career. I don't think I'll do that if people think we're sleeping together."

"Yeah, I guess you're right," Ava said, and she knew he was. She also knew there would be people who thought that anyway, and that there was only so much they could do about it. But best to keep it all aboveboard, for now.

For now. Ava repeated the words to herself as she left his apartment that night. After the recital was over, they would no longer be working together. So what then?

What then is he's flying to Los Angeles to record his new album, she reminded herself as she got in her car. *Take the boost he's giving you as a musician and move on. That's all this can ever be. Even if we both wish otherwise.*

The night of the recital, Ava paced backstage. She wasn't nervous, exactly—she had gotten past stage fright a long time ago—more so amped up, full of energy and ready to go. She just wanted to get out there and sing already.

Vivian sat in a chair and watched her pace. "You look gorgeous," she told Ava. "I'm so glad you picked that dress."

Ava smiled at her. They'd gone shopping for it the weekend before, and Vivian had helped her pick out the light, airy, floor-length red gown with a corset-style top. "It's exactly what I wanted," Ava said. "And I've learned by now not to ever disagree with your fashion advice."

Vivian laughed. "Good. You better not." Vivian herself looked perfect, as always, in a royal blue wrap dress that seemed to glow against her dark skin and her Afro circling her head like a halo. She raised her eyebrows and gave Ava a once-over again, from her carefully curled and pinned back hair to her dark, smoky eye makeup to her black satin flats. "I'm sure Killian will think you look gorgeous, too."

Ava had, of course, confided all to Vivian. "I don't care if he does," Ava said. "I just want to give the best performance I possibly can."

CHAPTER 10

Vivian raised an eyebrow again, but Ava meant it. She was in full-on performance mode now, and nothing else mattered but the music.

Still, just then, when the door opened and Killian stepped into the green room, Ava was nevertheless gratified to see his eyes widen and his body momentarily freeze as he caught sight of her. "Ava, you look…perfect." He smiled at her, a warm smile meant just for her. "You're just as beautiful as your voice."

She knew she was blushing. "Killian, this is my best friend, Vivian Williams," she said.

Vivian got up from her chair. "Nice to meet you, Killian," she said. "The famous rock star. I've heard a lot about you."

Killian laughed. "Ava talks about you a lot as well."

"I hope she didn't tell you what a bad influence I am." Vivian threw a wink in Ava's direction. "Well, I'll leave you two to warm up or have a pep talk or whatever it is you musical types do. Gotta get to my front-row seat." With that, she slipped out the door and left them alone.

Ava turned back to Killian. "You look great as well." And he did. He was wearing a fitted, well-tailored black suit with a gray shirt underneath and no tie. His long hair was loose around his shoulders.

He smiled. "Thanks, but believe me, no one's going to be looking at me."

She felt herself flush. "Oh, stop."

"And that's as it should be," he said. "Nervous?"

"No. I don't really do nervous."

"Good. You've got nothing to be nervous about. Not even the fact that it's a full house."

Ava's eyes lit up. "Is it really?" She knew the majority of the audience would be fans of Killian's and fans of the band. But people had come and would hear her, and that was all she cared about. And it was a big hall—a bit austere and modern, with cream walls and pale wood details on the theatre seats, but it was big. If it was full, that meant she had one heck of an audience.

Killian nodded, grinning. "Yep. Every seat is filled."

Quickly, before she could think better of it, Ava reached out and took Killian's hand. "Thank you, Killian," she said softly, catching his eyes with hers. "You didn't have to do this, but you did. I don't know how I'll ever thank you."

He lifted her hand to his lips and kissed it, never taking his eyes from her. "I'm selfish," he said softly. "I just want to hear you sing. And I want others to hear you, too." He squeezed her hand once, then let it go. "Ready?"

She nodded. "I'm ready." And together they left the green room and walked out onto the stage.

There was applause as they stepped out onstage, a few cheers and whoops. Ava nodded in acknowledgement, and Killian nodded and waved before sitting down at the piano. Ava took her spot, standing just in front of the bend in the grand piano, and looked out into the audience. With the house lights down and the stage lights up, it was hard to see the rest of the hall; it was hard to tell that, as Killian had told her, it was full. That was probably for the best, Ava realized. This was the biggest audience, and the biggest venue, she'd ever performed in solo, and there was a split second where nerves threatened to take over. But she could just barely make out the sight of Vivian sitting beside her mother, both of them next to Ava's parents in the front row, all of them beaming with pride and encouragement. She glanced back at Killian and saw him give her a similar smile of encouragement. She nodded to him to let him know she was ready, and he began playing.

After that, the recital passed mostly in a blur, with certain moments standing out in her mind; it was always so when she performed. She remembered wobbling a bit on a pitch halfway through "Vissi d'arte", and she'd glanced back at Killian ever so slightly, only to see him nod encouragingly once again. She forged through, knowing there would be plenty of time to beat herself up over it later. Her Mozart was a bit heavier than it maybe should have been, but it was nothing someone without a

CHAPTER 10

trained ear would likely have noticed. The *Stabat Mater* flowed just as effortlessly as it had in rehearsal, and she got a standing ovation for both "Una voce poco fa" and the Card Aria, as Killian had predicted she would.

Perhaps the one moment she knew she would always recall mostly clearly was at the end of "Tu dormi in tante pene". The last line of the aria were the words "Amato bene", repeated twice, which meant "I love you well". As she sang them, she again turned her head slightly to glance at Killian, and found that he was looking back at her. He mouthed the words with her as she sang, and it was only when the piece concluded that she turned again to face the audience. She got that weak-in-the-knees feeling again, and a part of her immediately began puzzling over what it meant, yet the dominant performer side pushed such thoughts aside to be examined later.

Just before "Starlight", the last song, Ava stepped closer to the edge of the stage and spoke. "Thank you so much for coming, everyone," she said. "I've had a lot of fun up here tonight, and I hope you've had a lot of fun listening.

"My next and final piece is one I'm very excited about. It is, in fact, the world premiere of a new song by a man I'm sure you all know to be a very gifted composer." She turned to acknowledge Killian, who waved briefly in response to the applause that followed her words. "It is my great honor to be the first person ever to sing it. I absolutely adore this song, and I know you will, too."

With that, she stepped back into position and nodded to Killian, who began to play.

As soon as she began singing, she was lost in the music, lost in the emotion, as though she were telling the audience how she felt about all of them. As though she were telling everyone how she felt about Killian. And maybe, just maybe, he was telling them all how he felt about her.

When she finished, the applause was again thunderous, with everyone in the hall rising to their feet. She took her bow, then held out her hand to acknowledge Killian. He nodded to the audience from his seat, seeming—and she could hardly believe it—bashful about the acclaim. She bowed twice more, and then the two of them went backstage.

The applause was still continuing as she turned to say something to Killian, only to have him gently but firmly take her face in his hands and kiss her hungrily. She was surprised for a moment, but then she responded swiftly, kissing him back with all the desire she had been saving the last few weeks.

When they finally broke apart, they were both breathing heavily. "You were glorious," he whispered to her.

"It was the best I ever sang in my life," she said. And she knew it was true.

They stayed there for a moment, holding on to each other in the darkness just offstage. Both of them realized at the same time that the audience was still applauding, still cheering, calling for an encore. "Told you," Killian said, giving her that half smile she had come to love so much in the weeks they had been working together.

They had prepared an encore piece at Killian's insistence, even though Ava had scoffed at the idea that they would need one. "Maybe people call for encores from big name performers—or from rock stars," she'd teased. "But I think we'll be safe."

Now she was glad for his foresight. "Alright," she said. "Let's do it."

Pulling apart and straightening their clothing and hair, they walked back out onstage, much to the audience's delight. "Since you asked so nicely," Ava said, once the noise had died down, "we'll give you one more."

She nodded to Killian, who began to play the immediately recognizable bars of the introduction. There was a smattering of laughter and applause from people in the audience as they realized what it was.

Ava had sung the famous "Habanera" from *Carmen* several times before; it was a blast to sing and, as possibly the most

CHAPTER 10

recognizable aria in all of opera, it was always a crowd-pleaser. She tried not to overuse it and had of late been focusing on learning newer and slightly more obscure repertoire—like arias from Vivaldi's operas, and more music by often overlooked female composers—but Killian had made the point that it would be a perfect encore piece. Now she saw that he was right.

And she was going to have fun with it. There was a seductive, Carmen-like woman somewhere deep inside Ava who didn't often get a chance to come out, she knew. She would let her out tonight, right now.

She slowly leaned over the end of the piano as she sang the languid first line, letting her arm slide slowly across the polished black lid, her eyes on Killian. He looked up at her, and she saw the heat in his eyes.

She walked slowly around the back of the piano as she sang the long, sparkling melodic lines on the word "L'amour", and when she reached Killian as she broke into the chorus, she placed a hand on his shoulder and let it trail across his back as she walked back around to the front of the piano again.

As she began the second verse, she decided to get even more daring. She sat on the piano bench next to him, leaning against him and turning to face the audience as she sang. When she rose, she caught a glimpse of his face, the amused smile coupled with the same desire in his eyes that had been there before. She walked a few steps away from him, feeling him watching her all the while. It seemed to her that perhaps he was striking the keys a bit harder than he strictly needed to, and she let her lips curl into a smile at this thought. She plunged into the chorus again, this time moving to stand behind Killian, placing her hands on his shoulders and letting them roam down over his chest as she sang about love, unpredictable love. She couldn't imagine when she'd become so daring.

As she approached the last phrase, with its final note, she moved back to center stage and delivered the last line—"Si je'taime, prendez guardois toi!"—with one hand pointing in

Killian's direction, as though the words of Carmen's warning were for him, too: "If you love me, beware!" When the last chord faded, she snapped her gaze forward again to face the audience, and once again, instantaneously, the applause rolled through the hall like thunder.

Killian rose from the piano bench, applauding as well. He met her at center stage and wrapped an arm around her waist. Together they bowed, once, twice, three times, and then they turned and went backstage.

Once they were out of sight of the audience, he wrapped an arm around her waist and drew her close. "My, my, Miss Tomei," he murmured, "a little handsy out there, weren't you?"

She grinned at him. The spirit of Carmen, it seemed, still had not left her. "Did you mind?"

"No," he said, resting his forehead against hers. "No, I didn't. All part of the performance, after all."

Instead of faltering at these words, she pressed on. "It wasn't completely a performance on my part."

He moved closer, so that their lips were only a breath away. "No. Not on mine either."

They were about to kiss again when someone nearby cleared their throat. They jumped apart like two guilty teenagers who had snuck off to make out during prom, but Ava was relieved to see that it was Vivian. "There's a few people on their way backstage to see you two," she said, a hint of a smile on her face. "Including my mother and your parents, Ava," Vivian added pointedly.

Ava winced slightly. She had somehow forgotten that her parents were in the audience when she'd put on her seductive siren act. Hopefully they wouldn't mention it, and it would never be spoken of amongst them, ever.

"And," Vivian went on, "I wanted to be the first to congratulate you. You killed it, babe."

Smiling, Ava drew away from Killian and gave Vivian a tight hug. "Thank you so much for being here," she said.

"I wouldn't be anywhere else," she said. "That was the best

CHAPTER 10

I've ever heard you sing. Seriously, Ava."

"Here come your adoring fans," Killian said, as a group of people, Ava's parents in the lead, came backstage. He smiled at her. "Enjoy it."

"Ava, you were wonderful!" her mother said, immediately drawing her into a hug. "I don't think I've ever heard you sing so well!"

"Me neither," her father added, hugging her as well.

Ava laughed. "That seems to be the general consensus," she said.

"But how do *you* feel about it?" her father asked her.

She smiled. It was the question he always asked her, understanding that, no matter how great she might have sounded, it wasn't a successful performance unless she herself was happy with it. "I think everyone is right," she said.

Her father beamed and patted her shoulder.

"And what about your encore, hmm?" her mother asked, raising her eyebrows. "I didn't know that you and Killian were together..."

Ava felt her face go red. So much for never speaking of it with her parents. "Um, we're not," she said. "That was just a... you know, a performance."

"Hmmm," her mother said again, the look on her face clearly saying she didn't believe it.

"Well, he seems like a good guy," her father said, a touch awkwardly. "A great musician, that's for sure. It was nice of him to help you put this all together."

"Yes, it was," Ava said, seizing on this safer topic. "Let me introduce you, actually. Killian—"

But when she turned to find him, he had gone and was already talking to friends and acquaintances. She moved to get his attention, but her mother stopped her.

"Oh, don't worry about it, sweetie. We're going to get out of your way now, anyway—you need to enjoy your moment. But we'll see you for dinner tomorrow night, right?"

"Yes, for sure," Ava said. Her parents were taking her out to dinner the next night before driving home to Batavia. At first she'd suggested they go that night after the recital, but her parents had said they hadn't wanted to rush her after her performance, and now she was glad they'd talked her out of it. She had some unfinished business with Killian, after all.

She hugged both her parents again. "Thank you both so much for coming," she said. "Really."

"Of course," her father said. "Now, have fun." He smiled as he took in all the people waiting to speak to his daughter.

Vivian's mother was next, congratulating her and inviting her to Sunday lunch the following weekend at her house. "Been too long since Viv has brought you to see me!" she said.

Ava laughed. "I'll see you then, Mrs. Williams. Looking forward to it!"

"Ava!" Killian called out to her. "There's someone here I want you to meet!"

Soon Ava was caught up in a whirlwind of introductions to people Killian knew, from his contact at Buff State that had booked them the hall to other local musicians, including some from the Buffalo Philharmonic Orchestra. Everyone was full of effusive praise for her performance, and Ava was sure she sounded like a robot after a while, nodding and smiling and saying "Thank you so much" and "Thanks for coming" to everyone, while not completely remembering their names. As the crowd of well-wishers and acquaintances of Killian's moved back out into the auditorium itself, Ava saw many more of her friends and co-workers, who she chatted with briefly before Killian came to find her to introduce her to someone else she just had to meet.

It was overwhelming and chaotic, and it passed in a blur in a much different way than the performance. Ava imagined that being a bride at a wedding reception must feel something like this: everyone wanted to see her, to have a quick word with her, and she had to make sure she greeted everyone.

Once the hall had finally emptied out, leaving only Killian

CHAPTER 10

speaking to a friend of his, Ava went back to the green room to gather her things. She was exhausted—the kind of pleasant and sad exhaustion that follows exhilaration—but somehow not entirely ready to go home.

Carrying her purse and tote bag, she went back out into the auditorium to find Killian alone, pushing the piano back into its storage spot in the wings of the stage. "Heading out?" he asked her, pausing and straightening up as she approached.

"Yes," she said, stopping a few paces away from him. In the whirlwind of introductions and chatter that had followed the performance, she hadn't had time to think about their backstage embraces. But now that they were alone again, it all came roaring back. What had it meant? Had it just been a post-performance high, a moment of adrenaline for them both? Were they going to talk about it? She grasped in vain for some vestiges of Carmen, of the seductive, confident spirit that had possessed her onstage so that she might ask him about it, point blank, but that part of Ava had fled, it seemed, retreated deep down to wherever it was she laid dormant, and Ava did not know how to rouse her again. "I...I don't know how I can ever thank you, Killian. This night...it was perfect. It was a performance I could barely have dreamt up."

He was silent for a moment, studying her. "I felt like I was the one dreaming," he said softly. "To hear you sing...to hear something I wrote performed like that..." He trailed off but did not look away from her. "I think we were made for each other."

Ava's heart began to pound. "What...what do you mean?"

"I should think it was obvious. I've never been more inspired by anyone. Never had someone occupy my thoughts so completely. Not until I met you." He sighed, heavily. "I don't know how it could work. Not when we live such different lives. But I need you, Ava."

Never before had a man been so honest with her, so forthright, so clear. He wanted her. He needed her. She closed the distance between them and kissed him, right there onstage, without any hesitation or self-consciousness. He returned the kiss with equal passion, his hands tangling in the curly strands of her hair.

After a moment, she drew back. "What happened to being professional?" she asked, half-teasing, but half in earnest—was it really happening this time?

His eyes burned blue, like coals. "The recital is over. We're not working together anymore." With that, he pulled her into the wings offstage and pressed her back up against the brick wall, kissing her again.

For a moment, Ava hesitated. Had this been his motivation all along, for putting the recital together, for trying to boost her career? Had he just wanted to sleep with her and so did something to make her feel indebted to him? But, no, that didn't make any sense, she concluded. They had been somewhat seeing each other before he'd proposed the recital, and she'd made it clear that she was into him. She would have slept with him anyway, even if he had not gone to such lengths for her. Because she…she hesitated to form the word "love", even in her mind, as though doing so was to cross a bridge that would burn behind her. Instead, she melted against him, returning his kiss just as passionately as he gave it.

They stayed there for a while, lips locked, hands roaming. It was only when Killian was tugging down the strap of her dress and she had her hands up under his shirt that she drew back. "Wait, wait," she whispered.

He met her eyes, and she knew he understood what she meant: she didn't want him to stop; just to pause for time being. "Where?" he asked, breathing heavily. "Your place or mine?"

"Mine is closer."

So they went out and got in Ava's car, and even then they couldn't keep their hands off each other. He leaned over and kissed her neck as she was driving, prompting her to admonish, "I'm going to crash this car." In truth, she wasn't resisting very forcefully.

"Then at least I'll die happy."

CHAPTER 10

"I'd be a lot happier if we made it to my bedroom before we die."

"Fair enough. Then focus on driving and don't say anything else that will turn me on quite like that."

Luckily, Ava's apartment was only a few blocks away. She parked on the street and they both hurried into the building and up the stairs. They kicked off their shoes, and she led him down the short hallway to her bedroom. She spared just a few seconds wishing she had straightened up her room and didn't have books, notebooks, and piles of laundry waiting to be put away everywhere, but those thoughts vanished from her mind almost instantly—and certainly Killian didn't notice. He pulled his shirt off over his head immediately, and seemed to be debating about even bothering to remove her dress. Ava found herself wishing he would just shove it up around her waist and throw her on the bed; he chuckled low in his throat, as if he knew what she was thinking.

"No," he murmured. "If we took the time to drive all the way over here, we'd better do this right."

He spun her around and unzipped her dress, pushing it down to the floor. Ava felt his hands fumble at the clasp of her strapless bra, and she almost couldn't breathe with anticipation. Soon he removed that and let it fall to the floor, and she spun to face him. His eyes took in her breasts unashamedly.

She stepped close to him and kissed him, and the feeling of her bare breasts against his chest drove her wild. He moaned against her mouth, and she knew he felt the same.

She undid his pants and pushed them down, and they both shed their underwear. For a moment they paused and just looked at each other, took one another in, and then all further pretense at slowing things down vanished.

Killian produced a condom and hurriedly rolled it on. They fell onto her bed, kissing, and Killian began to move his mouth down her body, sucking one nipple, then the other. She moaned and arched beneath him, wrapping her arms around his back and drawing his lips back up to hers.

"Now," she breathed. "I can't wait any longer."

Evidently he couldn't either, for he made no protest. She wrapped her legs around his waist and he thrust into her, hard, and she cried out with relief and pleasure. His thrusts were almost rough, and her body moved with his, matching his hunger, spending the desire that had been building between them for the past few weeks.

He came first, and she followed soon after, both of their voices mingling before they collapsed together, spent. He withdrew and lay beside her on his back, drawing her against his side.

"I've been dreaming about that for weeks now," he said, after a moment had passed and they'd both caught their breath. "But it was even better than I thought it would be."

"Same," was all the reply Ava managed, and they both laughed.

He drew her closer, burying his face in her hair. "You are magnificent," he whispered. "In every single way."

She kissed him. "I don't remember ever being so happy."

"Not even when you were up on that stage a little while ago?"

She smiled. "Okay. That comes pretty close. I'd better be careful I don't use up my life's allotment of happiness all in one day."

"If I have anything to say about it," Killian murmured, "you'll be this happy every day of your life."

chapter 11

Album #5
2016

One night after they'd finished recording for the day—Joel was well into tracking the guitar parts by then—Ava finally met Vivian for dinner.

Usually she loved being in the studio. She loved recording—for all the ways in which it was unlike performing—because it gave her crazy life balance: the quiet, measured way they all played or sang, thinking carefully about each note and its meaning and purpose; meditating on the lyrics and the emotions she wanted to make sure to bring to the forefront; the measured, slow-building thrill of seeing something they had built coming together layer by layer. But for this album, there was too much tension crowding out all of that, and she couldn't wait to get away from it and spend time with her friend instead.

She and Vivian were those kind of friends for whom time and distance seemed to have no effect. No matter how long they went without talking or seeing each other, they were always able to pick up right where they had left off, no questions asked or forgiveness needed. It was the one thing Ava regretted about joining the band and setting off on such a whirlwind adventure—it gave her less time for her family and friends. But Vivian understood and always had. She worked as a developer at a software startup in the city, and her work often kept her busy as well, what with sprints and the occasional last-minute client demo.

They met for dinner at Cole's, one of their old favorite haunts and not far from either of their apartments. It was in a prime spot right on Elmwood, the green awning out front marking it out to passersby, one of many restaurants in the line of two-story buildings along the strip. "Hey, girl," Vivian said when she walked in and saw Ava already waiting at the bar, crowded in among college kids, hipsters, and the odd middle-aged couple from the suburbs. She gave her a quick hug. "Long time! How's the album going?"

Ava rolled her eyes. "I don't even want to talk about it."

CHAPTER 11

Vivian raised her eyebrows questioningly. "Oh really? That good, huh?"

Ava sighed as the hostess led them to their table. "I wouldn't even know where to start."

"Well, now you're gonna have to tell me," Vivian said as they sat down. "I'm especially intrigued."

Ava didn't answer, instead picking up her menu.

Vivian picked up her own menu. But out of her peripherals Ava could see Vivian eyeing her from across the table. Finally she put the menu down and said, "Okay, spill."

Ava hesitated. "Shouldn't we decide first?"

Vivian waved a hand dismissively, causing her collection of silver bangles to jingle noisily. "We both always get the same thing here like we're a couple of old ladies. So: spill."

Ava hesitated. She knew she was going to tell Vivian everything that was going on—had to tell her, in fact. Yet even so she had still hoped she'd be able to forget about everything, just for a few hours. "Okay," she said. "But after this we're not talking about it anymore for the rest of the night, okay? I need to take my mind off things."

Vivian studied her for a moment, her dark eyes solemn. She nodded.

Ava filled Vivian in on everything that was happening between her and Killian, not sparing any of the bloody details. Ava had told her friend that things had been rough, telling her here and there about fights that she and Killian had had, but she had deliberately not given her the full picture, making multiple mental excuses to the effect that she didn't want Viv to worry or didn't want to get into it at any particular time. Once she started talking, though, it was plain how long she had needed to get it all out—she began to feel better even as she spoke.

They were briefly interrupted when their waitress came to take their orders, and after she'd gone Ava told Vivian all about her song, how Killian had asked her to play it for him, and how she had resisted—but not very hard. How he made her play it for the rest of the band, and how now it was going on the album.

Vivian listened patiently, her face going from surprised to shocked to angry to worried as Ava spoke. When Ava finally finished, she sat back in her chair, as though she was exhausted just from listening. "Damn, girl," she said. Her face took on a worried expression again. "Ava, I had no idea things had gotten so bad. Why didn't you tell me?"

Ava shrugged. "If I didn't tell you, it wasn't real, I guess," she said. "But I should have." She smiled. "I feel better already."

Vivian still didn't look convinced. "So...what are you going to do?"

"See what happens, I guess."

"What does that mean?" Vivian asked. "You guys can't go on like this. God, Ava, it's...not healthy."

"What am I supposed to do?" Ava asked. "Leave him? Leave him but stay in the band?"

"So you're just going to stay with him because you feel like you have no *choice*?"

Ava paused, considering her words. It was the same thing, essentially, that she had said to Killian a few nights ago when they had argued. *I don't want to be with you because I'm your default.* But was that all that was really keeping her with him?

Did she really want to leave him? Would it maybe be easier for them to remain in the band together if they stopped trying to keep up the pretense that everything was fine?

She realized Vivian was still waiting for an answer. "It's so much more complicated than that," she said.

Vivian snorted. "It always is."

"It is," Ava insisted. "I still love him."

And that, she realized, was the heart of the matter, the root of the problem. In spite of everything, she did still love him, even though she felt like she shouldn't. The very thing that had brought them together—music—now became the wedge between them.

She didn't know quite how it had happened, but she was

CHAPTER 11

no longer content to just be Killian's muse. The words he put in her mouth were no longer enough for her. She had things to say, and she wanted the world to hear them. She wanted *him* to hear them. But he didn't seem to know what to do with her when she wanted to step outside the role he had put her in.

Vivian sighed. "Look, it's your relationship. But I'm worried about you. I could tell that you and Killian haven't been on the same page for a while now." She reached across the table and took Ava's hand, squeezed it. "I just want you to be happy."

"I want to be, too."

They fell silent for a moment, sipping their beers. Vivian's lips curled into a knowing smile. "So a song you wrote is going on a Handel's Messiah album."

Ava felt a flush of pleasure at hearing the words spoken aloud. "Yeah."

"Well, cheers to that," she said, raising her glass. Ava smiled and clinked her glass against Vivian's. "No matter how Killian feels about it."

"I mean, it was his idea to put it on the album," Ava said.

"But why?" Vivian asked. "Why does it have to be his idea?"

Ava suddenly wondered why she felt she needed to defend Killian to Vivian. Why pretend that Vivian wasn't saying the very thing that Ava was thinking, that she was upset about, if you boiled the whole messy, complicated brew down to its source? "Damned if I know," Ava said at last. She laughed. "Because everything needs to be Killian's idea. The music, the album titles, me being in the band. Some days even our relationship feels like his idea…and that if it was ever going to end, he would need to be the one to decide he was done."

"You don't owe him anything, you know," Vivian said. "Just because he gave you this opportunity doesn't mean you're obligated to him for the rest of your life."

"I know that," Ava said. "But, Vivian, he finally heard me. When I wrote this song…he finally heard me. I made him hear me." She looked down at the varnished tabletop. "And maybe it was the worst thing I could have done for our relationship, but it was the best thing I could have done for me."

Vivian shook her head. "Your voice shouldn't break your relationship."

Ava shrugged. "I guess I...I just got in the habit of letting him take control," she said. "Creatively, anyway. He's...so talented I didn't feel like I could speak up."

"Damn," Vivian said, as the waitress appeared with their food and set it down before them. "Sounds to me like the great Mr. Sterling has a test to pass right about now." She picked up a French fry and pointed it at her friend. "We—mostly *you*—need some serious drinks after this. You hear me? *Serious* drinks."

Ava laughed and picked up her Buffalo chicken wrap. "I won't argue with that."

◦○◦

The rest of Ava's night out with Vivian was something of a blur. After they finished eating, they went to the bar and had some drinks, then when Cole's got too crowded they went next door to Mr. Goodbar for more drinks. They met a couple guys who recognized Ava and bought them a round of shots—or maybe it had been two rounds. Ava couldn't quite remember, come to think of it.

They had ended up stumbling outside and calling a cab—Vivian lived a bit further than Ava did, and even drunk off her ass Ava wanted to make sure her friend got home safe—at about 2 a.m. It had taken Vivian that long to shake off her admirer at Goodbar. "He was cute, Viv," Ava slurred when they were in the cab, aware that she was probably talking way too loudly but unsure of what to do about it. "You should've given him your number."

"*Please*," Vivian said. "I'm pretty sure he was in college. I need me a *man*, not a boy."

This had sent them both into a giggle fit, and that was the last clear memory Ava had of the night.

CHAPTER 11

She knew she'd gotten home and into bed because that was where she woke up the next morning—the same morning, technically. She groaned when she saw the clock read 9 a.m.—she was supposed to be at the studio in half an hour.

What if I don't go? she asked herself. *They don't need me for Joel to keep recording, and if there's one thing I need, it's a day away from Killian.* In the end, though, that thought was what propelled her from the bed and into the arms of her waiting hangover. If she just didn't show up—even if she texted Killian with an excuse—he would blow the whole thing way out of proportion, take it as some sort of silent statement she was making. And she knew that their current, if icy, state of affairs would be easier for her to deal with than that.

As she showered, though, she wondered if it might not be better to just goad Killian into a fight, get it all out in the open once and for all, and see what could be salvaged from the wreckage afterward. *Maybe,* she thought, letting the hot water stream over her body, all of which seemed to ache, *but I'll save that for a day when I'm not hungover.*

It was almost ten when she headed out of her apartment to make her way to the studio. When she walked in, Joel was in the middle of a take, so she just loitered near the door, not saying anything or announcing her presence as the rest of the band listened to him finish up.

As soon as Joel was done, though, Killian swiveled around on his seat immediately when he heard her come in. "Where have you been?" he demanded.

Ava flopped onto the couch that sat against the back wall. "Woke up late," she said. Her voice came out raspy, and she took a swig from the bottle of water she'd brought with her, praying for the Advil she'd tossed down on her way out the door to kick in soon.

"Jesus, Ava," he said. "Are you hungover?"

She glared at him. "So what if I am?" she asked, knowing that she sounded like a defiant teenager.

"Are you kidding me? In the middle of recording?" he asked, just as Joel walked in from the booth.

"Jesus Christ, calm the fuck down, Killian," Ava said. "I went out with Vivian last night. What are you, my father?"

"Vivian?" Rafael interjected hopefully from the other side of the room. "And you didn't invite me?" Vivian had met the guys in the band several times by then, and she had made a big impression on Rafael. *I really should set them up,* Ava thought idly, but she had more pressing matters to deal with just then—like that fact that Killian had apparently been thinking along the same lines as her that morning and was determined to pick a fight.

"It's just unprofessional," Killian said, ignoring Rafael.

Ava rolled her eyes. "I'm not recording today, am I? So what's the big deal?"

"The big deal is—"

"Shut up, Killian," Ava snapped. The room went silent for a moment, and she heard her words bouncing off the wood-paneled walls. She didn't think she had ever spoken that way to Killian before, let alone in front of the rest of the band. And Rich. "I'm not into your domineering, puppet master bullshit today, okay? Or ever, for that matter."

"What the fuck is that supposed to mean?" he asked.

"You know exactly what it means. Listen to yourself for a change."

"No, you know what? I'd rather hear it in your own words for once," he said.

"Yeah, well, I wrote you a song about it, didn't I?" she said. "I'm sick of being your marionette. I'm sick of dancing to your tune. I'm sick of you thinking you can order me around and mold me into what you want me to be. Is that clear enough for you?"

There was dead silence for a moment. "Clear as fucking crystal," Killian said. He got up and left the room, somehow managing not to slam the door behind him.

Ava took her eyes from him to see the rest of the guys

CHAPTER 11

staring at her. When they saw her looking back, they all quickly shifted their gaze away. The silence in the room stretched on uncomfortably.

"Well," Rafael said finally. "That was awkward."

Ava sighed. "I'm sorry, guys. I didn't mean to do that in front of you. But the way he was, like, scolding me…it just pushed me over the edge. I'm sorry."

"I'm staying out of this," Rich said, eyes fixed on the control board in front of him.

"No comment," Ben said.

"Yeah, I'm gonna just plead the fifth," Joel said. "Maybe I should do another take?"

"Shouldn't someone go talk to Killian or something?" Rafael said.

Ben snorted. "Be my guest, dude. I am not getting into the middle of that." He glanced guiltily at Ava. "No offense."

"None taken."

They all looked at each other expectantly, waiting for someone to decide what to do.

No, Ava thought, *they're waiting for me to say I'll go talk to Killian. And maybe I should, but I have absolutely no desire to say anything else to him right now, let alone apologize for something I'm not sorry for.* Ava knew, though, that she shouldn't have let Killian goad her into starting a fight in front of the guys. Hangover or not, *that* was unprofessional and would only cause bad things for the band.

Still, she was pretty sure going after Killian just then wasn't actually going to help matters very much or she would have. Or so she told herself.

He might be producing this album with Rich, but they could carry on without him for now. "Whatever," she finally said aloud. "He'll come back whenever he's ready, and then he and I will work out our issues in private, I promise." She addressed Rich. "Let's play back that last take and see what we think, yeah?"

Killian came back in after about an hour, and by then Joel had moved on to recording a different song. Killian came into the production room and stood in the doorway, arms crossed as he listened. The rest of the band members turned to glance at him as he came in, but no one said anything until Joel had finished.

"Joel did another take of that first song right after you left, and we thought it sounded good, so we moved on," Ben informed Killian neutrally.

Killian nodded, seeming to look anywhere but at Ava—or so she fancied. "Good," he said. "That last one sounded good, too, from what I heard."

"Yeah," Ava said. "He's been through that one three times now, and that was the best take, just now. Still a few more parts for that song, though."

Finally Killian looked at her, but only briefly. "Good," he said again, sitting down the couch. "Don't mind me, then. Let's keep going."

At the end of recording that day, Joel was almost finished—one more day and guitars would be done. Killian barely moved from the couch and offered very little input—mostly just agreeing when any of the other members thought a take needed to be redone or sounded good and thought they were ready to move on. It was the quietest and most unobtrusive he had ever been in regards to anything the band was doing, and Ava couldn't help but feel that this was no coincidence in light of her words to him earlier. She had apparently, finally, struck home.

Ava gathered her things at the end of the day, looking forward to doing nothing more strenuous than going home and laying around watching Netflix for the rest of the evening. So she was disappointed but not surprised when, as the guys were

CHAPTER 11

heading out, Killian said, "Ava. Can you stay? I think we need to talk."

She sighed and set down her bag, not wanting to do this now but knowing that, in light of what had happened earlier, she had no choice. The rest of the guys studiously avoided her eyes—or Killian's, for that matter—as they filed out of the room. When the door closed behind Ben, the last to leave, Killian and Ava stared at each other across the room for a moment in silence.

Finally Killian cleared his throat. "I want to apologize for attacking you earlier," he said. "It was uncalled for, especially in front of the guys. What you do on your own time isn't my business, and I shouldn't criticize you for it."

Ava was surprised. This was not the way she had envisioned this conversation beginning. "Thank you for that," she said. "And I apologize for saying those things to you in front of everyone. After you left I promised them that from now on we would...work out our issues in private. We can't put them in that position. It's not fair to anyone."

"Agreed," Killian said. He looked at her almost expectantly, as though waiting for her to say something else.

Ava, however, had nothing further to say. She shifted her weight awkwardly. "Well," she said. "I'm gonna head home—not feeling well, obviously, so I better rest up before—"

"Wait," Killian said. "Is that all?"

Ava was at a loss. "Is what all?"

"Don't you think..." He paused. "Don't you think you owe me an apology, too?"

"I thought I just did apologize."

"For getting into it in front of the guys, yeah. But I apologized for the things I said, so I thought—"

Ava felt her prickly, hot rage from earlier begin to return. "I *am* sorry for saying it in front of the guys, yeah, but I'm not sorry for what I said."

"But, Ava," he said, and, unbelievably, he smiled, like she was a child who didn't understand what was happening. "You can't think—you can't really think that. You didn't mean it."

"Don't tell me what I do or don't mean," she said. "If you really can't see it, if you really don't know what I'm talking about, then you have some reflection to do, I think."

She moved toward the door, but he stepped in front of her, putting his hands lightly on her shoulders to stop her.

"I can't see how this is news to you," Ava said, before he could speak again. "I shouldn't have brought up the song because I never meant for it to be another wedge between us, but it's all in there. Everything I've been feeling. I thought that's why you were upset about it."

"A song is a song. It's poetry: it can be exaggeration or oversimplification."

Ava could not believe what she was hearing. "Are you kidding? What was it you said to me just a couple weeks ago?" She pretended to be thinking hard about it. "Oh, yeah. 'The songs are me saying what I mean. I don't have any other way to say it.'"

"You're twisting my words."

"How convenient," Ava snapped. "Nothing you say is ever what you mean."

"That's not true."

"How am I supposed to know?" she demanded. "How am I ever supposed to know what you really mean anymore? But I can tell you this—I mean every word of that song. I meant it when I wrote it, and I mean it now." They were standing close together now, and she could see the emotion in every muscle of his face, every twitch and every movement of his eyes. He was hurt, and while a part of her wanted to kiss him, to make it all better, to erase everything that had happened between them in the last few weeks and months, she couldn't seem to stop herself. "Maybe," she said, her voice low, "what upset you most about the song is that you're not the only talented songwriter in this band. Maybe you're mad that I might finally be as good as you."

Killian looked as though he wanted to scream, to swear at her, to yell. Instead he kissed her.

CHAPTER 11

It was a hard kiss, and he bit painfully down on her lower lip. She gasped but didn't move away.

Finally he drew back. "That is bullshit," he growled. "But here's something that isn't. I love you, Ava. I love you as much as I hate you right now."

Ava kissed him again, then shoved him backward onto the couch. "Thank God," she said. "Finally, you've said something honest."

She dropped her bag, took off her coat, and then straddled him on the couch. *This is a terrible idea,* she screamed at herself as she kissed him again. *Terrible! Sex has never solved anything for us.*

Of course, her brain was not what was in control just then. She fumbled to undo his pants and push them down, then her own, even as his hands roamed up under her shirt, inside her bra. She lowered herself onto him, taking him inside her, furious at and disgusted with herself even as she moaned aloud and began to move atop him. He groaned and gripped her hips tightly, his fingers digging into her skin hard enough that she knew she would have bruises later, but at the moment it only heightened the pleasure.

Killian came first, tightening his grip as he shuddered beneath her. She kept grinding her hips into his until she felt her own orgasm building, and she threw her head back and let herself come as well, gasping.

When they were both finished, Killian wrapped his arms around her and lay back on the old couch, drawing her down against his chest. Spent, exhausted in more ways than one, Ava let him, resting her cheek on his chest.

After a while, she spoke. "Is this how it's always going to be?" she asked. "Loving and hating each other and going around in circles?"

He was silent for a moment, his fingers stroking the base of her spine. "That's how we know it's real," he said at last.

There are so many ways I drown without you.

Ava wanted to be angry at that, but all she felt was tired. "Maybe that's true in songs," she said. "I don't like that idea as much in real life."

He sighed. "You know what? I don't think I do, either."

They were silent for a moment, then Killian brushed her hair away from her eyes, prompting her to look up at him. "Come home with me?" he asked.

Ava hesitated for a moment, but just for a moment. "Okay."

chapter 12

Shoreline
2009–2010

A few weeks after their first night together, Killian was gone, off to record Handel's Messiah's new album in Los Angeles.

They had spent as much time as they could together before he'd left, to the exclusion of almost all else. The only exception had been for Ava to spend some time with her parents while they were in town for her recital and for Killian to finish writing some of the new songs. And for Ava to go to work, of course. She had never liked her job all that much, but it chafed even more when she had to be there knowing that Killian would soon be gone. He'd be off to Los Angeles, then after that he'd be on a world tour, on the road for who knew how long. She took a few days off during his last week, but even that was not enough.

While the band was recording, Killian called or texted her every day, giving her updates, asking how she was, telling her how much he missed her. She missed him, too—constantly—but she tried to stay both optimistic and realistic. Their attraction was strong enough that they wouldn't go down without a fight, she knew—yet what if the distance and time apart was too much? And, really, what did a couple weeks, a few nights in bed together, prove? She went back and forth within her own head, elated one minute and discouraged the next. Vivian was no doubt sick of hearing her go on about Killian, speculating and worrying and planning. But she couldn't help herself. It also didn't help matters that she had no projects of her own to distract her—she didn't have any performances coming up, work was as miserable as ever, and she didn't seem to have the focus to compose something.

"Girl, you just need to get laid again," Vivian advised her one night over drinks. "That'll help fix your head."

Ava laughed. "Oh, yeah, let me just fly out to Los Angeles and show up at his hotel."

Viv arched an eyebrow at her. "There are worse ideas." She shrugged. "Or…"

"Or what?" Ava asked suspiciously, sensing she wasn't going to like what was coming.

CHAPTER 12

"You could, you know, keep looking around here," Vivian said. "Keep your options open."

"Viv, seriously?" Ava said. "I don't want anyone else. *He* doesn't want anyone else." At least, she was pretty certain that was the case. "We talk every day. It's the best we can do at this point."

"I know," Vivian said. "I just…I think you should keep your options open in case this doesn't work out, okay? He's a rock star. He lives a different life from the rest of us."

Ava was well and truly annoyed by this point, mostly because she knew Vivian was right. Vivian was usually right. "I don't want to talk about this anymore," she said into her drink.

"Okay. That's cool." Vivian changed the subject, and they didn't mention Killian the rest of the night.

For a few days, Ava did toy with the idea of flying out to Los Angeles to surprise Killian, but she realized that Vivian, damn her, had a point. Their relationship wasn't familiar or comfortable enough for her to take such a bold step. *So I am just going to sit around here, waiting for him,* she thought. It was an uncomfortable thought, but she knew it was the truth.

It wasn't until a couple months later, when the album was completely finished, that Killian came home. He had a month off for the holidays—more than he had expected, he told her—before he would have to leave again to start doing press and promo for the album, and then hitting the road on tour before the album even came out. Their first week together they spent mostly in Ava's apartment, only venturing out for takeout or more wine. After that, they rejoined society a bit, going on dates as they had when they first met. Ava introduced him to Vivian properly, who even admitted that she was a) not only impressed but b) had most likely been wrong about him.

"I still think ya'll need some more time to play this thing out," she said to Ava as they escaped to the bathroom to chat, "but he's crazy about you, that's obvious." She smiled widely at her friend. "And he's just your type, too. The brooding, tortured artist type."

Ava smiled, almost silly with happiness and alcohol.

※

They spent almost all of Killian's month home together, with the exception of the few days Ava went home to Batavia for Christmas. He spent most nights at her apartment, as having given up his own place he was crashing with his parents for the time being. His parents lived in an old house in South Buffalo, where Killian had grown up. They first invited Ava over for dinner a few days before Christmas, a step in her and Killian's relationship that felt very "official". They were both very kind and she liked them at once. Killian's mother was a nurse at ECMC and had lots of crazy stories from the emergency room. His father was a musician as well and played guitar in a few local cover bands. He had been a radio DJ before retiring a few years before, and it was clear where Killian got his love of music from. Ava wondered if it was difficult for Killian to live at home with his parents after so long living either alone or on the road; after all, much as she loved her parents, she wasn't sure she could ever move back in with them. But she could tell, during the couple evenings she spent at the Sterling house, that Killian genuinely enjoyed having that time with his parents, no doubt because he was away so much. He helped his mom in the kitchen—he could cook, Ava was pleased to learn—and discussed wine pairings with her, something they could both talk passionately about. He talked music and the music business with his dad, and helped him with fixing and cleaning things around the house. It made Ava miss her own family.

One night, as Ava and Killian were having dinner at a restaurant near her apartment, he asked if she'd found any new performance opportunities. "Nothing solid yet," she said. "One of your contacts from the recital got in touch with me, the one who plays in the BPO. He said he thinks he might be able to get me a spot singing with them next fall, which would

CHAPTER 12

be amazing. But that's a ways off yet. After the holidays, I'll do some more digging."

He shook his head. "I wish I'd be around more to help you. You've got to do something," he said. "You're too talented to labor in obscurity. I'll keep my ears open, too."

She felt herself blush with pleasure at his words. "Well, thank you," she said.

He leaned forward. "If you could do anything with your voice," he asked, his eyes on hers, "what would it be?"

She hesitated for a moment, feeling uncertain about making this confession to him of all people. Would it sound like she was using him? Could either of them still really be in doubt of the other's feelings, after all the time spent together and the sex and the music? "I…I would love to sing in a band. If I could do anything."

He raised an eyebrow at this, a slight smile on his lips. "Really?"

"Yes," she said, feeling like she was blushing and wishing she would stop.

"Interesting. Not the Met?"

She laughed. "I've dreamt of that too, believe me. That would be amazing. But the odds…they seem so astronomical."

"Well, that's something to keep in mind. You of all people could make it, though. Whatever path you choose to take." Then, abruptly, he asked, "Do you compose?"

"I…play around with it," she admitted. "I'm nowhere near as good as you. But sometimes I try to write songs, and see how they sound…" she trailed off awkwardly. She much preferred it when they were talking about her voice, her singing, an area in which she actually had talent.

He smiled at her over the rim of his glass. "I want to hear something."

She laughed. "I don't think that's—"

"No. I mean it. Tonight."

"I don't think I really have anything that's ready for you to hear…"

"Believe me, songs are never really 'ready'. I just want to hear a little something. Please?"

She smiled nervously. "Okay. When we get back to my apartment," she said, confident that once they got there she would be able to employ a very effective distraction, and he would forget all about it.

He didn't mention it again the rest of the dinner, so Ava thought that maybe he had forgotten all on his own. But when they got back to her apartment, he pulled off his coat and went to stand meaningfully in front of her electric keyboard. "So?"

"What?" she asked, deliberately misunderstanding him even as her body went tight.

"I was promised a song," he said.

"Now?" she asked, looking away from him, feeling a tightness creeping up her shoulders.

"Why not?"

She gave what was supposed to be a seductive smile, but probably looked a bit shaky. "I can think of other things I'd rather do, that's why." She crossed the room to him and kissed him, willing her body to relax.

He pulled away. "Nice try, Ava. It almost worked, too." He swept her an exaggerated bow, gesturing toward the keyboard.

Sensing she had no other out, she sat down on the stool in front of the keyboard as though it was an electric chair. He pulled out a chair from her tiny dining room table and sat down expectantly. Taking a deep breath, she began to play. It was just the piano part at this point; she had lyrics in mind, but no melody had yet presented itself. She thought it was the most polished of the songs she had written lately—or attempted to write, anyway— but she still felt hot and prickly and uncomfortable as she played, knowing he was watching her, knowing he was listening with that ear that missed nothing. Her fingers felt awkward and heavy on the keys, and she knew she was striking them too hard in sections where the music should have been softer, but at least she played the correct notes. Tension pooled at the base of her spine, and she couldn't relax into the keys, lean into them the way she did when she played this alone. When she finished, she could barely meet his eye.

"Good," he said. "It's nice, Ava. I like it. Is there a vocal line? Are you planning to write one? And lyrics?"

"Yes," she mumbled. "I just haven't gotten that far yet."

"Hmmm." When she finally stole a glance at his face, he looked deep in thought. "Yes." He jumped up and came to stand next to her. "So, this part…" He hummed back a few bars of the first verse. "It goes like this, right?" He played that section back exactly.

"Yeah," she said.

"So use *this* chord instead of *this* one here…" he demonstrated, playing both chords.

"Killian," she began, mortified.

He didn't seem to hear her. "And then when you play this passage…" He played it again, this time with his alteration included, "it flows more naturally into that pre-chorus sort of section. See?"

"Killian, I—"

"Don't you hear it?" he asked, as though she hadn't spoken.

"Yes, I hear it," she said finally. "Killian, don't worry about it. It's just…it's just a silly song. I—"

He took her face in his hands. "It's not silly. You wrote it, love." He released her and turned back to the keyboard. "Now, this next part I think can be improved by—"

"It's okay, Killian," she said, louder now. "Really. It's not a big deal."

He paused, his hands still resting on the keys. After a moment he straightened up. "Okay," he said. "I was just trying to help."

"I know you were," she said. "It's just that I…it's not really finished yet. I shouldn't have played it for you at all."

He shrugged. "If you say so, Ava."

She walked past him into the kitchen, her cheeks burning,

mumbling something about getting some wine. Mostly she just needed to be away from him for a moment. Didn't he see that on top of everything else, she admired him? She had wanted to play something she'd written for him—eventually. She shouldn't have let him goad her into it. Couldn't he see how hard it was for her to have shared that with him, and then for it to be found wanting, as she'd known it would be? She should have refused, and she wished with every fiber of her being that she had.

In early January, Killian went back out to Los Angeles to do some promo for the record, and then the band hit the road on tour. They were playing some club shows in the U.S. before launching a European tour—Handel's Messiah was big in Europe—and then coming back to the States for a full-blown North American headlining tour. The album, which was entitled *Shoreline,* would be released midway through the European tour. Ava, for one, couldn't wait to hear it; Killian had been a terrible tease and wouldn't let her hear any of the tracks, nor so much as describe them to her.

"But I'm your biggest fan," she wheedled one night while they were in bed together.

He laughed and kissed her. "Oh, I know," he said. "Believe me, I know."

Killian had told her that once they were touring, he wouldn't be able to be in touch as much, due to their crazy road schedule—from traveling between cities to doing radio interviews or acoustic sets in whatever city they were in to playing the actual shows to doing fan meet-and-greets. Ava understood, even if she didn't like it. While they were in the U.S. he texted at least once a day and called her every few days, but when the band got to Europe, the time difference—not to mention international phone plans—made things more difficult.

Yet Killian managed to send her a postcard from every city the band visited. Sometimes they would arrive in bunches, and sometimes days would pass in between them: London and Manchester and Edinburgh and Dublin, then Paris and Lyon

CHAPTER 12

and Lisbon and Madrid and Barcelona. Then Italy: Milan and Florence and Rome and Naples. Then back up north, from Vienna to Prague to Munich to Cologne to Berlin to Frankfurt to Hamburg, then Amsterdam and Utrecht and Copenhagen and Stockholm and Helsinki and Tampere and Moscow and St. Petersburg. She put them all up on the walls of her bedroom, imagining all those places she'd never been and wondering what it would be like to see them with Killian beside her. Maybe someday she would.

Meanwhile, the album was released. Ava made sure she got her hands on a copy the day it came out. *I'll have to ask Killian to sign it for me when I see him again,* she thought, smiling, as she put the disc in her CD player. She was one of the few people she knew who still bought physical CDs, though Killian had been getting her into vinyl a bit as well.

Having such high expectations for the album made Ava nervous. How could it possibly live up to what she'd come to expect, both as a fan and from getting to know Killian, from being involved with him and seeing his talent firsthand? Entwined with her high expectations was an almost equal fear of being disappointed.

Yet, as it turned out, she shouldn't have worried. *Shoreline* completely exceeded her expectations. It was everything she had loved about Handel's Messiah's first album, yet amplified: the power and unyielding drive of the guitars and drums coupled with the passion and delicate beauty of the strings and piano, all set off by the indisputable majesty of Celeste's voice and the passion and romance of Killian's lyrics. Celeste, Ava could tell, had grown more confident and sure with her voice. And Killian, too, had grown as a songwriter and composer. He went bigger with the orchestra and choir arrangements, many of the parts—both instrumental and vocal—were much more complex, and he was playing with song form a bit more, straying from the traditional verse-chorus-verse-bridge format of most rock songs. The closing track of the album entitled "Cathedral" was over ten minutes long, a perfect melding of metal and symphonic classical styles.

There was one song on the album that Ava thought, fancied, hoped, wished had been written for her. It was one of the three slower songs, probably what would be considered a power ballad, called "Dark River". The lyrics of the chorus went:

It's a dark river that takes me under
When you are far away,
I'm gladly torn asunder
By our unfinished passion play,
I see you across the dark river
And all I want to do is return,
Hold me close, make me shiver
Pull me from the cold water and make me burn.

But her very favorite line in the song was the one repeated at the end of both the first and second verses: "There are so many ways I drown without you."

The more she heard it, the more Ava was certain it had been written for her. In some ways, hearing Celeste sing it felt wrong—she wanted to hear Killian whisper it in her ear, for just the two of them to hear. Yet it was no small thing, hearing a song written for her by the man she loved on an album that had gone out into the world, to be listened to by the thousands and thousands of the band's fans.

She loved Killian, she realized on what was probably her fifth or sixth listen to "Dark River". She had shied away from the word "love" before now, afraid it was too much too soon, even for her to bear on her own. But in listening to the song he'd written for her, she couldn't deny it anymore. And why should she? She laughed aloud in that moment, in realizing that she was really, truly in love.

Ava listened to the album over and over again, just as she had done with *The Art of Escape,* until she knew almost all the

CHAPTER 12

words and could sing with every track. A couple of the songs, though, proved difficult for her to sing, even with her trained voice—such was the ambition of Killian's songwriting.

When the band finally arrived back in the States—in Miami, from where they would kick off the North American headlining tour—Ava spoke to Killian on the phone for the first time since he'd been in Berlin, over two weeks before. He sounded completely exhausted, but happy to talk to her.

"How do you like the album?" he asked almost immediately.

"I love it," she told him. "Beyond words. Really, Killian. It's even better than I had imagined it would be."

"And do you have a favorite song?" he asked.

She hesitated for a moment before answering. "I think 'Dark River'."

She was sure she could hear him smiling through the phone. "I was hoping that would be your favorite."

***

And so the band toured North America, a massive tour that would wind its way up the east coast into Canada before hitting the Midwest, the west coast, three cities in Mexico, and then winding up in Buffalo, on home turf. Ava knew that after the final show—which she was anticipating almost as much as getting to see Killian again—the band would have a couple months off before hitting the road again, and she couldn't wait.

Yet soon something extraordinary and completely unexpected happened.

"Ava," Killian said when she picked up the phone, late one night. "You have to come. You have to meet us."

Ava tried to rub the sleep out of her eyes. It was well after midnight on a Thursday; she had fallen asleep on her couch watching reruns of *CSI*. "Killian? Come where? What are you talking about?"

"You need to come to New York," he said. "We just played

our first show here, and we have another one tomorrow night—tonight, I guess, and—"

Only now was Ava awake enough to pick up on the distress, the urgency in his tired voice. "Killian, what happened?" she demanded.

"Celeste quit," he said. "She got into a screaming fight with us after the show and walked out." He paused, and she thought she heard a catch in his voice. "I—we all made it clear to her that if she left, that was it, and she could never come back. I guess she didn't—*doesn't*—care."

"Jesus, Killian," Ava said. "That's…unbelievably shitty."

He sighed. "I'll explain everything—what I understand, anyway—once you get here, I promise. But we don't have much time. There's the show tonight, and we'll need to rehearse before then, and—"

"Wait," Ava said, realizing she must not be completely awake, because she didn't seem to grasp what he was saying. "When I get there? To New York? Why would I come to New York?"

Killian was silent for a moment, as though he couldn't believe she hadn't understood the situation. "We need you to fill in, Ava," he said. "For Celeste."

"For…in the band? Wait…you mean for the rest of the tour?"

Killian laughed humorlessly. "Well, my biggest concern right now is getting through this next show. It's sold out. But, yeah, ideally you would fill in for the rest of the tour. We're not even halfway through, and we can't cancel it now. We just can't, Ava."

"Why me?"

"Who else? You're not far, you already know most of the songs—we can adjust the set list however you want, don't worry—and your voice, Ava. Your voice is incredible. You're perfect."

He fell silent for a moment, a silence that was crowded by all her fears and anxiety and self-doubt about what he was asking her to do. *Could I?* she wondered. *Should I? Do I dare? Am I good enough?* All of this warred with the excitement that was beginning to bubble in the pit of her stomach. *How many*

CHAPTER 12

people ever get this chance, to sing lead for one of their favorite bands? Isn't this the break I've been wishing for, and then some? Isn't this what I've fantasized about, and more?

Then, softly, he added, "And because I love you. Please, Ava."

It was the first time he had said he loved her. She didn't think about it too much in the moment, but later she would wonder if he was aware that that was the first time he had ever said it. If he had used that to convince her. Or if he just hadn't realized he hadn't said it before. For years after that moment, Ava would spend a lot of time pondering what had truly convinced her, what had caused her to take the biggest plunge of her personal and professional life: his words or her own desire. Then there would be dark nights when she would wonder whether it had been worth it.

But at that moment, she didn't know or consider any of that. All she said was, "Yes. Of course I'll do it. Of course I'll come."

chapter 13

Album #5
2016

CHAPTER 13

The next morning, Ava and Killian arrived back at the studio together, and if the guys noticed, no one said anything. They hadn't talked much more the night before; they'd had wine and pizza for dinner, then gone to bed, where they'd made love again. This time, Ava had managed to banish her doubt and guilt and fear of what would happen to them tomorrow. She had thought about nothing but how good he felt inside her, and how wonderful, how *right* it felt to be so close to this person she loved so much.

Things weren't perfect. They were a long way from perfect. But they were better than they had been in a long time.

Joel finished recording his parts, and they decided to break early for the day and get started with Ava's vocals the next day. "Which song do you want to start with?" Killian asked her. His eyes were warm as he looked at her, and they'd been much more affectionate—albeit subtly so—with each other all day than they had been in some time. "It's up to you."

She looked over their roster of songs. "Let's start with 'Dark Lady'," she said, smiling at him. It was a song he'd written for her.

He nodded. "Okay, then. 'Dark Lady' it is. It's all yours tomorrow. Better get home and rest up that voice."

Ava wasn't sure what to make of those words. Did that mean he didn't want to spend time with her? That probably wasn't a bad idea, all things considered—it would be best to tread slowly around this new peace they'd found.

Or maybe, she said to herself irritably, *it means exactly what it sounds like. He wants you to go home and rest for recording tomorrow.*

She gathered her things as the rest of the guys began to shuffle out. "I'll see you tomorrow, then," she said to Killian.

He looked up at her, the warmth still in his eyes. "Yes. See you tomorrow."

She smiled and left. She would take his advice and go home and have some soup and some tea, and then go to bed early so that her voice was in prime shape for the next day. The album was what they both should be focusing on—was what they should have been focusing on all along. As Ava left the studio that day, she felt happier than she had in a long time.

The next day found Ava not feeling quite as cheery. "Dark Lady", she realized, had not been the best choice for starting to record, even if she was feeling good about her relationship with Killian and wanted to hold on to that. The song had a bit more of a doom/goth metal sort of sound, more so than anything from Handel's Messiah's recent albums. In addition, it had layer upon layer of vocals, lots of harmony and backing vocals. Ava knew the finished product would sound gorgeous, but recording it was nothing short of a pain in the ass.

It took them four days to nail it down, and then they moved on to "Chains of Gold", a hard, heavy song that they were considering for the first single. This was the one, Ava knew, that she should have started with—it was pretty easy and straightforward after "Dark Lady". But then, maybe it was better to get the more difficult song out of the way first, when she was fresh.

As the days wore on, they went through their roster of songs—seventeen in all, with the addition of Ava's. Ava kept the lyrics sheet for each song in front of her as she recorded—she had everything mostly memorized, but when recording she wanted to bring out as much emotion and nuance into each word as could, and so she wanted to be able to focus on that. There wasn't always time for that in a live show—time to slow down and think. All the emotional artistry had to happen now, so it could be heard on the album.

A little over a week into vocals, Ava finished up one night with "Memories", a beautiful, acoustic ballad that was almost folk-like, with gorgeous and poetic lyrics. Killian had never written anything quite like it before, and Ava loved it and loved

CHAPTER 13

that his talent could still surprise her.

"So what's up for tomorrow?" Rich asked that night as they all prepared to leave. "There's three songs left, right? Ava, what about your song?"

Ava couldn't help it—she stole a glance at Killian, who was not looking at her. She hadn't been avoiding her song, per se, but she hadn't wanted to bring it up with things between her and Killian going so well. Yet she was excited, still, to record it. *Damn it,* she thought, *here we go again. I'm afraid of the things I want because of him. Because I'm too worried about what he thinks and feels.* "Yeah," Ava said, the word coming out a bit more sharply than she had intended. "Yeah, let's start with that one tomorrow. I think it's time."

Ava showed up at the studio the next morning ready to record her song. The importance of the occasion was hitting her in a way it hadn't when she'd recorded the piano part. That had been new and different enough on its own that she almost didn't have room for any of the emotions she was feeling today. She would be singing a song that she had written, and it would be going on a Handel's Messiah album.

Killian caught her eye when she came into the production room and smiled at her, but she thought it was a tight smile. Or was she just imagining it? Was the fact that she was singing her song today really bringing back all their old tension or was it just in her head?

Either way, she refused to feel guilty about this in any way. This was her accomplishment, and it meant something to her. She wasn't going to let Killian—and how he may or may not be feeling—ruin this moment for her. For what kind of a relationship was that, that would break apart so easily?

It was so simple, too simple: a few thoughts, a few brain synapses firing, and she was right back where she had been with

Killian a few days ago. Their fragile reconciliation, their newborn fresh start, had been shattered in just seconds. Ava glanced at Killian, who was standing at the control board with his back to her. Could he feel it? She thought she could: the very air between them had changed; it was thicker and heavier and darker.

Ava waited on the couch—trying not to remember what had happened there just a few days ago—for the rest of the guys to show up. She smiled at them as they came in but didn't say anything. They were used to it: she tried not to speak unnecessarily on days when she was recording, to make sure her voice was at its freshest and strongest.

When everyone was there, Killian turned to look at her. "Ready to go with 'Appassionata'?" he asked.

She nodded and got up to walk into the booth.

"Wait—here." Killian passed her the binder of all the lyrics that she used when recording.

Ava shook her heard. "I don't need it for this one."

"Right. Of course," he said.

She went into the booth, donned her headphones, and positioned herself in front of the mic. She waited for the red light to come on, telling her it was time to start. When it did, and the music began, she closed her eyes and let it envelop her, the piano part—gentle at first, then quickening—that she herself had played, making her mark on a digital file forever; the other parts, guitar and bass and drums, that she had written, that had not existed in the world until she plucked them from her head and wrote them down and gave them to her fellow musicians. She felt heady, powerful with the knowledge that she had created something and it was living, was ringing in the air around her, existed separately from herself where it could travel into her ears and brain and heart and soon, very soon, would travel into the ears and brains and hearts of other people. These were people she had never met and probably never would, people who might understand her or might not, might like the song or might not. But they would all be able to hear it, regardless, and that was the beauty of it.

CHAPTER 13

She opened her mouth and began to sing.

She had sung so many songs in her life, ones she had written but mostly, largely, ones she had not, ones that she took and made her own without them ever really belonging to her. This was different, and it felt different. This was nothing like singing the words of some long dead composer or even like singing Killian's words—Killian, who seemed in so many ways an extension of herself, all the things she was not and sometimes wished to be. These words were hers, just as the music on which they rested that supported and transformed them, was hers. The emotion with which she sang them was hers, as were the thoughts and memories and desires and hopes and dread she brought to bear on them. It was all hers and had never been anyone else's before it was hers. She put herself back into that moment in the production room, just minutes before, when she had felt the tender thread between herself and Killian fray and snap; yet, this time, she welcomed that realization and the pain and fear that it brought. It was exactly what she needed; without it, this song would not sound the way it needed to sound. Perhaps when she stopped singing and stepped out of the booth, things would be different; she hoped they would be different. But right now everything within herself was exactly as it needed to be.

She stopped singing at the end and closed her eyes, taking a moment to collect herself, then removed her headphones and stepped out of the booth.

She walked back into the production room and found five faces staring at her in—there was no other word for it—awe. When no one said anything, she spoke. "How was it? Should I do it again?"

Joel shook his head. "Nah. Definitely not."

"Wait—what? You mean…we're using the first take?"

Rich nodded. "I would think so, yeah."

Killian looked up at her, and she found the expression on his face impossible to read. "I don't see how you could possibly sing it any better."

She couldn't stop the wide grin that spread across her face, nor did she want to hide her joy. "Good," she said.

◦§◦

Ava spent the rest of the day doing backing vocals for "Appassionata", then did a take of the second-to-last song on the roster called "Sky Before a Storm". By the time they finished up for the day, she was exhausted in every way a person can be: physically, mentally, and definitely emotionally. Yet part of her wanted to just keep going. She was in a groove where her voice was sounding exactly how she wanted it to, where she had complete control over it and over her emotions. She wanted to just keep singing until she'd finished the last two songs, but knew she couldn't—and, really, probably shouldn't. She just hoped she could get back to this same state the next day.

◦§◦

Killian stopped her in the parking lot of the studio as they were all leaving. "Hey," he said.

"Hey," she said, and when he didn't immediately speak, she asked, "Did you want to get dinner or something?"

"No, I'm feeling pretty tired," he said. And he looked it—something Ava hadn't noticed until just that moment. He continued, "And you should save your voice, anyway."

He's still telling me what to do, she thought. She instantly regretted thinking it.

"I just wanted to say that…that take you did of your song today," he said, "I think that's the best I've heard you sing. Ever."

Ava was taken aback. "Wow…thank you," she said. "That means a lot coming from you." She smiled. "After all, you've heard me sing quite a bit."

He nodded, staring off into the distance. "I just wanted you

CHAPTER 13

to know that," he said. "Maybe you write better for your voice than I ever will."

Ava shifted her weight uncomfortably. "Not per se... I mean, you can hear my voice from the outside, which I can't, not really." She was willing to offer him that much of an olive branch.

"Maybe."

They stood awkwardly in the parking lot, not looking at each other. *Was it the song? Was that really all it took?*

"Well," Killian said, causing her to start slightly. "I'm gonna head home and get some rest."

"Yeah," she said. "You...don't take this the wrong way, Killian, but you look like you need it."

He scrutinized her again with that impassable wall behind his eyes. "Yeah," he said. "It's been a rough few weeks to say the least."

As he walked to his car, part of Ava felt that she should be offended. But he was right, after all. It had certainly been a rough few weeks—and longer, really—for her as well. And at least he was speaking plainly, honestly. Wasn't that what they both wanted?

chapter 14

Shoreline
2010

CHAPTER 14

Ava arrived in New York that Friday morning exhausted—there hadn't been time to get back to sleep after Killian had called her, of course, so she'd packed a bag and waited for him to call her back with the flight arrangements.

Yet even packing a bag was more difficult than she would have thought. How long would she be gone? What did one bring on tour with a metal band? She needed a stage outfit, at the very least, if she was really doing this. And she seemed to be. After much—*much*—deliberation, she chose a mid-thigh black and red plaid skirt, fishnets, a black top with long lace sleeves, and combat boots. It was a little Hot Topic, maybe, but it would do. It would have to do.

The rest of the time was spent stressing about what she was going to tell her job. She settled for emailing her boss saying that she needed an emergency personal day and wouldn't be in. After all, she hadn't officially agreed to fill in for the rest of the tour yet, though it was obvious that someone would need to, and soon. She had the weekend to figure out her next move.

If it even mattered. If she could even get through this one show without completely disgracing herself.

Killian called back around 5:30 a.m., saying they had booked her on a 9:00 a.m. flight from Buffalo to LaGuardia. Since there was no point in waiting around her apartment any longer, she called a cab and headed to the airport, even though she was going to be ridiculously early. She found she needed to be in motion, to avoid thinking too much about what she had agreed to and worrying if she could really pull it off.

On the way, she texted her parents in their family group chat, as well as Vivian, letting them know what was happening and where she was going. Their shocked replies to her texts came in immediately:

Dad: You're doing what?
Mom: Is this some kind of joke, honey?

HEAVY METAL SYMPHONY

Meanwhile,
Vivian: Girl, is this for real????

Mom: Are you sure about this, Ava?
Dad: Good luck with the show, then. A bit different from a recital!
Mom: Yes, of course, good luck! Let us know how it goes!

Vivian: YOU'RE GOING TO KICK ASS!!!!!!!!!

Ava smiled and dumped her phone back in her bag. She could understand the surprise, appreciated the enthusiasm, but found she didn't have the emotional energy to deal with either just then.

She checked in, took her carry-on bag through security (and people could say what they wanted about Buffalo, but she had never moved through airport security faster anywhere, that was for sure), found her gate, and settled in to wait. She had brought a book with her, but reading was proving an exercise in futility. Though normally a favorite pastime of hers, she found that all it was doing at the moment was allowing her mind to wander. What had she been thinking to agree to this? Of course she wanted to help Killian when he needed it, but was she really cut out for this? Could she really do this crazy thing: go on stage with a metal band—a band that had been one of her favorites for years—and sing their songs and perform in front of their fans and do a credible job? She had plenty of performing experience, of course, but none like this, as her father had pointed out. She knew he meant well, but now she was doubting herself. What if she was awful? What if everyone hated her? What if she got booed offstage? Ava didn't know what would be more upsetting about that scenario should it come to pass: letting herself down or letting Killian down.

Then there were the other guys in the band, whom Ava had

CHAPTER 14

never even met. Had they signed on to this? Were they okay with it, with her coming in to take over, a woman they had never met, a singer they had probably never heard, nor heard of? Or had they not had much of a choice but to go along with it, to take a gamble on Killian's girlfriend?

Ava had just under two hours to go until her flight, and she knew she'd go crazy if she spent it sitting at the gate, thinking these thoughts that scratched at her like an itchy sweater. So she got up and wandered around the terminal, poking in and out of the gift shops and magazine stands, and finally getting a massive blended coffee and chocolate concoction from the Coffee Beanery just past the security checkpoint. She figured if there was ever a day to indulge, this was it; and besides, she'd need all this caffeine and more before the night was over.

Finally, finally, it was time to board, and Ava settled into her seat (a window seat, thankfully) and pulled out her iPod as the plane prepared for takeoff. It was a little over an hour flight from Buffalo to New York, and she was going to use all the time she could to study up on Handel's Messiah's songs. She knew the ones from *The Art of Escape* well enough—she had listened to the album obsessively when it had first come out, and she had kept it in pretty heavy rotation since—so she was going to have to go through *Shoreline*. She hadn't had it as long, of course, and so didn't know the songs as well—problematic to say the least, since the set list was sure to be heavy on songs from the new album. She had practiced singing most of them—in her car, in her apartment when she was alone—simply because that was how she interacted with her favorite music. She couldn't *not* sing it and sing along with it. Still, singing something just for fun—even though she might *imagine* she was rocking out onstage while doing it—was very, very different from performing it.

She only made it through the album once by the time the plane landed. *I should have just listened to a few songs over and over, so at least I'd know those better,* she cursed herself as she gathered her things and disembarked.

Despite all the signs, the sheer size of the terminal and the masses of people hurrying in all directions ensured that it took her a few minutes—longer than she would have liked—to find the exit.

Thank God Killian was waiting for her once she got there. With him was a guy whom Ava recognized as Rafael, the band's bass player. "Ava," Killian said when he saw her, her name on his lips a prayer and an exclamation and a sigh of relief. He drew her into an embrace and gave her a quick kiss. Any further expressions of their happiness at seeing one another for the first time in months were delayed for the time being by the urgency of the situation. "Thank you for doing this," he said when they drew apart. "I will never be able to thank you enough."

She laughed, somewhat self-consciously. "Let's just hope I don't make a wreck of things."

"You won't. I know you won't." He gestured to Rafael. "Ava, this is Rafael Sanchez, our bass player, as you probably know. Raf, this Ava Tomei, my girlfriend."

Rafael reached out and shook her hand. "Nice to finally meet you," he said. "I've heard a lot about you, especially being on the road with this guy for months at a time." Rafael rolled his eyes good-naturedly, and Ava laughed, appreciating that he was trying to put her at ease.

"That's just Raf's polite way of saying I haven't shut up about you," Killian said.

Ava smiled at Rafael. "Nice to finally meet you as well," she said. "As I'm sure Killian's told you, I'm a big fan."

Rafael nodded. "That's good to hear," he says. "I was actually at your recital at Buff State, though I had to take off before Killian could introduce us. You were incredible. I think you'll be fine tonight."

Ava felt herself blushing, which wasn't very rock star. "Thanks," she said, feeling something akin to relief at this endorsement.

"Alright, we better go," Killian said. Without asking, he reached over and took her bag from her and began leading them

CHAPTER 14

out of the airport. "There's nothing else going on at the venue today, thank God, so they said we can use it as a rehearsal space all day if we need. We're going to have to go through the whole set list at least once, just to be safe." He tossed a reassuring smile over his shoulder at Ava. "And to make sure you're comfortable, Ava. We can go over a few songs more than once if you want. Whatever you need."

Rafael sighed as they all piled into a cab just outside the terminal. "It's going to be a very long day after a very long night."

"Yeah, well," Killian replied, having given the taxi driver the address of the venue, "we knew that last night when Celeste threw her bitch fit."

This seemed to be the opening Ava had been waiting for. "Yeah, what happened?" she asked tentatively. "I mean, that's… so crazy."

Killian and Rafael exchanged a look. "Who knows," Killian said. "We can talk about it later."

Ava wanted to press him, but something about the look on his face told her that that wasn't a good idea. Not now, anyway.

This, however, only brought to the forefront something that had been bothering Ava ever since Killian had called, a worm that had been burrowing away in the back of her brain and that now emerged in the very front. It was strange that Celeste would walk away from her band, just as Handel's Messiah had just released a very successful album and was becoming even more well-known. There had to have been some kind of massive falling-out, and/or long buried and simmering resentment and anger of some kind.

When Ava had first gotten into the band, she'd read quite a few reviews and articles about them, as well as interviews. There had been quite a bit of speculation that Killian and Celeste were a couple. Ava had never been sure why the speculation had centered on Killian, rather than any of the other guys in the band. Perhaps because he was the mastermind behind the songs? Perhaps because it had been Killian and Celeste who had first founded Handel's Messiah between the two of them?

Whatever the reason, such rumors had been part of the discourse surrounding the band since they had first emerged onto the scene. Only in one interview that Ava had read had Celeste and Killian been asked directly about their relationship status, and Killian had dismissed the question with a rather slick, disdainful line that Ava remembered being impressed by at the time: "Just because a woman is fronting a metal band, she has to be dating one of the guys in the band? That's a little sexist, don't you think? Let's get back to talking about the music, if you don't mind."

She had never asked Killian if there had ever been anything between him and Celeste. The fact that he threw himself so enthusiastically—and publicly—into a relationship with Ava clearly indicated that there was no current romantic attachment between him and Celeste or anyone else. Whether there had been in the past, well, Ava wasn't sure. Neither of them had thus far volunteered information about their exes—it hadn't seemed relevant or necessary yet, when they had still been in that period of feverish honeymoon, getting to know one another and discovering all the ways that they needed and desired and longed for each other. And so Ava had not wanted to bring it up, even when questions crossed her mind, even when jealousy—yes, she would admit to it—flowered within her at the thought of Killian spending all those hours and days and weeks with Celeste in the recording studio and on stage and on the road in the close confines of a tour bus.

Now Ava began to wonder if they would need to have that conversation whether they wanted to or not.

"What's important now," Killian went on, "is getting through this show and making sure you have everything you need."

"And then after that, we've gotta worry about getting through the tour," Rafael interjected.

Killian glared at him. "One step at a time."

Rafael shrugged. "Sorry, man. I'm not trying to freak her out or anything, but it's something we gotta figure out real soon."

"Yeah, I know. Later," Killian said, in a tone that brooked no argument.

CHAPTER 14

Rafael shrugged. "So, Ava," he said. "Where else have you performed?"

The rest of the cab ride passed as Ava talked about her performances, with Rafael asking genuinely interested questions about her musical background and career. Whether it was intentional on Rafael's part or not, talking about her training and performance history made Ava feel just a bit more confident, with the added bonus of making her forget (for the time being) about Celeste and Killian and what may or may not have happened in their history together. Ava *had* done all those things, after all; given all those performances and been reviewed well (on those occasions when a reviewer showed up) and gotten all sorts of experience. And she had decided, after that one holiday concert while she was still in college, that once she had sung the solo in Mendelssohn's "I Waited for the Lord" in front of five hundred people, there was really nothing else in life to get nervous about ever again.

If only that college girl could see what she now faced.

As Ava and Rafael chatted, Killian kept his face turned toward the window, watching the city go by. Ava wished he would chime in to the conversation, help put her at ease, but then, she realized, he probably had the weight of the world on his mind. She needed to remember that and try to do the best she could. For him. For her, too. Because didn't she deserve to give her best performance tonight? For the first time, it occurred to her that maybe this was the big break she'd been waiting for, that maybe instead of nerves and doubt and anxiety, she should be feeling optimism and excitement. Maybe she had been meant to meet Killian for more than one reason.

Maybe this was the day everything in her life would change.

The confidence and optimism Ava had begun feeling in the cab vanished quickly when they got to the venue.

First of all, it was bigger than she had been picturing—much bigger. And Killian had said it was sold out, hadn't he? Any shame or embarrassment she suffered tonight would not be able to be safely swept away. Not with that many people in the audience.

Then there were the other two band members, Ben Brooks and Joel Radley, as well as a man she didn't recognize. They were waiting in the large pit area before the stage, chatting idly, but broke off as soon as Killian burst through the doors with Rafael and Ava behind him. One look at the expressions on their faces told Ava that perhaps Rafael had been the only one to welcome her at the airport because he was the only one who wanted to.

"Guys," Killian said as they approached. "This is Ava Tomei. Ava, Joel Radley and Ben Brooks." He turned to the third man. "And this is Billy Mikowski, our manager."

Ava stepped forward and shook all of their hands. "Nice to meet all of you," Ava said, trying and failing to banish the queasy, uneasy feeling in her stomach.

"Likewise," Billy said. At least he sounded friendly.

"We've heard a lot about you," Ben said finally.

"Thanks," Ava said, even if it wasn't a compliment, really. "I'm…I hope I can help out."

Joel snorted, crossing his arms over his chest. "Yeah, I hope you can too."

"Joel, what the fuck?" Killian said.

"I'm sorry, Killian," Joel said, even though he didn't sound it. "But this sucks, you know? Celeste is gone, and we're stuck with your new girlfriend, who only you and Raf have ever heard before, and who has no experience singing in a band." He tossed Ava an apologetic look. "Sorry. It's nothing personal. We just have no idea what the hell we're getting into right now."

Ava felt as though she had been slapped, yet it was a slap she had seen coming, truthfully. As happy as Killian had seemed that she had come, even he seemed nervous about how she would do, how the show would go. And really, she couldn't blame any of them for being nervous. She tried to open her mouth to tell Joel she understood, yet the words seemed to stick in her throat.

CHAPTER 14

"Guys, let's just all get along and make the best of this, okay?" Billy said. "Let's be professionals here."

"Well, what the fuck, Joel?" Killian said again, as if Billy hadn't spoken. "What were we supposed to do? Did you have any other bright ideas? I'm telling you, Ava will nail it. She's perfect."

"According to you," Ben said. "And, no offense, dude, but she's your girlfriend. Of course you're going to think she's great." He, too, tossed an apologetic look in Ava's direction.

"Guys, calm down," Rafael said. "I've heard her, and I think she's a great singer. Obviously Celeste leaving in the middle of the tour is not ideal, but—"

"Yeah, and whose fault is that?" Joel asked, tossing a glare in Killian's direction.

"Me? How the fuck is it my fault?" Killian asked.

"You should know."

"This is bullshit," Killian said. "I'm not sure how I was apparently supposed to stop Celeste from walking out, but that's beside the point right now. Ava is here, and I would have thought you guys had a little more respect for me as a musician then to think I would have someone sing with us who isn't the real deal."

"And not for anything," Rafael said, "Celeste had never sung in a band before we got started. I don't think Killian had played in one either, right?"

Joel crossed his arms over his chest again. "Not the same thing, man. We were all kids then. This is different. The stakes are much higher."

"I still don't hear you coming up with any brilliant ideas for what we should have done besides calling Ava," Killian said.

"*You* should have—"

"Okay, enough!" Ava shouted, sick of standing there and listening to them talk about her as if she wasn't even there, eroding her confidence while they were at it. "Listen, I appreciate that this is really difficult for you guys. And I understand that I was not everyone's first choice, nor is this situation ideal." She cast Joel a pointed look. "I do. But I came all the way here, and you're wasting time arguing like this." She cleared her throat and looked around at all of them. "At least hear me sing first. If I suck, I'll go all the way back to Buffalo if that makes you feel better."

Killian looked about to argue, but Ava silenced him with a look.

"Well, we don't have much choice *now*," Joel grumbled. Ava ignored him, and thankfully everyone else followed suit.

"Okay," Ben said. "Let's hear you."

Ava stalked up the stage and positioned herself in front of the mic stand, moving it up to accommodate her 5' 10" height.

"Is this ready to go?" Killian asked, of no one in particular.

"Yeah," Ben said. "Everything's ready."

The guys got themselves into position: Ben behind his drum kit, Killian at his keyboards, and Joel and Rafael strapped on their guitars. Billy walked to the back of the room to listen.

Ava fancied that she could hear her own pounding heartbeat amplified throughout the huge, empty room by the live mic in front of where she stood. She understood why they were all upset, she did, but she was also pissed. She wanted to show them she could do it and show Killian that she was better than simply the only person he could call on short notice.

She glanced back at the band members positioned behind her, looking at her expectantly. "Play 'Believer'," she said. "Believer" was the band's big single off their first album and was so far their most popular song: catchy while still being heavy, and with relatable lyrics about leaving behind misguided beliefs. The video had even gotten some plays on MTV, which was odd for a metal band. Frankly, Ava thought most of their other songs were better, both lyrically and musically, but she did like it, and—more importantly—she knew she could sing it like no one's business. And since it would definitely be in the set list, it seemed like as good a song as any to start with.

There was a moment of silence behind her, then she heard Killian launch into the piano intro to the song. Then the guitar, bass, and drums kicked up into the riff that was heavy but still

CHAPTER 14

catchy and not too overpowering, which was one of the things that helped make the song so popular.

Ava took a few slow, abdominal breaths before her entrance, as she always did. Her heart rate spiked as the measure approached, and she opened her mouth and began to sing.

To her horror and frustration, the voice that came out was just a shadow of her own, quiet and wispy and breathy. She didn't turn around, but she imagined that Joel and Ben were exchanging glances or that Rafael was looking at Killian questioningly.

Pull it together, Ava, she admonished herself. *You can do this.* As she moved through the pre-chorus and the chorus, she began to slip into the performance groove, accessing the place in her muscle memory where this song was stored so that she barely had to even think about it.

She had as much formal classical training as Celeste—probably more—yet Ava also had a solid belting voice that she'd developed from years of musical theatre in high school. She kept it in shape, too, because she liked having versatility in her voice. And that, she knew, was what could set her apart and potentially make her even better in the band than Celeste had been.

She managed to mix her belting voice and classical voice for the song, giving it power and force without making it sound too formal, too inaccessible. She sang it just like she did in her living room, in her car, in her shower, when she was relaxed and having fun and had nothing to prove. And, somehow, it worked. Her big, powerful mezzo-soprano rang out through the empty theatre like she had been born for this.

"*I once was a believer,*" Ava sang on the final chorus, when the song had changed to a slightly higher key that suited her voice even better,

> *But I had to turn away*
> *I had to tear down your altar*
> *Had to leave you dead with no hope of resurrection*

Had to demolish the shrine
And save myself
I once was your believer...

Ava took a deep breath and stepped back from the mic as the band finished up the instrumental outro to the song. She waited until the music had cut out before she turned around.

What she saw were looks of surprise—pleasant surprise. Killian was beaming hugely at her, yet even he seemed surprised that she had done so well.

Ben nodded from behind his drum kit. "I'm satisfied."

"Yeah," Joel said, somewhat grudgingly.

"I told you so," Killian said. "Ava, that was amazing. Really."

"That was perfect, Ava!" Billy called from the back of the venue.

"Hopefully you can sing everything as well as you can that one," Ben said.

Ava laughed, feeling much more at ease than she had five minutes ago. "Just about, I think."

Killian reached down and picked up a couple sheets of paper from the floor beside him. He beckoned everyone over, and they gathered around his keyboard. "Okay," he said. "This has been our set list for this tour so far." He handed Ava the first sheet. "This is all the songs we rehearsed before hitting the road—we did a few different ones for the European tour. And this way we can change things up so we don't get bored." He handed her the second sheet. "You pick whichever songs you can do. We definitely want 'Believer' in there, which won't be a problem, and 'Dreamscape', since that's the new single."

"For sure," Ava said. She loved "Dreamscape" and knew she could sing it.

"Everything else is up to you," Killian said.

"Well, we need more of the new stuff in there," Joel said.

Killian shot him a look but didn't say anything.

CHAPTER 14

Ava looked over the master list in front of her and began working through it, telling them which ones she could sing. She glanced up and smiled at Killian when she got to "Dark River". "This one, definitely," she said.

He caught her eye and smiled back, and she wished right then that the two of them were alone. It had been so long since they'd seen each other, after all...

Focus, Ava. She turned her attention back to the list. She had a job to do. They all did. Everything else could wait.

"Mmm, 'Gothic Romance', for sure," she said, naming a song from the band's first album. She had always loved the lyrics; Killian had worked with themes and images from different gothic novels, which had always been her favorite in her literature classes as a student. She would need to bust out her high range for that song.

"Oh, and 'Dream Specter'," she said excitedly. It had been her favorite song from *The Art of Escape,* with beautiful lyrics about falling in love with someone in a dream. Another one she knew she could sing perfectly.

Last on the list was 'Cathedral', the epic, ten-minute closing track from *Shoreline*. To Ava's dismay, she saw it had been in the set list from the night before—it had closed out the show, in fact. "Umm, I don't think I can do 'Cathedral'," she said, looking up at Killian. "I don't really know it all that well." Also, the vocal part was quite difficult, as Killian no doubt knew, but she didn't say that out loud.

"No problem," he said. "You can always learn it later."

"Well," Joel said. "If it comes to that."

Killian just ignored him, and everyone else followed suit.

In the end, they had a set list of thirteen songs, plus an encore. It was heavier on songs from the first album, but oh well, Ava thought. It couldn't be helped.

They all studied the final list for a moment, which began with "Who I Am", the opening track from *Shoreline.* An appropriate choice, Ava realized, for her first official moment with the band—perhaps the first of many. Maybe.

Killian clapped his hands lightly. "All right. Let's get to work," he said. "The whole set list, one by one."

They all returned to their positions on stage and began.

Ava stood just offstage, listening to Rafael address the crowd—not quite full yet—before the opening band began that night. They had all nominated him to go out and fill in the audience on the recent developments before the show got started.

"This way," Killian had said, "we're not throwing Ava to the wolves, so to speak. No one will be shocked or disappointed when she hits the stage."

"Plus," Ben had added, "we need to be up front with the fans. We've got nothing to hide."

Ava couldn't help but wonder how much the people now crowded into the concert venue already knew. What with social media reporting things as soon as they happened, surely rumors about Celeste were already out, somehow.

"You all may have heard the rumors," Rafael was saying, echoing Ava's thoughts, "that Celeste has left Handel's Messiah. And unfortunately we have to confirm that they are true."

The audience seemed to gasp as one.

"She decided to leave the band last night due to personal and creative differences with the rest of the band members," he went on. "So, rather than cancel our show for all you lovely people tonight, we've brought in a replacement. The beautiful and talented Ava Tomei, a fellow Buffalonian, will be singing with us tonight, and let me tell you, you guys are in for a real treat. The show is going to go on, so let's all have a great time tonight!"

There was a pregnant moment of silence, and then the crowd cheered dutifully.

"Alright!" Rafael said. "Let's do this!" He left the stage, and the opening band, a rock-rap quintet, filed onto the stage

CHAPTER 14

and picked up their waiting instruments.

Killian clapped Rafael on the back as he joined them just offstage. "Nice job," he said.

"Yeah," Rafael said. He turned and grinned at Ava. "The rest is up to you, baby."

"No pressure," Ben added jokingly.

Ava smiled tightly. She had felt good during rehearsal earlier, despite a few mistakes and some sections of songs that had not gone as smoothly as she—or any of them—would have wanted, but that was to be expected. She couldn't be perfect. But, she was realizing now, she would need to be as close to it as possible.

She seemed to have won over the band. Joel had come up to her a bit sheepishly after rehearsal and pulled her aside backstage.

"Hey," he'd said. "I just wanted to apologize for how I acted earlier. None of this is your fault, obviously. And you sounded awesome in rehearsal, by the way."

"Thanks," Ava said, surprised but pleased. She had very much gotten the impression that Joel didn't like her. "I appreciate that. And like I said, I get that this is tough for everyone."

He laughed shortly. "Understatement," he said. "Things have been…rough with Celeste for months now, honestly. She and Killian were just at each other's throats, and…well, I won't get into all that. We've all been stressed and tense and so that's what you were seeing today, honestly. After everything we'd already been through on this tour, it was tough to wrap my head around playing with someone I'd never heard before. It's not about you, I promise."

"Well, thank you," Ava said again. She desperately wanted to press him about why Celeste and Killian had been at each other's throats, but realized it wasn't the time. She didn't need that distraction before going onstage, so she let the comment pass. And in the moment, it almost made her feel better: whatever might have happened between Celeste and Killian in the past, there had certainly been no lingering romantic feelings. "I won't say I'm not nervous, and I'm sorry you guys were dealing with all that, but this show is…really a dream come true for me. I won't let you down."

"You'll kill it," Joel said. "I'm looking forward to it. Honestly."

After that, they'd headed backstage, where Ben enthusiastically high-fived her and offered to go over some lyrics with her if she wanted. So at least her new—and perhaps temporary—band mates had accepted her, for this show at least.

As she stood just offstage and listened to the opening band without really hearing them, she realized that the real hurdle would be winning over Handel's Messiah's devoted fans.

chapter 15

Album #5
2016

Ava spent the rest of the next day finishing up "Sky Before a Storm", and then the following day she would begin the last song, called "Hostage". They had all agreed early on that this was another song that had single potential, though of course they couldn't know for sure until they'd heard the final recorded version.

The excitement in the air was palpable. They were almost done; it was so close. Just another couple days, maybe three, and they would wrap. Then there would be a night out for dinner and some drinks to celebrate—a tradition. There was still a lot of work to be done, of course—Killian had to fly out to Los Angeles for the recording of the orchestra and the choir, and then there was mixing and mastering to be done. But soon, the heavy lifting for the band members themselves would be done.

"Okay," Killian said when Joel—the last to arrive—was there. "One thing before we get started. I finally thought of a name for the album." He paused dramatically.

"Well, don't keep us in suspense," Rafael said.

Killian smiled. "I'm thinking we should call it *Messiah Complex*."

Rafael hooted with laughter. "I love it!"

"How have we not had an album called that by now?" Ben said.

Joel grinned. "It gets the thumbs up from me."

"Me, too," Ava said.

"Okay. Well. That was easy," Killian said. "No one has any counter proposals?"

"I don't see how any of us could come up with anything better," Ava said.

"Alright, then. That's settled." He slid over to sit at the sound board beside Rich. "Ava, just give us a few minutes to get this set up, then you can start." He glanced up at her. "'Hostage' is the last one, right?"

"Yup," she said, already flipping through her lyric binder to find the right page.

CHAPTER 15

"Okay," he said, and he turned away from her.

She found the lyrics sheet for "Hostage" and began to read through it. As she did so, her heart rate sped up, and she felt her face redden.

How had she not seen it before? How had she not realized what this song was really about? Or was it simply that before she had written a song capable of wounding Killian, she had never thought him capable of the same?

Taking a couple deep breaths, she went back to the beginning and began to reread the lyrics, wanting to be sure that she was right, that she wasn't overreacting.

> *Some days you're the gun to my head,*
> *Your eyes locked and loaded*
> *And warning me not to move;*
> *Some days I've got Stockholm syndrome,*
> *And I want nothing more*
> *Than to stay in this prison of yours.*
>
> *You've always got a bullet in the chamber, love,*
> *And any moment could be our last.*
>
> *I'm your willing hostage,*
> *Hands tied,*
> *Bound here by the rusting chains*
> *Of a love I can't let go;*
> *I'm your unwilling hostage,*
> *Hands tied,*
> *Bound here by the decaying chains*
> *Of a love that won't let me go.*
>
> *Some days you've got the gun to your own head,*
> *Your words locked and loaded*
> *And making sure I don't move;*
> *Some days we're both ready to die,*

*And end this standoff
Even though there might be nothing
   waiting on the other side.*

*You've always got a bullet in the chamber, love,
And any moment could be our last.*

*I'm your willing hostage,
Hands tied,
Bound here by the rusting chains
Of a love I can't let go;
I'm your unwilling hostage,
Hands tied,
Bound here by the decaying chains
Of a love that won't let me go.*

*Some days I am in control,
And some days you're the one with the gun,
At some point the captive became the captured
As purgatory opened and swallowed us whole.*

*I'm your willing hostage,
Hands tied,
Bound here by the rusting chains
Of a love I won't let go;
I'm your unwilling hostage,
Hands tied,
Bound here by the decaying chains
Of a love that can't let me go.*

Ava's heart was pounding in her ears anew, drowning out any and all sound around her. The lyrics were blunt in a way that Killian's lyrics, so often heavy with more obscure metaphors, usually were not. How had she missed it? How had she rehearsed this song so many times, letting her voice carry her through the

CHAPTER 15

powerful vocal line, focusing on remembering the switch of "won't" to "can't" in the final chorus, and not have realized?

It certainly wouldn't be the first time that Killian had been vindictive in his lyrics. There had been a song on *Terra Nova*, Ava's first album with the band, called "Prima Donna" that was very obviously about Celeste.

Yet maybe "vindictive" wasn't the right word here. Ava was hurt, yes, but hadn't he always written about what he was thinking and feeling? How could she have thought that the difficulty in their relationship *wouldn't* appear in his lyrics? If she had the right to write about it, didn't he?

He probably assumed she knew and was okay with it—or at least that she was in agreement—since she hadn't objected to recording the song. Not that she would have in any case—over the years there had been a couple songs that she hadn't loved, but she'd never said anything, not wanting to invite comparisons to Celeste.

"Ava? Ava!"

Ava started, then looked up from the binder to find the entire room staring at her. "Sorry. What?"

Killian looked slightly annoyed. "We're ready. It's time for you to start."

She stood up quickly, binder in her hand. "Sorry. I'm ready." She met his eyes, hoping he saw the challenge in them.

She stalked into the booth, set the lyrics binder on the stand, and donned her headphones. She nodded toward the window, letting them know she was ready. A few seconds later, the red light came on, and the music started playing through her headphones.

The music for "Hostage" was true metal with crunchy guitars and a fast and driving rhythm that would definitely get fans headbanging at the shows. Killian's synths underpinned the whole thing subtly, not detracting from the song's harsh power.

The vocals, too, needed to be powerful for this song to work, and this was one, ironically, that Ava had nailed in rehearsal right from the beginning, finding it was very comfortable in her voice. At the time, it had given her a flush of pleasure and confidence, knowing that she would not have been able to sing something like this so easily—or perhaps at all—when she'd first joined the band.

Now, as she waited for her entrance, she realized that she could use Killian's song, his own words, to send him a message. She could turn his own song on him. That was the danger of writing about the person in whose very mouth you were putting the words: she could take them and make them her own.

Because, really, Ava related to the song. She was the only person who could possibly feel the words as deeply as Killian did. And she was definitely going to make him feel them.

She took her two customary deep, silent breaths a couple measures before her entrance, then she began to sing.

She let the words pour out of her, breathing deeply and using all the air she could to power her voice, to lift and bear up her rage and push it from her throat for everyone to hear. At the moment, though, she didn't care who heard her, so long as Killian did. There was an edge to her voice, now, she realized, letting her tongue spear words like "chains" and curl around the word "hostage". It was an edge that wasn't usually there, and it made her voice heavier and not as nimble, but quick and light was not what was needed for this song. She chewed the words and spat them out, her voice racing along with the music, refusing to be drowned out or left behind. She made sure her voice soared over all, taking control of the song from the inside out.

It was an altogether different experience from recording "Appassionata", when she had let herself sink into the music, let it absorb her. Here, she fought with the song, beat it into submission until it could no longer harm her, and used it her for own ends instead.

When she was done, and the red light winked off, she stayed still for a moment, taking another couple deep breaths to calm herself down, to come down from her angry high. Then she left the booth and walked back into the production room.

The expressions on the guys' faces were similar to what they had been after she'd recorded "Appassionata". She let a

CHAPTER 15

smile curl her lips. "What? That bad, huh?"

"Psssh." Rafael looked at her incredulously. "You know that was kickass, right?"

Ava shrugged. "It felt pretty good, that's all I know. How did it sound?"

"Perfect," Ben said instantly.

"Yeah, that was killer, Ava," Rich agreed.

"That's another one-taker," Joel said. "Two in one album. I think that's a Handel's Messiah record, right?"

Ava didn't answer, but rather looked at Killian, waiting to hear his reaction.

"Another perfect take," he said, his eyes meeting and holding hers.

He knew. He knew exactly what she had done, what she'd been thinking and really saying as she sang. And she was glad. She looked back coolly at him. "Like I said, it felt good."

chapter 16

Shoreline
2010

CHAPTER 16

The lights were down in the venue, and the crowd—packed to the gills, just as Killian had promised—was chanting Handel's Messiah's name. The music that had been playing over the speakers while the opening band broke down their equipment and Handel's Messiah's was being put into place had been cut, so the audience knew the band was coming out in a matter of minutes, maybe even seconds. The anticipation hovered in an almost corporeal cloud over the heads of the audience. Meanwhile, the band members were all gathered just offstage in the dark, waiting to go on: Killian, Ben, Rafael, Joel, and Ava. Billy, the manager, was there too. He gave Ava an encouraging smile. She felt like she was going to throw up.

What am I doing here? Ava asked herself, not for the first time that day. Had she really been in her apartment in Buffalo only that morning?

"Okay, guys. And girl," Killian said, and Ava could see his smile even through the dark. "This is it. This is a big moment for us. You ready?"

"Yeah!" everyone said in unison.

"Okay," Killian said. "Let's go."

With that, he and the rest of the guys filed onto the stage, taking their places, and the crowd screamed with enthusiasm, seeing their shapes even in the darkness. Then the lights popped on and Joel kicked off the show with the opening riff to "Who I Am." The crowed went nuts.

Still waiting in the wings, Ava took several slow, abdominal breaths as she usually did, but she found that this time it wasn't calming her down, wasn't focusing her. The noise of the crowd and of the band itself—louder now, so much louder than it had been during rehearsal, somehow—was all around her, a physical presence worming its way into her head, and she couldn't think, couldn't clear her mind the way she always did—needed to do—before a performance.

In an instant of clarity, she realized that she was approaching this all wrong. She was used to classical performance, of course, and trying to prepare for a metal show in the same way as she did for a recital or an opera was ludicrous. There was no peace and quiet here for her to clear her head, nor should there be. That was the point. She needed to take the noise, the pounding drums and throbbing bass and chugging guitar and the screaming of the crowd, and use it. These things weren't a wall through which she would have to push. They were the wave that would carry her forward, to the horizon and beyond—as far, potentially, as she wanted.

And then it was time for her to walk onto the stage, at a strategic pause in the music, and somehow—she didn't really consciously know how—she was out on the stage, moving to the front and center, where her mic stand was. The crowd roared even louder than before, and in some part of her mind she realized they were screaming for *her.*

She bowed, waving and smiling at the blur of faces in front of her, shadowy though they were beyond the stage lights, which nearly blinded her. The boards of the stage rattled slightly beneath her combat boots from the sheer force of the sound, and she let that energize her as well. *This is it,* she thought. *I am really doing this.* Then she stepped up to the mic as her entrance approached. She opened her mouth and began to sing.

Her voice came out big and smooth—thankfully—yet once the initial rush of adrenaline from hitting the stage ebbed away slightly, Ava found that though her mind was ready to go, her body still reacted in a nervous way. Her legs shook slightly and breathing was more difficult—a major issue for a singer, to say the least.

As such, the middle verse of the song was a bit shaky, and she stayed almost rigidly in front of the mic stand, afraid to move or walk around the stage in case she fell over. She kept her eyes closed as she sang, afraid, now, of what she would see when she opened them.

Yet as she worked into the bridge of the song, she felt herself get slightly more comfortable. *This is their introduction to me as*

CHAPTER 16

a singer and as the potential permanent lead singer of Handel's Messiah, she reminded herself. *I better make this good. The best that I can. The best that I've ever sung.*

As she launched into the chorus at the end of the song, she felt the words in a way her nervous, overstimulated mind hadn't before, and she belted them out with new force and confidence. "*And you might be surprised by who I am*," she sang, feeling a big smile stretch across her face.

I am different from who you thought I was
Your eyes are playing tricks on you again
Listen to me tell you who I am
And someday you'll open your eyes
And you'll see me as I really am.

The chorus repeated once more, and then the song closed with a crash of guitar and synths, and the crowd went nuts. Ava felt her grin grow even wider, and she dared to sneak a glance at Killian, who was positioned to her right and slightly behind. He gave her a quick thumbs up, love and pride shining on his face.

Ava turned back to face the crowd as the band started to play "Sunstorm", a fan favorite from the first album.

Even if nothing else comes of this, Ava thought, feeling her legs solidify under her and beginning to move her hips slightly to the music, *how many people can say they got to play a show onstage with one of their favorite bands? I need to enjoy this. That's all.*

"Open your eyes to blindness," she sang, beginning the song, "*and breathe the heat into your lungs…*"

After "Sunstorm", there was a pause in the set list where Rafael would again address the crowd.

"How ya doing, New York?" he said into his mic—he occasionally sang basic backing vocals. He proceeded to repeat his explanation from earlier about Celeste leaving the band. "So here tonight, doing us a solid, is the lovely and talented Miss

Ava Tomei of Buffalo." The crowd gave what Ava thought was a gratifying loud cheer. "As you can hear, we didn't let you guys down in calling up Ava. So let's make her feel welcome, yeah?"

There was another cheer, and Ava stepped back up to her microphone so that she could also speak to the crowd briefly, as they'd all discussed. This, she thought, might be even harder than singing. "What's up, New York?" she cried, announcer style, and got another loud response. "This is Handel's Messiah, and I just wanted to say thank you for having me tonight and listening to me sing with these ridiculously talented guys. I've always been a big fan of the band, so this is really a dream come true!" Everyone cheered.

"We're gonna have some fun tonight," she went on, wondering where this confidence had come from, "and since I think you all know this next one, I hope that, since I'm new here, you all can sing along and help me out."

With that, she turned around and gave a quick nod to Ben, who clicked his drumsticks together and started them off with "Dreamscape".

The rest of the show passed in a blur. Ava talked to the crowd when it was indicated in the set list, and it was much more natural than she would have imagined. She could feel them being won over between her patter and her singing—or at least she thought so, anyway. She got much more comfortable on stage, as though she had been doing this her whole life: headbanging and swinging her hair around, pumping her fist and urging the crowd to get louder. She took the mic off the stand and walked around, rocking out face-to-face with Rafael and singing next to Killian. For "Gothic Romance", though, she found she had to stand more or less completely still—the high tessitura and overall difficult vocal lines of the moody, spooky song demanded she give it her full energy and attention.

About halfway through the show came "Dark River". The crowd obligingly busted out their cell phones, holding up the glowing screens and swaying in time to the music as she sang.

CHAPTER 16

She could feel Killian's gaze on her from behind as she sang the beautiful, melancholy, longing words, and her whole body, every inch of her skin, felt as though it was electrified. Despite being surrounded by the other band members, as well as the hundreds of audience members packed into the venue, she felt as though she and Killian were completely alone, as though she was singing for him and only him. Exactly as she had wanted to ever since hearing the song for the first time.

She could tell it was her best performance of the night.

The band closed with "Believer", and then they filed off stage. Right as Ava stepped into the wings, Killian wrapped his arms around her, hard, both of their damp, sweaty bodies pressed tightly together. "You were amazing," he said into her ear, loud enough that she could hear him over the roar of the crowd just beyond the stage. "Amazing. You blew everyone away, Ava. You blew me away."

She drew away from him, suddenly feeling exhausted but exhilarated. "Thank you," she said. "That means more than I can say."

It was all she had time to say before the rest of the band descended on her, hugging her and slapping her on the back. "You killed 'em, Ava," Ben said.

"Long live the queen!" Rafael cried, somewhat nonsensically.

Joel clapped her on the back. "That was kickass, Ava," he said. "I mean it. You were incredible."

The crowd was growing even louder, chanting the band's name, calling for an encore. Then Ava realized that some of them were chanting something else: her name.

A-va! A-va! A-va!

They were calling for her.

"Alright, guys," Killian said, but he was looking at Ava. "You got enough left for one more?"

Ava nodded, her smile stretching across her face. "Definitely."

The band went back out onstage, and the cheers rose to a deafening level. "Okay, guys," Ava said, grabbing the mic again.

"You've been such a wonderful crowd tonight, we figure you deserve one more. Sound good?"

Everyone screamed in agreement.

Ava closed her eyes briefly as the band started playing "Shoreline", the title track from the new album. This one, it occurred to her for the first time as she began to sing, was maybe another one that Killian had written for her.

> *I see your light guiding me home*
> *Always beckoning me back*
> *My eyes stay fixed on the shoreline*
> *The promise of so many destinations in one...*

Backstage after the show, the band members, Ava, Billy, and their road crew celebrated with a few bottles of champagne Billy had ordered for them. There had been a lot of whooping, shouting, fist bumps, and high fives as they came off stage after their encore, and Ava had been swept up in their exhilaration and, yes, relief. It was obvious now how tense they had all been in the hours leading up to the show, the guys perhaps most of all. Their reputation had been on the line, and they had put it in Ava's hands. Ava knew she had risen to the challenge as well as she possibly could.

The guys wasted no time in letting her know what a great job she'd done and how hard she rocked. That the show had gone better than anyone had dreamed it would was obvious. Ava let herself bask in the exultation and in the satisfaction of the feeling that she had proved any initial doubts wrong.

"Whew," Rafael said, after most of the champagne was gone and they had relived their favorite moments of the show several times over. "We should get to bed. I know none of us slept well last night, so it's probably time to get some rest."

Ava nodded agreement, only realizing when Raf spoke just how tired she was. The adrenaline that had carried her through the show had long since faded, and the champagne

CHAPTER 16

wasn't helping her keep her eyes open.

"Wait," Killian said. "First we need to decide what we're doing for the rest of the tour."

"What do you mean?" Joel asked.

"What we're doing for a lead singer for the rest of the tour," Killian clarified.

Rafael looked confused. "Well...Ava, of course."

"Yeah," Billy said. "I thought that was sort of a foregone conclusion."

Killian threw up his hands, a wide smile on his lips. "I just wanted to make sure we all agree."

"Well, obviously," Ben said. "After that performance, I think we're set. We couldn't find anyone who would do a better job, even if we wanted to." He smiled at Ava.

"And Ava?" Killian asked formally, turning to her. "Do you accept?"

The words *of course* sprang to her lips, but she found herself hesitating. She wanted to join them on tour, more than anything. But the practical considerations she hadn't had time for over the course of the last whirlwind day now took up residence in the front of her mind. She'd have to quit her job without notice—that would certainly burn some bridges. And how would she pay her bills? She had some savings, but student loans—manageable though hers were, compared to a lot of her friends—and rent payments hadn't left her with a lot of financial wiggle room. And then there was the basic matter of clothes, toiletries, underwear, not to mention stage clothes—she'd only brought enough things for a night or two. She'd need to go back home, pack, get someone to keep an eye on her apartment...

"Ava?" Killian asked, somewhat worriedly.

She blinked once and looked up at him. "I want to, of course," she said. "I would love to. More than anything. But... it's just not that easy."

"It is, Ava," Killian said earnestly. "What are you worried about? We can help you."

She hesitated, glancing at the rest of the guys. It felt like they were approaching a more intimate conversation now, one she would feel much more comfortable having with just Killian. Yet if she was in—if she was in this band, at least temporarily—they would need to know her reservations, too. "I mean…I have a job, I have bills…"

"Quit your job," Killian said, too easily. "You don't even like it! And obviously you'll get paid for playing with us. You should be fine. I'll make sure you're fine."

"Killian," she said, uncomfortably aware of the rest of the guys' eyes on them, "it's not that simple. I can't just drop everything to go on tour with you. As much as you know I want to."

"You can, Ava," he said. "This is what you've always dreamed about. How can you think twice?" He paused, and when he spoke again he had lowered his voice. "And I need you." He looked up at the rest of the guys. "We need you," he said, louder this time.

"Yeah, we do," Ben said. "You gotta help us out, Ava. Whatever you need, we'll take care of it."

"We'll make sure the label gets you Celeste's cut for the tour," Joel said.

Billy held up his cell phone. "I'll call them right now."

Killian discreetly took her hand and squeezed it once. Maybe it was just that she was so exhausted, but Ava felt tears begin to well in her eyes. The guys really believed in her. They really wanted her to tour with them. Killian believed in her. He was right—she was being given a chance, on a silver platter, to do what she had always dreamed of doing. And who knew? Once the tour was over, they would need a new lead singer, permanently. She was in prime position to step into the role for good, provided the rest of the tour went well. So what if she was late on some bills? Was she really going to let an entry-level job—that, as Killian had pointed out, she didn't like—stand in her way?

"All right," she said aloud. "I'll do it. Of course I'll do it."

Everyone cheered.

CHAPTER 16

"We've got a show in Toronto tomorrow night," Killian said. "I'll fly back to Buffalo with you so you can get some of your things, and we'll meet everyone else in Toronto."

Billy nodded and began dialing on his phone. "I'll set everything up."

Ben stood up and stretched. "I'll go hail us a cab back to the hotel."

"Hotel, huh?" Ava said, following the guys out of the dressing room. "You guys live pretty large on the road."

Rafael laughed. "Not usually, believe me. Killian only talked the label into it since we were here two nights. I think he got you your own room for tonight, too." He grinned. "Not that you'll probably get it all to yourself—I'm sure he'll be joining you, the lucky bastard."

Ava blushed, but laughed along with the rest of the guys. If they were going to be touring together (and living in very close quarters together) for the foreseeable future, there was no point in being coy about her and Killian's relationship.

"I'm the real lucky one here," Ben said. "If Killian is shacking up with Ava, then I'm the one who gets a room to himself."

"I don't think anyone can blame Killian for preferring Ava over you as a roommate," Rafael said.

They gathered all their things from backstage while Billy talked to the label and made travel arrangements. Half an hour later, they went out to the curb, everyone carrying their bags, and Billy joined them as they waited for a cab. "Everything's arranged," he told Ava. "You and Killian have a flight to Buffalo at 10 a.m. tomorrow, then once you're packed we've got a car rented for you both to drive to Toronto."

Ava smiled at him gratefully. "Thank you."

Billy wandered away, and Killian came up beside her. He slipped a hand around her waist and kissed her deeply. "I know we both need our rest tonight," he murmured, low enough so that the rest of the guys couldn't hear, "but I can think of a few things I'd rather do than sleep."

It had been so long since they'd been together that Ava was aroused by his very words, by his hand on her waist. "I can think of more than a few things," she said softly in response.

He lowered his voice further, speaking right into her ear. "I was rock hard on stage tonight, listening to you sing my music." He drew her hips against his so she could feel the truth of his words.

Ava felt certain her knees would have given out and she would have melted to the pavement had he not been holding her up.

"How far is the hotel?" she all but gasped.

"Too far," he said, releasing her.

Ben hailed a cab, and they all moved to pile into it, with Joel hopping into the front seat. Ava was about to climb in after Rafael when Killian tightened his grip, holding her back for a moment. "I'm going to pay the rent on your apartment while you're touring with us," he said quietly. "I want you to have to worry about as little as possible. You're doing us a favor, after all."

"Killian, no," Ava said. "You don't have to do that. I should be fine for a few—"

He cut her off with a quick kiss. "I'm gonna take care of it," he said. "I want to." He nudged her toward the cab, and she had no choice but to get in. She tossed him a glare that she hoped said *This conversation isn't over,* but he just gave her a cat-that-ate-the-canary smile as the cab pulled away from the curb.

I'll bring it up again once we're in our room, she told herself, but she knew that once they were alone—and in close proximity to a bed—Killian would very definitely be able to keep her distracted.

chapter 17

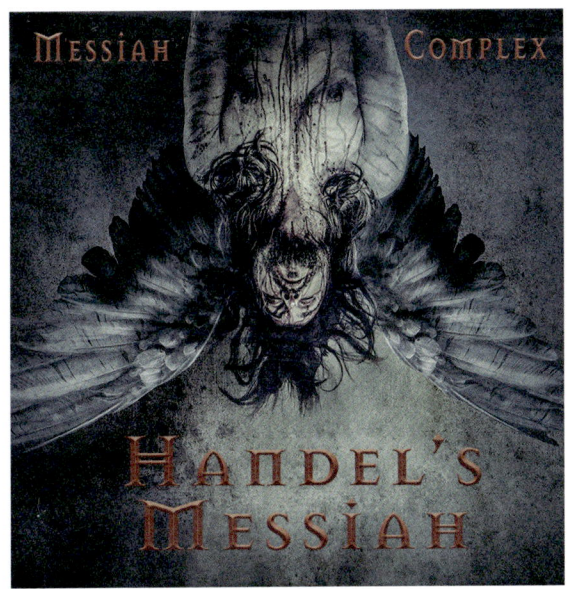

Messiah Complex
2016

It took Ava another day to record the backing vocals for "Hostage", and then they were done. Done recording. Ava could hardly believe it. It was always like this: they spent so long rehearsing the new songs, working on them and tweaking them so they would be just right, then spent just as long in the studio, recording them through take after take. And then, just like that, it was over.

For their customary post-recording celebration, they decided on dinner at Toutant, a newer restaurant downtown. They ordered several bottles of champagne and spared no expense on the food. When they sensed they were getting a bit too rowdy for such a fine establishment, they all squished themselves into a cab—Ava sat on Killian's lap in the back seat, while Joel tried to get on Rafael's in the front seat, much to the cab driver's chagrin—and they headed over to Cole's on Elmwood.

It was a Thursday night, so the crowd there wasn't weekend-level heavy, but as the night wore on it began to fill up.

"Jesus Christ," Ava said, to anyone who would listen. "Why is it that suddenly, every time we come in here, it's always college kids?"

"Didn't you come here when you were in college?" Ben asked. Everyone in the band was from Buffalo originally. Ben had gone to Buff State, just up the road from the bar, while Joel had gone to UB and Killian and Rafael had gone to SUNY Fredonia, an hour away, where they had met. And where they had both met Celeste.

"I did not," she said primly. "I was *far* too busy studying and taking care of my voice."

"Bullshit," Ben said, ruffling her already unruly curls.

The night got a bit hazy after that. At about two in the morning, the party began to break up, and Ava stumbled out of the bar with Killian's arm around her shoulders. She couldn't have said where the rest of the guys went or when they'd left.

"Why is it that every time I'm in that bar, I end up drunk off my ass?" Ava slurred.

CHAPTER 17

"Dunno," Killian said, for once almost as drunk as she was. "Weren't you drunk with Viv at…that other place, the other night? Mr. Goodbar!" he exclaimed triumphantly.

Ava shoved him, and in his current state he stumbled and almost fell to the ground. "What a stalker!" she cried. "How did you know where I was?"

"You told me," he mumbled, getting back to his feet.

"Oh."

"My spies follow you everywhere," he joked.

She shoved him again, but this time he was ready for her. "Jerk."

"Maybe," he agreed. "Maybe I am. Maybe that's the problem."

Ava was too drunk to make any sense of that, just as Killian was no doubt too drunk to know what he had said. Somehow, they made it back to Ava's apartment and into her bed, though neither of them had the ability to remove their own clothes, let alone do anything more strenuous.

Ava woke up early in the morning—too early, given how late they had been out the night before. Even the weak morning sunlight filtering through her sheer curtains hurt her eyes, and she moaned aloud at the realization of just how bad her headache was. Well, she should have known better. She wasn't twenty-three anymore and could no longer drink whatever she wanted without feeling it the next day.

Beside her, Killian's eyes fluttered open. "It shouldn't be this romantic to wake up in bed with you with a hangover," he said, his voice rough. "But somehow it is."

Ava half-laughed, half-groaned. "That hangover is exactly why your attempts at seduction will get you nowhere this morning."

But he didn't laugh or even smile. "I'm not trying to seduce you," he said. "I just wanted to tell you that…waking up in bed with you is always perfect. I think maybe I've lost sight of that lately."

Ava was quiet, not sure how to respond. "Maybe we've lost

sight of a lot of things," she said finally. "Maybe all we've been able to see are things we should let go."

He reached out and wrapped his arms around her. "Maybe we can start over?" he whispered against her hair.

She thought about this. After everything, could it really be so easy? Maybe it could be that easy if they both wanted it to be.

"I think it's worth a try," she said.

chapter 18

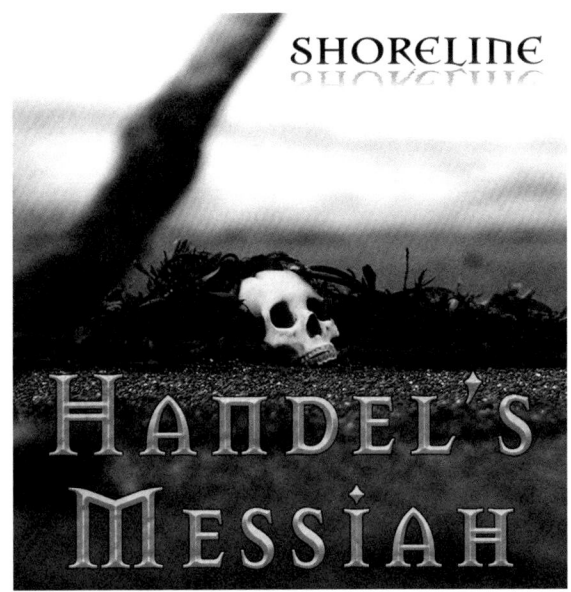

Shoreline
2010

The day following Ava's first show with Handel's Messiah was a whirlwind of activity, as she had expected. She and Killian woke up and got ready in time to catch their flight back to Buffalo—which was thankfully on time—and once they'd landed, they took a cab straight to Ava's apartment.

"Do you need any help?" Killian asked, standing in the doorway of Ava's bedroom as she reached around under the bed, looking for her suitcase.

"No," she said, twisting to look up at him from her awkward (and unflattering) position on the floor, one arm and half of her face under the bed. "I'm just gonna grab a bunch of things." Her fingers struck the handle of the suitcase, and she wriggled backward, pulling it along with her. "I'll have to try to pull together as many stage outfits as I can—I don't really have a ton of stuff, but I'll do what I can. Maybe I can go shopping in one of the cities along the way and get some things."

He stepped toward her, took her face in his hands, and kissed her. "Whatever you do will be perfect," he said, his hands sliding down to her waist. "You were extremely sexy on very short notice last night, so I have every confidence in you."

She pushed him away with mock sternness. "No time for any funny business, Mr. Sterling," she said. "I don't know if you've heard, but I have a tour to save." She stepped back. "Besides, 'sexy' is not the goal. Being taken seriously as a musician is."

He gave her a smile that made her very much wish that they *did* have time for some funny business, especially since opportunities for that sort of thing were likely to be in short supply in the close confines of a tour bus. "You're the whole package," he said. "You're both." He retreated back to the doorway. "Alright, then. I'll get out of your way. Just let me know if you need help." He disappeared, presumably to wait for her in the living room.

Within forty-five minutes, Ava had dug out some appropriate lead-singer-of-a-metal-band attire—and, as she'd told Killian, what she did have was not much—as well as a few pairs of jeans,

CHAPTER 18

some T-shirts and also nicer skirts and tops in case she needed to take part in interviews or other press events, as well as two pairs of combat-type boots, one pair of ballet flats, and some pajamas, sweatpants, and lots of clean bras and underwear. She didn't know how one went about doing laundry on tour and was a little afraid to find out. Then she gathered together toiletries, as well as personal items like some books, her Nook, and her laptop, along with all the necessary chargers.

Her suitcase was full to bursting by the time she was done, in addition to her purse and stuffed laptop bag that she'd be carrying onto the plane. Even so, it still didn't feel like enough for a month of touring, but there was no help for it now.

Before she left her bedroom and rejoined Killian, she figured it was time to call her parents—and Vivian, of course—to let them know how things had gone. And were going.

She called her parents first. She had the feeling that would be the more difficult conversation than the one with Vivian, so better get that over with.

"Hello?"

"Hi, Mom. Is Dad there?"

"Ava? How was your show? You really went on and sang with Killian's band? Hold on, your father's around here somewhere..."

"Can you put me on speaker?" Ava asked. "I have something to tell you both."

There was a pause, then her mother said, "Of course." Ava heard her call, "Bob! Come here, it's Ava!"

A moment later, her dad said, "We're here, Ava. What's going on? How was the show?"

She smiled. "The show was great, Dad. I did great. So great, in fact, that, um, the band asked me to keep touring with them."

There was a stunned silence.

"And I'm going to do it," she added, just in case there was any confusion.

"Oh, Ava," her mother said. "Really?"

"Yes, Mom. I can't turn down this opportunity. This is a dream come true!"

"But what about your job, your apartment…"

Ava winced slightly, hearing her mother list all the objections she herself had made the night before. "I'm going to quit my job," she said. "I'm not going to let that place stop me. And my bills and everything will be fine. I'm getting paid to tour with the guys, you know."

"Back up," her father said. "What band is this again? Killian's band?"

"YES, Dad. Handel's Messiah. It was all in the text I sent you."

"So this is Killian's idea?" her mother asked.

Ava sighed. She had told her parents that she and Killian were dating, of course, but they had yet to meet him—they had gone home a couple days after her recital, then hadn't been back in town since, and of course Killian had been away recording the album and then on tour for much of their relationship. "I mean, it's his band, so he asked me to fill in for the New York show, yes. But the rest of the band wants me to tour with them, too."

"Are you sure about this, Ava?" her father asked. "This is… this is really something. You're going on tour with a metal band? Is this…something you're ready for?"

"Yes, Dad," she said. "I killed it at the show last night. This is literally a dream come true. I'll be ready for it."

Both her parents were silent. "I don't know about this, Ava," her mother said finally. "You don't know anything about this lifestyle, or any of it. And you and Killian only just started dating. And isn't he a lot older than you? I just worry—"

"Mom," Ava interrupted. "All that is true. But I'm doing this. And I'm thrilled about it. I'll…figure everything out as I go."

Silence again. She could just picture them communicating silently with one another beside the phone, the way she'd seen them do plenty of times.

Finally her mother sighed. "If you're sure, Ava."

"I'm sure."

CHAPTER 18

"Be careful out there," her mother admonished. "Please."

"I will."

"Let us know if you need anything," her father added. "And keep in touch, okay?"

"I will."

"Good. Knock 'em dead, kiddo," he said.

She smiled. "I will."

"We're here, supporting you," her mother said. "And Ava?"

"Yeah?"

"Have fun."

Her smiled widened. "Oh, I will."

She hung up, taking a deep breath. That had gone better than expected, really.

Her next call was to Vivian, and it was both shorter and more enthusiastic than the one with her parents. "OH MY GOD YOU ARE TOURING WITH THE BAND HOLY SHIT AVA THIS IS AMAZING YOU WILL BE INCREDIBLE I JUST KNOW IT," Vivian shouted without even taking a breath. "You better text me every day! Tell me *everything!*"

Ava laughed. "I will, I will!"

"I want to hear all about it! Oh, man, I wish I could make it up to Toronto tonight to see you!"

"It's okay," she said. "The last show of the tour is in Buffalo, anyway."

Vivian shrieked again, and Ava could hear the clicking of a keyboard. "Okay," she said. "I bought a ticket. Just now. I'll be there with the biggest bells on."

Somewhat unexpectedly, Ava felt herself tear up. "Thanks, Viv. Love you," she sniffed.

"Ava, babe, you know I love *you.* Now get out there with your sexy man and melt their faces off!"

Ava laughed, said goodbye, and hung up.

Then it was time to get on the road.

When she came down the short hallway and into her living room, she saw Killian was stretched out on the couch, asleep.

She smiled sadly, watching him. He had hardly gotten any sleep in the last couple days, and the stress he had been carrying was obvious. How the band weathered this crisis would reflect on all the guys, sure, but on Killian more than anyone else: he was seen as the leader of the band, after all. Ava's performance as his replacement choice would be to his credit or detriment, even as he would no doubt face a barrage of questions in the coming days about why Celeste had left and how the band could carry on without her. Ava's status as Killian's girlfriend, she realized for the first time, would only heighten the scrutiny on both of them, many times over.

That thought made Ava want to lay down and take a nap herself and hardly encouraged her to wake Killian. Still, they had another show to play tonight, and the sooner they got to Toronto, the more time they would have to collect themselves. She went and knelt beside the head of the couch. "Killian," she said gently. She reached out and stroked his face, brushing away a strand of his long hair that had fallen over his eyes.

His eyes slowly opened, and he blinked a few times before fixing his gaze on her face. "Was it all a dream?" he asked her softly.

Her heart almost broke at the sadness in his voice. "No," she said. "But you'll get through this." Her fingers played lightly with his hair. "We'll get through this."

※

They picked up their rented car and headed north to Toronto. Since it was a Saturday, the wait at the Rainbow Bridge to go through customs was a long one, certainly longer than they would have liked. Still, there was no help for it, so they talked and listened to music to pass the time. Killian put on *Shoreline*, suggesting that the drive would be a good time for Ava to learn some new songs. "Don't worry about it for tonight's show," he said as they sat on the bridge. "We'll just use the same set list we did last night. But for the rest of the tour it'll be good if we can

CHAPTER 18

shake things up, and add some more of the new songs."

Neither of them paid much attention to the view of Niagara Falls just outside the window of their rented car. Having both been born and raised in or near Buffalo meant that they were pretty much over the sight, even if it was one of the wonders of the world.

Once they finally got through customs, they were on the road and would hopefully make it to Toronto in little more than an hour. On the way, Ava brought up the topic of her rent again, but Killian wouldn't budge.

"Ava, no," he said. "The band is doing really well financially, so it's no problem for me, and you're doing me and the guys a huge favor. Why can't I do one for you too?"

"It's just not necessary," she protested. "I can work it all out, really."

He reached out and took her hand, taking his eyes briefly from the road. "I want to. You're my girlfriend. Just let me do something nice for you. If for no other reason than that."

Ava smiled at him, then turned her gaze back out the window, deciding not to argue about it anymore. It was a financial load off her mind, that much was true, but it still made her a little uncomfortable. It didn't seem like she and Killian had been together all that long, really, especially when you considered that for most of their relationship they had not physically been in the same city. Not to mention the fact that everything between them had gone so quickly as it was...

But was that a bad thing? They loved each other, and they knew it. Why take things slow when neither of them really had any doubts about what they felt?

Such thoughts were, Ava knew, beside the point now. They would be touring together now, and she didn't think there was any tried-and-true, *Cosmopolitan*-approved relationship advice for when you had to fill in on tour with your boyfriend's metal band. Their relationship would either hold up to this test or it wouldn't.

Ava, for one, was not worried.

They made good time the rest of the way to Toronto, dropped off the rental car, then took a taxi to the venue to meet the rest of the band. The tour bus was already there—they had left before Killian and Ava's flight to Buffalo—and were getting ready for sound check when Ava and Killian walked in.

"Okay," Killian said, when all their equipment was set up. "Let's use this as a bit of rehearsal time, too. Ava and I decided that tonight we'll stick with the same set list from last night, and she'll work on learning some more songs along the way."

The rest of the guys nodded agreement.

Killian turned to Ava. "Anything from last night that you thought didn't go so well? Any songs you want to work on?"

Ava thought for a minute. "I can do 'Sunstorm' better, I think," she said. "And I think 'Clock Tower' may have been a little out of my comfort zone, as it turned out."

Killian nodded. "Good. We'll do those two, then, and maybe a couple others. I think everything else sounded fine."

Ava went to warm up quickly, then she took the stage and the band started 'Sunstorm'. They rehearsed for a little over half an hour, then agreed it was time to head back to the bus and get some rest before the show. Killian showed Ava to her bunk, the one that had been Celeste's. It was completely bare, with nothing—no personal possessions, not so much as a bobby pin—left behind. That Celeste had managed to so completely clean out her space made Ava wonder how hasty her predecessor's departure had been, really. Had she been planning it for some time? And why had Celeste left, really? Killian had promised her an explanation, but so far he—and, to be fair, the rest of the band members as well—hadn't been exactly forthcoming with that information.

Ava lay down on the bunk, her suitcase on the floor beside her—she'd unpack everything later. Really, she thought, as she began to drift off to sleep almost instantly, did it really matter why Celeste had left, in the long run? It wouldn't change anything. She, Ava, was here now, and that was how things would be for

CHAPTER 18

the foreseeable future. All that knowing would do, really, was satisfy her curiosity.

Ava woke up a couple hours later and headed into the venue dressing room with her clothes and supplies to get ready for the show. She did her makeup—dark eyeliner and shadow, with some silvery sparkles around her eyes that she thought would pop well from stage—and decided to just let her curly hair go wild. She put on the outfit she'd been mulling over on the car ride, and it looked perfect: a shredded-looking, just-above-knee-length black skirt with a layer of fishnet poking out under the hem, and a black and red corset that she'd once bought at Charlotte Russe at the mall for $6, thinking it might be a good Halloween costume piece one day. She topped it off with a pair of boots with lots of silver studs and a pair of black and gray arm warmers with zippers running along them.

"Wow," Killian said, coming into the dressing room behind her. She could hear the opening band getting started out on the stage. He leaned against the doorframe and studied her. "How come you've never worn that corset for me before?"

Ava laughed. "I forgot I had it, honestly. I just found it in the back of my closet today when I was looking for stuff to bring."

"Hmmm." Killian stepped closer, wrapped his hands around her waist, and kissed her. "I won't be able to forget you have that, now," he whispered in her ear. "How am I supposed to focus on stage tonight?"

She laughed and pushed him away. "You'll just have to find a way," she said. "The show must go on, after all."

His lips curled into just a hint of a smile. "You're right."

Once ready, Ava warmed up again and drank some water to make sure her voice was in good shape. She waited in the green room with the rest of the guys, and they joked and bantered while waiting for the opening band to finish and their gear to be cleared away. Ava couldn't help but marvel at the difference between the atmosphere that night and the night before. Tonight everyone was relaxed, ready, excited to get out there and play. There was none of the anxiety, the apprehension that had plagued them. They had gotten through one show without Celeste, and Ava had delivered. If they could do it once, they all knew, they could do it again, and surely it would just keep getting better.

Finally, it was almost time, and they crowded into the wings, listening to the noise of the audience in the darkened venue, chanting the band's name.

"Alright," Killian said. "Let's do this."

The crowd roared as he and the guys headed out onto the stage, as the lights went up and the music of "Who I Am" blared to life. Ava waited for her cue, a few measures before she would start singing, and stepped out onto the stage, nearly jogging to her mic stand at center stage. At the sight of her, the crowd cheered anew, and the sound was like a drug injected straight into her veins.

As she opened her mouth and began to sing, she knew that she wanted to do this for the rest of her life.

>We're sure that by now the rumors have spread and the news is more or less out. Still, for those of you who haven't been at our last couple shows, we want you to hear the news from us. Celeste Perinot has left Handel's Messiah due to creative and personal differences with the rest of the band members. While we respect her decision and wish her well, her departure in the middle of a massive tour promoting Shoreline has put us in a very difficult position.
>
>However, the show(s) will go on! We were lucky enough to quickly find a replacement singer: the lovely, talented, and kickass Ava Tomei, a friend of the band and an extremely gifted musician. Ava hails from our native Buffalo and has performed quite a bit locally. Following Celeste's departure, we sent Ava an

CHAPTER 18

SOS and she came to our aid. Those of you who were lucky enough to be at our New York or Toronto shows in the last couple days have already had the privilege of hearing her and seeing her rock in person.

Ava has very graciously agreed to fill in for the rest of our North American tour, so you can look forward to seeing her on the road in the next few weeks. We hope all our fans will give her a big welcome!

As soon as we are able, we will make some decisions as a band about a permanent lead vocalist. Rest assured that Handel's Messiah will continue on and be stronger than ever in the future. Thanks for all your support, and we look forward to seeing you all on the road!

The announcement, drafted by the band and approved by Billy, as well as someone at the record label, was posted on their website and all their social media accounts in the wee hours of the morning following the Toronto show. It was the first chance they had really had to make an official announcement, given the upheaval immediately following Celeste's departure.

Ava, quite frankly, didn't think too much about the fans' reaction: she knew they would be disappointed, especially the most die-hard fans. But she had other things on her mind, like adjusting to life on the road and, when Monday morning rolled around (after their incredible show in Montreal Sunday night), calling to quit her job.

The conversation with her boss, whom she called from the tour bus right at 9 a.m., didn't go particularly well, but Ava had expected as much. She felt bad, because she had liked Rachel well enough—who told her stiffly that quitting this way, by the phone and with no notice, was "unprofessional" and even "immature". Ava hung up the phone immensely relieved that that conversation was over, even if she had burned that bridge behind her. If she ever needed a reference in the future, she knew who *not* to call.

Ava was not entirely prepared for what started happening next.

It started one morning on the bus, when they were en route to Chicago. Ava woke up to find Rafael and Ben huddled over someone's laptop, talking in low voices.

"Hey, guys," she said, flopping into a seat near them. "What's up?"

Rafael whipped the lid of the laptop shut. "Nothing."

Ava laughed. "What are you looking at, porn? Don't worry, I won't tell your mothers."

Neither of them laughed or responded; instead, they only exchanged a look.

"Seriously, guys?" she said. "That was a joke. I'm not offended, or whatever—"

"We weren't looking at porn," Ben said.

"Yeah," Rafael said. "What dudes look at porn together? That's just weird."

"Oookay," Ava said. "Like I said, I was just joking. But come on. What's the big secret?"

They exchanged a guilty look again, which only made Ava more curious—and a bit apprehensive.

"What is it?" she asked again in a very different tone.

Rafael sighed. "Ava, look—"

"Dude!" Ben said. "What are you trying to do?"

"She's gonna see it eventually, anyway," Rafael said. "Maybe hearing it from us will be better."

Ava's first thought was, *Killian is cheating on me.* It was something she had wondered about, of course, worried about, before she had come to join the band. Killian was attractive and ridiculously talented and played in a band. Surely he had women throwing themselves at him when he toured. She would never have thought that he would dare with her there, though...

So, in a way, when Rafael opened the laptop and Ava saw the web browser was open to YouTube—to a bootleg video of

CHAPTER 18

"Believer" from their Montreal show, in fact—she was relieved. "What am I looking at?" she asked. "What's the big deal?"

Yet before either of the guys could say anything, Ava's eyes zeroed in on the comments.

They weren't all bad—some were along the lines of *"They sound great!"* and *"Idk who this chick is but she rocks"* and even one *"This girl is way better than Celeste*!!!!!!" Yet, for some reason, Ava was drawn not to those but to many of the other comments.

"Where the fuck did they find this train wreck??"

"Who is this bitch??"

"This is bullshit. BRING BACK CELESTE."

"This Ava chick SUCKS. Handel's Messiah sucks without Celeste."

"She sounds like a dying goat."

"How'd this bitch get into one of the best metal bands around? She must be sleeping with someone in the band."

That last comment had a reply. *"She's prbly sleeping with all of them. WHORE."*

Ava felt a tear spill onto her cheek; she hadn't even realized she was crying. She moved to wipe it away, quickly, but the guys had already seen.

"What the fuck, Raf," Ben said, punching him on the arm. "I told you not to—"

"Shut up, Ben," Rafael said. "Ava, hon, don't cry. Seriously, this is bullshit. These people on the internet—they have no lives. There's shit like that posted on all of our videos—they call Celeste a slut too, and say we're all talentless scumbags. You can't read this shit."

"But you were reading it," Ava said in a watery voice.

They exchanged a guilty look.

"Ava, seriously, don't let it get you down," Rafael said. "You're never gonna please everyone, you know? You gotta make peace with that in this business."

"Yeah," Ben added. "A bunch of fans hate the new album. Think we sounded better on the first one. That's just how it goes."

Ava shook her head but didn't speak. She knew what they were saying, but this was different. This felt so personal. They were attacking her, specifically, and for things that had nothing to do with her musical talent, in some cases.

And what hurt the most, perhaps, what prevented her from really being able to just shrug it off, was that she wasn't entirely sure they were wrong. After all, she *was* sleeping with someone in the band. She knew perfectly well that if she wasn't Killian's girlfriend, she wouldn't be where she was. Wasn't that why he had called her, after all? First and foremost? She knew he legitimately thought she was talented, but wasn't even his judgment clouded where she was concerned?

"What's going on? Ava, are you okay?"

Ava looked up to see Killian looking at her concernedly. She quickly reached out and slapped the laptop closed, just as Rafael had done when she approached. "Nothing. It's nothing."

"Why are you crying? Hey, come here..."

He reached out to try to take her arm and draw her away from the other two guys, but she pulled away. "It's nothing. I'm fine." She got up and went back to her bunk under the pretense of digging around in her suitcase for something—a pretense that wouldn't last very long, since her suitcase wasn't that big.

Part of her wanted to tell Killian everything, to let him see how upset she was and let him comfort her. But pride held her back. She wanted him to know she could handle this. She knew that Ben and Raf were right, and that this sort of thing went along with the so-called rock star lifestyle, with being in the public eye in any way. If she wanted to make a case for being Handel's Messiah's permanent lead vocalist, she needed to show that she could play the part in every way. That she could handle the pressure.

For the first time, though, she considered whether that was really what she wanted. Did she want to put herself out there for people's scrutiny for the rest of her life? Did she want to constantly be on the receiving end of criticism, justified or not? It

CHAPTER 18

was something that she had somehow never managed to consider in all her years of working and yearning for a performing career, for acclaim, even fame. No one thought about this part, it seemed, until it happened. But she'd made the choice a long time ago to be a performer, and she couldn't go back now, not when she loved doing it so much.

Yet it was a choice, she realized now, that she had made without all the information. And going through life as a target of criticism and even hate and pretending it didn't bother you seemed exhausting. *Maybe that's life,* Ava thought, vaguely aware that by now the amount of time she had spent rummaging was ridiculous, *but life sucks.*

A shadow fell across her open suitcase. "Ava," Killian said quietly.

She looked up quickly. "What?"

"Look, the guys—"

"I don't want to talk about it," she said, looking back down so that her hair swung across her face, hiding her tears from him. "It's fine. It's not a big deal."

He crouched down next to her. "It is a big deal, and you're allowed to be upset. It's—"

"I know," she interrupted, still not looking at him. "Raf and Ben already told me. It's something that happens. I just have to ignore it."

Killian studied her for a moment, as though decided whether or not to press the issue. "Alright," he said. He leaned over to kiss her quickly, and then spoke into her ear, his voice low. "You know what those idiots said is bullshit, right? You're not here just because we're dating. You're here because you deserve to be."

Ava nodded quickly. "Yeah. I guess."

She could feel his eyes on her, hot and hard. "You guess? You mean you don't believe that?"

"I do."

He brushed her hair away from her face so her could see her red-rimmed eyes, her tearstained cheeks. "Ava," he said. "Listen to me. I—and the rest of the guys—can't carry on being the only ones telling you how awesome and how amazing you are. You're going to have to start telling it to yourself, too."

With that, he stood up and walked away, leaving her alone.

Ava spent the rest of the bus ride to the venue curled up on her bunk, thinking and trying not to think.

The next few days were dark ones. The show that same night, in Chicago, was by far Ava's worse yet. Every note and word she sang, every move she made on stage, terrified her. She imagined nameless, faceless detractors in the crowd, ready to criticize everything, and it was all she could do to keep herself on stage. She tripped once, mid-song, and even her voice felt like it was betraying her: it was heavy, clumsy, and she could not make it move or fly in the ways she wanted, needed it to. It was as though she had to drag it out from down in the deepest depths of herself. If it retreated any farther within her, she knew, she would never be able to reach it. She missed a few high notes—simply knew she could not reach them, and let her voice die out on the way. She thought that she heard booing from the crowd on more than one occasion, but that may well have been only in her imagination. Or it may well not have: she did deserve it, after all.

At Killian's suggestion, she set her personal Facebook page to private: it had been public before, in case anyone had wanted to look her up for performing engagements. By the time she did so, though, there was already a plethora of nasty messages on her page. They were all in the same vein as the YouTube comments she had seen: words like "slut", "whore", "bitch", and "cunt" abounded; they attacked her voice, her clothes, her face, her hair, her body. And message after message about how she had to be fucking every guy in the band and at their label to have become Celeste's replacement. She painstakingly read each one before deleting it, then changed her privacy settings

CHAPTER 18

so that only her friends could view her page. It got better after that—any comments posted to the band's official Facebook page were moderated, so she had a layer of protection, however thin, against the onslaught. But comments on posts the band made, or on videos posted on YouTube, could be made freely.

The guys in the band would usually go to the stage door of the venue after each show to say hi to the fans who had hung around to see them, take some pictures, sign some autographs. Killian had asked her if she wanted to join them after the Minneapolis show, and she'd begged off. He hadn't pressed her and neither had any of the other guys. A few days before, she might have been a little nervous but excited at the idea of meeting fans, of being someone that they wanted to meet. But after seeing all the filth spewed at her online, she couldn't bring herself to do it. It was one thing to read those things on a computer screen, but what would she do if someone said any of it to her face? Would anyone dare, when they didn't have the anonymity of that computer screen? Maybe not, but she had no desire to find out. She couldn't, not if she was going to get through this tour.

One day, Ben happened by her bunk while she was reading through the comments on a video the band had posted on their Facebook page. "Ava, you've got to stop that," he said, causing her to quickly shut her phone off.

"What?" she asked in an attempt at innocence.

He sat next to her on the bunk. "Don't do that to yourself. Take it from me: you can't let that shit get into your head. It's just going to fuck you up and take away your passion for doing what you love."

"Easy for you to say," she snapped, suddenly no longer able to hold it together. "No one's accusing you of fucking every guy in the music industry or calling you a whore or a cunt or..." She trailed off, hating the sound of the words coming out of her mouth.

Ben was quiet for a moment, and when he finally spoke again she could hear the anger in his voice. "No," he said tightly. "But I'm a Black man in a metal band. It's a pretty white genre, in case you haven't noticed. Both the musicians and the fans, for the most part. So I'm sure you can imagine a few of the choice words that have been used to describe me over the years."

Ava fell silent, intensely regretting her words of just seconds ago. She'd been too consumed in her own drama, her own feelings of victimization, to consider that he might have been through worse. "That's horrible," she said at last. "I'm so sorry, Ben. So sorry you've had to deal with that. I should have realized…"

He shook his head. "Don't be sorry," he said. "Just be better. And know that this shit happens. It's not okay and it blows, but you gotta just keep going. Like I said, don't let these stupid fucking trolls take away your love for what you do. Let your music do the talking." With that, he got up and walked away. Ava watched him go, and then she shoved her phone in her suitcase and left it there.

chapter 19

Messiah Complex
2016

A week after recording wrapped, Killian, Ava, and Joel flew out to Los Angeles for the recording of the strings and choirs for the album. Killian had sent scores on ahead—adding the one Ava created for her song after the fact—and everything and everyone was ready when they got there. Ava had come along for this portion for all of the Handel's Messiah albums, mostly to be able to spend some one-on-one time with Killian. Yet this time was different—this time, she'd be hearing the orchestra record something she'd written.

Joel, having collaborated with Killian on a few songs on the last couple albums, was coming to help oversee things as well. Rafael and Ben had opted out, deciding to spend some time at home with their family and friends before promo and touring started.

They had already nailed down a big North American tour around the time of the album's slated release and were finishing up the details of a European tour to follow. Soon after that, no doubt, would come plans for other continents—Asia, South America, Australia—and bookings for festivals in the summer. Each album cycle went much the same, logistically speaking, but Ava loved it every time. It never got old for her.

Hearing the orchestra record her song, play the parts she had written, was, as Ava had anticipated, magical. It gave her song a whole new life that she had only as yet imagined and never been able to hear aloud. Again she felt a renewed appreciation for Killian. Could she entirely blame him if he was distant at times? It was only natural, wasn't it, that he would live in his head more often than not, trying to capture and recreate all those experiences all over again?

Then, before she knew it, they went back to Buffalo, and Killian and Rich went back to the studio to mix and master the album, a process about which Ava still didn't know very much, despite having recorded multiple albums. In the meantime, the North American tour was announced, tickets went on sale, and hype was high for the new Handel's Messiah album.

And, as Killian helped with the mixing, Ava could finally

CHAPTER 19

spend time with him outside of the band. He only spent a few hours each day in the studio, and then the two of them would do something, go somewhere, and not talk about Handel's Messiah. It felt like when they had first started dating, those first few weeks before he'd left to go to Los Angeles to record *Shoreline*, just months before Ava had joined the band in New York six years ago. They tried new restaurants, they went to the movies, and they went shopping together. They also went away for a weekend, driving north and checking out wineries just across the border in Canada. And Ava spent almost every night at Killian's house. She had forgotten how much she loved being with him, just being: that they could both be reading a book in the same room, on opposite ends of the couch, and it could be the most fun she'd had in a while. At least, until the next day they spent together.

One night they went dancing at a little club in Buffalo, something they both loved to do but rarely had time for. It was dark enough that no one recognized them, and they didn't have much to drink, preferring to spend most of their time on the dance floor. Ava remembered the first time they had gone dancing together, in a club in Barcelona—one of their favorite cities—when they'd had a day off while on tour. It had just been the two of them—none of the rest of the guys in the band had wanted to come—and they'd hardly spoken, just danced and reveled in each other's closeness.

This night was much like that. In that smoky darkness, Ava dancing with Killian pressed close behind her, both of them moving to and being consumed by music that neither of them had performed or written, it felt like another kind of closeness: physical, but not sex; emotional, but without words. For the first time in a long time, it felt as though they were in sync again. As though they both finally had the rhythm right.

Maybe they could write music together. And maybe, she realized, there was a future for them after all, outside of the band, and they could put each other first. Maybe they were growing up.

After they got back from dancing, they were laying in Killian's bed together, breathing hard after making love. After a moment, Killian rolled onto his side to face her, propping himself up on one arm.

"Do you think we can do it?" he asked. "Put it all behind us."

She looked away from him. "I thought that's what we've been doing."

"Is it really?" He didn't speak again until she looked up at him. "Because if we are, then that's great. I just want to make sure that's really what's happening and that we're not just skating over all the shit that's frozen under the surface. I want to make sure we're not just biding our time until our next fight."

Ava thought about this, really thought. The past couple weeks had been wonderful, and most of the time she'd forgotten about all the things she'd been so angry about: the things he had done and, more importantly, hadn't done. Did that mean those things no longer mattered? Maybe not. Maybe they could matter, but she could decide that they didn't matter enough. Not more than how much she loved Killian; not more than what they had.

But maybe it was time to put it all out there, make sure they were really and truly playing the same song at last.

"I want to make sure, too," she said. She turned onto her side, facing him. "My song."

She thought he flinched slightly, but she might have imagined it. "Yes."

"I want you to know that it's truly a dream come true for a song I wrote—and that song in particular—to be going on a Handel's Messiah album. It's what I've wanted for a long time."

"You should have said—"

"I did," she interrupted. "Or I thought I did. Maybe I wasn't as clear as I should have been, but you never seemed to take any of my songs seriously, until that one. And I didn't write it to hurt you, Killian. I didn't. It was just what I was feeling at the time."

He remained silent.

"I want to do more, in the future," she continued. "I want

CHAPTER 19

to write songs. With you…and maybe alone. I'm not saying they all have to go on an album—I don't expect that. But I want my voice, my creativity, to be heard. I don't…" She bit her lip. "I don't want to be just your muse anymore, Killian. That isn't…it isn't enough for me."

He ran a hand over her hip, stroking her bare skin lightly. "I never want you to be something you don't want to be," he said softly. "I want everything we have to be enough for you. To be more than enough."

She smiled, feeling tears sting her eyes. "I…I'm really happy to hear you say that. Then…yes. I think we can put it all behind us."

"Me too," he said. "On one condition."

She went still. "What?" she asked warily.

"You have to still let me write a song about how much I love you from time to time, okay? I can't just quit."

She laughed. "Fine, I'll still allow it," she said.

He kissed her and drew her on top of him. "Good."

chapter 20

Shoreline
2010

CHAPTER 20

For the first couple of weeks that Ava was on tour, Killian—sometimes with Joel or Rafael, and sometimes alone—handled all their press requests: radio interviews; interviews for magazines, newspapers, and webzines; interviews for television and podcasts. In the past, it had always been Killian and Celeste as the faces of the band. Ava read and watched what interviews she could, and the questions were pretty standard: a few about Celeste and her departure, which Killian answered with the standard "creative and personal differences" and more or less refusing to elaborate any further; then questions about Ava and how the band knew her. These Killian answered with the truth, saying that he had seen her perform at a concert in Buffalo and gotten to know her, and had later done a performance with her. He never mentioned their relationship, and thankfully no one asked. Ava knew they couldn't hide it forever, but she was dreading the moment when it came out into the open and the further speculation and nasty comments it would provoke amongst the band's fandom. *Although,* she sometimes thought, *isn't the truth better than what they're thinking and saying now?*

Usually left for the end of the interviews, almost as an afterthought, were questions about the new album and songs. The recent drama surrounding Handel's Messiah seemed to dwarf their music for the time being, even though *Shoreline* had already outsold *The Art of Escape* and continued to sell steadily. But no doubt the band had the recent drama to thank for at least some of those sales.

When they got to Los Angeles, an interview had been lined up with Amplified TV, a channel dedicated to rock and metal music, and Billy told them that the network, in no uncertain terms, wanted the whole band—Ava included.

Killian tried to prep her as best he could. "Let me do the talking where possible," he said. "I'm sure they'll ask you to talk about how you ended up filling in, and how you like touring and performing, and what your plans are for the future. We haven't made any permanent plans for a new lead singer yet, and everything else you can answer."

Ava knew he was trying to be helpful, to prepare her and put her more at ease, but his high-handedness annoyed her. "I got it, thanks," she said. "And what do I say if they ask if we're dating? Or if I'm dating someone in the band?"

Killian scowled. "I don't think they'll ask you that. That would be ridiculous."

"They might."

"No one's asked me that yet."

"But I bet you they'll ask me."

Killian rolled his eyes, as if he didn't have time for such foolishness. "Well, you can't lie about it," he said, and that ended their conversation on the topic.

When they got to the small studio where the interview was taking place, they were shown in and offered bottles of water, which Ava gratefully accepted. Her mouth and throat were so dry she was beginning to think that she wouldn't be able to speak at all should she be asked any questions. Ben was no help; he had been grumbling for two days about how much he was dreading this. He was, Ava had been surprised to learn, quite shy, more so than one would expect of a metal drummer. He had avoided interviews like the plague for so long that no one ever even asked him to do them anymore, except in situations like this, where the whole band was needed.

"But you get up on stage every night and play in front of hundreds, sometimes thousands, of people," she pointed out.

He had shrugged. "That's different. I'm playing music. That makes me forget all the rest." He smiled. "Plus everyone can barely see me behind my kit."

Once they'd had some water and been welcomed by the producers and interviewer, they were led to the interview room, where the whole band was directed to sit on one long couch. Killian sat at the end closest to the interviewer, with Ava next to him. Rafael was on her other side, then Joel, then Ben at the

CHAPTER 20

end, as though he was hoping no one would notice him.

Once they were settled, the red light on the camera facing them went on, and the cameraman gave the thumbs up.

"Welcome," the interviewer began in his British accent. He had introduced himself as Cook, and whether that was his first name, last name, or some sort of stage name, Ava wasn't sure. "I'm with symphonic metal outfit Handel's Messiah, who are here in Los Angeles on their North American tour supporting their sophomore album, *Shoreline*. Of course, as all you metalheads out there will know, the band's been in the news for other reasons recently, what with the sudden departure of vocalist Celeste Perinot early on in this very tour. As a result, the band's got a new face here with them—replacement vocalist Ava Tomei. We here at Amplified are thrilled to be bringing you Ava's first interview since joining the band." He turned from the camera to the band. "First, let me welcome you all and thank you for being here. Now, let me ask the question that's on everyone's mind these days: what prompted Celeste's rather unceremonious exit?" His grin widened. "And none of that 'creative and personal differences', if you please." He laughed. "What's the *real* reason?"

Ava could feel Killian tense next to her, and she got the sense that this was going to be a very long interview indeed. "There really is nothing more scandalous to it than that," Killian answered smoothly. "Some tension had grown between Celeste and the rest of the band during the recording of *Shoreline*, and it spilled over into the tour. So, she ultimately decided to leave, and while, as we said in our statement, this certainly put us in a very difficult spot, we respected her decision and agreed that it was best for the band, in light of everything. And we do wish her the best."

The rest of the guys nodded, so Ava did too, thinking it would look odd if she didn't. In reality she didn't really care what happened to Celeste.

"But this tension you mentioned," Cook said, "what was the source of it? There had to be something in particular that Celeste was unhappy about."

"You'd have to ask her about that," Killian said.

"But surely she brought up whatever it was? Surely you all, as a band, talked about it and tried to work it out?"

Killian allowed himself a small sigh. "I know that she wasn't thrilled with some of the music and lyrics I'd written for her for *Shoreline*."

Ava was surprised but tried her best not to show it. This was the first she was hearing of that.

"Ahh, yes. You are the principal songwriter for the band, correct?"

"Yes."

"And what was it in particular that Celeste objected to, do you recall?"

On her other side, Ava felt Rafael shift uncomfortably.

"Again, you'd have to ask her for the full details," Killian said. "I'm not in the habit of airing the band's dirty laundry."

Killian's tone said in no uncertain terms that the subject was closed, and Ava felt a tiny bit of relief. Surely now they would move on—though who knew if what came next would be any better.

Thankfully, Cook took the hint. "Fair enough, then. Now, Ava," he said, shifting his attention. "I've some questions for you, if you don't mind."

"Sure," Ava said, smiling widely.

"Now, you were a vocal performance major at, let me see—" he consulted some notes on his cue cards. "Canisius College in Buffalo, New York, is that correct?" He pronounced it "Ca-NEE-see-us", instead of "Ca-NEESH-us", but Ava let it slide.

"Yes."

"Classical voice?"

"Yes."

"And you performed quite extensively in the local area, which is how you and Killian met, yes?"

"I don't know about extensively," Ava said. "Certainly not as extensively as I would have liked. But, yes, Killian's sister was my roommate in college, and she brought Killian to a concert I

CHAPTER 20

was doing at a church one night. She introduced us afterwards, and we got to talking."

"And did you know who he was?"

"Yes," she said, beginning to relax slightly at the benign nature of the questions. "I did. I was—and still am, really—a big Handel's Messiah fan."

"Interesting, that you come from such a classical background, and yet your singing style, from what clips I've heard from your live shows online, is not strictly classical, like Celeste's was."

"No," Ava agreed. "I have just a bit of a musical theatre background too, and in my private rehearsal time I would try to develop my belting voice as well. I feel like it gives me much more range and versatility as a singer, and so I'm trying to use that to its fullest advantage with the band."

"Actually," Rafael interjected from beside her, "I came from a classical background as well, with the upright bass. So did Killian." Killian nodded in acknowledgement. "It's not as uncommon amongst metal musicians as you might think."

"Indeed," Cook said. "Well, it certainly seems to have worked out well for all of you, and Ava, your style works very well with the band's music from what I've heard, I must say."

She smiled genuinely. "Thank you."

"So when Celeste made her exit, you were the first person the band called, yes?"

"Killian called me," Ava clarified, then wondered why she had done so.

"I see. And why do you think you were his—the band's—first choice?"

"I don't know that I was, necessarily," she said, with a self-deprecating laugh. *Jesus, I'm better at this putting on an act business than I ever would have thought,* she mused. "But Killian knew my voice, and I was close, in Buffalo. They needed me in New York for the show that night."

"Ava is too modest," Killian said. "It was handy that she wasn't far, but I knew she'd be perfect, and being a fan of the band she already knew many of our songs. The guys agreed, once they heard her."

Ben, Joel, and Rafael nodded.

"Ahh," Cook said. "So you didn't know the rest of the band when you flew to New York to join them?"

"No," Ava said.

"Just Killian here?"

"Yes."

"That must have been quite intimidating, jumping right into things like that." Without giving her a chance to answer or comment, Cook scooted his chair somewhat closer to them, leaning in conspiratorially. "So then, Ava, if you would just answer for us the question we're all dying to know about: are you and Killian *an item?*"

Ava could feel Killian go practically rigid with tension. Her stomach dropped practically to the toes of her boots, and she could feel her face begin to flush. *I told him,* she thought petulantly, thinking of their earlier conversation. *I told him they would ask.*

Still, since she'd known it was coming, she'd had time to think about how to play it. She had taken to heart—or tried to, anyway—Killian's words a couple weeks ago: *I can't carry on being the only one telling you how awesome, how amazing you are. You're going to have to start telling it to yourself, too.* He was right, she had come to realize. If she believed she was only there because she was Killian's girlfriend, then there was no reason for anyone else to believe otherwise. But if she owned it—with the confidence she knew she should and could have—then what could anyone say?

Her lips curved into a smile. "Yeah," she said. "Yeah, actually, we are."

Cook's bleached blonde eyebrows disappeared into his hairline. "Oh, indeed? And why has the happy couple not mentioned this before?"

Ava shrugged, leaning back against the couch. "No one asked."

CHAPTER 20

"I find that hard to believe. The Internet's been buzzing with rumors, as surely you know."

Ava shrugged again. "I don't pay attention to any of that stuff. And, like you said earlier, this is my first interview. No one's asked Killian because men don't tend to get asked questions like that. Just women."

Cook had the grace to look slightly abashed as he changed the subject.

He asked her a few more questions, like how she liked touring and performing—"I love it. I have seriously loved every minute of it"—as well as how she felt, as a fan, to be asked to step in and front one of her favorite bands. "It sounds corny, but it is literally a dream come true," Ava said. "You know how many times I'd go for a run around my neighborhood, listening to Handel's Messiah and imagining I was on stage with them?"

Cook then moved on, asking the rest of the guys about the recording process for the new album, how they'd liked their tour in Europe, what everyone's favorite song to play live was—Ava's was "Dark River", Ben's was "Sunstorm", Rafael's was "Shoreline", Joel's was "Who I Am", and Killian's was "Beyond the Veil". He ended the interview by asking if the world might expect Ava to be Handel's Messiah's new lead vocalist permanently.

"We haven't made any decisions yet," Killian said. "Right now, we're just trying to have some fun."

After the interview, they headed back to the venue, as there wasn't much time left before the show started. Ava was grabbing the things she'd need to take into the dressing room when Killian appeared, looking for something near his bunk.

"Hey," she said, setting down her bag. She'd been meaning to have a word with him ever since the interview.

He straightened up. "Hey. What's up?"

"So…Celeste didn't like the songs for *Shoreline*?" she asked. "I didn't know that."

"Yeah." Killian shrugged. "That was a big part of the whole thing. I guess." He sighed and ran his fingers through his long hair. "When I told him he'd have to ask Celeste for the details, that wasn't just a line. I really don't know what caused her to go so fucking crazy."

"Well…you never really told me the story," Ava said. "Any of it. So I was just curious." She hadn't forgotten how, when she'd first shown up in New York, Joel had insinuated that Celeste's departure had been Killian's fault, both when she'd arrived and later, when he had apologized to her after rehearsing. It was about time she got some answers about the person who had started feeling a bit like the other woman, both in her relationship and in the band.

"Does it really matter?" Killian asked.

"Yeah, actually," Ava said. "It does matter. Even if I'm just curious and nothing else. I flew out to New York at the last minute. I quit my job to come on tour. I think I deserve to know why."

Killian laughed. "It's really not that big a deal, Ava. You don't have to cash in all the big favors. Besides, I thought you were here because you want to be."

"I am. I am, Killian. You know that. But since I got to New York, it's felt like there was something bigger going on here that I've been on the outside of. I'd just like for us all to be on the same page."

Killian sighed. "That's fair. I'm sorry. I have been meaning to tell you, it's just…everything's been so crazy."

"I get it. But…the songs," Ava said, trying to bring the conversation back on track. "What didn't she like?"

Killian sighed and sank down onto his bunk, which was right across from Ava's—the closest they could get to sleeping in the same bed while on the bus. "She thought the vocal parts didn't fit her voice very well," he said. "She wanted me to redo most of them, actually. She said they were too difficult for her to sing."

CHAPTER 20

"I mean, there are some tricky vocal parts in there," Ava said. "But she sounds fantastic on *Shoreline*. Better than on *The Art of Escape*."

"I know. We all know that. Even she knows that, though she'd be damned if she would admit it to any of us." He reached up and tied back his long hair. "I knew what I was doing. I knew she'd have to stretch her voice for some of the songs, that she'd have to sing in ways she hadn't on the early stuff or the first record. That's what I wanted. I don't want to be one of those bands that sounds the same all the time, that just keeps making the same record over and over again." He rolled his eyes. "But Celeste didn't want to leave her comfort zone."

"I can see that, I guess," Ava said. "And the lyrics?"

"That too," he said. "She didn't like the lyrics for some of the songs, God knows why. She never made a fuss about anything I gave her to sing before that. I told her she could rewrite some of them, however she wanted, and she couldn't be bothered. She was just throwing a diva fit for no reason."

"Hmmm," Ava said. "I never met her, obviously, but I always thought she seemed like kind of a prima donna to be honest with you."

Killian rolled his eyes. "You have no idea," he said. "When *The Art of Escape* came out, we got pretty big, obviously, and Celeste...well, you followed the band, you probably remember—people made a big deal out of her. There's not a lot of metal bands with female members, and she was in that magazine—what was that issue? 'The Sexiest Rocker Chicks' or something like that. And everyone wanted to interview her, and the fans were always all over her—guys and girls. She started acting differently, even at the end of the touring cycle for the first album. It all went to her head."

But Ava's curiosity wasn't quite satisfied. "Which ones didn't she like?"

"Hmm?"

"Which lyrics didn't she like."

"Oh." You would have to know Killian as well as Ava did to see it, but he had tensed up, closed off, ever so slightly. "I think…she didn't like 'Who I Am'; she said she thought it was boring and derivative. And she didn't like 'Dreamscape'; she thought it was stupid. She hated 'Beyond the Veil', too, damned if I remember why. Oh, and she didn't really like 'Dark River', particularly."

"Oh?" Ava said. "Why not? What was her problem with that one?"

"She just didn't like it," he said. "Didn't like the lyrics."

"The song you wrote for me."

"Yeah," he said. "Of course it's for you, Ava. 'Shoreline' is for you, too."

"Why would she not like that song in particular?"

"It wasn't just that one, obviously," Killian said, exasperated. "I told you all the other ones she didn't like."

"But I'm just wondering why—"

"Go ahead and say it, Ava," he interrupted, his voice dangerous and low. "Go ahead and ask me what you've really been wanting to ask me."

There was silence for a moment as Ava both considered and rejected the idea of pretending that she didn't know what he was talking about. "Did you and Celeste ever date?"

"Yes," he bit out. "For a while. It started when we were in college. We broke up when the band got serious, though. It had kind of run its course, and we figured it was for the best."

"You could have told me."

"It didn't come up."

"And you were worried that if I knew, I wouldn't be okay with you going on tour with her."

"That crossed my mind, yeah."

"What do you take me for?" Ava demanded. "Some nagging, shrewish, sitcom girlfriend who doesn't trust you?"

"Ava, the whole thing was so new," he said. "I wasn't sure what you'd do. And since Celeste and I hadn't been together in a

CHAPTER 20

while, I told myself it wasn't relevant. I *still* don't think it's really relevant, although, yeah, I guess you do have a right to know." He sighed, his shoulders slumping, and seemed suddenly very tired. "This is still so new, you and I, if you think about it."

"Yeah," Ava said. "I guess it is."

Ava knew she should leave it there, but God help her, she still had to prod a little bit more. "So…Celeste was jealous. That's why she didn't like 'Dark River'."

Killian sighed again, irritated. "Yes. I guess so. God knows why. We'd been friends for years since we'd broken up, obviously, and worked together in the band, and everything was fine. She dated a few people, I dated a few people—though never anyone seriously, until you. It was obvious, when I showed up in Los Angeles to rehearse and record the album, that I was serious about you. And apparently she didn't like that."

He paused, considering what he was about to say before speaking again. "And…I didn't realize it consciously at first, but…the songs. I was writing for your voice." He lifted his head to look at her, and Ava was surprised to see his eyes rimmed with red. "It took me a while to realize it. I'd written a few of the songs before I met you, but the rest—I was writing for you. And I think Celeste picked up on that, somehow." He shook his head. "It wasn't the whole reason, but I'm sure it was part of it."

Ava stared at him in wonder, shocked and thrilled and horrified in equal parts by what she was hearing, by the implications of it. "So I…I caused Celeste to leave Handel's Messiah," she whispered. "It's all because of me."

Killian's hand shot out and grabbed hers, tightly. "No. Never think that." He squeezed harder. "It's all because of Celeste. She caused this, with her ego and her misplaced jealousy. The more I think about it, the more I'm sure it would have come sooner or later, whether I had met you or not. The way fame was going to her head, our past…I think it was inevitable. But, Ava." She looked up to meet his gaze, and the look in his eyes caused her to want to run into his arms, to hold him tightly and never let go, to make love to him right there and damn anyone who might walk in on them. "You are my muse. It's right that you're here. You are supposed to be here with me."

chapter 21

Messiah Complex
2016

Killian seemed true to his word about wanting a fresh start, about being more equal artistic partners. One night, he dropped by her apartment after he finished at the studio, and she was at her piano, hard at work on a new song, as she had been often lately. Her instinct was to get up from the piano bench before he came up, to put away the notes for the song she'd been working on so he couldn't ask her about it. But she stayed where she was, kept playing. They were past all that, after all.

He came into the apartment and closed the door behind him. "What's that?" he asked over the sound of the piano.

She smiled at him. "A new song."

"Someone's on fire," he remarked, coming to sit on the piano bench next to her.

"I have been, lately," she said, stopping. "You know how it is."

He smiled at her. "I do. And I love that you do too." He hesitated. "Can I hear some more of it?"

She hesitated, as well. "Sure," she said, pushing past her knee-jerk response of "no." "I haven't finished the lyrics yet, but I've got some, and the melody is shaping up, so…" She trailed off and began to play the song from the beginning, humming a melody where she didn't have lyrics yet, and singing them where she did—just for the chorus, so far:

No need to catch me,
From up here I can fly,
This is where I was meant to be,
I can't fall from here, won't fall from this high.

She stopped there and turned to smile at him. "Like I said, a work in progress. I'm trying to capture how I feel when I'm up onstage, when I'm in the groove and the crowd is into it and nothing can knock me out of it." She shrugged. "It's getting there."

CHAPTER 21

Killian held up his arm, and she saw that he had goose bumps. "You captured it, exactly," he said softly. "Between the lyrics and that melody—it's exactly what that onstage rush feels like."

Warmth spread through her abdomen; not only joy but pride that something she had written had affected him so much. "Well, thanks," she said awkwardly. "I'm off to a good start, then, I guess."

"I'll say." He slid an arm around her waist and kissed her. "You've got time, though, since this one will have to wait for the next album," he said, a smile crinkling the corners of his eyes. "Even we can't record this one that last minute."

She grinned and kissed him again, reveling in his words that were both a promise and the fulfillment of one.

Once the mixing and mastering was done, the band convened at Killian's house to listen to the tracks, all seventeen that they had recorded, and make their final choices. They had decided that the album itself would have fourteen tracks, and the remaining three—as usually happened with any that didn't make the final cut—could be released as bonus tracks or B-sides at some point in the future. Since Killian had taken over on producing this album, he—and the rest of the band—had much more control over the album as a finished product.

They also had some artwork to go over for the album cover and booklet, which had been sent over by the artist they usually worked with. Ava gasped when she saw the image: it was an upside-down image of a long-haired, shirtless man with angel wings sprouting from his back. The color palette was cool, grays and blues and blacks. The band's name and the title of the album were on the front, of course, but subtly, in such a way so as not to distract from the striking image. The whole band agreed on it unanimously and enthusiastically, and then they moved on to the music.

They sat in Killian's spacious living room, the disc on his top-of-the-line stereo, and listened to each and every track in its final, finished form. For Ava, it was the first time hearing every song through with all the elements and production in place and, as always, she was filled with a feeling of pride in their hard work and happiness in how everything had come together; coupled with a sense of awe that these were really their songs. Despite knowing them inside and out during the recording and rehearsal processes, there was always an element of the unfamiliar, the magical, in hearing the shiny and clean recordings for the first time, with the strings added in and all the post-production touches.

Per their usual practice, they played one track at a time, then talked about that song, if they felt the need. Each band member had a pad of paper and a pen to write down their ideal track listing for the album (albeit with no regard for order—that would come later). Then, at the end, if there were any discrepancies, they would discuss it.

The songs had been burned onto the disc in no particular order, and Ava's was second, after the 7-minute, epically tinged "Map of the End of the World". She almost wasn't prepared for it, but there it was, her smooth piano playing, the guitar and bass and drums, the build up of the song and of the emotion, the urgent and soaring strings. She, of course, put her song on her list. Of the two tracks they'd listened to so far, she had two written down.

They went on through the list, this time not saying too much after each track, except to compliment each other on a certain section, a certain passage. They went through "Hostage"—"Seriously, that might be your most killer vocal yet, Ava," Rafael said when it was over—and the folk-like ballad "Memories"—"It sounds weird for a metal band, because it's just so *pretty*," Ben said—through to the last track on the disc, the epic, 14-minute long "Archangel".

By the time they reached the end, Ava knew they had

CHAPTER 21

some impossible choices to make. *Messiah Complex* was aptly named; she could already tell that, no matter what the fans thought or what the sales ended up being, this was their best album to date. It was the strongest—musically, lyrically, and technically—that the band had ever been. And though it was still a brand new creation, Ava already felt that familiar twist of anxiety at the thought that somehow, next time, they would need to top it.

"I think we can all agree that 'Archangel' is in, and that it should go at the end," Ben said.

"Definitely," Joel said. "None of us recorded that beast so it could *not* go on the album."

"Tell me about it," Killian said. "I saved that one for last because I knew my fingers would take days to recover." The song pushed them all to the edge of their musical abilities, but most notably Killian. It had a fiendishly difficult keyboard part, one that Killian had lamented and regretted writing several times.

"I take it we're not playing it live, then?" Rafael said.

"Killian is just gonna need to deal with it," Ava said, only half-teasing. "We all will. That obviously needs to be our closer for the shows." She frowned. "Although I don't know that it should go last on the album. Maybe second last, with 'Map of the End of the World' as the closer."

"That's not a bad idea," Joel said.

"Yeah. I kinda like it, actually," Rafael said.

"Okay, let's focus, shall we?" Killian said. "Track order comes later. That's the easy part. We're going to have to cut three of these songs, and we better get that out of the way." He turned to Ava. "Ladies first. Which ones didn't make the cut for you?"

Ava sighed and picked up her list. "Let me preface this by saying that this was the hardest time I've had deciding, out of all of our albums. So if anyone thinks any of these *should* be on the album, I won't argue with you." She smiled. "Not too strenuously, anyway, depending on which ones you all want to leave off." She glanced down at her list. "Okay. I have

'Deception', 'Colossus', and 'Sky Before a Storm'."

"'Colossus'?" Joel demanded. "You sound killer on that one! I think we all sound killer, actually."

Ava threw up her hands. "I can be talked out of it! What did you have?"

Joel looked at his pad. "I've got 'Deception', 'Sky Before a Storm', and 'To Hell and Back'."

"Really? I love 'To Hell and Back'," Ava said.

"I love them all," Joel said. "This is really tough. Can't we just put them all on the album?"

Killian laughed. "I wish, but I don't think so. Okay, Ben?"

Ben had the same three as Joel, as did Rafael.

Ava sighed. "I guess I'm overruled on 'To Hell and Back', then."

Rafael laughed. "Apparently there's no love for 'Sky Before a Storm' or 'Deception', though."

"The more I think about it, the more I feel like 'Deception' is not our best work," Joel said. "And what's crazy is it would have been the strongest song on *The Art of Escape*, but among this group, it's not up to snuff."

"Agreed," Killian said.

"And 'Sky Before a Storm'...I *like* it," Ava said, and the guys all nodded. "I do. But not as much as I like the rest of the songs."

"Yeah," Rafael said. "Same."

"Killian, what did you have?" Joel asked.

"Oh." He glanced down at his list. "I had 'Deception' and 'Sky Before a Storm' also. And 'Appassionata'."

There was dead silence in the room.

Ava could not believe he had said it. She could feel the rest of the guys glancing at her out of the corners of her eyes, but she didn't turn her head. She stared straight at Killian, who was studiously avoiding her gaze.

"No way," Ben said finally.

"That's one of the best songs here," Joel said.

"Yeah," Rafael said. "Sorry, man. Majority rules."

CHAPTER 21

"I know it does," Killian said. "But I just wanted to give my opinion."

The blood began pounding in Ava's temples, and she felt the heat rising in her face. *How is this happening? After I was honest with him about what I wanted and needed from him, and after he agreed? After we decided to start fresh?*

"Listen, Killian," Rafael said. "I probably shouldn't say anything because I don't really want to get involved, but I would have thought you could put your personal issues aside on this one. I thought you had—because you wanted us to record it in the first place."

"What did I just say?" Killian demanded. "Majority rules. It's going on the album. Fine."

"It's not fine," Ava said quietly, and all heads turned toward her. Her entire body was vibrating with rage, and it was all she could do not to scream, to break something, to slap him. "Why?"

"What do you mean, why?" Killian said.

"You know exactly what I mean. Why, after you pushed me to play the song for you, and then for everyone, pushed us to rehearse it and record it when I hadn't even planned that myself, why would you turn around and say you don't want it to go on the album?"

"I don't know—"

"I want to hear you say it."

"Look, after listening to everything, I thought it wasn't quite at the level of the rest of them—"

"Not quite at the level of the ones you wrote, you mean?"

"That's bullshit, Ava. Anyway, it doesn't matter. It's going on the album."

"It *does* matter," Ava said, her voice rising, finally. "It does matter that you even said such a thing."

"I don't see—"

Ava stood up from her spot on the carpet. "I promised we wouldn't do this in front of the guys ever again," she said. "Can I have a moment, Killian?"

Killian got up from the couch without saying anything and followed Ava into the kitchen—the scene of another argument not so long ago, she realized. There were a lot of places that had been scenes of arguments of theirs, lately. When she looked around their world, the spaces they inhabited, it seemed that now she remembered most of them for the fights they had had there and not any of the joyful, happy moments.

Ava walked into the kitchen, and she heard the door close behind Killian as he came in, but still she didn't turn to face him. She kept herself facing away from him, her whole body rigid, so much so that she thought a single wrong move would shatter her completely and utterly, into enough pieces that she would never be able to collect them all again, let alone put them back together in the right order. It was just such damage that she had been fearing all along, that she had been dancing around these past few months.

Finally, she turned to face him and was somewhat surprised to find him on the offensive. "I don't know what you want from me, Ava."

"I told you exactly what I want a couple weeks ago. You acted like you were on board. And I want just what I said in there," she said. "I want to hear you say it. I want to hear your voice saying the words to explain to me why, after you moved heaven and earth to get it done, after I *told* you how much this means to me, you don't want my song on the album. I know it's going on anyway," she said, holding up a hand to forestall the argument he had just opened his mouth to repeat. "Believe me, I know. Because you will not take that from me, not now. I just want to know why you thought you would try anyway. And so everything you said about wanting a new start, was that all bullshit, too? Your usual manipulative bullshit?"

"No," he said. "Damn it, no, Ava, it wasn't. I meant that."

"I don't know if I believe you. I feel like I never should have believed you."

"I shouldn't have said anything. It was *because* we made a

CHAPTER 21

new start that I thought, maybe, it shouldn't go on the album. That those feelings you had were part of what we should be leaving in the past."

"Are you fucking kidding me?" she demanded. "My God, I *told* you how important this was to me! The fact that you have been trying to control me creatively has been the biggest part of the problem all along! And this is your fucking solution?"

"I just thought maybe we could leave this one song behind, is all," he said. "You've been writing so many new ones! Like that one you played for me the other night. I love what you have of that song! You can write however many you want for the next album, I swear! You'll have your moment. Why does it have to be this song?"

"Because this song is the one that's most important to me," she shot back. "Because finally, finally, I said everything I needed to say. Because it's the one that finally got you to *hear me.*"

She thought he would explode in response to that, but he didn't. He looked away from her, down at the floor, for a long time. Ava felt her rage build with every second that he didn't speak. Finally, he looked up, and she saw that his eyes were hollow and empty, somehow. "What do you want me to say, Ava? I made a mistake. I did. I thought I could handle it. Thought I could handle having that song on the album because it deserves to be. I mean that, and I always did. The guys are right. It's one of the best songs out of the seventeen we recorded. I'm not denying that, and I never will. But can you blame me for wanting to hold on to the songwriting, the one thing that I thought you might still need me for?"

"What the fuck is that supposed to mean?"

"You've been pulling away from me for the last, what, over a year now? Almost two?" He shrugged. "Can you blame me for worrying that you had gotten what you needed from me and didn't want me anymore?"

"You can't really think—"

"I don't know that I do. But it's crossed my mind, more than once."

Ava shook hear head, unable to believe what she was hearing. "So you thought you'd deny me the chance to let the world hear my song," she said. "The chance for it to matter to anyone else except me. All to keep some kind of...hold over me?"

He shrugged. "I'm not proud of myself," he said. "Of any of it."

I'll be damned, Ava thought as he spoke, in wonder that bordered on admiration. *The bastard actually has the balls to look me in the eye.*

"If that makes you feel any better," he went on, "I'm not proud of myself at all. I thought I was a bigger man than this. But I guess I'm not. I guess I don't want our dirty laundry aired for all our fans, all the world, to hear."

"Are you kidding me?" Ava cried, her voice rising to the level of a screech. She heard how she sounded, but could do nothing about it. "What about 'Hostage', for Christ's sake? What about 'The Fine Line'? I admit I didn't see it at first—with either of them—but how are those songs not you airing our dirty laundry for everyone to hear?"

"Neither of them says anything that isn't true. You know that better than anyone."

"And my song is full of slanderous lies? Bullshit, Killian. Truth is not what this is about. This is about your ego and nothing else."

"You're right, it is," he said, finally raising his voice. "It's about my ego. There, are you happy now? Does it get you off that I finally said it? Does it fix everything that's broken here?"

"Fuck you, Killian," she said, and she walked past him toward the door.

"I used to have you for that," he said.

She turned back to face him, her hand on the door. "You're right, you used to. Not anymore. Go find some new girl to fuck who will let you keep thinking you're some...some genius master of the universe."

With that, she stalked out of the kitchen and out of Killian's

CHAPTER 21

house, past the rest of the band, open-mouthed, in the living room.

But not, she swore to herself, out of the band. And she knew it was happening, knew it *had* happened, the thing that Marissa Martin and Celeste Perinot had both warned her about. She had had to choose between her band and her relationship, and she had chosen her band. She would be sticking around if it was the last thing she did, and if Killian couldn't deal with it, then he could get out. They could be fine without him.

She could be fine without him.

chapter 22

Shoreline
2010

CHAPTER 22

The North American tour rolled on, heading further south from Los Angeles and then snaking its way back east, hitting cities like Phoenix and Albuquerque before venturing into Mexico for a few shows. Then they headed through Texas and across the Midwest. While they were touring, the band's management booked them a South American tour, and soon they were also booked for some of the big European festivals: Wacken Open Air and Rock am Ring in Germany, the Download Festival in the UK, Pinkpop in the Netherlands, and the Female Metal Voices Festival in Belgium. It was assumed that Ava would be coming, though Killian did say, as an afterthought one night as the band was discussing the new dates, "Wait, you're going to keep touring with us, right?" to which Ava replied, "Just try to get rid of me." They had all laughed, already looking forward to the next adventure.

Ava was certainly in no hurry to get back to Buffalo, what with no job and only an empty apartment waiting for her. She was afraid of the day when the touring would be done, as though it was all a magical spell cast by some sort of heavy metal fairy godmother, and when she stepped off of the tour bus for good it would all be over as if it had never been. There was still no mention of her joining the band permanently, which she started to worry over sometimes, privately. Was that, too, a foregone conclusion? Or did they think she was fine enough for the tour, but wanted someone better, different, for the long haul?

She had never wanted something so badly in her life, yet she tried to put it from her mind as much as possible and just enjoy the tour. She would be visiting places and countries she had never been to and had never even dreamed of going to. Not to mention that Wacken Open Air and the Female Metal Voices Festival had long been on her bucket list. It blew her mind that the first time she would be going to either one she would be appearing as a performer.

And singing on stage was the biggest rush, an addiction that Ava knew she would never be able to kick. As much as she had loved recitals and church concerts and the opera stage, and she knew she wouldn't turn down a chance to perform in such a way again should it be offered to her, singing with the band was such a different animal: untamed and free and wild, built on all the aggression and catharsis that clean and controlled classical music so often lacked. As much as she had tried to imagine what singing with a band would be like—since it had always been something she'd wanted to do—it was all just so much more than she had thought: bigger and louder and more exciting. It was an adrenaline thrill ride that she never wanted to get off. And she hoped that she wouldn't have to.

The North American tour ended up back home in Buffalo for what promised to be a triumphant homecoming. The Town Ballroom was completely sold out, and Ava was excited that her friends and family would be able to see her perform. Then the band would have a couple weeks at home to recuperate before flying to Rio de Janeiro to kick off the South American tour.

The set list looked a bit different than it had for Ava's first few shows. She had managed to learn "Cathedral", and so they had been closing out shows with that, keeping "Shoreline" as the encore. They'd also added "Crystalline"—another song that required Ava to use her best classical high range—"The Neverending War", and "I Want You Gone" from *Shoreline*, which Ava had also learned along the way, thus enabling them to change up the set list a bit here and there every night.

They had a longer show planned for their homecoming, so all the songs they'd been performing were on the set list. Ava tried not to talk to any of the guys that day and drank tea with honey like it was her job, trying to make sure her voice was in the best possible shape.

She hadn't realized—though, of course, she should have—the wear on her voice that would occur from singing in such a manner just about every night. There had definitely been shows along the way where she had woken up knowing her voice wasn't at its best, but she'd had to get back out there anyway and make

CHAPTER 22

the best of it. Tea with honey became her best friend, she avoided dairy like the plague, and began to give herself more time to warm up before shows. She wished she knew more singers in the business so she could ask for some tips, but so far her routine seemed to be working well enough. As much as she was going to miss performing for the two weeks they would be off, she knew her voice needed a break. And she had learned, for the next time, how better to save her voice and pace herself.

There was no opening band for this show—it was all them, hence the longer set list. The venue filled up almost as soon as the doors opened, and Ava could hear them, even backstage, even over the music that was playing over the venue speakers. Soon, the crowd began chanting the band's name.

Ava felt a thrill at the sound, ringing through what she thought of as her home venue, where she'd seen so many of her favorite bands over the years. The interior was nothing special: a floor in front of the stage with standing room risers behind it, everything painted in shades of black and red, with a bit of a dive-bar feel. But she loved it all the same. In a way, she was almost as nervous as she had been for her first show with the band in New York: this was her city, her crowd, and she knew there were a lot of people she knew in the audience. It made for nerves of a different kind, yet she was also confident in a way she had not been before the New York show. She had learned a lot over the course of the tour, had had great shows and bad shows and just okay shows and knew what made the difference.

Soon enough, the band was all crowded just offstage, and the lights went down, and the screaming and cheering intensified. Then the guys took the stage, and started the music to "Who I Am", just as they had almost every night for the last few weeks. Except this night was not just like all the others.

Ava practically ran out onto the stage, sending the crowd into a new frenzy. She bowed, tears springing to her eyes, then grabbed the mic and began to sing.

Though she had sung them many times now, the lyrics of the

song took on a new, heightened meaning here in her hometown. She was not the same person, or the same singer, that had left Buffalo a few weeks ago, and it was time that everyone knew it.

"*Now you see me, now you don't,*" she sang, beginning the song.

Don't look for me where I was before
The night has fallen and the past is buried
The sirens are singing different songs to me now
And it's time I walk into their sea.

"*And you might be surprised by who I am,*" she sang on the chorus.

I am different from who you thought I was
Your eyes are playing tricks on you again
Listen to me tell you who I am
And someday you'll open your eyes
And you'll see me as I really am.

After that song, with barely a pause, the band launched into "Sunstorm", and then it was time for Ava to speak to the crowd.

"Buffalo!" she cried, and an enthusiastic roar greeted her. "Oh, I think you can be louder than that!" The audience obliged her by screaming even louder. "We are your very own Handel's Messiah, Buffalo-born and bred!"

The crowd cheered again.

"As you probably know, the guys here were in a bit of a bind recently, and so they called me to come help out," she said. "I've had the time of my life on the road with them, and now we're bringing the party back home! So let's keep it going!"

She turned to Ben, smiling, to let him know she was ready and, clicking his drumsticks together, he launched them into "Wintersoul" from *Shoreline*.

Ava powered through the set list, giving each and every song

CHAPTER 22

everything she had. She roamed the whole stage, holding out the mic for the crowd to sing along for some of the more well-known songs like "Dreamscape" and "Believer". She jumped up and down, pumped her fist, and headbanged between singing. Her adrenaline was amped up as high as it could go, and not once did she start to feel tired or like her voice needed a rest.

It wasn't just her. The rest of the guys were giving it everything they had, too, playing harder and with more energy than she had ever seen. She rocked out with Joel, sang back-to-back with Rafael, and crossed the stage to the keyboards and sang to Killian at a few points. The guys, too, kept up the headbanging, gesturing at the crowd to be louder, to jump higher. It was the last night of the tour, and no one was holding anything back.

About halfway through the set, Ben had a drum solo, giving Ava a break and the rest of the guys a chance to rest as well. Ava was covered in sweat and drank almost a whole bottle of water before the solo ended and they trooped back out on stage to keep going.

Before "Cathedral", Ava spoke to the crowd again.

"Buffalo," she said, "we have to thank you so much for being the best crowd of the whole tour, and being here for our best show of the tour. But then we expect nothing less when we come home!" She paused for the cheers. "Let me thank you, too, for making me feel so welcome up here," she went on. "It's been tough on everyone at times, but I just want to thank you, the fans, for rocking with me, and the guys of Handel's Messiah for giving me this chance.

"This is our last song," she said, "so I'm gonna need you all to be louder and crazier than you have been all night. Can you do that for me, Buffalo?"

The crowd roared their approval, and Killian began the ominous keyboard into of "Cathedral".

Ava hadn't thought she had anything left to give, but she found a little more for that last song. She sank into the dark atmosphere of the song and took the crowd with her, wanting to bring them into this same perfect musical zone that she was in.

"*And the weight of my sins is too dark and too heavy,*" she sang, as the song built in intensity toward the ending,

> *and they scream at me, echoing through the vast*
>   *space of the cathedral*
> *All is gray, all is cold stone*
> *And I am alone and cannot see*
> *The angels have all left me*
> *The weight of my sins is enough to bury me*
> *And I am alone and cannot see*
> *The distance between damnation and salvation*
> *Is enough to obliterate me.*

The music continued on long after Ava stopped singing, the guitar and bass crashing and the drums rumbling behind her, the keys frantically racing on. On the album, the song continued until it faded out, so the band kept it up for a minute, then abruptly brought it all to a stop.

The crowd was deafening, louder than they had been all night, as the band filed off the stage. As they gathered just off stage, waiting a few moments before going back out for their encore, they all pulled one another into an enormous, sweaty group hug. They were all laughing and cheering nonsensically, and as Ava found herself in the middle, laughing so hard tears sprung to her eyes, she knew she had found her home: with the guys, on stage, inside the music.

.ೋ෴ೋ.

The morning after the Buffalo show, Ava woke up somewhat disoriented: she was back in her own bed, in her apartment, with Killian next to her. For a moment, she wasn't sure where she was or what was happening. She remembered feeling this way after the first night she'd spent with Killian, as well. Had it all been a dream?

CHAPTER 22

But then she saw her suitcase on the floor where she'd dumped it when she came in, and her stage outfit from the night before draped over her butterfly chair. She smiled, closed her eyes, and burrowed in closer to Killian. It hadn't been a dream. This was her life now.

In the two weeks they were home, Killian effectively moved in with Ava, since he'd let the lease on the house he'd been renting go when they went on tour. Yet they also spent some time apart, seeing friends and relatives they'd been away from for a while. Ava's parents, who had been shocked when she'd called them from the road to tell them that she'd quit her job and was touring with Handel's Messiah, read her an extended version of the lecture they'd given her over the phone, but eventually accepted that she was happy, and taking a chance on something she loved, at least. They'd been at the Town Ballroom show, and even though Handel's Messiah wasn't exactly their kind of music, they admitted that she was something special as the band's front woman.

It was nice to be home, and it was nice to relax for a while and rest her voice. She hung out with Vivian, got to know Killian's parents a little better, and spent some time with Denise, who was thrilled at her success in introducing Ava to her brother and declared that she'd always known Ava was her sister from another mister.

Yet after a week, Ava was already anxious to hit the road again and see more places she'd never been and perform for more people she'd never met.

The only wave of disturbance on the smooth sea of Ava's two weeks at home came from, of course, Celeste.

Killian found out from a mutual friend not long after they got home that Celeste had moved to New York—why or for what, no one quite knew yet. Killian was obviously relieved by this news, and Ava was too, since they didn't need to worry about running into her anywhere. It might have been the second biggest city in New York State, but Buffalo was a small town at heart.

Just a few days before the band was leaving for the South American tour, though, Metal Planet published an interview with Celeste on their website. Rafael texted Ava to tell her about it, guessing (probably rightly) that Killian wouldn't tell her. Ava, of course, read it immediately, then emailed the link to Vivian and waited by her cell phone for Viv to call her.

She wasn't disappointed. "Girl," Vivian said as soon as Ava picked up the phone. "This chick is crazy."

"Right?" Ava squealed indignantly. She loved the guys (Killian especially, of course) but she had really missed having another woman to talk to at a moment's notice. "I can't believe this crap. Listen to this: 'The band is right when they say I left because of creative and personal differences, but it goes so much deeper than that. The guys—and Killian especially, as the songwriter—really didn't respect my talent and my abilities. It was a very depressing working environment, especially since making music shouldn't be work.' Give me a break," Ava said. "Killian *told* her he would change the songs for her, that she could rewrite the lyrics if she wanted. I notice she doesn't mention that."

"Well, she wouldn't," Viv said. "I really like the beginning where she says 'I'm so happy to finally be able to tell my side of the story!' You mean, make excuses for why you ran out on your boys in the middle of a tour? Okay."

"Right?" Ava said again. "And, of course, she had to take a dig at me. When the interviewer asked her what she thought of me. 'Well, I've only heard live clips online so far, so it's really hard to tell based on that, of course. It would be interesting to hear what she sounds like on a professional studio recording—if they decide to stick with her, that is.' Would it kill her to pay me a compliment?"

"It just might," Vivian said.

"And why *wouldn't* they stick with me? *She's* hoping they don't, of course. That would be her worst nightmare—first I

CHAPTER 22

get Killian, then I get her spot in the band."

"You better not let her get to you," Vivian said. "You kick way more ass than her. I never liked her screechy-ass voice anyway."

Ava laughed. "Well, thanks," she said. "Maybe you should call the record label up and tell them that, and make sure the band keeps me around."

"You don't think they will?" Vivian said. "Like you just said—why wouldn't they?"

Ava shrugged, even though Vivian couldn't see her. "I mean, it makes the most sense, obviously," she said. "But if that's what they wanted, wouldn't they have told me by now? I mean, why wait?"

"Got me," Vivian said. "I guess they just want to wait until all the touring is over and everything calms down? And," she added, sounding as though she'd just thought of something, "all the drama probably sells more albums and brings more people out to the shows, right? People are probably curious to hear you, and they think this might be their only chance. Why resolve that quite yet?"

"Yeah," Ava said, feeling heartened by this explanation. "That makes sense. That's probably it."

They chatted for a while longer before hanging up. Ava felt better having vented about the interview because that meant she wouldn't feel the need to vent about it to Killian. In fact, maybe they wouldn't even need to talk about it.

That, of course, ended up being wishful thinking, mostly because of what Celeste had revealed at the end of the interview.

Killian came back to the apartment before they went to dinner the same night the interview went live. Ava could only guess what expression was on her face because as soon as he saw her, he said, "You read it."

"Read what?" Ava asked innocently.

Killian groaned and flopped onto the couch.

"Honestly, Killian," Ava said, sitting down next to him. "What's the big deal? I have a right to know that she's badmouthing me."

Killian opened one eye, a near-smile on his lips. "She didn't badmouth you, exactly."

"It was implied."

He laughed shortly. "Well, that's Celeste for you." He sighed and sat up. "I just don't want you to get dragged into any of this bullshit, that's all."

Ava laughed. "Well, I think it's a little late for that. But I don't mind, I promise. You've livened up my existence; think of it that way." She leaned over and gave him a quick kiss. "Come on, let's go eat."

Ava thought that was the end of the discussion, and they could forget all about the interview. Yet later that night, she woke up and found Killian sitting on the edge of the bed, staring out the small window.

"Killian?" she asked sleepily. She sat up. "What...are you doing? Is everything okay?"

He didn't answer her for so long that she thought he was actually asleep after all. But then, finally, he said, "She's starting a new band. You saw that, right?"

Ava remained still. "Yes." It had been at the end of the interview. The interviewer had asked Celeste how she was liking New York and what her plans were. "I'm in the process of starting a new band, a band of my own," she'd said. "I don't want to say too much yet, but it's all coming together pretty nicely!"

"How could she?" he asked softly. "After everything...she had my music to sing. We were perfect together. How could she just forget that so quickly?"

"Killian, I—"

"It's just difficult, you know?" he said, turning toward her. "We were such a good team, musically, even before the other guys got involved. And it's like it didn't matter to her at all."

Ava didn't know what to say to that.

He shook his head. "I'm sorry. You don't want to hear about this." He leaned over to her and kissed her forehead. "I love you, Ava. More than I've ever loved anyone. Never doubt that."

CHAPTER 22

With that, he laid down beside her and was soon asleep.

Ava, however, would lay awake much longer, wondering what to make of what she had just heard. Wondering whether he had been more asleep than awake when he'd said it—and wondering which was worse.

chapter 23

Messiah Complex
2016

CHAPTER 23

After her screaming match—*after the breakup, you mean*, a spiteful little voice in her head reminded her—with Killian, Ava went home. She screamed into her pillow; she cried on her bed for hours with despair and anguish and rage. Rage, it sometimes seemed, most of all: that he should treat her so; that he should say such things; that he was still capable, after all this time and after all they had been through together, of breaking her heart.

Yet most of all, she was angry because she still loved him. If she didn't, none of it would have hurt so much.

Once the anger drained away, she was left with only sadness and regret. How had something that had started out so promising, and gone on for so long, shattered so horribly all in an instant?

Yet it hadn't been an instant, not really. There had been so many things all along the way that had caused the cracks to appear. But, like a broken pane of glass, they had managed to keep their relationship in place for a long time. Until today, when they'd thrown a rock through the whole thing.

To try to stave off the vast, heavy emptiness she felt growing inside her, Ava thought back all the way to the beginning and moved forward over their whole relationship. What could she have done differently? At what road could she have made a different turn, a turn that would not have led them to this place, but elsewhere?

Maybe she should have told him no, when he had called and asked her to join the band on tour. Or, failing that, maybe she should have filled in for the rest of the tour and then told them she was out, that they would need to find a different permanent singer. That was the moment when she could have put her relationship with Killian before the band, before anything else, if that was what she had wanted most.

But how could she have said no then? It had seemed so easy, at the time, the idea that she could have him and the band and therefore everything she wanted.

Or maybe the truth was that the band had meant more to her than her relationship with Killian all along. Much as it stung to admit it, made her feel dirty and grasping, hadn't part of her falling in love with him been about who he was, what he could do for her?

No. That wasn't entirely true, either. She loved him for himself. Or she had, once.

She did now. But had that been how it started? Would she have fallen in love with him if he had been some guy she'd met in a bar, and not Killian Sterling of Handel's Messiah?

Was it even possible to say? So much of their connection, their attraction, was the music, and had always been. Take it away, and neither of them was the same person.

But she had loved all of him, all this time, she knew. If she hadn't, this wouldn't hurt so much. So what could she have done? Could she have done any of it differently?

She could have stifled her voice, she realized with a pang. She could have never written that song. Never expressed herself. Never spoken up.

She went to her record player and put on her vinyl copy of *Terra Nova,* Handel's Messiah's third album and the first one she had recorded with them. It was chock full of songs Killian had written for her, love songs, songs specifically for her voice. A voice he only wanted to hear if he had it on a leash, it seemed. She curled up in her bed, still wearing her clothes, and eventually fell asleep.

Ava woke up the next morning, eyes red and nearly swollen shut from crying, her head aching so much that she felt as if she was hung over. And she was, in a way, she realized as she stared at her bleak reflection in the mirror. The entire six years of her relationship with Killian had been like one long drinking binge, with her as the happy, giddy drunk. And,

CHAPTER 23

lately, an angry one. Now the time had come to purge.

Except that she couldn't purge, not really. She still had to be in the band with him. She'd never be able to fully remove him from underneath her skin. Her voice was on those albums, singing his songs. And for that she had no one to thank but herself, for joining the band anyway when everyone knew that this was a possibility. No one had told her how much it would hurt her, though, and if they had she wouldn't have listened. Not then, not when they'd both been so in love and dreaming of touring together their whole lives. A rock-and-roll love story for the ages.

She took a shower, put on her pajamas, and went back to bed. She had no commitments with the band today, thank God, so she planned on doing exactly nothing. Unfortunately, she was not going to get her wish.

She dozed off, and she wasn't sure for how long she had been asleep when she was awoken by the buzzer sounding in her empty apartment. She rolled over, intending to ignore it until whoever it was got the message and went away. She was in no state for company.

Whoever it was, though, was persistent, and the buzzing repeated, over and over until Ava flung herself from the bed with a scream of frustration and went out into the living room. "What?" she snapped into the intercom.

"Ava, it's Viv. Let us—let me up."

Ava hesitated. Vivian's slip had told her that there was someone else with her. Vivian was about the only person Ava felt capable of talking to, but no matter who was with her, she couldn't let Vivian stand outside all day. Whoever Viv had brought with her, it wouldn't be Killian, that much she knew. Anyone else she could probably handle for now, until she got them to go away.

She buzzed them up and waited, arms crossed, by the door. A minute later, Vivian came in, followed by—much to Ava's surprise—Rafael.

"Jesus, Ava," Vivian said. "What's the matter with you?

You couldn't answer any of my texts?"

"I..." Ava had a vague recollection of turning her phone off when she got home, not wanting to have to field any potential apology texts or calls from Killian. And if he didn't text or call at all, that was worse, and she didn't want to know. "My phone's been off."

"I guess so." Vivian kicked off her shoes and tugged off her coat, making herself at home.

"What are you guys even doing here?" Ava asked.

"Checking on you," Vivian said.

Ava looked uncomprehendingly between her friend and Rafael. "But...Viv, how do you even know what happened?"

"Ah," Rafael began, looking uncomfortable. "That would be me. Killian unceremoniously threw us out after you left last night. We..." his face turned red. "We figured out what happened from what we heard of your argument," he said, as delicately as he was able. "And we wanted to talk to you. The three of us were trying to call you, but it kept going right to voicemail." He inclined his head in Vivian's direction. "We were starting to get worried about you, so I called Vivian."

"You had Viv's phone number?" Ava asked.

"Um." Ava had never seen goofy, outgoing Rafael look so flustered and awkward in all the time she'd known him, nor had she ever guessed that he was capable of being either of those things. "I had, uh, asked Killian for her number a while ago, but then I never actually called her."

Vivian's lips curled up in just the barest hint of a smile at this admission, but she held out one finger in his direction authoritatively. "And we will get to that later." She turned her attention back to Ava. "Ava...what happened? Are you okay?"

Ava opened her mouth to retort angrily that yes, she was fine, but instead she burst into tears.

"Oh, honey." Vivian came over and put an arm around Ava's shoulders, steering her toward the couch.

"I'll just...go make us some coffee," Rafael mumbled,

CHAPTER 23

heading for the kitchen.

"Put some Bailey's in it," Vivian called after him. "I know she's got some in there."

In spite of herself, Ava laughed through her tears.

Vivian waited until her tears faded, rubbing small circles on her back. "Do you want to tell me what happened?" she asked. "You don't have to."

Ava drew a shuddering breath. "No, I will. Maybe I'll feel better after."

She told Vivian the whole story, starting with the listening session for the album and ending with the fight between her and Killian after he wanted to leave her song off.

"Wow," Vivian said, when Ava finished. "Ava. That's horrible. I don't even know what to say except that I am so, so sorry."

Ava shrugged. "I should have known. I should have known this new start was bullshit, should have known he'd never change."

"I have half a mind to show up on his doorstep and rearrange that pretty face of his," Vivian said.

Ava laughed, a watery sound.

"I'll do it, if you want." She held up her fists in front of her face. "For you, I will throw these hands."

"I'll keep that in mind," Ava said. "As long as you don't ruin *his* hands. That's the only part of him that's useful to any of us right now."

Vivian went still. "So…you're going to stay in the band?"

"Of course," Ava said.

"Are you sure you're up for that?"

"No," Ava answered truthfully. "But I won't give it up, Vivian. I can't. It's the thing I love most. Not to mention that I can't do that to the rest of the guys. If Killian has a problem, he can leave."

As if on cue, Rafael appeared, carrying a tray that Ava had forgotten she had with three steaming mugs of coffee on it, each one topped with a small mountain of whipped cream. "Three Irish coffees, as requested," he said. He set the tray on the coffee table.

"When he's not slappin' da bass, he's a domestic wizard," Vivian said, reaching for a mug.

"Always a good quality in a man," Ava said, winking at Vivian. In theory, the romance that was potentially blossoming between Vivian and Rafael should have been the last thing Ava wanted to think about right then, but she surprised herself by being happy for them in spite of everything. If something good could come out of the wreckage of her and Killian, maybe it hadn't all been for nothing.

For nothing. Was it? Had it all been for nothing, the whole six years? Had it been a complete waste? Ava felt her eyes well with tears at the thought.

Yet before she could allow herself to fall any further down the rabbit hole of that particular idea, Vivian changed the subject somewhat by asking how the album sounded, and Rafael answered her enthusiastically. Ava chimed in here and there. It was so nice to have them there distracting her that she completely forgot to throw them out.

They stayed for a few hours before leaving to go get dinner. They invited Ava to join them, but she declined. "I'm exhausted," she said. "I'll probably just watch some TV and then go to bed early." This was true, but she didn't mention the fact that being the third wheel on their first date—which was no doubt what this would turn into—was more than she could handle at the moment.

Before they stood up to leave, Rafael looked directly at her. "Look, the guys and I have known we can't really take sides in this," he said. "In what was going on between you and Killian. But I just want to say that I got your back, and the other guys do too. We...well, we may have happened to overhear..."

"It's fine," Ava said quickly, not wanting to rehash it, but appreciating his attempt to be delicate. "We weren't exactly quiet."

"Well, anyway," Rafael said, looking relieved that she had rescued him, "a lot of what he said to you was complete bullshit and way out of line. We don't want you to go anywhere, and if he

CHAPTER 23

can't deal then we'll tell him to get lost. If this is how he's going to start acting, then we'd be better off without him."

Ava felt touched and guilty all at once. "Thanks, Raf," she said. "If you see Ben and Joel before I do, tell them I will definitely be sticking around. Hopefully we can all act like professionals through this."

Rafael engulfed her in a big bear hug. "We got you," he said again.

Vivian got up and hugged her as well. "You call me whenever you need to talk," she said. "Whenever, you hear me? I don't care what time it is. And I'm coming to take you to lunch tomorrow."

Ava smiled, her eyes tearing up again. "Thanks, Viv," she whispered in her ear.

"Don't mention it." Vivian stepped back. "You sure you don't want to come? You want us to bring you something? Anything you want, babe. I'll bring you some of those Korean beef tacos from Cantina Loco that you like so much."

Ava smiled. "No, thanks. You guys go. I'll be fine."

They gathered their things and headed out, leaving Ava alone and resolved not to fall back into wallowing. She read a while, a book she hadn't had much time for lately, then did in fact turn on the TV.

Don't think about him, her mind whispered whenever her sorrow threatened to break through again. *It's over. Let it go.*

She couldn't imagine how she'd be ready to face him in two days for their next album meeting when the thought of him still threatened to destroy what was left of her. After the show she was watching ended, she turned off the TV, went over to the piano, sat down, and played and sang "Appassionata", twice through.

This is what I gave him up for, she told herself as she sang the words she herself had written, the most honest thing she had ever said. *This feeling.*

She started, just barely, to remember why it had been worth it.

chapter 24

Shoreline
2010

CHAPTER 24

Before she knew it, Ava was back on the road with the band. The fans in South America absolutely blew her away with their energy and enthusiasm at the shows. And the places they visited were absolutely beautiful. She particularly loved Rio de Janeiro, surrounded by lush greenery and the turquoise of the ocean and the blue of the sky; and Buenos Aires, a stately, cosmopolitan city with gorgeous architecture. She spent every spare minute she could sightseeing, a practice that would continue everywhere they went.

Then it was over to Europe for the festivals, which were a completely different animal from the club shows they'd been playing. Some of Ava's nerves came back, and how could they not, when within the space of a few months she'd gone from being a complete unknown to playing the main stage at Wacken? Her Wacken performance started out shaky, she knew, but she managed to bring it around soon enough, and the fans responded better than she had imagined. Thank God they hadn't been one of the headliners, she'd told herself afterwards. Luckily, there were still so many shows to play that she had no choice but to put her less-than-ideal performance behind her and move on.

The Female Metal Voices Festival in Belgium was her favorite: it was a bit smaller, and so she was able to relax a bit and have more fun. The venue was a low building that looked like an arched warehouse from the outside, and inside, lights had been strung along the curve of the roof with a stage set up at one end. The crowd was mostly metalheads, come from all over, and it would be fewer people than Wacken but more than at their club shows—a perfect size, in Ava's opinion. And Ava was thrilled that some of her idols were present and would be listening to her. She got to meet many of the singers whose music she had discovered and was coming to love, like Simone Simons from Epica, and Charlotte Wessels from Delain. And she was beyond thrilled to finally meet her old hero, Marissa Martin of Wavelength.

Wavelength was headlining the first day—they had gotten even more popular over the years and had a huge fanbase all over the world for their gothically-tinged mix of hard rock and nu-metal—and Ava and the guys were just checking out the backstage area the first day when they ran into Marissa. "Hey! You're Ava Tomei, right?" Marissa said, walking up to her and shaking her hand. "Marissa Martin."

"Yeah! I mean, yes I am," Ava nearly babbled, shaking Marissa's hand in return. "And yeah, I totally know who you are. I'm a huge fan. Wavelength is one of my favorite bands, and you've always been a hero of mine." She wondered if she sounded like a total dork, then decided she didn't care. She was meeting a woman she'd looked up to for a long time, and she was absolutely going to tell her so.

"Thank you so much! That means a lot." Marissa took a step back and studied Ava for a moment. "I've been hearing a lot about you—obviously, it was big news when you stepped in with Handel's Messiah here. Major props to you for jumping into the spotlight like that. It couldn't have been easy."

"Thanks," Ava said, still hardly able to believe that Marissa Martin actually knew who she was, let alone had given her a compliment. "Yeah, it's been tough at times, but I couldn't not help out when Killian called me. And honestly, this is a dream come true."

"I'm sure. Well, this is a crazy life. Don't let it burn you out."

"I'm trying not to," Ava said with a laugh. "I'm finding that just pure adrenaline can't always take you the whole way, though."

"No, definitely not. As I'm sure you're finding, it's so important to rest and eat healthy and all that, so you don't collapse from exhaustion." She checked the chunky black watch on her wrist. "I've got a little time before I need to be anywhere. Want to grab lunch? There's a great little café I know just outside the venue here."

Ava couldn't believe that this was happening, that this was her life. "Yeah, absolutely. Let me just let the guys know." She waved over Killian, who was talking to Mark Jansen from Epica, and told him she was going to lunch with Marissa—who he

CHAPTER 24

seemed to already know. Then she followed her hero—and new friend, it seemed—out the back door of the venue and down the street until they came to a charming-looking café with lots of outdoor seating.

Once they were seated, Marissa pulled back her long, thick black hair and donned a pair of oversized sunglasses. "Good to get away from all the bustle for a little bit," she commented.

"Yeah," Ava agreed, wishing she could think of something more intelligent to say. But in truth it was nice, not spending the whole day in the venue, away from the hive of activity that was the backstage area at any festival. She felt like she could take a breath for the first time in weeks.

"I'm really looking forward to your set," Marissa said after they'd ordered coffees and some sandwiches. "I've seen some clips of you online, and you sound phenomenal. You look great onstage, too. It's hard to believe you've never done this before."

"Wow, thank you," Ava said, flattered. "I did have a lot of performance experience before joining the band, just not, you know, this kind."

Marissa nodded. "And will you stay on permanently?" she asked. She waved a hand to forestall Ava's objection before she spoke. "I know you have to tell the media and everyone that you don't know yet, but you can tell me."

"I wish I knew," she said. "I don't think the band or the label have made any decision yet, and if they have they didn't tell me."

Ava could tell Marissa was studying her from behind her dark sunglasses. "And do you want to stay on?" she asked. "Join the band permanently? You want this to be your life?"

Ava didn't hesitate. "Yes. More than anything."

"I admire that. But this business can really take a lot out of you: mentally, emotionally, physically. I'm sure you're already finding all that, but you should know that going in that all of that never lets up. You just have to learn how to deal with it." She smiled. "I'd ask if you'd let me give you some advice, though I don't know as it'll make any difference."

"No, please," Ava said eagerly.

Marissa hesitated for a moment. "I would tell you not to date anyone you work with," she said slowly, "but I think it's too late for that, isn't it?"

Ava stiffened slightly but did not reply.

"From what I hear, you and Killian are together, right?"

"Yes," Ava said. "And you're right, it is too late. We were together before he asked me to fill in for Celeste."

Marissa sighed. "Well, take it from me: that can be a very difficult relationship. Because loving someone and sleeping with someone and being with someone is very intense, and making music and touring is all very intense as well. It can really be...too much intensity for a couple to bear."

Ava remained silent. There had been rumors about Marissa Martin and Jeremy Belmont, the former lead guitarist and founding member of Wavelength. In a situation remarkably similar to Handel's Messiah's, Jeremy had left the band midway through the long, grueling tour for their third album. They had both given the excuse of "creative differences" as well, but rumors had circulated of infighting among the band, as well as people claiming that Marissa and Jeremy had gone through a bad breakup. Neither of them had ever confirmed it, though it seemed now that Marissa was confessing as much to Ava.

"I would have thought that Killian knew better, after Celeste," Marissa commented. She shrugged. "But then, you're both grown-ups. Both phenomenally talented, from what I can see. Just...keep that in mind. I hope you never reach a day where you have to choose between your band and your relationship."

"I hope not, too," Ava said a bit tightly. Thrilled as she was to be having lunch with Marissa Martin, she couldn't help but feel a little irritated at the other woman's bleak view of her relationship with Killian. After all, she barely knew either of them.

Their lunches arrived just then, and luckily their talk turned to other things as they ate. Ava asked Marissa for advice on

CHAPTER 24

preserving her voice over the long touring schedule, and Marissa asked Ava about her classical training and her practice regimen. By the time they were walking back to the venue, Ava's mood had lifted again, and she was picking Marissa's brain about the writing process behind her favorite Wavelength songs. They swapped phone numbers and email addresses and promised to keep in touch.

"Us women need to stick together," Marissa said just before she headed off to her dressing room. "There's not many of us in this scene, so we need to support each other."

"I agree," Ava said. "And thank you. I can't wait for your set tonight."

"And I'm looking forward to yours tomorrow."

And the next evening, Ava gave what she was certain was one of her best performances since joining the band. No doubt it was because, she realized, she was finally starting to feel like she belonged.

Handel's Messiah came home again for a few weeks in October, then they were off again for a tour of Australia, which wrapped up before Thanksgiving.

"For the last record we went back to Europe for another tour, then did another, shorter U.S. tour after that," Killian told her on the flight to Sydney—the longest flight Ava had ever been on, which she had been dreading. "But based on what Billy and the label have been saying, though, it looks like we're done after this for *Shoreline*. They think the promotion has been enough—it's sold four times what *The Art of Escape* did already—and, quite frankly, the feeling is that with all of the drama it'll be best for us to get into the studio and record a new album, and show everyone that we're coming back stronger than ever."

It made sense. And, admittedly, the drama had died down quite a bit. People kept asking about Celeste in interviews, both in South America and at the festivals, but it remained more of a footnote to the rest of the interview, due to the fact that the band hadn't deviated from their stock answers. Happily, most of the interviewers seemed more interested in the future of the band—something Ava herself wanted to know more about.

The band came home just before Thanksgiving, and right after the holiday the guys had a meeting with management and their label in New York to discuss a permanent replacement for Celeste. Ava was not invited, a fact which she somewhat resented; nor, Killian told her, was he bringing her to New York at all, even though she had imagined she might at least come along for the trip and do some sightseeing.

"I'm sorry," Killian told her when he broke the news of it to her. "I wanted you to be there, but management vetoed me. They want to discuss whether you're the best choice permanently, and that would be awkward to do right in front of you. And even you being in the city might not be good."

Ava could understand that, but it didn't make waiting around any easier. Luckily she had made enough money from touring that she didn't need to look for another job right away—there would be no point before she knew for sure what her future with Handel's Messiah was—but that didn't mean she wasn't antsy. "So…so what do you think?" Ava asked. "Am I in? Do I have anything to worry about?"

Killian hesitated, and that was all she really needed to know. "You know you're my first choice," he said. "You're the obvious choice. And the guys agree with me, for the most part."

"For the *most* part?" she demanded, feeling betrayed.

"Look, everyone has some concerns because we're dating," he said. "They're worried that if we break up or have problems, it'll adversely affect the band, and no one wants another situation like this, ever."

"But that's…" Ava trailed off. What was she going to say? Ridiculous? Because it wasn't, not really. Much as she may have wanted to, she couldn't forget Marissa Martin's warning to her, even as she knew it wouldn't stop her from joining the band permanently if asked.

CHAPTER 24

"I know," Killian said. "I'll let you know everything that happens. I promise."

~∽~

Ava was understandably on edge the day of the meeting. She didn't know what time it was happening precisely—why hadn't she thought to ask Killian?—and so stayed near her phone all day.

She also tried not to think about what the backlash among the fans would be if she made it in. It had been horrible enough when she was just filling in, and though she had gotten better at ignoring it, at avoiding the places online where people would be most likely to post nasty comments about her, she still knew it was out there, and in her more perverse moments she couldn't resist. In the days leading up the meeting in New York, she took to scrolling through YouTube and some online message boards, as if to steel herself by reminding her what she would not miss if she didn't make it. Somehow the nasty comments still loomed large, overshadowing the love many of the fans had for her.

When the waiting began to drive her crazy, she texted Vivian, and the two of them headed up to the Galleria Mall to fight the Christmas shopping crowds.

"What do you think of this?" Vivian asked, stepping out of a dressing room. She was wearing a sparkly silver top that clung to her curves in all the right places. "New Year's Eve, maybe?" She frowned when she saw Ava hadn't looked up from her phone. "Girl, if he doesn't get you the first time, he will call you back."

Ava looked up, smiling sheepishly. "I know. It's just…my whole future is at stake right now, you know?"

"I know. I do. But there is nothing you can do about it. You gave it your all on tour, and that's the most you could have done. What you *can* do is make my future a little less uncertain and tell me how this top looks."

Ava laughed. "You're right. And it looks perfect. But then,

everything you ever put on looks perfect. I don't know how you do it."

"Easy," Vivian said, admiring her reflection in the mirror. "I pick the right things to put on."

"If I get into the band, you're gonna have to help me shop for some new stage clothes," Ava said.

"Okay, this is not you distracting yourself," Vivian said. "Let's bring it back to me. The question is, is this outfit gonna draw the men like flies, or not?"

Ava laughed again. "I don't think there's any question about that."

Vivian turned to face her. "You try anything on?"

Ava held up a slinky black top. "I like this one—for reasons that I'm supposed to be forgetting about."

Vivian laughed. "Okay. I'm getting changed, we'll check out, and then we're going to Frederick's so you can buy Killian a welcome home present, if you know what I mean." She threw Ava a wink. "If that doesn't distract you, then I don't know what will."

They had fun at Frederick's, though neither of them ended up buying anything. Then Vivian insisted on dragging Ava off to The Cheesecake Factory for dinner—dessert was not optional—and then they headed home. There was still no call from Killian.

It wasn't until about eleven o'clock that night, when Ava was home, that her phone finally rang. She pounced on it, her heart pounding wildly. "Hello?" she said.

"Hello, my love," Killian said. Ava couldn't really glean anything from his tone besides the fact that he was tired. "Good news. You're in."

Ava closed her eyes, fighting back the urge to scream in joy. "Really?" she said, her voice coming out pinched and strangled. "I am?"

"You are," he said. "I'll be honest with you, it was a hard sell."

"What? Why?"

"Exactly what I said before I left," he said. "Everyone is worried about what happens if we have problems or if we break

CHAPTER 24

up. Even some of the guys said they were concerned."

"Really?" Ava said, feeling hurt.

"Don't hold it against them, Ava. I see why they would be worried."

"You do?"

"Yes. I mean—not like that, Ava." He lowered his voice slightly. "I see why, in theory, they're concerned about us dating and being in the band at the same time. I do not think that, in reality, those concerns will come to fruition."

Ava's whole body relaxed. "Me neither."

"I don't anticipate us breaking up, Ava," he said. "Not in the near future. If I have my way, not ever."

She closed her eyes again, tears welling. Why had she ever been worried, about anything? She had everything she wanted, and she would hold onto it all. "Yes," she said. "I feel the same way."

She could hear him smiling into the phone. "Ava…are you crying?"

She nodded, even though he couldn't see her. "Yes."

"Why?"

The tears came faster. "Because I've just been told I can have the two things I want most in the world. And regret."

"Regret?"

"That I didn't buy the ensemble I tried on at Frederick's of Hollywood today."

There was a split second of silence, then Killian burst out laughing. "I regret that too."

<hr />

The guys came home a few days later, and they all took her out to dinner to celebrate her official membership in the band. They were all genuinely excited to have her, and so Ava hoped that whatever Killian had said had put their fears to rest.

Ava also moved into a new apartment, leaving her old one on Bird and moving into a bigger one in a building a bit further up Elmwood. It had a bigger kitchen with a separate dining area, a big living room, and a master bedroom with the bath attached and a walk-in closet, as well as a small guest bedroom that she took to using for storage and for her bookshelves and record collection. She was thrilled to have more space, and thrilled that she could now afford it with the money she'd made on tour—and that being a working, performing musician was now her only job. It was what she'd always dreamed of, only better, somehow.

One day Ava came home to her new apartment and found Killian waiting for her with the baby grand piano, and as unsettled as it made her for him to be so extravagant, she couldn't help but thrill at her life, at what it had become. She had everything she could ever possibly want.

Then, after Christmas, it was time to get back to work.

They had a studio in Los Angeles booked for the month of May. That meant Killian had to finish writing the album, and they would need to rehearse the songs to get them ready to be recorded before then. It seemed like a daunting task, and Ava, as a newcomer, had no idea how the process worked. Luckily the guys were, of course, veterans. And as Killian had started writing some new songs months before—he'd been writing a bit while they were on the road—they had a head start.

One night, Ava awoke to the sound of piano music coming from her living room. In her disoriented state, she thought that there must be a radio on or perhaps the TV. Once she came to a bit more, though, she quickly realized that it was Killian, playing the baby grand piano he'd bought for her.

It was something she'd never heard before, something romantic and flowing and beautiful. She got out of bed, pulled her robe on over her naked body and went out to the living room.

He had put two lit on candles on the piano lid, closed to help dampen the sound. He didn't have candles everywhere, the way he did in his piano room at the house he'd bought when

CHAPTER 24

they'd come home from tour, but it still lent the same dark, mysterious aura as he played. He didn't notice her at first, but continued playing, his hands moving fluidly over the keys, the music pouring from him more so than from the piano.

He had, she noticed, taken the manuscript paper and lyric sheet of a song she'd been working on off the music stand and placed them on the lid of the piano, out of his way. She had no way of knowing if he had looked at it or what he thought if he had.

After a few moments, he looked up and saw her, but he didn't stop playing. He held her gaze in the dim, flickering candlelight, the music spilling from his fingers and pouring onto the floor at her feet, like an offering.

She crossed the room to stand beside him, sliding her hands down his shoulders and over his bare chest, resting her chin on his left shoulder and closing her eyes as she listened. Part of her wanted to imagine her singing to this music, her voice soaring over this rich, beautiful accompaniment, but she resisted the temptation and just listened, and drowned.

When he finally stopped, they remained where they were for a moment, then he drew her into his lap. "I've had that song in my head for weeks now," he murmured against her hair. "But I never had the time I needed to work it out; didn't have the right piano when we were on the road. Finally I've got it. Finally it's come."

He drew back so that he could see her face. "It's for you. It's called 'Muse.'"

She shivered with pleasure and fear and the pure force of the moment. "It's beautiful. It might be the most beautiful thing you've ever written."

"It should be." He kissed her hair. "It's about the most beautiful woman I've ever known."

It was, they found, quite inconvenient and impractical to make love on a piano bench, so they moved to the floor, unwilling to take the time to go anywhere else.

chapter 25

Messiah Complex
2016

CHAPTER 25

True to her word, Vivian arrived the next day to take Ava to lunch, and they went out to the outlet mall in Niagara Falls to fit in some retail therapy as well. It had been Vivian's suggestion, and Ava knew why: not only would they be able to keep her distracted for a few hours, but the chances were slim that they would run into Killian, much slimmer than if they stayed in their home territory of the Elmwood Village.

Ava tried to ask how Vivian's dinner with Rafael had gone the night before, but Vivian would only smile secretly and shake her head. "We'll talk about my love life some other time. That's not what you need to be worrying about right now." Yet this very response—and the fact that Ava caught Vivian checking her texts and grinning a few times throughout the day—told her that it had gone very well indeed.

When Ava finally looked at her phone later that day, there was still nothing from Killian, but she did have a text from his sister.

Denise: Ava! What did my idiot brother do??

Ava wasn't sure how to respond. She had been friends with Denise since before she ever met Killian, after all, and hoped that that friendship wasn't going to be a casualty of the breakup. Still, no matter how sympathetic Denise seemed in that one text, could Ava expect her to do anything but take her brother's side?

Ava: It's complicated. We both had our reasons, I guess.
Denise: I'm sure it isn't more complicated than Killian being an idiot. My parents are pissed at him too. Would love to see you soon!
Ava: Sure. Let's plan something.

She left it at that. She would need some more time to process her feelings before seeing Denise again. She couldn't deal with anything else just then other than how she was going to get through the launch of this album.

The next day Ava's respite came to an end. The band was set to meet to listen to the album again, confirm their song selections, and decide on an order for the official track list. They had originally planned to meet at Killian's house again, but Rafael had texted her while she was out shopping with Vivian to let her know that it would be at his place. Ava was a little embarrassed at the need for a venue change and was aware that everyone knew why, but she was grateful nonetheless.

She was so anxious about having to face Killian again that she ended up being the first person to show up. Rafael lived in a big house—purchased after their tour for the last album, *Gifts from the Devil*—on Auburn, between Elmwood and Delaware. Ava always teased him that it was way too big a house for a bachelor, and he would just shrug and grin at her. "I like having all this space just because I can," he would say. He had grown up in a tiny apartment on the West Side, raised by a single mother, so Ava could certainly see where he was coming from. "Maybe someday," he sometimes added, "I'll want to share it. Not yet, though."

Ava smiled slightly, thinking of these oft-uttered words as she walked in and Rafael, always a gracious host, took her coat. Maybe he had finally found the woman he was ready to share his space with. She hoped so.

Rafael showed her into the living room and poured her a glass of wine, then disappeared back into his kitchen. Her stomach knotted itself when she heard the front door open and shut, but she relaxed immediately when Joel walked into the room. "Hey," he said to her. "How are you, Ava? You doin' okay?"

She smiled. "As well as can be expected."

He nodded and sat next to her. "Yeah. Well—I'm glad you're here."

"There's no place I'd rather be."

That wasn't strictly true, she knew, especially when Killian walked in a few minutes later. She saw his whole body tense

CHAPTER 25

when he saw her—only because she knew him so well could she see it—then collect himself. He gave Rafael his coat, said hello to Joel, and nodded tightly to her. After a moment of consideration, he took the armchair as far from her as he could possibly get.

Ava almost laughed. It would be funny, his obvious awkwardness and discomfort, if being in the same room with him didn't make her feel like she was about to vomit.

None of the three of them said anything, and Ava had to fight back to urge to fidget. *This cannot be how it's going to be,* she told herself. *It cannot be this awkward forever. I'll never be able to bear it.*

Rafael came back in and sat down next to Ava, and she instantly felt a bit better. Having Joel on one side and big, bear-like Rafael on the other made her feel safe, protected. Like they were the big brothers she'd never had. She loved them for it.

Ben arrived last and Rafael got everyone their beverage of choice without even having to ask: Jack and Coke for Joel and himself, red wine for Ava and Killian, and raspberry wheat beer for Ben.

"Here's your fruity girly beer," Rafael said, handing Ben the bottle.

"Fuck you, man," Ben said good-naturedly, well-used to the jokes about his beer choices. "Have you tried this stuff? It's great."

"No, because if I liked it then I couldn't give you shit about it," Rafael said.

"I get it, you're pissed because I'm more secure in my masculinity than you, it's fine," Ben said, grinning and taking a swig of his beer.

Ava laughed and glanced over at Killian, out of habit, wanting to roll her eyes with him at this whole schtick like they always did. He must have forgotten, too, because he was looking over at her with a faint smile on his lips as well. But when their eyes met, they both remembered again, both recalled the way things really were between them, and quickly looked away again.

This is going to be so much harder than I ever imagined, Ava thought, fighting back tears.

But luckily then Rafael put in the CD, and they listened to the whole thing from start to finish, sipping their beverages in silence, making a few comments here and there.

As Ava had anticipated, it was hard for her to hear all the songs through. She almost burst into tears during "Dark Lady", written when she and Killian still loved each other, and which she had sung when she had thought that, maybe, things were getting better. "The Fine Line" just made her angry, wishing she could turn off her own voice, mocking her with the lyrics whose true meaning she had missed for so long. *"Here I am before you,"* the recorded version of herself sang on the second verse,

My life awash in blood
Because it was always leading up to this moment
Drenched in blistering hatred
But you're still so beautiful.

Then the song moved into the chorus:

There's a thin, fine line
Between love
And hate
Between you
And me,
Between life
And the death I'll die for you tonight.

Ava glanced in Killian's direction on this last line and found that he was already looking at her. When their eyes met, he simply looked away.

Coincidentally, "Hostage" was the next song and, to Ava's surprise, she found herself taking a savage pleasure in the near brutality of her voice, the way she spat the words at the listener.

CHAPTER 25

Her rage, her feelings of betrayal, were captured for all to hear. She didn't even try to stop a satisfied smile from spreading over her face.

It was over an hour by the time they'd listened to everything, and once they were through Rafael got up and turned the stereo off.

"Well," he said. "I stand by our picks from the other day."

Everyone nodded agreement.

Killian had pulled out his laptop and booted it up. "Okay," he said, and the sound of his voice was enough to send both longing and anger through Ava. "So. Order. What do we like for the opener?"

"I kind of like 'Say Goodbye' for the opener," Joel said. It was one he had written with Killian, since Killian readily admitted that he needed a guitar player's input from time to time, and the two of them had never lost the habit of just jamming together that they'd picked up in college. "The title makes it kind of unexpected, and it has the right rocking sort of feel to start off the album."

Everyone agreed, so they marked it down. They agreed with Ava's idea of a few days before, that "Map of the End of the World" made a perfect closer, with "Archangel" coming before it as song number thirteen. Then they went down the roster of songs, assigning each one a spot.

"Okay. 'Appassionata'?" Rafael asked, after they'd placed "Teller of Tales" as song four.

Ava could feel, ever so subtly, the tension in the room ratchet up. She caught both Ben and Joel sneaking glances between her and Killian.

"Ummm." Ava avoided their eyes and glanced down at her notepad, where she'd been keeping her own copy of the list. "Maybe number six? In the first half of the album?"

"Sounds good to me," Joel said. Ben and Rafael nodded.

Not looking up, Killian typed it in. "Okay. Number six," he mumbled.

And that was that.

HEAVY METAL SYMPHONY

Once they'd gone through their fourteen chosen songs, Killian spun his laptop around so they could all see the screen. Ava leaned in and, in spite of everything, felt a shiver of excitement at seeing it all there on the screen, in black and white typeface and beginning to look official.

HANDEL'S MESSIAH – MESSIAH COMPLEX
ALBUM #5

- Say Goodbye
- Hostage
- Chains of Gold
- Teller of Tales
- Depths
- Appassionata
- Colossus
- Die for Me
- Poisonous Idols
- The Fine Line
- Dark Lady
- Memories
- Archangel
- Map of the End of the World

Rafael let out a whoop. "Looks good!"

Ava smiled. It was all happening, just like it did every time, yet it never failed to make her excited and even a little awed to see all their hard work coming to fruition. And even as she was coming apart on the inside, with Killian just feet away but no longer hers to touch, to hold, to love, it began to heal her, just a little bit, to see everything else coming together.

Once they were finished, Killian reminded them that they were starting rehearsal the week after next for the upcoming tour. Then he left, the first of them to go. He hadn't said a single word to Ava the entire time.

CHAPTER 25

That night, when Ava got home, she opened up her laptop and scrolled to the digital file of the final mix of the album that she'd been sent. She immediately clicked on the track that was "Appassionata", turned up the volume as high as it would go, and sat back in her chair to listen. To really listen to the final version of her song, to feel it in a way she hadn't truly been able to with the rest of the band there today. And perhaps especially with Killian there.

She knew it wasn't perfect, knew that no song was ever perfect, but in that moment, it felt perfect to her. Every note exactly in place, played with the exact emotion she'd wanted it to be played with. The strings, swelling gently before building later on in the song. The piano, the backbone of the song, driving it throughout. Ben giving just enough on the drums but not too much; Rafael and Joel playing their lines just as she'd heard them in her head as the song was being born.

And her voice. She knew that this was one of her best vocal performances, of any song, in any setting. And why shouldn't it be? Of course she knew how to write for her voice best; knew how to use it exactly as the song required. And in each word of the lyrics, she heard her pain and her sorrow and her anguish, but also her determination to be done. To be heard, finally. No matter the cost.

And Killian, she realized, was nowhere on this song. She had recorded the piano for the album, after all. He hadn't touched it. It was truly and fully hers.

Oh, he would need to play the piano part live, if they decided to add it to the setlist—and Ava was determined that they would. But this recording of it, the way most of the world would hear it first and most often, was all hers. And that meant something to her. Even if it had been Killian who had inspired it, Killian who had given her the word "Appassionata" at the top of the score of a song he had written for her. She had taken his word and made it her own. She had raised her voice louder and louder until he finally heard her. Until he had no choice but to hear her. And she realized then that she would never, ever regret that.

Goosebumps had broken out over her skin from the first note and didn't fade until long after the song had ended. This was her song, and it was written and recorded and finished and was going on a Handel's Messiah album. In that moment, the weight and import of that fact truly struck her.

Grabbing her phone, she sent Vivian a text.

Ava: Can you come with me somewhere tomorrow after you get out of work? There's something I need to do.
Vivian: Sure. Where?
Ava: You'll see.

The next day, Ava brought Vivian with her to Cowpok, the tattoo and piercing parlor on Elmwood where she'd gotten her "Vissi d'arte" tattoo. With Vivian there for moral support—Ava had never liked needles—Ava had an artist add the word "Appassionata" in a beautiful, scrolling font just above where the music staff began.

chapter 26

Terra Nova
2011

While Handel's Messiah was still touring for *Shoreline,* Celeste Perinot had been busy as well. Her new band, Poisoned Smile, wasted no time, perhaps hoping to capitalize on the drama and publicity surrounding her hasty exit from Handel's Messiah. They wrote and recorded their debut album, entitled *Strangers,* and it was released just as Handel's Messiah was preparing to go into the studio to record their third album, and Ava's first as a member of the band.

Ava was desperately curious to hear what Celeste's new band sounded like, and while she struggled briefly with the question of whether or not she should support Celeste's career and what Killian would think, she eventually caved and downloaded the album from iTunes. She had to know.

Ava tried her best to keep an open mind while listening to the album, but found it impossible to fully divorce her personal feelings about Celeste and the situation from the music. It was a decent album, she could readily acknowledge, but not anything particularly exceptional. Not as good as *The Art of Escape* had been, and certainly not as good as the songs Killian had written for the new album, and which they were in the process of rehearsing. The sound was still symphonic metal, but perhaps a bit lighter, poppier. Maybe it was just the familiarity of hearing Celeste's voice in such a context, but Ava couldn't help but think that Poisoned Smile was basically what Handel's Messiah would be if they didn't have a songwriter as gifted as Killian. But in spite of herself, Ava did have to admit to really liking some of the songs, particularly "Witch", a hard-rocking song blasting sexism that Ava could certainly relate to, and "Dreaming in Daylight", an absolutely gorgeous power ballad.

In keeping with Celeste's reasons for leaving Handel's Messiah, she had a songwriting credit on all of the songs. And, in a move that would no doubt satisfy those looking for drama in the album, two of the songs—"Behind Me" and the title track, "Strangers"—seemed to directly address her departure from

CHAPTER 26

Handel's Messiah, with the latter seeming to be aimed at Killian in particular.

"*Now we're nothing but strangers passing in the crowd,*" Celeste sang on the chorus of "Strangers".

*Let you make me into nothing, and I'm not proud
Thought you needed me like I needed you
Thought we could hold on, thought we could get through
You said I left, but you were already gone
I realized I'd never be anything more than your pawn
But now you're nothing but a stranger in my crowd.*

The lyrics—nowhere near as good as Killian's, certainly—made Ava angry on her boyfriend's behalf. Celeste had deserted her band when they'd needed her; hadn't taken the chances Killian had given her to make changes to the songs and to work through their issues. How was any of this his fault?

Ava knew, of course, that there were two sides to every story, but she found she didn't particularly care what Celeste's side was. Or so she told herself.

Still, the album was solid, and Celeste had plenty of die-hard fans from her Handel's Messiah days—as Ava well knew, since lots of them had voiced their preference for her online—and no doubt would pick up some new ones. Ava read a couple reviews of it, both of which were positive, and then told herself not to think about it or what Celeste was doing anymore. It had nothing to do with her, after all, and so ultimately it didn't matter.

She was certainly not about to bring up Celeste's album—let alone the fact that she had listened to it—with any of the guys in the band, and especially not with Killian. Yet a little less than a week after the album's release, she showed up to rehearsal to find that it was already a topic of conversation, albeit in a way she hadn't expected.

She walked into their rented rehearsal space in Allentown to hear Killian saying, his voice tight and almost angry, "No, of course not. Why would I?"

Joel, who had apparently asked the question he'd been responding to, shrugged. "Figured you'd be curious. I was."

"Well, I'm not," Killian said from where he was standing behind his keyboard rig.

"But Killian," Rafael said from beside Joel, bass already strapped on and ready to go, "the thing is—"

Killian glanced up when he noticed Ava, and his face changed, softened. "Hello, love. We're just waiting on Ben, and— "

"I'm here," Ben said, walking through the door behind Ava.

"Did you guys hear it?" Joel asked Ava and Ben.

"Hear what?" Ben asked.

"The Poisoned Smile album. Celeste's new band."

"Oh, shit, is it out?" Ben asked.

Joel rolled his eyes. "You living under a rock?"

Ben waved a hand dismissively. "I don't pay attention to the scene too much when we're not on tour," he said. "You know that. I need a break from it all."

"I, um," Ava said hesitantly. "I listened to it, yeah."

"Can we stop talking about this and get to work?" Killian demanded.

"I don't think we can," Rafael said reluctantly. "Because there's something you should know, Killian."

"About what? Celeste's new band? I told you, I don't give a shit."

"Well, you're gonna give a shit about this," Joel said. He crossed his arms over his chest. "Remember that song you wrote for Celeste back in college, when we were just getting the band started? She sang it at her senior recital, or something."

Killian went still. "Yeah, I remember."

Ava felt a pit open up in her stomach. Killian had written a song for Celeste, an art song, for a recital she'd given? And Ava had thought she was so special, that he had done the same for her.

How can you be surprised, though? a somewhat annoying inner voice asked her. *He's a composer, a songwriter. It's what he*

CHAPTER 26

does. He was writing songs for Celeste for years before he met you. They started the band together!

"Well, Celeste put it on her fucking album."

Dead silence followed Joel's announcement. Ava's mouth dropped open, and she glanced around at the rest of the guys in turn. Joel looked grim, as though he'd known he needed to break this news but hadn't been looking forward to it; Rafael looked chagrined, as he had plainly listened to the album and recognized the song as well; and Ben looked as shocked as Ava felt.

Killian, though, had gone utterly rigid with something very like rage. Slowly, slowly, he came out from behind his keyboards. "She did what?" he asked from between gritted teeth.

"Celeste put it on her band's new album," Joel repeated. "She arranged it for guitar and everything else, obviously, and recorded it for the album. She made it a power ballad."

"'Dreaming in Daylight'," Killian said. "That song."

Ava gasped; she couldn't help it.

"Yes, dude. That's what I'm telling you."

"Are you *fucking* kidding me," Killian spat, almost but not quite shouting. "She actually had the fucking nerve…"

"But…wait," Ava said, not really wanting to interject, but feeling like she should. "I…I listened to the album, and I read through the liner notes," she said. "Killian's name wasn't listed for any of the songs. Maybe it has the same title, or something, but—"

"That's the point," Joel said tersely. "Not only did she record a song Killian wrote without his permission, but she's claiming *she* wrote it. The only songwriter credited on that song is Celeste Perinot."

"Jesus Christ," Ben muttered.

"That's… a lot of nerve," Ava said, woefully aware of how inadequate her words were.

Killian's hands clenched into fists. "She actually did this. She really fucking did it."

"Yeah, she sure did," Rafael said.

"I figured you should know," Joel said.

"Yeah, you're fucking right I should know," Killian said. "Someone play it. I need to hear it. I need to hear what she did."

Joel laughed. "It's not like I'm carrying the goddamn album around with me, dude."

"Um." Ava produced her iPod from her bag. "I've got it on here."

Killian grabbed the iPod from her and plugged it into the sound system in the rehearsal space. He scrolled through until he found the song, and pressed Play.

The song spilled through the speakers, with its beautiful piano intro. Soon the piano was joined by Celeste's—admittedly beautiful—voice, singing the shimmering first verse. The drums, guitars, and bass kicked in on the chorus, the lyrics of which hit Ava very differently now that she knew Killian had written it for Celeste:

So much more than what I thought could be real
Love beyond what I thought I could feel
I'm dreaming in daylight, drowning in sunlight
I open my eyes to morning's bright
And somehow you're still here with me.

It made sense why this had been Ava's favorite song on the Poisoned Smile album, since Killian had written it. She could hear how his songwriting had matured since he had written this, both musically and lyrically, yet it still stood out among the songs Celeste and her band had written. The ones they had actually written, that was.

Killian listened to the song all the way through, not speaking, not moving, save for a single muscle working in his jaw. When the song ended, he jabbed almost violently at the iPod's pause button to shut it off.

No one said anything.

Suddenly Killian stalked angrily toward the door, then at the last minute turned and walked back toward his bandmates.

CHAPTER 26

"I'm going to sue her," he ground out. "I'm going to take her for everything she's got, every penny she got off this stupid fucking record, and she's going to be sorry."

"Good," Ava said. "You should."

"Now, hold on," Rafael said.

Killian whirled to face him. "Hold on?" he shouted. "Hold on for what? You fucking heard it, Raf. You know I wrote that song."

"I know you did," he said. "I recognized it as soon as I heard it. But—"

"As if it isn't bad enough she recorded it and put it on there without my permission," Killian seethed. "She's actually *claiming she wrote it!*"

"*Did* she write any of it?" Joel asked.

"No," Killian snapped. "Well…she gave me some ideas for the vocal line. But I wrote the lyrics, and—*I wrote the fucking song!*"

"Yeah, but…" Rafael hesitated. "Can you prove it?"

"Prove it? You *know* I wrote it—"

"I know. I know you did," Rafael said. "But could you prove it, like, legally? She's going to claim she collaborated on it, at the very least, and could you prove in court that you actually wrote it? Did you ever record it, or publish it, or—"

"No," Killian bit out. "We were kids. We were in college. I wrote it for her recital. I gave her the sheet music; I have no idea what happened to the original. She performed it that once, and then it sat. We all agreed it wasn't right for Handel's Messiah, so that was the end of it."

"I'm no lawyer," Ben said, "but is that enough?"

"Who cares? I have to at least try! She fucking stole my song!"

"Do you, though?" Rafael asked. "I know she stole it, dude. I know. And it was unbelievably shitty. But, come on—we all know Celeste. She did this to provoke you. To get a rise just like this."

"Oh, she'll get a rise alright," Killian said.

"But that's what she wants," Ben said. "More drama, more gossip, and more publicity for her and her band."

"And—I'm not trying to defend her or anything—but if she collaborated on it with you, maybe she thought it was genuinely hers to use," Rafael said. "Yeah, she was still taking a shot at you by doing it, but maybe—"

"Oh, she knew exactly what she was doing," Joel said.

"So don't give her what she wants," Rafael urged Killian. "Let it go."

"Let it go," he spat. "She stole a song I wrote, and claimed to write it herself, and you think I should just let it go."

"It's not like you'd probably get that much money out of her anyway, even if you could prove it—"

"The money isn't the point," Killian said. "It's the principle of the thing!"

"I know it is, and you shouldn't give her the satisfaction," Rafael said. "Nothing will chafe her ass more than if she thinks you don't care. And why should you? You've written lots of other songs, better ones. Let her have this one."

"I can't just—"

"Sure you can," Rafael said. "Let it go; don't give her what she wants. Don't get tied up in some legal battle. Just wash your hands of her, like she did of us."

Silence fell as Killian considered this.

Ava had been silent for most of the argument, sensing that no good would come of her getting involved. She'd been shocked to hear Rafael argue against Killian suing Celeste, yet the wisdom of what he was saying had begun to sink in. Part of her wanted Killian to do it just for the principle of the thing, as he'd said, and yet…wasn't it better to just leave Celeste and everything to do with her in the past? Wasn't that the best not only for the band, but for Ava and Killian's relationship?

"I think Raf might be right," Joel said, a bit reluctantly. "We're about to start recording a new album, the first one with Ava. Then we'll be going on tour. A lawsuit would just distract

CHAPTER 26

attention from all that—the fans' attention *and* ours. And I think we all deserve better than that. Raf's right. Let's just wash our hands of Celeste and move on."

"And Ava deserves all the attention to be on her with the new album," Ben said. "This is her chance to really win over the fans. And our chance to show we can go on without Celeste. I don't think any of us want Celeste to take that away from Ava and the rest of us."

Ava shot Ben a grateful smile. She had just begun thinking the same thing herself, but hadn't necessarily wanted to say it.

Killian turned to look at Ava, for maybe the first time since she had come in. "Yes," he said. "Ava deserves all that and more."

"It's for the best, man," Rafael said.

Killian sighed, and while he was plainly still upset, most of the anger had drained away. "It still feels like letting her get away with something," he said. "She probably counted on me letting it go for those very reasons."

Joel shrugged. "Maybe. Personally I think she was hoping for drama, though, because she's always hoping for drama. But either way, don't give her any free publicity. It's only the one song. Her band is going to have to succeed on their own merits, just like everyone else."

"And they're not as good as we are," Rafael said. "They're just not."

"Definitely not," Ava said.

Killian turned to her. "What do you think I should do?" he asked, his voice low, plainly just asking her, even though everyone in the room could hear.

Ava hesitated for a moment. Part of her still thought that Killian should sue, but that part was being firmly drowned out by the things Rafael and Joel had said, all the solid, reasonable points they'd made.

And by the fact that, more than anything, she didn't want Celeste to take this moment from her.

And for whatever reason, Ava was suddenly powerfully

certain that, in this moment, about this, Killian would do whatever she told him he should do.

Ava met Killian's eyes. "I think you should let it go," she said. "Forget it and move on. Let's focus on *our* music."

Killian held her gaze a moment, then nodded. "Okay," he said. "Fine. Let's forget it."

The tension palpably leaked from the room at that.

"We should get to work," Killian said, returning to his keyboards. "We've wasted enough time today."

Rafael exhaled. "That's more like it!"

They all took their places at their instruments, and Ava at her microphone, and got back to work.

chapter 27

Messiah Complex
2016

Part of Vivian's campaign to take Ava's mind off of her break up included another night out. "You never know," she said, as they walked up Elmwood toward Mr. Goodbar. One of Buffalo's busiest sections of town was alive and bustling on a Friday night, with people walking to and from the restaurants and bars that lined the street, the shops interspersed among them closed for the night. "You might meet someone new!"

Ava rolled her eyes. "A rebound is the last thing I need."

"I disagree," Vivian said. "I think it's exactly what you need."

"Why bother meeting someone?" Ava said. "I'm never here, always on tour, and—"

"Excuse me, when did I say you needed to start a whole ass relationship with someone?" Vivian asked. "Think *rebound*. A fling. Just something to remind you there's other men out there than old moody what's-his-face."

Ava laughed in spite of herself. "You know that's not really my style, Viv."

"You can always try something new, is all I'm saying."

Ava stopped walking and let out a weary sigh. Vivian stopped and turned around to face her. "I…" Ava began. She sighed again. "I still love him, Viv, is the thing." Her voice was teary, tremulous, though she was doing her damnedest not to cry and ruin the makeup Vivian had so carefully applied for her.

Instantly Vivian was at her side, wrapping an arm around her shoulders. "Oh, honey," she said. "I know. It's okay. It's gonna take time. I'll stop with my rebound nonsense now. You just relax, have a good time tonight, and don't think about him, okay? That's all."

Ava nodded. "Okay. You're right."

"But if you *do* see a fine man you'd like a piece of, let me know, and I will make sure you get it."

Ava laughed and playfully shoved her friend. "You're incorrigible."

"Okay, time to get some booze into you so you stop using words like 'incorrigible'," Vivian said, pulling open the door of the bar and following Ava inside.

CHAPTER 27

"Goddamn, why do we still come to this shitty bar?" Vivian shouted at Ava an hour and a half—and several vodka cranberries—later. Goodbar was packed and the music was blasting. A typical Friday night.

"What?" Ava yelled back.

Vivian rolled her eyes. "My point exactly. I said, why do we still come here? You're a rock star now. Shouldn't you be partying somewhere classier and bringing me with you?"

Ava shrugged. "Because it's familiar? Because this is always where we've come? Because it makes us feel younger?"

"Okay, I'm sorry I asked," Vivian said, her eyes flicking to the door behind Ava's shoulder.

"What's with you?" Ava asked.

"Hmmm?"

"You keep looking at the door. Are you waiting for someone?" A terrible thought occurred to Ava. "Oh, shit. Viv. You didn't invite someone here to meet me? Like a set up or something?"

Vivian's eyes darted back to her friend's. "What? No! Of course not. I'd never do that without asking you, babe." For a moment, Vivian looked almost sheepish, an expression Ava could not remember ever having seen on her face before. "It's just that I, uh, might have told Rafael where we'd be tonight, in case he wanted to drop by."

"Oh." Ava wasn't sure what to say. She'd know they'd been casually seeing each other, but she hadn't expected Vivian to invite him out with them.

"Is that okay?" Vivian asked hurriedly. "Shit. I'm sorry. I just figured, you know, you and him are tight, so you wouldn't mind. But. Shit. This is supposed to be girls' night out, getting your mind off things." She pulled her phone out of her clutch. "I'm gonna text him and tell him not to come."

"No, no," Ava said. "It's fine. Really it is, Viv."

"No, that was stupid of me. You don't need to be feeling like a third wheel when—"

Ava put her hand over Vivian's phone screen. "Really, Viv. It's fine. If anything, Raf is the one who's about to feel like a third wheel."

Vivian snort-laughed. "I know that's right." But her face grew serious again. "But you're sure?"

"Yes. Really. It's fine. I love Raf, you know that."

"Well. Okay. If you're sure." Her face relaxed into the warmest and happiest of smiles. "I haven't seen him since we grabbed dinner on Wednesday, so…"

"*Wednesday?* Vivian, that was *two days* ago."

She shrugged. "I don't know. Seemed like a long time."

"Ohhhh my god," Ava said, grinning. "You *like* him. You've got it *bad*."

"Shut up," Vivian said, but she was beaming.

"Hot damn," Ava crowed. "When was the last time we saw *this?*"

"It's been too damn long, for your information," Vivian said. "And to think he was right there the whole time…"

But she trailed off, and her biggest smile yet came over her face as Rafael walked in. He saw them immediately and fought his way through the crowd to get to the spot they'd staked out at the end of the bar. "Evening, ladies," he said. He drew Vivian into his arms and gave her an enthusiastic kiss. Ava couldn't help a pang at the sight, but she smirked with self-satisfaction anyway. They had met because of her, after all. She'd be able to remind Vivian of that accordingly. When they drew apart, Rafael grinned at her. "What are we drinking? Next round's on me!"

The rest of the night passed in a boozy, happy haze. They didn't have to buy too many more rounds, since some girls at the other end of the bar recognized Rafael and Ava and kept sending them drinks. One of them kept tossing winks in Rafael's direction, which got Vivian steamed up. "This white

CHAPTER 27

girl is *not* making eyes at my man," Vivian said, glaring at the blonde in question.

"*Making eyes?*" Ava screeched. "You sound like my grandmother!"

But beside Ava, Rafael had gone still. "Your man?" he asked with a casual air, but Ava could see the look on his face. Joy, but a fear that it was too premature.

Vivian turned her head back to face him. "Of course you're my man," she said. "What did you think we were doing here?"

Rafael wore a bigger grin than usual the rest of the night.

As Ava watched the new couple throughout the evening, she realized that, her earlier teasing of Vivian aside, this was the real thing. A few times Rafael drifted away to talk to some acquaintances he saw in the crowd, but every few minutes he would glance back at Vivian, as if to reassure himself that she was still there. And Vivian, no matter what she and Ava were talking about, would let her eyes drift over to Raf, as if she didn't even realized she was doing it. When their eyes met, Ava was surprised the sparks that flew didn't catch and burn down the whole bar. The old dive was definitely flammable.

Ava should have felt sadder, perhaps, watching them. Regretful for what she used to have with Killian, worried she might never have it again. But she wasn't. It was hard to feel that way when two people she loved so much were so happy.

The fact that she had always been a giddy drunk certainly didn't hurt.

At one in the morning, they stumbled outside, and Rafael called them a cab. She assumed they'd drop off Vivian first, since she lived closest, but the cab sped past her side street.

She turned to look at Vivian, eyebrows raised. "Oh?" she asked.

Vivian nodded, closing her eyes and leaning her head against Rafael's shoulder. "Yup."

The cab let Ava out in front of her apartment building, and then drove away with its two lovebirds.

And, somehow, as Ava went up to her apartment, managed to pull on some pajamas, and got into bed, she felt better than she had in a long time.

chapter 28

Terra Nova
2011–2012

Ava got swept up in her first album recording experience. She worked with Killian on many of the songs before he showed them to the rest of the band, with him handing her a new score for her to sing through every few days, it seemed. He had never written so much so quickly, he told her, and the set of songs they selected to record were full of songs for her, about her: "Muse", "Savior", "Soul's Fire", and "Annabel Lee", the famous poem which Killian had set to music for her after seeing an Edgar Allan Poe anthology on her nightstand one night. Then, of course, once they started recording, came "The Lighthouse", which Killian wrote and had the band learn during recording so that they could add it. "*Appassionata*", he'd written as the marking at the top of the score he'd given her.

Then after the recording there were photo shoots for the album, which they did in California right after recording: some of the band in the desert, some on cliffs beside the ocean. Then came a music video shoot for "Crescendo", the first song on the album and also the first single; then lots of interviews and promotion. The interviewers were eager to get Ava's take on how she felt to be a permanent part of the band; how the recording process had gone for her; how she felt about the new songs; what she thought of the fan reaction. It had been decidedly mixed: people seemed to either love her or hate her, though she gathered, from one of her Internet-scouring sessions, that there were a large number of people who were reserving judgment on her until they heard the new record. This had been an extra pressure in the back of her mind while recording, knowing that this might be her one chance to win over fans who had yet to see her live.

And, of course, in between giving interviews the band rehearsed seemingly nonstop for the upcoming tour, choosing which new songs to add to the set list, and also learning a cover song: "Fairies Wear Boots" by Black Sabbath, which had been Ava's idea.

The night before *Terra Nova* was released and they were

CHAPTER 28

to play their hometown release show, an enormous bouquet of flowers was delivered to Ava's apartment—two dozen deep red roses, her favorite. The card attached read: *For Ava. This album is your best performance yet, and I can't wait for the whole world to hear you like I do. Love, Killian.*

Tears welled in Ava's eyes as she read the note—tears of love, joy, pride. She went and got her biggest vase and arranged the flowers in it, placing them on the lid of her piano.

For their headlining North American tour, they'd offered meet-and-greet packages for the fans to meet the band and have their picture taken with them before the show. Therefore their first official tour stop after their release show—at the PlayStation Theater in Times Square—would be Ava's first face-to-face interaction with the band's fans.

She was nervous; she couldn't help it. The guys had never asked her to do this on the tours for *Shoreline,* given that she wasn't an official member of the band yet. Had she wanted to join the guys at stage doors after shows and things like that, they certainly would have welcomed her, but she hadn't—though she was disappointed in her own cowardice—and so no one had pressed her. She couldn't help but think that, had she never seen any of the online hate directed at her, she would have done it gladly and without a second thought.

But this tour, she'd be able to take the opportunity—had to take the opportunity, really. And while there was a part of her that was excited, a greater part of her was terrified.

"You'll be fine," Killian assured her just before they went out to the lobby of the venue, where the meet-and-greet was being held. "You'll be better than fine. You'll be great."

She gave him a nervous smile but didn't reply. She felt like she was about to throw up.

Then the band filed out to the table in the lobby where

they'd be sitting to sign posters for the fans and to take pictures. Ava sat down and grabbed the Sharpie that had been left at her seat and smiled vapidly.

And then it began. The first fan came up to the table, shook everyone's hands, had each of them sign his poster. He was a tall, skinny white kid with dark hair, there with a friend—or boyfriend? Ava wasn't sure. When he got to her, he smiled shyly. "Hi," he said. "Nice to meet you."

"Nice to meet you," Ava said, shaking his hand and signing the poster Ben, beside her, had passed her. Then, because she felt she should say something else, she asked, "Are you looking forward to the show tonight?"

The kid's face lit up. "Oh, yeah," he said enthusiastically. "Been counting down the days. I absolutely love *Terra Nova*."

Ava smiled—what felt like her first genuine smile in hours. "Well, thank you," she said. "I'm so happy to hear that."

With a grin and quick flash of the "rock on" horns, the kid moved down to talk to Killian.

And so it went. Some fans did little more than nod, some enthusiastically told her how much they loved the album; some said how thrilled they were to meet her, to be there. And some seemed downright nervous.

They're more nervous than I am, Ava thought, as a young woman who had giggled her way through most of the conversation moved on. *Imagine that.*

But it was a young woman in her early twenties, about midway through the line of fans, who struck Ava the most. She confidently shook Ava's hand, then told her, "It's such a thrill to meet you. I'm studying classical voice at Julliard, but I'd love to sing in a band. You're…" Her face flushed slightly. "You're kind of my hero."

Julliard? And she looked up to *Ava?* Ava couldn't help it. She got up from her chair, reached out, and gave the girl a quick hug over the table. "That's so sweet of you to say," she said, when they drew apart. "And that means a lot. What's your name?"

CHAPTER 28

"Victoria Lessing," the girl said, grinning.

Ava returned the grin. "I'll remember the name," she said. "Thanks for coming tonight."

"Oh my gosh, thank *you*," Victoria gushed.

It had all been worth it, everything, Ava realized, watching Victoria go, if just for that. If only for that.

―⁂―

Soon interacting with the fans was one of Ava's favorite parts of show days. Either the online haters didn't come out to their shows or they had at least enough manners not to say anything nasty to Ava's face. But every show there were people who told Ava how much they loved the album, how much the band's music meant to them, who would share what specific songs meant to them. How the band's music, or certain songs, had gotten them through hard times. And girls and women who told Ava how much she inspired them, how much they looked up to her, how much more at home they felt in the metal scene when their favorite band was fronted by a woman. Fellow vocalists who loved the work she was doing, and simply those who loved the music, who had heard Ava's voice and felt it spoke to them, specifically. More than once when talking to the fans, she would brush away tears.

And it wasn't just her. She would see aspiring young Black musicians talking to Ben, asking for advice. Latinx kids who looked up to Rafael. And guitarists of all genders and races who idolized Joel, and budding composers and pianists who seemed completely in awe of Killian.

One time, as they filed back to their dressing room, she turned to grin at Ben, who had handed a set of his drumsticks to a Black teenage boy in a Handel's Messiah T-shirt who had been one of the last through the line. He had a big, happy smile on his face. He caught her eye and nodded. "This is what it's all about, man," he said, jerking his thumb over his shoulder in the direction of the room. "What we do, it means something to people. It's always nice to be reminded of that, and that it's an honor and privilege to do what we do."

Ava nodded. "It absolutely is," she said. "And I'll never take it for granted."

⁓∞⁓

"The Lighthouse", a rocking power ballad, would go on to become the second single from the aptly named *Terra Nova,* with a video made for it as well in between tour stops, on the same stretch of California coast where they'd shot the promo pictures for the album. It helped propel *Terra Nova* to even higher sales than *Shoreline,* and it became the most successful song in the band's history thus far, even more so than "Believer".

Handel's Messiah toured all over the world in support of *Terra Nova,* starting with a massive North American headlining tour this time, then following up with an equally huge European tour. Ava tried to make sure they had time to see the sights in as many cities as possible, something there hadn't really been room in the schedule for when they'd hit all the European festivals while touring for *Shoreline.* They went to St. Peter's and the Castel Sant'Angelo in Rome; the great gothic Duomo in Milan; the Hofburg in Vienna; St. Basil's Cathedral in Moscow; the Brandenburg gate in Berlin; they went to the Sagrada Familia and to the top of Mount Tibidabo in Barcelona. Ava saw so many things in such a short period of time that she felt as though her world had completely exploded, expanding further and further outward to become big enough to encompass all of these things she now knew; all of the experiences she now had.

One night, at the end of their day off in Rome, Ava and Killian went for dinner alone in the Trastevere neighborhood, then walked back to the hotel they'd booked for themselves for the night, which was in the neighborhood behind Vatican City. Hand in hand, they walked along the Tiber River, its illuminated

CHAPTER 28

bridges reflecting in the dark water below.

The bustle of Rome around them contrasted with the calm of the riverside walkway; the perfectly clear sky above, peppered with stars and a beautiful crescent moon; the graceful old stone bridges and their lights. Killian there beside her. For a moment, it was all too much for Ava, and she began to laugh.

Killian looked at her strangely. "Something I said?"

She stopped and faced him, swinging their interlaced hands between them. "It's just…I mean, look at this!" She gestured to the river, the city, the illuminated Castel Sant'Angelo just visible up ahead. She looked back at him. "And you. And me. Here, together. About to play a metal show tomorrow night. Just… how is this my life?"

Killian laughed and stepped close to her, gently taking her face in his hands. "It's your life because you're the most beautiful, talented, wonderful woman I've ever known, and you deserve all this and more," he said. "You deserve the world."

He kissed her, deeply, and she kissed him back, and it was a kiss that was maybe not quite appropriate for a public place. But it was night, it was dark, and they were in a city that had seen thousands of years of love stories and passion and everything else that humans could experience. Ava liked to think that the Eternal City approved.

She would always remember it as one of the best moments of her life.

The band went to Australia after Europe, then they went through North America again as the opening band for Korn. Then it was off to South America, then came their first ever Asian tour. After that, they went back to Europe over the summer for the big festivals, playing Wacken and Download again as well as some new ones that they had never played before.

And it was at the Download Festival in the U.K. that Ava

finally came face-to-face with Celeste Perinot.

Poisoned Smile had been touring pretty steadily since their album had been released. No one in Handel's Messiah seemed to realize that Poisoned Smile was also booked for Download—their hectic touring schedule was such that no one had really had the time or the inclination to pour over the lineup. It was only when they arrived at Donington Park, the racing circuit where the festival was held, the day before it was due to start that anyone realized.

"Shit. Killian. Did you see this?" Joel asked, climbing onto the bus and brandishing the festival poster.

Killian barely glanced at it from where he was sitting at the table with his laptop. "The poster? Yeah. I've seen it."

"No. I mean have you seen *this*." Joel slapped the piece of paper down on the table and jabbed his finger at one spot on it. Ava got up from her bunk and came over to see.

She saw Killian freeze, then followed his gaze to see what his eyes were locked on. There, somewhere in the middle of the list of bands, was the name. *Poisoned Smile*. Ava sucked in her breath sharply.

"Yeah," Joel said, correctly interpreting the heavy silence that had slithered onto the bus. "I didn't realize."

Killian shrugged again, trying to act as though he wasn't bothered, but Ava could tell that he was rattled all the same. "It's a huge festival," he said, and Ava wondered if Joel could also hear the dark undertone in his voice. "We probably won't even see her."

Joel smirked. "Don't kid yourself, man. You know Celeste better than anyone. She'll make sure we see her."

Joel was right, of course. They were in the area just off to the side of one of the smaller stages the next day, listening to the band that was playing. Celeste's band was coming up soon, and

CHAPTER 28

Ava wondered if any of her bandmates would stick around for the set—she was planning to, unobtrusively, in spite of herself. She was curious to hear how they would sound.

Yet she didn't have to wait until Celeste took the stage to see her. Ava was walking off toward the row of Johnny on the Spots—which she had for most of her life refused to use, until realizing that part of the so-called glamorous rock star life meant sometimes not having any other choice—when she saw Celeste walking toward her, in the direction of the stage, her makeup and long, glossy dark hair perfect and performance-ready.

For a second Ava wondered if she could turn and go in another direction, so they wouldn't need to pass each other. Then she thought that perhaps Celeste didn't even know who she was. It was possible, though not probable. The next second, though, Celeste's eyes locked on her, and it was too late to go anywhere else. And there was no doubt that she knew exactly who Ava was.

"Well," she said, stopping in front of Ava and putting her hands on her corseted hips. "If it isn't Ava Tomei. I suppose it's about time we met." She stuck out a hand, encased in a lace fingerless glove. "Celeste Perinot."

"Yeah, I know," Ava said, shaking the other woman's hand in return. She noted with some dismay that Celeste was nearly as tall as she was. Ava had never thought of her height as much of an advantage—and indeed there were times when it seemed like very much the opposite—but at that moment she would very much have liked to tower over Celeste. "Nice to finally meet you."

Celeste laughed at that, her voice musical yet with a note of harshness in it, somehow. "Good that you think so," she said. She gave Ava a slow once over, making her feel as though she was back in high school. "I have to compliment you," she said at last. "*Terra Nova* is a great album."

Ava was surprised at this olive branch. "Thank you," she said. "We're all thrilled with it." She thought about reciprocating the peacemaking and saying that she had liked *Strangers*—not untrue—but then remembered that Celeste had stolen a song Killian had written and so said nothing.

Celeste smiled. "I think the new songs are Killian's best work yet," she said, as if Ava hadn't spoken. "But then, that shouldn't surprise me, I guess. He got what he wanted."

"What do you mean?" Ava asked, defensive now and realizing she probably shouldn't even have asked; she probably should have just smiled, wished her a good show, and walked away, back to the Handel's Messiah tour bus parked across the stretch of green space at the race track or gone into one of the tents set up for performers to get something to eat. Or some liquor.

Celeste smiled again, but it was a bitter, pointed smile this time. "He got what he wanted," she repeated, "and so did you, it seems."

"Look, I'm not trying to start a fight or anything," Ava said. "I don't know you. You don't know me. I'm not really sure what your problem is with me."

"Oh, come on," Celeste said, rolling her eyes. "Don't be coy. Ever since he met you and worked with you on your little recital, he wanted you in the band. He wanted me out and you in, and you wanted the same thing."

Ava was so stunned she didn't know what to say.

"I was at your recital, you know," she went on. "Killian and I were broken up, and we had still been fighting about some of the music he was writing for the band. We hadn't spoken in a while, and so I came there to see him, to try to talk to him after. But I saw you onstage, saw how he looked at you." She sniffed. "Saw how you were all over him during your encore. I knew we were really over then, he and I. Did he tell you he talked to me after?"

Ava still couldn't speak. Killian hadn't told her Celeste had been at her recital that night, that he had spoken to her. The night she and Killian had first had sex. It seemed obvious, now, why he would hide something like that.

"I told him I saw that he really had moved on from me. But

CHAPTER 28

that I would still be professional if he could." She laughed, a hard sound. "But we see how that worked out. He had met you and he wanted me out. All those songs...it was obvious he was writing for your voice. Not mine. They didn't play to my strengths, and I didn't like them, and he didn't care."

"Did he tell you that?" Ava demanded. It was exactly what Killian had said to her when she'd pressed him about Celeste's departure from the band: *It took me a while to realize it. I'd written a few of the songs before I met you, but the rest—I was writing for you. And I think Celeste picked up on that, somehow.*

"No," Celeste said. "He didn't have to. I knew."

"Believe me when I say I never tried to force you out of the band," Ava said stiffly. "I never dreamed of such a thing. I was always a fan of yours, to be perfectly honest. If...if Killian was playing some kind of game like you're claiming, I had nothing to do with it. I didn't know about any of this until he called and asked me to fill in after you left them high and dry."

Celeste looked down. "Yeah. Well." When she looked back up, Ava was shocked to see tears sparkling in her eyes. "He found his new muse, and he didn't need me anymore," she said. "So you better watch out. He used his music to make you love him, but he can use it to make you hate him too."

With that, Celeste whirled and stalked toward the stage, swallowed into the crowd.

Ava stared after her, mouth agape, and most of all surprised that the dominant emotion she was feeling toward Celeste just then was pity.

What bothered her the most, she realized, was the way Celeste knew Killian's music so intimately, without having to be told what he was saying or feeling or doing. She knew it inside out in a way that Ava did not. Still. Yet.

She knew she would not tell Killian about this conversation.

chapter 29

Messiah Complex
2016

CHAPTER 29

With the final track list set, the incredible artwork ready, and the band's acknowledgements written during the last days of recording, the album was off for production of physical copies and preparation for sales.

Killian did several interviews with print magazines and webzines in the couple weeks they had before they started rehearsing, and he took them all alone. There was one exception—an interview with an online metal magazine that exclusively covered female-fronted bands—which he asked Ava to do. He texted her the information and asked if she would mind doing it instead of him—the first text or any other kind of communication between them since the breakup.

Ava did it, and though she usually loved talking about their music and their process, this time it felt different. It felt like she was hiding things, but she didn't want her and Killian's breakup—and the resulting tension in the band—to become public knowledge. The fact that they weren't together would get out eventually, but as she had barely come to terms with it herself, she couldn't bear for the wider world to know or to comment on it just yet.

So she answered the questions about the recording process, about the new songs, about what the sound would be, with as much enthusiasm as she could and avoided specifics and personal details as much as possible. Handel's Messiah was all she had left, it seemed, so she would do her best for it.

Meanwhile, things were happening: the band officially announced the title of the album, then the track list, then the release date: almost three months away at the end of January. They also announced their European headlining tour, to follow the North American tour for which tickets had been on sale for about a month. They had originally planned to release "Chains of Gold" as the first single, but with the results of the U.S. presidential election, they unanimously agreed to make "Poisonous Idols", an angry, hard-rocking song with political themes, the first single instead. Killian had never really gotten overtly political in his lyrics before, but he'd written the song in early 2016 as the presidential race was heating up, in response to all the hate and bigotry that seemed to be bubbling to the surface in the country. Ava loved the song; she found it cathartic to sing in a very new way. Making the song their first single would be their own statement of protest in the wake of Donald Trump's election.

Ava felt stirrings of the usual excitement that she always felt at this point: eagerness to get back on the road, pride at the thought of the album—their best yet—going out into the world, excitement to see and hear the fans' reactions to it. But it was all muted this time, as though she were at a show with earmuffs over her ears. She was mostly just tired, and she fantasized about sleeping through the next few months of pain and awkwardness between her and Killian.

If only it could be so easy.

***

A few days before rehearsals, Ava met Vivian and Rafael for coffee at Public Espresso downtown. The up-and-coming coffee shop was located inside the lobby of the gorgeous and lovingly restored Hotel Lafayette, which had been built during Buffalo's heyday at the turn of the century and designed by America's first professional female architect, Louise Blanchard Bethune. Ava always felt like she was stepping back in time whenever she came inside, even though the couches and tables around Public Espresso's bar gave the lobby a homey, casual feel.

Despite Vivian and Rafael's overt lovebird vibes, they were also still the only people Ava could really stand to be around, though she knew she'd have to rejoin the world eventually. But when she sat down across from them on one of the couches, she noticed they were shooting each other warning looks. "What'd I miss?" she asked uneasily.

"Nothing. You didn't miss anything," Vivian said firmly.

"Viv, come on—" Rafael began.

CHAPTER 29

"No. Nothing," she said, glaring at him.

"Okay, something's going on," Ava said. She could just tell it was bad news; her stomach was already clenching.

"Nope," Vivian insisted.

"Jesus Christ, Vivian," Ava snapped. "Something is up. Just tell me already before you make me crazy."

"We need to tell her, Viv," Rafael said, exasperated. "Better that she hear it from us than someone else."

Vivian crossed her arms over her chest and sat back against the couch, lips pursed, not willing to say anything herself but clearly done trying to stop Rafael.

"It's really not *that* big of a deal, Ava," Rafael began. "I just figured you should know."

"Would you please spit it out already?"

"I ran into Killian a couple of days ago, and he was…with Celeste."

Ava felt like she had been punched. Bile rose in her throat, and for a moment she was sure she was going to vomit. "What?" she almost gasped.

"Not…like, it wasn't a date or anything," Rafael assured her. "I don't think so, anyway. They were just talking, laughing a little…"

"Where was this?" Ava asked.

"Spot Coffee on Elmwood," Vivian interjected. "Almost as if he wanted every-damn-body to see him."

"What…what is she even doing here?" Ava demanded. "She lives in New York now, doesn't she? Why the fuck is she in Buffalo?"

"She's from here. She has family and friends here," Rafael said. He shrugged. "Look, they weren't, like, all over each other or anything. I just figured word would get out and rumors would start, and I wanted you to hear it from us." Vivian cleared her throat pointedly and Rafael amended, "From me."

Ava sat back, and closed her eyes, wishing she could go back to the start of this day, before she had heard any of this.

"Well, we broke up. He can do what he wants," she said through clenched teeth. "But I…" She could feel tears welling in her eyes and hated it. "Should I be worried about my job?"

Rafael looked surprised. "In the band? God, no. None of us would have her back, and even Killian isn't that big of a fool."

Ava closed her eyes, hearing again Celeste's words to her the only time they'd met, at the Download Festival, about how Killian had grown tired of her and needed a new muse. And how Ava had wondered if that would happen to her, too.

He used his music to make you love him, but he can use it to make you hate him too.

"This is bullshit," Ava said out loud. "Bullshit."

"I know that's right," Vivian said.

But, inevitably, they had to start rehearsing.

Ava showed up to the studio—which had a rehearsal room—on the first day, not sure what to expect. She hadn't been in the same room with Killian since the day they'd decided on the track list for the album. It was probably the longest she had gone without him since they had started dating, save for that first tour for *Shoreline* before she'd joined the band, and she felt strangely weightless, while at the same time always cognizant of the loss.

Killian was there when she arrived, but luckily so was Joel. "Hey, guys," she said, and they both nodded at her in greeting, though Killian didn't quite meet her eyes.

Her heart screamed at the sight of him, his physical presence bringing back all the wonderful things, all the happy memories, all the times that everything had seemed perfect between them. She wanted to touch him and knew she never could again. She took a deep breath and tried to hold on to her anger at him. That would allow her to get through this—and all the days to come—in a way that her sadness and grief and regret never could.

"Everything set up?" she asked, walking to their makeshift

CHAPTER 29

stage. Killian and Rafael had been here a few days ago to supervise the setup of their gear. She walked up to her mic and, as she'd known she would have to, adjusted the stand so it was a bit higher.

"Yeah," Joel answered her, when it became clear that Killian wasn't going to. "We should be good to go as soon as Ben and Raf get here."

Ava could feel Killian's eyes on her, and she glanced his way to see that he was looking at her new tattoo, at the word "Appassionata" on the inside of her wrist. She met and held his gaze, chin lifted defiantly, daring him to say something. But he didn't.

Ben and Rafael arrived right on each other's heels, and once everyone was present they all crowded around an amp case, atop which Killian had placed a blank sheet of paper.

"Okay," he said. "First things first. Let's decide which of the new songs we want to rehearse, and then we'll go back and pick some older ones."

"Um, and don't forget about our cover of that song from Hocus Pocus," Rafael added.

Ava felt a twisting in her heart as she remembered that day: how much fun they'd all been having, how loose and comfortable everyone had been. Killian's eyes flickered up to hers, briefly, so quickly she thought she might have imagined it. But then he laughed. "Right, okay," he said, and wrote down "Come Little Children" at the top of the page.

"I'm thinking—for the album release show, should we just play the whole new album? Nothing else?" Joel asked.

There was a pause as everyone considered this.

"Let's not," Killian said, "only because the fans usually want to hear some older songs too, and we won't be playing in Buffalo again after the release show. Not for a long time, at least."

Everyone agreed, and so they began naming tracks from the new album for the set list. "Poisonous Idols" was obvious, since it was the first single, as was "Chains of Gold", since that would likely be the second one. They also agreed on "Say Goodbye",

"Hostage" (though not without some furtive looks in Ava's direction), "Memories", "The Fine Line", "Teller of Tales", "Depths", and "Map of the End of the World".

"Okay, so what about 'Archangel'?" Rafael wanted to know.

Killian groaned. "I don't know. And if we do it, I don't know if it would be better to put it at the end of the show, so no one has to play anything else after, or at the beginning, when we're fresh."

"Let's rehearse it and see how it goes," Joel suggested. "I like what Ava said before, that it would be a killer closing song."

Killian added "Archangel" to the list.

"Maybe I'm just sentimental since it didn't make the album, but what about 'To Hell and Back'?" Ava said. "I like that one, and it might be kind of cool to mix it in here and there. Definitely for the release show."

Everyone agreed, and Killian added it to the list as well.

"And 'Appassionata'," Rafael said firmly.

Ava exhaled ever so slightly. She had been planning to mention it herself if no one else did, but couldn't help feeling relieved that someone else had brought it up.

"Yeah, I think so too," Joel said.

All eyes were on Killian. He hesitated for a moment, not looking at any of them.

Don't you dare, Ava thought, wanting to spit the words at him. *Don't you dare, you bastard.*

But then the moment of tension passed, and Killian wrote the song down. Ava exhaled again, louder now, and didn't care if anyone noticed.

They finished up with the songs from *Messiah Complex* and moved on to the other albums. When they were done, they had a list of songs that Ava thought could form a greatest hits album someday:

CHAPTER 29

HANDEL'S MESSIAH – MESSIAH COMPLEX WORLD TOUR

Come Little Children
Chains of Gold
Poisonous Idols
Say Goodbye
Hostage
Colossus
Teller of Tales
Depths
Memories
Map of the End of the World
Archangel
To Hell and Back
The Fine Line
Appassionata
Believer
Gothic Romance
Dream Specter
Shoreline
Wintersoul
Dreamscape
Clock Tower
Crescendo
The Lighthouse
Diabolus in Musica
Murder of Crows
The Philosopher
Fortune's Fool
Bridge of Sighs
Sing for Me
Dark October Sky
Odyssey
Tibidabo
Inferno

"Jesus," Ben said, when the list was complete. "That's a lot. Should we cut that back a bit?"

"It's gonna be a long tour cycle," Joel said. "We'll need all that."

"I had to hold myself back," Rafael said. "We could have added 'Muse' and 'Sense in Madness', too, as far as I'm concerned."

At the mention of "Muse", Ava and Killian's eyes unconsciously sought each other out then, just as quickly, they both looked away. They had each avoided most of the songs that directly referred to their relationship, like "Dark Lady", "Soul's Fire", "Savior", and "Dark River", and thankfully none of the other guys had brought them up—no doubt they'd sensed it would be a bad idea. Some, of course, like "The Lighthouse", couldn't be avoided.

"We can always add more songs, too, before the touring cycle is over," Killian said. "Some more of the news ones, maybe. But we've got plenty of work to do for right now, so let's get started."

They put the list up on the wall where they could all see it and decided to just go in the order they'd written the songs down in, except for "Come Little Children"—they agreed that once they got back in the swing of playing together, they'd turn their attention to working out the cover. The new songs would need the most rehearsal anyway, along with a few older ones that they'd never played live before. Songs like "Believer", "Shoreline", and "Dreamscape" they would hardly have to go over.

Some of the new songs were a bit shaky, as was to be expected, and "Archangel" was almost an unmitigated disaster—Rafael's bass was tuned in the wrong key to begin with, and Killian kept missing notes in the piano part—completely unlike him, but then he had never written anything quite so difficult before. Ben was off tempo a few times, and as a result dragged the rest of the band with him.

"How did we even record this?" Ava asked when they were done. She hadn't been too happy with how she sounded, either. A

CHAPTER 29

singer could never truly hear herself, but it just hadn't felt right, so she was sure it hadn't sounded right either.

"We got lucky, apparently," Rafael said.

"Maybe we should just scrap this one," Joel suggested.

"No," Ava and Killian said in unison. They both glanced at each other, startled, then quickly looked away. "I mean," Ava went on, when Killian didn't immediately speak, "that was so bad that now I want us to do it just for the principle of the thing."

"I agree," Killian said.

Everyone was silent for a moment, though whether they were considering what Ava had said or in shock that she and Killian had agreed about something, Ava couldn't be sure.

"Okay," Rafael said.

"Fine," said Ben.

"Okay," Joel said, but added, "but if we keep rehearsing it and it keeps sucking, then I say we abandon ship."

Everyone agreed, and they moved on to the next song, "To Hell and Back".

After that came "Appassionata."

Ava could feel the tension snaking up her spine as she stood at the mic stand, willing herself not to turn and look at Killian. Everyone confirmed that they were ready and waited for him to start the piano intro.

He waited long enough that it began to seem that he was making a point, and Ava wondered just how far he'd take it. But then, just as she was getting ready to turn around and demand to know what his problem was, he started playing.

The intro was smooth enough, and the rest of the guys came in perfectly, just as they had rehearsed when preparing to record it. Ava was relaxing into the song, feeling like she was ready to spread her wings, when behind her Killian began making mistakes in the piano part. Minor at first—in fact, the rest of the guys might not even have noticed, not knowing the song inside out as she did—but soon they became more blatant. She carried on, though, as did the rest of the band.

As soon as the song came to a close, she whirled to face him. "What the hell, Killian?" she said.

"Calm down, Maestro," he said coolly. "You recorded this song, remember? I haven't had as much practice with it as you have."

"Well, learn it," Ava snapped.

"Don't you—"

"Okay," Rafael interrupted, stepping between them with his bass. "We have plenty of time still. Killian has plenty of time to get it. Let's just move on."

Ava took a deep breath and spun away from Killian, putting her back to him again.

They continued on through the list, getting through the new songs and beginning to polish up some of the old ones. Everything was going smoothly until they ran through "Wintersoul".

"You need a bit more opera in your voice in the verses and pre-chorus of this one, Ava," Killian commented after they'd finished.

She turned and glared at him. "I think the way I do it is just fine."

"It's not the way I wrote it. You need to sing it a bit more like Celeste there."

Ava could feel a collective intake of breath from the rest of the guys as she exploded. "Oh, really?" she bit out. "Interesting comparison, since you're apparently seeing Celeste again."

Killian shot a dark look at Rafael. "You told her?"

"You were in Spot Coffee, man. Half the Elmwood Village saw you guys."

Killian looked back to Ava. "Not that it's any of your business—because we broke up, remember?—but I'm not dating her. Hell no. She was in town and reached out, and we got coffee and decided to bury the hatchet."

"Where, in my back?" Ava said. She had a moment of startling clarity where she realized, *This is how Celeste must have felt, when she saw me perform with Killian all those years ago.* And she knew that it wasn't Celeste she was angry with. That it had never been Celeste she was angry with.

"This is some juvenile bullshit, Ava. I'm just trying to give

CHAPTER 29

you notes on your performance like I always have."

Ava knew it *was* juvenile bullshit, and that only made her angrier. "Whatever. Just as long as you're not getting ready to swap the two of us again." With that, she turned her back to him again, unable to see the look on his face.

It was going to be a long three weeks of rehearsal.

chapter 30

Terra Nova
2013

CHAPTER 30

When they finished touring for *Terra Nova,* Ava couldn't believe how fast the time had gone. She had still not tired of performing the new songs: "The Lighthouse", of course, had earned itself a permanent place in the set list, along with "Crescendo"; she also loved performing "Heaven and Hell", "Journey to a New World", and "Muse". She'd loved singing "Prima Donna", the band's biting shot at Celeste, at first; but after she'd met the woman, she felt a little uncomfortable with it.

Being onstage never got old, and Ava didn't think it ever would. When the music started, when her voice was ringing out perfectly and completely under her control to the point where she barely had to even think about it, when the songs were fully in her muscle memory and she could just sing, perform, that was when something magical happened. Ava could feel herself dissolving into the music, her muscles and bones and sinews changing from solid matter to molecules of sound, losing herself in the service of the larger whole. She remembered something of the same feeling from being in the front row at her favorite bands' shows, but when she was the one onstage it was amplified by ten thousand.

She didn't get to that perfect, musical nirvana every show, though. Some nights she was exhausted from the grueling touring schedule; some days her voice was tired, and she could feel it, whether the audience heard it or not; some days she woke up and, for whatever reason—the weather or the environment or what she had drunk or eaten the day before or how much sleep she had gotten—her voice just didn't sound its best. She learned to let those days go as best she could, and it kept her searching for that high, trying to get to it as often as possible.

In a way, Ava was surprised at how well her relationship with Killian flourished throughout all the touring. Things were still new between them the first time around, so she had been a bit anxious setting out this time. In a small, yet often worried-over corner of her heart that she didn't discuss with anyone, she wondered if the two of them spending so much time together—

constantly, for months at a time, and in close quarters besides—would be more detrimental than anything. Surely they'd get on each other's nerves or get sick of each other?

What she found was quite the opposite. They got into minor arguments, just like any couple, but the presence of the other guys helped them keep such moments to a minimum. Yet for the most part, what they found was that being in such close quarters but rarely having any time alone together only fueled their love and desire for each other. It sometimes drove Ava crazy to have Killian right there and not be able to rip all his clothes off. And so when they did have the opportunity—a quickie on the bus or in the dressing room when no one else was around, a night in a hotel if they had a day off—the sex was as hot as it had been when they'd first met. More often than not it felt forbidden, and that only made it better.

This time, it soon became apparent that they would have a longer break between albums. Killian was still writing—he never stopped, it seemed—but he wasn't particularly satisfied with his work. In addition, they had all chipped in to purchase a recording studio in Buffalo, which would allow them to record at home from now on, as well as help cultivate some local talent. They had taken a local band called Devil's Hole (named for the infamous whirlpool near Niagara Falls) on tour with them across North America, and were planning to take them as support to Europe on the next album tour. Ava loved their sound; they reminded her a bit of Three Days Grace. They were also a ton of fun to hang out with on the road. That experience had prompted Killian—and everyone else, once he explained his idea—to want to give back to the Buffalo music scene, particularly the budding hard rock and metal scene.

They had been home from touring for five months, still with no studio plans, when Killian showed up unannounced at Ava's apartment one night. "I don't know what it is," he said as he walked in, by way of a greeting. "The songs keep appearing in my head, but once I play them out loud, once I write them down,

CHAPTER 30

they all crumble. It's like they can't hold up to the light of day. They can't bear to be outside my head."

Ava got up from the piano, where she'd been working on a new song of her own—if Killian was having writing trouble, she'd reasoned of late, maybe he'd be open to using some of her material for the new album, though she had yet to broach the subject with him and wasn't sure how to do so—and went to sit beside him on the couch. "Maybe you're trying to too hard," she said. "I've found that writing is like fishing, and some days they're just not biting. If you try to force it, you'll just make yourself even more frustrated." Part of her marveled at her nerve, giving Killian writing advice. But he had come here to talk to her about it, hadn't he?

"That's true," he said. "But the label is starting to lean on me a bit, asking what our timeline is. They want to know when we're going into the studio, and I don't even have enough songs I'm happy with for us to start rehearsing."

Ava shrugged. "Tell them you need more time."

"It's not that simple."

"Killian, what more can they want from you—from us? We recorded and released *Terra Nova* in practically record time. Every album can't be like that. Especially not with the kind of music that you write." She leaned her head against his shoulder and smiled. "You can't rush genius, after all."

She could feel him smile. "You flatter me," he murmured, draping an arm around her shoulders.

"No," she corrected. "I'm a supportive girlfriend."

"And I am your biggest fan," he said, leaning over and kissing her neck. In a whisper, he said, "Sing for me."

"Now?"

"Yes," he said. "I haven't heard you sing in a while. Maybe that's what I need. I need to hear your voice so I can start writing again."

His words calmed the doubt within her, the doubt that spoke with Celeste's voice. *He still needs me. I still inspire him.*

Ava got up from the couch and went back to her seat at the piano, heady in her role as muse. *Why not,* she told herself, seeing the notes she'd made for her new song. "This isn't quite finished yet, but here goes," she said aloud. "It's called 'Lose to Win'."

She played the introduction for herself, taking that time to slow her breathing and her rapid heartbeat. She began to sing, when she reached the proper measure, what she knew was one of the best melodies she'd ever written. The lyrics weren't set in stone yet, but she didn't worry about that just then: she let her voice stretch over the music she'd written, let it flex in a way that it never quite had when singing one of Killian's songs. As intimate as it was to make music with him, this was something more intimate still; something that had come from her and her alone and that she was sharing with him because she chose to. It was all hers now, and would become part his in the hearing, just as all music belongs partially to those who hear it. It was one of the things that had made Ava first fall in love with music: each song, each piece, would never sound quite the same, would never mean the same thing, to each person who heard it.

The song was about the fear of loving someone too deeply, but knowing you needed to give in to your feelings. It was up tempo, and Ava had no trouble imagining it as a hard rocking song played by the whole band, with Joel and Rafael fully flexing their muscles. She grew more and more confident as she went on, pouring more power and emotion into her voice, letting her fingers lean into the keys just a little more.

A few times during her impromptu performance, she glanced over at Killian; but he had no visible reaction. He was slouched down on the couch, his head resting against the back, eyes closed. She knew, though, that this meant he was listening.

She reached the end of the song and played the brief outro, which she heard in her head as a guitar riff. She kept her gaze down at the keys for a few moments, then finally looked up.

Killian was sitting forward, his elbows resting on his knees. He turned his head to look at her, smiling. "That was beautiful."

CHAPTER 30

He got up and came over to kiss her. "Beautiful." He pulled his keys out of his pocket. "That was exactly what I needed. I'm gonna head home and get back to work." He tossed her another smile over his shoulder as he opened the door. "I'll pick you up for dinner later."

Then, just like that, he was gone.

Ava rested her forehead against the top of the piano, feeling oddly drained. The spell she had cast—had thought she was casting—as she played was gone as if it had never been, and maybe it hadn't. Maybe it had all been in her head, in her hopes.

She had not thought that Killian could so completely miss the point of something, but he had.

True to form, Killian managed to get a few songs out of his so-called writer's block, which he titled "The Philosopher", "Fortune's Fool", and "Smile in the Dark". He showed them to Ava one at a time, over a period of a few weeks, and played them so she could sing. Each time, he was grinning widely as she finished. "Yes," he'd say. "That's it. Perfect."

As long as those songs took him, it seemed that eventually he was able to break down the dam. A month after he first showed "Smile in the Dark" to Ava, he had written seven more songs. Those, plus his three "writer's block" songs, as they had both taken to calling them, as well as four songs he had written some time before, made him feel that they finally had enough to start rehearsing. They blocked off some time a month away in the studio—no need to book it, since it was their studio—and began to rehearse.

A few nights before rehearsals were due to begin, Ava came over to Killian's house with a bottle of wine. "Hey," she called as she came in the door. She could hear him in the piano room, playing something she'd never heard before, something beautiful but aggressive. She went to stand in the doorway and listened. When he was finished, he looked up at her and smiled. She clapped. "I like that," she said. "What is it?"

"Something new I'm just finishing up," he said. "I think it'll go on the album. We'll have to add it to the rehearsals."

"You never know when to quit," she said. "What's it called?"

"It's called 'Lose to Win'."

Ava went stock still. "Are you serious?"

He glanced at her quizzically. "Yes."

She crossed the room to him and snatched the score and lyric sheet off the piano, scanning through them both. It wasn't her song—none of the music was the same, and the lyrics were completely different—but it was her title. "But that was the title of my song," she said, her voice tight with anger. "The one I played for you a couple months ago?"

"Yeah," he said. "It's a good title."

"But it's *my* title," she said, "for *my* song."

"Yeah, but this one is *not* your song," he said. He gestured to the papers she held in her hand. "As you can see. It just has the same title."

"It doesn't just *have* the same title. You *took* the title from a song that *I* wrote."

"So what?" he demanded. "I liked the title, so I used it, okay? It's not a big deal. Your song isn't going on the album."

"Why can't it?" she asked, furious now. "You liked it enough to use the title. You told me it was beautiful. Why isn't it good enough?"

"Ava, look, you're not as experienced a composer, okay? It's a great song, but I don't think it's quite ready yet."

At that, Ava turned and stalked out of the room and out of Killian's house. It was their first truly big fight.

chapter 31

Messiah Complex
2016

Rehearsals carried on, and they got the new songs down—they even, eventually, nailed "Archangel", which made them all very excited to play it live. Ava and Killian spoke to one another when they needed to, but not more than that, which suited her just fine. At least they weren't arguing.

They finally worked out their cover of "Come Little Children" from *Hocus Pocus,* and Ava couldn't remember ever having such an absolute blast with a song. None of them had written it, there were no strong emotions tied up in it. It was just a fun, nostalgic favorite that she knew would be a huge hit at the shows. Killian had added an eerie piano part, and the guitar and bass gave it a dark, sinister weight.

Then the band had some time off, with a few interviews and the like to promote the upcoming album. During this time, the band received their copies of the album from the label, and Ava felt like she might cry with pride and excitement and happiness. She flipped open the booklet to the page where the songwriting and composition credits were placed.

"*All music and lyrics by Killian Sterling,*" it read, "*except: tracks 1, 3, and 7, music by Killian Sterling and Joel Radley; and track 6, music and lyrics by Ava Tomei.*"

There it was, in print, her first songwriting credit. She knew it would be the first of many.

The band had one more week of rehearsal scheduled right before the first show to give them time to digest everything before having one more chance to polish. At the last rehearsal, with just four days to go before their album release show at the Town Ballroom, they ran through a few songs—"Archangel", "To Hell and Back", "Crisis of Conscience", and "Map of the End of the World"—before deciding to finish up early. They were ready, they knew. They weren't going to get more ready.

The last order of business was to select a starting set list for the tour—a mix of the new songs, old hits, and some that had just felt good during rehearsal—and then to select

CHAPTER 31

a different, special set list for the release show. It could be a little longer, which gave them a lot more choices.

They went through their list again, picking a handful of older songs, then began establishing an order, mixing them in with the newer songs. They had "Say Goodbye" at the beginning, just as on the album, followed by "Colossus", then into "Tibidabo" and "The Lighthouse". "Come Little Children", of course. They worked through the songs, trying to shake things up from previous tours and make sure the set would keep the energy high throughout.

"Okay, and then after 'Crescendo', let's do 'Appassionata'," Joel said.

Killian stopped writing. "No."

Ava froze, feeling anger begin to curdle in her stomach.

"No?" Joel asked in disbelief.

"What, do you want to put it later?" Rafael asked. "I don't think it should go any sooner—"

"No," Killian said again. "I mean, I don't want it in this set list at all."

Ava closed her eyes. *Please, not this again,* she prayed, to any god who was likely to be listening. She was so tired of this fight. So, so tired.

"Killian, what the hell—" Ben began.

Killian shrugged. "I don't want to play it at this show."

"This is bullshit, man," Joel said.

"We have it in the set list for the rest of the tour," Killian argued. "It's on the album. I just don't want to play it at this one show. Is that too much to ask?"

"Is it too much to ask that you put aside your ego and start to act like a professional?" Rafael shot back. "I'm getting real sick of your bullshit about this song, Killian. Ava only played it for us in the first place because you wanted her to. We all love it because it's a kickass song. Don't keep jerking everyone around. Don't keep jerking *Ava* around."

"I'm not," Killian said. "It's just one show, and I don't want to play it."

"Fine," Ava said. "I'll play it."

Killian paused. He hadn't been expecting that, it seems.

"Ava, you shouldn't have to pick up his slack," Joel said. "This is some bullshit, like I said. He's been rehearsing it, and you haven't."

"It doesn't matter," she said. "I could play it in my sleep."

Killian shrugged again. "Whatever," he said. "I just don't want to play it."

Ava looked around at the rest of the guys. "I will. I want to."

An uneasy silence fell.

"Look, maybe we shouldn't make it a big thing," Ben said. "If Killian doesn't want us to—"

"No," Rafael said. "Fuck that. I'm sick of this. Let's all act like adults, huh? We're playing the song, so long as Ava doesn't mind hitting the keyboards." He pointed at Killian. "You better get your shit together, dude. That's all I'm gonna say." He turned back to the list. "So. 'Crescendo', and then 'Appassionata'. Then how about 'Murder of Crows'?"

They finished off the set list with Killian barely saying a word. They would close with "Archangel", then come back out for their encore with "The Philosopher", which had been the second single off of *Gifts from the Devil,* followed by "Map of the End of the World."

"Looks good to me!" Joel said when they were finished.

"Okay. Rest up, everyone," Killian said. "In four days, we get to work."

Everyone gathered up their things and headed for the door. Ava was checking her phone quickly when she looked up to find that everyone had left except Killian. He was still standing by his keyboard on the makeshift stage, looking over their set lists.

As if he felt her watching him, he looked up and met her eyes. "It's not about you, you know," he said. "Not really."

She froze, instantly uncomfortable. They hadn't been alone in a room together since the fight that had led to their break up.

CHAPTER 31

"What isn't?" she asked, though she knew exactly what he was talking about.

"The song," he said, "and my...aversion to it." He put down the papers, stepped off the stage, and walked toward her. "The song, it...it makes me ashamed. Of some of the things I said and did."

Ava couldn't think how to respond. She had not expected this from him, ever. "It was meant to," she admitted, his honesty prompting her own. "At first. That's why I wanted to play it for you that night, but I never intended for anyone else to hear it."

"You were right, you know. When you accused me of punishing myself with the song." He ran his fingers through his hair. "I just overestimated how much pain I could take."

"Be that as it may," she said, "it's felt like it's about me, all this time. And if you're so ashamed of yourself, you're not doing yourself any favors with how you've been acting."

"I know that. I'm trying—"

But Ava wasn't done. "Killian, I thought you understood," she said. "Or that you would understand. You've always spoken to me in songs, and I knew that was how I wanted to say this."

"I thought you wanted plain words for a change."

She met his gaze levelly. "I did. And when you wouldn't give them to me, I replied in your language."

"And we see how that worked out," he said. Albeit with a rueful smile.

"Yes. I thought that you loved me enough to hear me. To let me have my own voice, no matter what it might cost you. But I guess you don't and never did."

He sighed. "You're right that I was...insecure," he said quietly. "That I was so used to putting you in the role of muse that I...I didn't know what to do when that didn't seem to be enough for you. I should have known better. It's not like it hadn't happened before."

Celeste. Her name was there in the air between them, but neither of them said it.

"And like I said when we...you know." He looked away, apparently unable to even say the words "broke up". "I got afraid that you didn't need me anymore. When we first met, I fell in love with you, but I wanted to help your career, too." He laughed mirthlessly. "I definitely did that. But then I started to worry that, once you were in the band, once you had what you'd always wanted, you wouldn't need me anymore."

"You can't have thought that," Ava said, both angry and heartbroken all at once. "You can't really have thought that of me. That I was using you like that."

"No," he said quickly. "No. I never thought that. I just thought, what if..." He looked at the floor. "What if you realized it was the band you wanted all along, and not me? At least if I was still the one writing the songs, maybe, you might still need me." He laughed again, a much harsher sound this time. "It's fucked up, and I know it. But I couldn't help but be afraid that someone as amazing as you would get tired of me. Would want... more." He shook his head. "It's like I said in so many of the songs I've written for you, Ava. 'Dark River'. 'Shoreline'. 'The Lighthouse'. You've always been the light on shore for me. The rope that keeps me from drowning."

There are so many ways I drown without you.

"Oh, Killian," Ava said. She wanted to strangle him and kiss him all at once and wasn't quite sure which one she wanted to do more. "I wanted both. You and the band. That was all I ever wanted. But I wanted to contribute to the band. I wanted to use my voice. *All* of my voice. But that doesn't mean I don't—didn't—love you. For you, and not what you could give me. I just..." She trailed off. "I can't always be your life raft. I can't keep swimming for the both of us."

"I know," he said. "I realize that now, when it's too late. And don't ever think that I didn't love you enough. That was never it. I did. I do. Even if I fucked it all up."

Tears sprang to her eyes. It was everything she had always wanted to hear him say. But what could it change now? She turned

CHAPTER 31

away from him, and just before she reached the door she stopped. "In the end, it wasn't what we did or didn't do that broke us," she said softly, though she knew that he could hear her. "It was all the things we imagined each other was capable of."

And as she walked out, she realized that this was the most honest they had been with each other in months—maybe longer. The sad part, of course, was that Killian was right—surely it was too late.

chapter 32

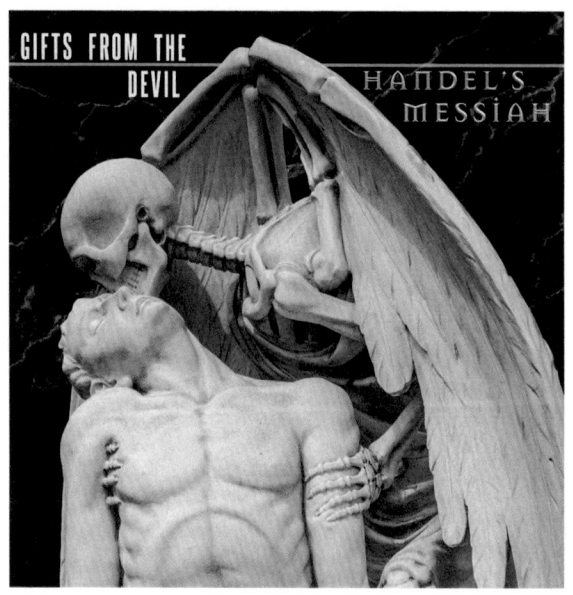

Gifts from the Devil
2013

CHAPTER 32

Ava and Killian didn't speak at all for a few days after their fight, but then the band was headed into rehearsal to learn all the new songs before they began recording the album, and they would no longer be able to avoid each other. Killian apologized, saying that he should have asked Ava if he could use the title, and that they would think about putting one of her songs on the next album.

Ava felt that his apology missed the point—especially since they were still rehearsing his new song with her title. But she let it go in the interest of patching things up, of working together. And, in truth, she missed him.

She told herself she forgave him, but the incident never stopped bugging her.

They got the new songs down within a few weeks, and then they headed into the studio. Ava was excited about the new material and even more excited to get back out onto the road and play live.

Yet soon things came crashing down in a way she had never expected.

One night, halfway through recording the album that would become *Gifts from the Devil,* Ava turned up at Killian's house, a drugstore plastic bag in her hand.

"Ava," Killian said, his face lighting up when he saw her on his doorstep. But he soon sobered when he saw the expression on her face. "What's the matter?"

Ava stepped past him and into the house, turning to face him as he shut the door behind her. "I was going to do this at my place, alone," she said, "but then I got nervous and came here." She reached into the plastic bag and pulled out the pregnancy test she had bought.

His eyes widened. "You...you think you might be...?"

"Yeah," she said. "Maybe. I'm over a week late, and that

never happens." She got regular birth control shots, since she'd heard too many horror stories about IUDs and it was way too easy to forget to take the pill while on tour and crossing different time zones. She hadn't missed a shot, but she also knew that nothing was a hundred percent.

Whatever reaction she'd been expecting, it wasn't the one she got. Killian rushed over to her and pulled her into his arms, jubilant. "Ava! You mean…we might be having a baby?"

"You—you're *happy* about this?" she demanded.

"Of course!" His joy faded as he drew back and saw the look on her face. "You—oh. You're not?"

She looked away from him, uncomfortable now in the face of his unexpected joy. But it wasn't like she could—or would—hide her true feelings from him now. "I don't know yet if there's anything to be happy about or not. But no, I won't be particularly happy if it turns out I am pregnant."

"But…why not?" he asked. "Why wouldn't you be happy about it?"

"Killian, we're going on tour in a few months," she said. "Or we're supposed to. If I'm pregnant, I'll be about six months pregnant when the tour is supposed to start. This is hardly the time—"

"Is there going to be a better time?"

"Yeah, a time when we'd maybe *planned* on having a baby would definitely be better. And to be honest, I didn't expect you to be happy about the idea—"

He looked at her, his eyes wet again. "Why the hell didn't you think I'd be happy? What kind of man do you think I am?"

"Because we're not in a good place for this! We're not *ready* for this! At least, I'm not." Ava closed her eyes and took a deep breath. "Okay. This is all getting away from us. Why don't I go take the damn pregnancy test and find out if I'm actually pregnant or not before we get any further."

Killian looked like he was going to protest, but then he sighed and nodded. "Yes. You're right. This…there might be nothing to argue about."

CHAPTER 32

"Correct." With that, Ava went into Killian's downstairs bathroom and closed the door. She opened the box with the pregnancy test, read the instructions over just to be sure she was doing it right—she had been through this once before, with Dan in college, but it had been a while—and then dutifully peed on the stick.

The brief time she waited for the result seemed like the longest moment of her life. But when the little negative sign appeared, she heaved a sigh of relief from her very bones.

She threw everything away, washed her hands, and came back out into the living room, where Killian was waiting expectantly.

"Well?" he asked.

"Not pregnant," she said, unable to hide the relief in her voice.

He, it seemed, was similarly unable to hide his disappointment. "Oh."

"It's for the best, Killian," Ava said, a bit more sympathetic now—and touched, even, that he'd been so excited—that she knew she was in the clear. "The album will be done soon, we'll be going out on tour…our lifestyle just isn't conducive to a kid."

"Is it ever going to be?"

"What…what do you mean?" Ava asked. This conversation seemed to be headed somewhere she wasn't prepared to go. Yet, she wondered, why wasn't she prepared to go there? They had been together, what, three years at that point? In reality, they should have had a conversation about their future—if marriage and kids were in the cards—a long time ago.

As if reading her mind, Killian asked, "Are you telling me you've never thought about our future? Thought about us getting married and having kids together? I guess I figured you wanted that. I do."

"I have," Ava said. "I do. Just…not right now."

"Then what are we waiting for, I guess is my question?"

"I don't know!" she cried. "I don't know, okay, Killian? I just know it can't be when we're about to leave on tour, for

Christ's sake. And, once again, I'm *not pregnant,* so this is all a moot point."

"I'm just saying, if you want to have kids, if we do, we can figure it out."

"But I *don't* want that," she said. "Not now, anyway."

"Then when? I'm not asking you for an answer right now," he said quickly, as she opened her mouth to retort angrily. "This all just made me realize that we haven't talked about any of this. And we probably should."

Ava threw up her hands. "Yeah. I guess you're right. It's just...it's all a lot right now, okay? I've gone through a lot of emotions today, and in the last half hour specifically. So can we maybe talk about this some other time?"

"Yeah," Killian said immediately, a hint of contrition in his voice. "Yeah, of course. Of course. Sorry, you just got me thinking..."

"Yeah, I can tell," Ava said, walking into his kitchen to pour herself a glass of wine.

Yet even with the negative test result, there was still a feeling of dread in her stomach that didn't quite go away.

A few days later, when they'd wrapped up recording for the day, Killian asked Ava to come back to his place with him, which she did. Things had seemed a little off between them since their argument—had it been an argument, really?—and the not-pregnancy, so she was eager for them to spend some time alone together and get back to normal.

Yet once they were settled on the couch at Killian's house, each with a glass of wine in their hand, Killian brought up a subject she—foolishly, perhaps—hadn't been expecting. "So I've been thinking," he said, draping an arm around Ava's shoulders and drawing her against him, "that maybe after the tour and everything for this album, we could take a bit of a break."

Ava froze for a moment, not sure she understood what he meant. "A...a break?"

"Yeah." He must have seen the panic on her face, because

CHAPTER 32

he rushed to reassure her. "No, not you and me! No, no, that's not what I meant at all."

"Okay, good," Ava said, with a nervous laugh.

"Yeah, no, not at all. I meant the band."

Ava went still again. This was hardly more welcome. "You want Handel's Messiah to take a break? Like, go on hiatus?"

"Not even anything as big as that. Just…take a year, maybe two, before we get started with the next album."

"But…why?" Ava asked, still not understanding. What would they do if they weren't recording, touring, performing, making music? What would she do? What would she even *want* to do, other than that?

"It's a pretty intense lifestyle, obviously. It takes a lot out of a person, which you know by now. And we wrote and recorded *Terra Nova* so quickly after *Shoreline,* and we're back at it again with this new one. I don't think it would hurt anyone to take a breather. Bands do it all the time."

"O-okay," Ava said, trying to be empathetic. She didn't feel like she needed a break, but she could appreciate that maybe Killian—and the rest of the guys as well—very well might. They had been at this a lot longer than her, after all; hustling to get their first record deal, then getting started with *The Art of Escape*. They had pretty much been writing, recording, and touring nonstop since then. And maybe after this album cycle, Ava herself might feel differently. Maybe by then she'd be ready for a break too.

"Okay," she said again. "Yeah, it's definitely something to think about. Have you mentioned it to the rest of the guys yet? Do they feel the same way?"

"I haven't, no," he said. "I wanted to see how you felt first."

"Well, I'll definitely have to think about it," she said. "I hadn't considered it before, but I will. And, you know, see how I feel at the end of the touring for this one. We don't have to decide anything right away, after all."

Killian was silent for a moment. "Well, I just thought," he

said, sounding almost hesitant, "that maybe if we had a couple years off, we could get around to getting married, having a baby."

Now it was Ava's turn to be silent.

"Maybe," he said. "If you wanted to."

She drew away from him, so that she could more clearly see his face. "I thought we just talked about this, Killian," she said. "I'm not ready for a baby. Marriage, I...well, I would say I'm open to that. But having kids? No. I'm not ready."

"Even if you knew we'd have some time off?" he pressed. "If you didn't have to worry about a tour coming up, or—"

"There would still be a tour coming up *eventually*," she said. "Eventually we'd get back out there. And then what would we do with our kid?" A horrible thought occurred to her. "You don't mean...you don't think I'm going to *retire* from the band to have kids, do you?"

"No!" he exclaimed. "Of course not! We'd cross that bridge when we come to it. There's lots of musicians that have kids and tour and all the rest. It's not impossible, Ava. We'd figure it out."

She shook her head. "But I don't *want* to figure it out. Not now, anyway. Maybe in a few years I'll feel differently. But I'm just...not there yet, Killian."

"Are you ever going to be there?"

She got up from the couch. "I don't know, okay?" she said. "I honestly don't know. I'm sorry, but I can't give you an answer to that right now. In these last few years, my life has taken a turn I never expected and never planned for. And I *love* it. Right now I don't want anything but what I already have. To be able to keep doing what I'm doing. What *we're* doing. Maybe a few years down the road, I'll feel differently. I get that this business takes a lot out of you. And I'm happy to take a break after this album cycle if that's what you need. But I won't be doing it so you can knock me up."

"Now hold on," Killian said, getting to his feet. "That isn't what I said. I just wanted us to have a discussion. To start thinking about it."

CHAPTER 32

"Well, I've thought about it, and there's my answer," Ava said. "I just gave it to you. I can't give you a timeline for when I'll be ready to have kids, Killian, if I ever am. And if you love me and want to be with me, you're just going to have to accept that."

He held up his hands. "I get that. I get it," he said. "I just wanted to make sure we're on the same page."

"Are we, though?"

They looked at each other in silence for a moment. "I guess not," he said. "But I can live with that because I love you."

But Ava suddenly wasn't sure if she could live with it. How could they go on from here without her constantly feeling like Killian was waiting for her to get that maternal instinct, to want to "settle down"? And how could she stand feeling like there was something he wanted that she wouldn't give him? What would that do to their relationship?

She took a deep breath. "I think I'm gonna go home," she said.

"What? No, Ava, don't go. I just—"

"I'm sorry," she cut him off. "It's just a lot to process, and I just need some space to…to process it. I think we both do."

"Okay. If that's what you need."

Ava didn't say anything else, just got her purse and left.

chapter 33

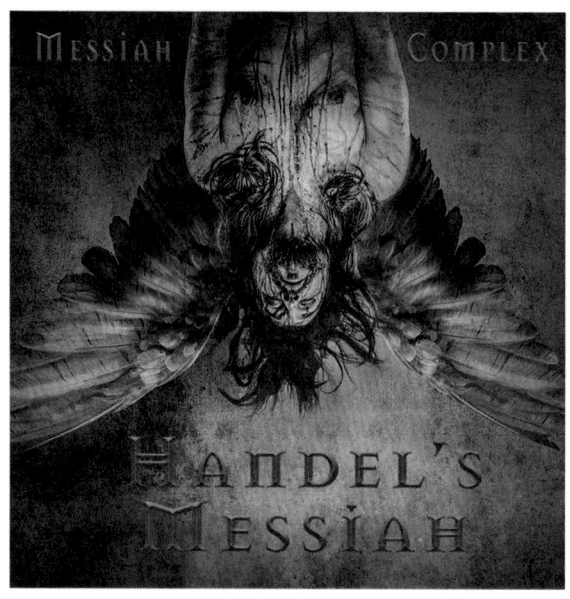

Messiah Complex
2017

CHAPTER 33

The day before the album release show for *Messiah Complex*—which would be at the Town Ballroom, as all their hometown shows were—Ava was at home, sitting at her piano and writing. She had been writing a lot in the past few days, as she'd found that she couldn't *not* write about her breakup with Killian and everything that had happened because of it. A couple of her new songs were angry, but most of them were sad, wistful, regretful. It had all gone so wrong, and while they both shared the blame, Ava was beginning to see that she had perhaps done everything she could have.

She didn't know what would become of these songs, but that wasn't really the point. Maybe they would make it onto a future Handel's Messiah album, but likely not. If she and Killian were going to continue to work together, they would probably need to keep their personal feelings out of the band and its music— the both of them. Maybe no one would ever hear these songs; maybe someday she would release her own record. She could if she wanted to, or not, if she decided against it. For so long she had thought that her creativity and her artistic future were inextricably linked to Killian, but now she saw that that simply wasn't true. And above all, she was disappointed in herself for not realizing it sooner.

As it neared five o' clock, someone buzzed up to her apartment. She got on the intercom, and the person downstairs said, "Delivery."

Puzzled, she said, "Okay," and buzzed him in. She waited by the door and opened it when the knock came. A florist delivery man stood there, holding a huge bouquet of flowers. "For Ava Tomei," he said, handing them to her.

"Thanks," she said, feeling her hands shaking slightly as she took the big paper-and-plastic wrapped bouquet. She stepped back inside her apartment and closed the door. Unwrapping the bouquet, she was surprised to see that it was two dozen red roses, just like the ones Killian had sent her just before the release of *Terra Nova* and again before the release of *Gifts from the Devil*.

She certainly hadn't been expecting them this time, though.
She removed the card from its small envelope and opened it.

To Ava,
This was your best performance yet. And you are as gifted a composer as anyone I know. It's long past time for the world—and me—to hear your true voice.
I'm sorry.
Love, Killian.

She stared at the card for a long time. It felt at once huge, momentous, finally what she had wanted to hear. And yet it still felt too late. But didn't it count for something that he had said it at all? That he had still sent the flowers?

Maybe. Maybe not. Almost more than the rest, it was the *I'm sorry* that gave her pause. Killian never apologized without meaning it.

But words were cheap, and Killian had always been good at them. If he was sorry, truly sorry, let him show her. Let him show her once and for all.

Ava got out her vase, filled it halfway with water, and arranged the roses in it, placing them in their usual spot on the lid of the piano. A part of her wanted to throw the card away, but she couldn't quite bear to. Instead, she stuck it in the junk drawer in her kitchen.

For once, out of sight didn't mean out of mind.

She sat back down and began to play again, not singing so as to save her voice for the show the next night, but wishing that she could in order to relieve the ache of the unshed tears in her throat.

chapter 34

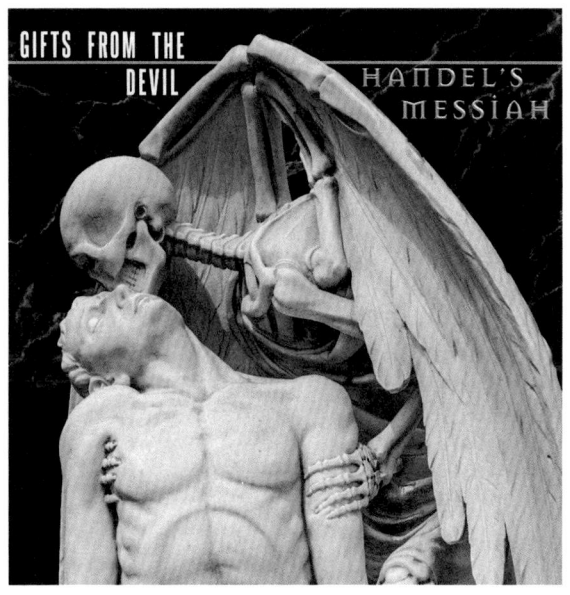

Gifts from the Devil
2013–2016

Killian gave Ava her space, she had to give him that much credit. They were both at the studio every day, but they didn't talk much, and didn't spend any time together outside of it. After a few days, they went to dinner together and talked it out. They agreed that they would see what would happen: maybe in the future, as Ava had said, she might change her mind, but for now they would live in the moment. What was most important right then was that they loved one another and wanted to stay together, to keep making music together.

Ava hoped it would be enough, even as she worried that it wouldn't be.

⁓⚬⁓

Ava began recording her vocals for the album right after they made up, and it happened that the song she recorded the first day was perhaps her favorite of the group, "Tibidabo". Killian had come up with the idea after their visit to Mount Tibidabo in Barcelona while on tour for *Terra Nova*. Atop the mountain was a church, large enough and tall enough in its perch on the mountain to be seen from most of the city, but surprisingly small and intimate inside. They had all been fascinated—but especially Killian—by the stained glass window inside the entryway to the church that illustrated the Bible story from which the church and mountain had gotten their name. The colored glass showed a winged and horned Lucifer, dressed in black and pointing to a panoramic city view—a view just like the one of Barcelona mere feet away—behind the haloed figure of Christ. Beneath the image were the words, "*Hace omnia tibi dabo, si cadens adoraveris me*", Latin for "All of this I can give to you, if you worship me". Killian had taken the story, and the experience of being up on the mountain, and made it into an epic, seven-minute long rocker of a song.

And a few days after their biggest fight—even though they'd

CHAPTER 34

made up—it was this song that Ava was recording.

She had expected that recording while she was in such a state of mind—while she was going through uncertainty in her personal life, beginning to doubt her drive and ambition for the first time, wondering if she was selfish for wanting the things she did and not what many people would say she should want—would make for an album that she didn't want to listen to again, that would dredge up painful memories for her to hear. What she found, though, was that every time she listened to "Tibidabo" in particular, she remembered the cathartic feel of channeling all her pain and frustration and confusion into the song as she sang. It would become one of her all-time favorite Handel's Messiah songs, and one of her favorite songs to perform live.

"*All of this I will give to you,*" she sang in the booth that day, in the extended first verse,

> *If you will fall down and worship me*
> *All of this can be yours*
> *All I've promised you and more*
> *Everything you've ever dared to dream*
> *And everything you haven't*
> *All of it will be yours*
> *If you will only worship me.*

Even as she sang in the booth that day, letting loose the jumble of chaos that was in her mind, she wondered who she was casting as the devil in her own personal temptation: Killian or her own guilt and ambition and the anger she felt at feeling guilty? She didn't know, but just to be able to articulate the question felt like enough.

"*These gifts from the devil crumble to ash in my hands,*" she sang, moving into the chorus.

> *All of this, he can give to me*
> *All but the hope of heaven*

HEAVY METAL SYMPHONY

All of this, he can give to me
If I admit that I am not enough...

The band finished recording *Gifts from the Devil* and did the usual promotion, and then they filmed a video for "Fortune's Fool", the first single. They embarked on another worldwide tour: North America, South America, Europe, Australia, Asia, and even a few cities in Africa, where they'd never been before.

Ava knew her voice was the strongest it had ever been, and that her performances on the *Gifts from the Devil* tour were the best yet. For all the struggles Killian had had in writing these songs, they still managed to be perfect, epic, beautiful; they were capable of showing off her voice and challenging it at the same time. Musically, it seemed, they had never been more in sync.

Offstage, though, things were different, and Ava was no longer sure who to blame. They both acted as though everything was fine, as though everything was normal and they were on the same page, but were they, really? It felt to Ava as though they were both holding on to something it would have been better to let go of, only they didn't know how. And so they were clinging to the wreckage in the hope that it would somehow reassemble itself.

A few hours before their show in Madrid, Killian found Ava alone in the dressing room, beginning to get ready. He closed the door behind him as he came in. "Don't get too fancy just yet," he said, coming up behind her and wrapping his arms around her waist. He slid his hands beneath her robe and down her bare stomach, dipping his fingers into her panties.

"Killian, please," Ava said, making to pull away.

"Yes," he murmured in her ear, mistaking her meaning. He began to steer her toward the couch nearby with his body, his hands undoing his jeans. His mouth was on hers, stifling her words.

"Killian, no," she said, pushing him off of her. He looked almost absurdly comical for a moment: his pants unbuttoned, his hair loose, his expression dumbfounded.

She stood up and retied her robe. "I mean," she began,

CHAPTER 34

awkwardly, "I still have to finish getting ready. I already did my makeup. I just don't want—"

"No, no," he said quickly, buttoning and zipping his jeans. "No, I get it. It's fine."

"I didn't mean—"

"No, no. You're right. This isn't the time."

"I—" Ava began, wanting to explain, apologize, something. But he was already gone.

That night, onstage, Ava sung the best she had in days, reached that musical heaven that she sought, night after night. She sang songs like "The Lighthouse" and "Dark River" and "Muse" and "Sing for Me"—one of the songs on *Gifts from the Devil* that had been written for her, about her—with more passion then she ever had, as though trying to call back the love that felt like it was slipping away from her—or that she was driving away. She wasn't sure which.

It felt as though she was singing right to Killian, asking him if he could understand, if he could come back to her. And it also felt as though she was singing to herself, asking, wondering, if she could forgive him.

The next day, they had moved on to Lisbon for the next show. "Let's do a little touching up here," Killian said during sound check.

"Which songs?" Ben asked. "I thought we were all really on last night."

"Yeah," Rafael agreed.

"Let's do 'Muse' and 'Sing for Me', for sure," Killian said. He looked right at Ava, standing by her custom chrome mic stand. "You were a little strident on both of those last night. A few other ones, too."

Joel frowned, oblivious to the tension that had manifested in the air, tangible and heavy and malicious. "I didn't hear that. I thought Ava sounded fantastic."

"Ben's right," Rafael said. "I thought that was one of our better shows lately, to be honest."

Killian shrugged, glancing at Ava again. "Like I said, I thought you were a bit strident. You need to pull back on those a little, especially 'Muse'. It needs to be softer than it was."

Ava met his eyes, hurt, confused. "It was amazing," she said. "The whole set felt better than it has for the last few shows, actually."

Killian shrugged. "I'm just telling you what I heard. Think about it."

Horrified, Ava felt like she was about to cry, but she forced the impulse down, clenching her jaw as the band began 'Muse' until she was in control again. And as she began to sing, she felt herself bringing it back, making it softer, almost without trying to. She hated herself for it, but she couldn't seem to make herself stop.

It seemed that he had heard her the night before, heard the questions and longing that she knew had been so naked in her voice. This was his answer.

After the band finished touring for *Gifts from the Devil*, Killian was right back to work on new songs. Ava was relieved to see it, even as she knew that things felt different between them still.

She had thought that so long as they shared the same true love, the same passion outside of each other, everything would be fine, and it would never become a competition or a struggle to balance it all. But she had been wrong. They both had. They'd thought that they could go full tilt at both their band and their relationship, but nothing could withstand that much intensity before it all went up in flames. She knew that now.

Yet Killian threw himself into the new songs like a man possessed—or like a man trying to outrun something.

The whole time, Ava remembered his promise that they would take another look at some of her songs for the next album. She remembered, but he, it seemed, did not. He didn't mention it, and she let it go, wanting him to remember on his own.

One night, he showed up at her apartment in a fit of inspiration, as he did from time to time while he was composing. His long hair was loose, and he was wearing old, faded jeans and

CHAPTER 34

a ratty T-shirt, as though he had simply pulled on whatever was closest to hand. "You need to hear this," he said, giving Ava a quick kiss before taking his smudged manuscript pages and sitting down at her piano. He set the pages right over the top of the score for a new song Ava had been working on and began to play.

Ava didn't even hear the beginning of the song, which would become the heartbreaking, yearning "Die for Me". She could only stare at the pages covering her own work and wonder if he saw what he had done. If he had seen and simply didn't care or if he hadn't even noticed.

And either way, she was so tired of not being heard.

chapter 35

Messiah Complex
2017

CHAPTER 35

The Town Ballroom was packed to the gills for the album release show. *Messiah Complex* wasn't officially on sale until the next day, but fans could purchase a copy early at the show, along with all of the new tour merch.

And, of course, they'd get to hear the songs first.

Not *first*, exactly, but before the majority of the world. The label had sent out promotional copies to various music magazines and outlets, of course, and so far the reviews had been only positive. The reviewers seemed to agree that this was Handel's Messiah's finest album to date; that the musicianship of the band members was at its finest; that the songwriting skills of Killian, Joel—and, yes, Ava—had never been better. A number of reviewers also devoted a couple paragraphs to Ava's performance in particular. "'Fans and critics alike have long extolled the virtues of Tomei's voice, and with ample reason'," went Ava's favorite review quote, from *Metal Planet,* " 'but everyone is in for a surprise with *Messiah Complex*. Tomei's voice transcends all her previous work, managing to be strong, intimate, beautiful, and brutal all at once.'" It was the phrase "beautiful and brutal" that Ava perhaps loved the most. It was the way she had always thought of and described Handel's Messiah's music, from way back when she was just a fan of the band and nothing more.

Now, Ava could not wait to see and hear the fan reactions to the new songs—both from the stage that night and online the next day via Twitter and Facebook and online Amazon and iTunes reviews. The hate directed at her and at the band as a whole had never really stopped, and she had come to accept it as she became much better at ignoring it. It would never not hurt, and it would never be fair, but she had long ago found that she didn't have the stores of emotional and mental energy necessary to obsess over it.

"Who let *you* in here?" Ava shouted playfully at Vivian as she entered the green room at the Ballroom and found her friend inside, perched on the arm of a couch next to Rafael as he warmed up.

Vivian grinned, then adopted a haughty tone. "I'm sorry, I don't know if anyone told you, but I'm with the band."

Ava laughed and went to hug her friend, glad she was there.

⁓✦⁓

Ava waited backstage, fully twenty minutes before they were going to go on, but too excited to do anything else. There was no opening band tonight—it was all them. The venue was packed, fans already pressing close to the stage, shouting and chanting and waiting, waiting for Handel's Messiah to hit the stage.

Ava was wearing the black and silver corset that she'd had made custom for her, the same one she was wearing in the promo pictures they'd done for the album. Her makeup was done, her long curly hair, streaked with blue now, wild and loose down her back.

It will never get old, she thought, unable to stop a wide smile from snaking its way onto her face as she peered out into the venue. *This will never get old. I will never not want this.*

And though she had long ago acknowledged that very thing, tonight, after everything, it seemed like a revelation all over again.

⁓✦⁓

The lights had gone down in the venue, and the crowd was screaming, shrieking, chanting the band's name over and over. The five members huddled in the wings, where Ava had been standing by herself just minutes before.

"A new chapter," Killian said, and in the dark it seemed that his eyes briefly settled on Ava's before flitting away, but she couldn't be sure. "Are you guys ready?"

"Yeah!" they all cried in unison.

"Let's do it!" Rafael said.

Under cover of the darkened lights, Killian, Ben, Rafael and Joel went out to take their positions on the stage. Ben set the tempo,

CHAPTER 35

and the lights flashed on at the same instant that the music blared to life, the first heavy, unrepentant chords of "Say Goodbye" flying loose and landing among the crowd, pounding into the floor and the walls until the crowd moved as one with the rhythm, headbanging and pumping their fists along with the music.

In the split second before she took the stage, Ava felt the familiar sensation of being about to leap, about to jump, about to fly. It was the first drop on a roller coaster, the feeling of missing a step on a staircase, the instant of not knowing if you'll make it or not, but knowing that you're all in either way.

She stalked out onto the stage and grabbed the mic. "What's up, Buffalo!" she cried, just before beginning to sing.

The star in the sky
That died years ago,
The heartfelt message
You wrote in the sand,
The dream you dreamed
And forgot when you woke,
The story you read
That never had an ending.

Then she burst into the simple yet soaring and powerful chorus:

Say goodbye
Say goodbye
Say goodbye
Say goodbye!

As they usually did, they launched right into the second song—tonight it was "Colossus"—before taking a pause to talk to the crowd. "Buffalo," Ava cried, and the crowd let out a roar of sound in response. "You all look beautiful tonight!"

After the screaming and applause died down, she said, "So

as you've no doubt figured out, those were two of the new songs: 'Say Goodbye' and 'Colossus'. What did you guys think?"

This, the loudest roar yet.

"We are so happy to hear that," Ava said. "Making this album was wonderful and amazing and difficult, too, and we're so, so proud of it, and we hope you guys love it. We think it's our finest work yet." Here, she paused and cast a smile around at the band members. They were her brothers: Rafael and Joel and Ben and even Killian. "You're gonna hear some more of it soon. This next song, though, is one of my favorites. Remember: never, ever take gifts from the devil."

The crowd cheered again, and the band began "Tibidado".

Maybe it was that they hadn't played live in so long; maybe Ava had forgotten the rush, just a little bit, the way you always do. But something about this show was perfect, was everything she had imagined being a rock star and performing would be. They were all completely in sync, in a way that didn't happen every night, even after months on the road. As they played, they all loved each other more than anyone else in the world.

After "Crescendo", Ava stepped back up to the mic. "All right, you guys," she said. "This next song is another new one. I wrote this one." She paused, grinning, to let the whoops and cheers fade. "So I'm really excited to be playing it live for you guys for the first time ever in my hometown."

She stepped away from the mic, turned, moving toward the keyboard, where she would replace Killian for this song. A mic with a stand waited off to the side for her to move it into place. But as she stepped toward him, he looked up, met her eyes, and did the very last thing she expected him to do.

He began to play. He began to play her song. He began to play "Appassionata".

She turned away again, back to her microphone stand at center stage, and closed her eyes, smiling. She could feel tears threatening beneath her lids, and she didn't care. She let them come.

And then she opened her mouth and let her voice fly free.

extras

HEAVY METAL SYMPHONY

The Art of Escape

Voices
The Legend Left Behind
Haunt Me
Believer
Prisoner in Your Chains
Sunstorm
The Sword
Gothic Romance
Dream Specter
Lady from the Sea
Escapism

ALYSSA PALOMBO

Shoreline

Who I Am
Dreamscape
Clock Tower
Raven
Shoreline
I Want You Gone
Beyond the Veil
Crystalline
Dark River
Blood Roses
Wintersoul
The Neverending War
Cathedral

HEAVY METAL SYMPHONY

Terra Nova

Crescendo
Heaven and Hell
Bridge of Sighs
Muse
Ashes
Soul's Fire
Prima Donna
Savior
The Lighthouse
Diabolus in Musica
Annabel Lee
Journey to a New World

ALYSSA PALOMBO

Gifts from the Devil

Sense in Madness
Smile in the Dark
Fortune's Fool
Murder of Crows
Dark October Sky
The Philosopher
Crisis of Conscience
Tibidabo
Sing for Me
Inferno
Lose to Win
Confession
Odyssey

HEAVY METAL SYMPHONY

Messiah Complex

Say Goodbye
Hostage
Chains of Gold
Teller of Tales
Depths
Appassionata
Colossus
Die for Me
Poisonous Idols
The Fine Line
Dark Lady
Memories
Archangel
Map of the End of the World

Believer

Once I mistook your words for my own,
Once I confused your thoughts for mine,
Now I too clearly see your rotting throne,
Now I see the rust where you used to shine.

Too long I've been on my knees
You'd keep me here forever if you could.

CHORUS
I once was a believer
But I had to turn away,
I had to tear down your altar
Had to leave you dead
With no hope of resurrection,
Had to demolish the shrine
And save myself,
I once was your believer...

Once the sun shone bright
Once the air was sweet,
It's all gone darker now, the light,
But I've finally gotten to my feet.

Too long I've been on my knees
You'd keep me there forever if you could.

CHORUS

Bridge
Roses shrivel, and turn to dust,
Rivers and streams run dry,
So much is gone, the faith, the trust,
It was all lies in the form of a lullaby.

CHORUS x2

Dream Specter

Awoken by tears
A pain in a phantom limb,
Was it real?
I can't forget and I can't remember.

But what about me,
I'm still here.

CHORUS
Hold my hand, dream specter,
Don't leave me behind,
You are but a shadow of someone from a fantasy,
Someone I once loved,
Or did I?

I fight to hold on
To this brittle, delusional warmth
That can't stand up to the light of day,
Fading ever more
When pierced by the sun's rays.

Except for me,
I'm still here…

CHORUS

Bridge

Don't abandon me to fade,
I'll erase the daylight from my eyes, dream specter
If you'll stay with me…

Dark River

Crushed by the weight of silence,
Lost in the void without your voice,
Suffocated by the emptiness of my bed,
There are so many ways I drown without you.

CHORUS
It's a dark river that takes me under
When you are far away,
I'm gladly torn asunder
By our unfinished passion play,
I see you across the dark river
And all I want to do is return,
Hold me close, make me shiver,
Pull me from the cold water and make me burn.

Tossed by storms
Submerged in desolation,
Kept barely afloat by the memory of my name in your voice,
There are so many ways I drown without you.

CHORUS

Let the sun rise,
Give me your hand,
And turn this dark river to gold.

Cathedral

All alone
Among the cold glass and stone,
A space too big to fill,
A pain heavy enough to kill.

Release me,
Bleed me,
Bury me,
Purge me.

A nothingness so vast
It swallows every last shadow cast,
This temple of divinity
So suffocating in its infinity.

Forgive me,
Forget me,

HEAVY METAL SYMPHONY

Bless me,
Damn me.

CHORUS
Why have you brought me here?
What is it within me that you fear?
I know I won't escape,
I know it's too late,
This has always been my fate,
Crushed forever under its weight.
No light breaks through,
There's a demon and an angel in my view,
No color anymore, no hope left,
All solace fled, leaving me bereft.

Condemn me,
Kill me,
Fail me,
Abandon me.

CHORUS

How can a place of so much beauty
Be so forbidding, so lonely?

CHORUS

And the weight of my sins
Is too dark and too heavy
And they scream at me
Echoing through the vast space of the cathedral,
All is gray, all is cold stone
And I am alone, and cannot see,
The angels have all left me;
The weight of my sins
Is enough to bury me,
And I am alone and cannot see,
The distance between damnation and salvation
Is enough to obliterate me.

Prima Donna

All the world's a stage to you,
All of us just lesser players to you,
You want to see us all bow down to you,
Pay worship, praise, and love to you.
Not this time.

CHORUS
What becomes of the leading lady
When the stage crumbles beneath her feet?
What becomes of the shining star
When her spotlight finally goes dark?
What becomes of the prima donna
When no one adores her anymore?
You took everything, left nothing at all for me,
Had nothing but disdain and spite for me,
But I'll step out of the shadow you cast for me,
Won't play the role you wrote for me.
Not this time.

CHORUS

Bridge
You played your last hand and had to fold,
We won't be your fools anymore,
Prima donna, never satisfied, always sanctified,
I hope you're happy now.

Goodbye, prima donna,
Farewell, prima donna,
Take your final bow.

Tibidabo

Every river, every mountain
Every blade of grass,
Every lake, every fountain
Every person that you see pass,

HEAVY METAL SYMPHONY

I can make you the master of it all.

All of this I will give to you
If you will fall down and worship me,
All of this can be yours
All I've promised you and more,
Everything you've ever dared to dream
And everything you haven't,
All of it will be yours
If you will only worship me.

CHORUS
These gifts from the devil
(Hace omnia tibi dabo)
Crumble to ash in my hands
(Si cadens adoraveris me)
All of this, he can give to me
(Hace omnia tibi dabo)
All but the hope of heaven
(Si cadens adoraveris me)
All of this he can give to me
If I admit that I am not enough.

Every road, every stream,
Every city, every town,
Every person you see dream,
You will sit above it in a crown,
I can make you master of it all.

All of this I will give to you
If you will fall down and worship me.

CHORUS

Bridge
Better to reign in hell
Than serve in heaven,
But what about on earth?
Tempt me not, devil,
Leave me, take away your evil,

Before I change my mind.

CHORUS x2

Poisonous Idols

You wear your hate like armor
As though it will protect you
Instead of smother you,
You'll burn everything to the ground
Just to be king of the ashes.

Be careful who you worship,
Even the devil can call himself God.

CHORUS
Tear down these idols,
Before their poison taints us all,
Tear down these idols,
All they can do is destroy.

How can you speak
When your hypocrisy should choke you,
Your every sin forgiven
Without even being acknowledged
Because you're saying what they want to hear.

Be careful who you worship,
Even the devil can call himself God.

CHORUS

Choose a side,
It's going to be a long ride.

Bridge
All the filth you fling
All the hate you stoke
All the souls you've bought and sold,
Soon you'll be covered in blood.

HEAVY METAL SYMPHONY

CHORUS

Tear down these idols
Before their poison taints us all,
Tear down these idols,
All they will do is destroy.

Memories

Memories abound
In every valley and under every rock,
In the trickle of the water
And the setting of the sun,
This twilight—
The most nostalgic time of day—
Seeps through me with its beautiful cool breeze,
Fills me with memories until I am whole,
And I am purified by every sight and scent,
Sensation and sound,
Memories abound.

The people we once were have never left us
Nor have they left this place,
They are here, in the changing colors of the leaves
And the pink tint of the fading sky.
I am never alone, so long as I can remember,
Oh, and I do.

The return of a feeling long since missed,
A yearning for a once found perfection,
It is here, in the dusk,
And may you never need look further.

The Fine Line

I'm on my knees before you
Awash in blood, both yours and mine,
Waiting for the blow
I know you will deal,

We have walked the fine line tonight.

CHORUS
There's a thin, fine line
Between love
And hate,
Between you
And me,
Between life
And the death I'll die for you tonight.

Here I am before you
My life awash in blood
Because it was always leading up to this moment
Drenched in blistering hatred,
But you're still so beautiful.

CHORUS

Bridge
And we have crossed the line tonight,
Love you, hate you, desire you,
Hate you, love you, hate you…

CHORUS

I'm dying now
Because I hate you
I'm dying
Because I hate you
(But I love you…)
I'm dying
Because I love to hate you.

acknowledgments

Back in the late summer/early fall of 2014, I was a writer who was struggling to write. I had recently sold my debut novel, *The Violinist of Venice,* to St. Martin's Griffin in a two-book deal. The book I was trying, mostly unsuccessfully, to write was the book that would go on to be my second novel, *The Most Beautiful Woman in Florence.* Second book syndrome, as I would later learn, is well known among novelists; that walking uphill through mud feeling of trying to write your first book under contract. Sure, I'd written one book, but could I do it again? What if it wasn't as good as the first one? What if I let down people other than myself (some of whom were paying me to do this)?

At the same time, the scraps of an idea I had about a woman who joins her boyfriend's metal band began to coalesce. That story came together with sharper clarity and urgency than the one I was writing, and wouldn't leave me alone. So I wrote a few chapters, thinking, okay, I'll just get this out of my system and then go back to the book I'm *supposed* to be writing.

Only that wasn't what happened. Once I started writing Ava and Killian's story, I found I couldn't stop. And, incredibly, I was having *fun* writing again. I worked on it every spare minute I could for a little over two months. At the end of November that year, I had written a full draft.

And once it was done? Well, then I went back and finished writing *The Most Beautiful Woman in Florence.* It scared me less by then. There was no worry about whether or not I could write another book. I'd just done it. The floodgates were opened.

And so what happened to that other book I wrote? Well, it sat on my computer. I revised it several times between other projects, would pick at it from time to time. Every time I would go back to it, I was reminded of how deeply and passionately I loved the characters and the story, of how much of myself and my love of heavy metal I'd put into its pages, even as it seemed like it might never see the light of day. I probably should have given up on it at a couple points, but I loved it too much to do that.

HEAVY METAL SYMPHONY

And now, of course, you are holding that book in your hands. *Heavy Metal Symphony* has been a piece of my heart for seven years now, so I have a lot of people to thank for helping it and me along in its journey.

First off, my very deepest of gratitude to my editor and publisher, Amanda Vink, for being the one to help me bring this book to the world. Under her guidance, it has become so much better and stronger than I ever could have made it on my own. She prompted me to think harder, to dig deeper about these characters and their motivations and emotions, and the book has improved immensely for it. Thank you so, so much, Amanda.

A standing ovation for Handel's Messiah's first fan, Lindsay Fowler. She's been listening to me talk about this book for SEVEN YEARS and somehow isn't sick of it. Thank you for always being just a text away, no matter what.

The world's biggest cheering crowd for my best friend (and now cover designer!!) Jennifer Hark-Hameister. So much about publishing this book has been a dream come true, and part of that has definitely been being able to work on it with you. Thank you for making visual magic out of my vague ideas. Thank you for helping to bring Handel's Messiah to life. And thank you for always being there, and for being willing to let me drag you to metal shows.

Much applause to the Canisius Alumni Writers, who workshopped the first draft of this novel: Caitie McAneney Klimchuk, Davidlee Klimchuk, Ryan Wolf, Joe Bieron, Cara Cotter, and Brittany Gray. Thank you for being the best group of early readers for this book. And a special and very heartfelt thanks to Caitie for putting me in touch with Amanda and Kaledena Press!

To my writing group, who has also heard me talk about this book for way too long: Adrienne, Dee, Kate, Jenn, Sandi, and Claudia. Thank you for all the encouragement!

Thank you to my rock star professors at Canisius College, of both creative writing and music, for giving me the all the tools to write this book: Mick Cochrane, Janet McNally, Eric Gansworth, Karen Schmid, Frank Scinta, and Melissa Thorburn.

Shout out to some of my favorite Buffalo spots that appeared in this book: Cole's, Toutant, Public Espresso (where I wrote lots of the first draft!), Spot Coffee, and of course, Mr. Goodbar. And to my favorite writing spots that didn't make an appearance in these pages, but that I still very much love: Caffe Aroma, Remedy House, and Platter's. And thank you, as always, to Talking Leaves Books and the wonderful staff there, who have been so supportive of me and my books!

And all my love to my hometown, Buffalo, New York. Stay weird and wonderful.

Endless cheers to my friends and family who continue to support me, especially: Amanda Beck, Andrea Bieniek, Alex Dockstader Schwob, Sandy Hark, Lisa and Joe Moore, Mike and Kathy Zimmerman, and Tom and Mary Zimmerman.

So many thanks to my dad, Tony Palombo. When I was fifteen and just starting to get into metal, he picked me up from my part-time job one day, took me to Best Buy on the way home, and bought me Black Sabbath's *Paranoid,* saying, "I think you should hear this." He was right. And thanks also for thinking that Handel's Messiah *was* a band name, making me realize that it really needed to be!

All of my gratitude to my mom, Debbie Palombo, who is better at promoting my books than I am, and whose musical tastes overlap at least a little with mine!

Thank you so much to my brother, Matt Palombo, for all his support and willingness to listen to whatever is playing in my car. Also, for the record, he once admitted I am the most metal person he knows.

Thank you to the world's best writing buddy and possessor of the world's best face (really! It's true!) Fenway the silky terrier.

This book is, of course, a love letter to music and to heavy metal, so I must thank all the bands and artists I love so much, and who helped inspire this book with their incredible music:

HEAVY METAL SYMPHONY

Nightwish, Evanescence, Delain, Lacuna Coil, Kamelot, Karmin, In This Moment, Flyleaf, Northward, The Dark Element, Fleetwood Mac, Halestorm Within Temptation, and Florence + the Machine. Music, other than books, is my very favorite thing in life. I'm so grateful for these artists and the inspiration they've given me. My life wouldn't be the same without them.

And, last but certainly not least, thank you to all the amazing women in rock and metal who have inspired me since I was a teenager and continue to do so, whose music has brought me so much joy and comfort and strength, and who showed me that there is a place for women in heavy music: Floor Jansen, Amy Lee, Charlotte Wessels, Sharon den Adel, Cristina Scabbia, and Simone Simons. Ava and I both owe you all so much.

Alyssa Palombo is the author of four historical novels: The Violinist of Venice, The Most Beautiful Woman in Florence, The Spellbook of Katrina Van Tassel, and The Borgia Confessions. She is a graduate of Canisius College with degrees in English and creative writing. A passionate music lover, she is a classically trained singer as well as a big fan of heavy metal. She lives in Buffalo, NY, where she is always at work on a new novel.

To find out more, visit
https://alyssapalombo.com/